Critical acc...

'Harlan Coben always ... ...ale to tell, and he knows how to present it with elegance, pace and loads of tension'   *Guardian*

'This is familiar Coben territory – dark, twisted and gripping'   *Daily Mail*

'Harlan Coben has made his intentions clear: he wants to fool his readers. And he makes a good job of doing so in *The Innocent* . . . The enjoyably intricate plot takes several turns before we are fooled for the last time and the villains and motive are revealed. A book to read in one gulp'   *Daily Telegraph*

'An electrifying thrill-ride of a novel that peeks behind the white picket fences of suburbia. *The Innocent* is at once a twisting, turning, emotionally-charged story, and a compelling tale of the choices people make and the repercussions that remain'   *Deadly Pleasures*

'Coben is becoming one of America's top thriller writers. This is his best book yet'   *Daily Mirror*

'If your taste for crime is novels that can be relied on to wrongfoot you in the most delightful way, you should . . . quickly pick up a copy of *The Innocent*'
                                           Daily Express

'Coben's electrifying New Jersey-based thriller plays games with notions of innocence and guilt . . . Adding to the enjoyment of this slicky crafted tale is the sharpness of the dialogue and the satisfying realism of the descriptive writing'   *The Times*

Harlan Coben is one of the most exciting talents in American crime writing. *The Innocent, Just One Look, No Second Chance, Tell No One* and *Gone For Good* were all international bestsellers, and are published in thirty-three languages. He was the first ever author to win all three major US crime awards, and established a bestselling series of crime novels starring his powerful creation, Myron Bolitar, before turning to stand-alone books. *Promise Me* is his latest novel in Orion paperback. Visit his website at www.harlancoben.com.

By Harlan Coben

The Innocent

HARLAN COBEN

An Orion paperback

First published in Great Britain in 2005
by Orion
This paperback edition published in 2005
by Orion Books Ltd,
Orion House, 5 Upper St Martin's Lane,
London WC2H 9EA

Reissued 2007

20 19 18 17 16 15 14 13 12

A CIP catalogue record for this book
is available from the British Library.

ISBN-13 978-1-4072-0815-2

Printed and bound by GGP Media GmbH, Poessneck

The Orion Publishing Group's policy is to use papers that
are natural, renewable and recyclable products and made from
wood grown in sustainable forests. The logging and manufacturing
processes are expected to conform to the environmental regulations
of the country of origin.

www.orionbooks.co.uk

In memory of Steven Z. Miller

To those of us fortunate enough to have been
    his friend –
We try to be thankful for the time we had,
    But it's so damn hard

And to Steve's family, especially Jesse, Maya T,
    and Nico –
When we're strong enough, we will talk about
    your father
Because he was the best man we've ever known

Prologue

You never meant to kill him.

Your name is Matt Hunter. You are twenty years old. You grew up in an upper-middle-class suburb in northern New Jersey, not far from Manhattan. You live on the poorer side of town, but it's a pretty wealthy town. Your parents work hard and love you unconditionally. You are a middle child. You have an older brother whom you worship, and a younger sister whom you tolerate.

Like every kid in your town, you grow up worrying about your future and what college you will get into. You work hard enough and get good, if not spectacular, grades. Your average is an A minus. You don't make the top ten percent but you're close. You have decent extracurricular activities, including a stint as treasurer of the school. You are a letterman for both the football and basketball team – good enough to play Division Three but not for a financial scholarship. You are a bit of a wiseass and naturally charming. In terms of popularity, you hover right below the top echelon. When you take your SATs, your high scores surprise your guidance counselor.

You shoot for the Ivy Leagues, but they are just a little out of your reach. Harvard and Yale reject you outright. Penn and Columbia waitlist you. You end up going to Bowdoin, a small elite college in Brunswick, Maine. You love it there. The class sizes are small. You make friends. You don't have a steady girlfriend, but you probably don't want one anyway. In your sophomore year, you start on the varsity football team as a defensive back. You play JV basketball right off the bat, and now that the senior point guard has graduated, you have a serious chance of getting valuable minutes.

It is then, heading back to campus between the first and second semester of your junior year, that you kill someone.

You have a wonderfully hectic holiday break with your family, but basketball practice beckons. You kiss your mother and father good-bye and drive back to campus with your best friend and roommate, Duff. Duff is from Westchester, New York. He is squat with thick legs. He plays right tackle on the football team and sits the bench for basketball. He is the biggest drinker on campus – Duff never loses a chugging contest.

You drive.

Duff wants to stop at UMass in Amherst, Massachusetts, on the way up. A high school buddy of his is a member of a wild frat there. They are having a huge party.

You're not enthusiastic, but you're no party pooper. You are more comfortable with smaller gatherings where you pretty much know everyone. Bowdoin has about 1,600 students. UMass has nearly 40,000. It is early January and freezing cold. There is snow on the ground. You see your breath as you walk into the frat house.

You and Duff throw your coats on the pile. You will think about that a lot over the years, that casual toss of the coats. If you'd kept the coat on, if you'd left it in the car, if you'd put it anyplace else . . .

But none of that happened.

The party is okay. It is wild, yes, but it feels to you like a forced wild. Duff's friend wants you both to spend the night in his room. You agree. You drink a fair amount – this is a college party, after all – though not nearly as much as Duff. The party winds down. At some point you both go to get your coats. Duff is holding his beer. He picks up his coat and swings it over his shoulder.

That is when some of his beer spills.

Not a lot. Just a splash. But it's enough.

The beer lands on a red Windbreaker. That's one of the things you remember. It was freezing cold outside, in the teens, and yet someone was wearing just a Windbreaker. The other thing you will never shake from your mind is that a Windbreaker is waterproof. The spilled beer, little as it was, would not harm the coat. It would not stain. It could so easily be rinsed away.

But someone yells, 'Hey!'

He, the owner of the red Windbreaker, is a big guy but not huge. Duff shrugs. He does not apologize. The guy, Mr. Red Windbreaker, gets in Duff's face. This is a mistake. You know that Duff is a great fighter with a short fuse. Every school has a Duff – the guy you can never imagine losing a fight.

That's the problem, of course. Every school has a Duff. And once in a while your Duff runs into their Duff.

You try to end it right there, try to laugh it off, but you have two serious beer-marinated headcases with reddening faces and tightening fists. A challenge is issued. You don't remember who made it. You all step outside into the frigid night, and you realize that you are in a heap of trouble.

The big guy with the red Windbreaker has friends with him.

Eight or nine of them. You and Duff are alone. You look for Duff's high school friend – Mark or Mike or something – but he is nowhere to be found.

The fight begins quickly.

Duff lowers his head bull-like and charges Red Windbreaker. Red Windbreaker steps to the side and catches Duff in a headlock. He punches Duff in the nose. Still holding Duff in the headlock, he punches him again. Then again. And again.

Duff's head is down. He is swinging wildly and with no effect. It is somewhere around the seventh or eighth punch that Duff stops swinging. Red Windbreaker's friends start cheering. Duff's arms drop to his sides.

You want to stop it, but you are not sure how. Red Windbreaker is going about his work methodically, taking his time with his punches, using big windups. His buddies are cheering him on now. They *ooh* and *ahh* with each splat.

You are terrified.

Your friend is taking a beating, but you are mostly worried about yourself. That shames you. You want to do something, but you are afraid, seriously afraid. You can't move. Your legs feel like rubber. Your arms tingle. And you hate yourself for that.

Red Windbreaker throws another punch straight into Duff's face. He releases the headlock. Duff drops to the ground like a bag of laundry. Red Windbreaker kicks Duff in the ribs.

You are the worst sort of friend. You are too scared to help. You will never forget that feeling. Cowardice. It is worse than a beating, you think. Your silence. This awful feeling of dishonor.

Another kick. Duff grunts and rolls onto his back. His face is streaked with crimson red. You will learn later that his injuries were minor. Duff will have two black eyes and numerous bruises. That will be about it. But right now he looks bad. You know that he would never

4

stand by and let you take a beating like this.

You can stand it no longer.

You jump out of the crowd.

All heads turn toward you. For a moment nobody moves. Nobody speaks. Red Windbreaker is breathing hard. You see his breath in the cold. You are shaking. You try to sound rational. Hey, you say, he's had enough. You spread your arms. You try the charming smile. He's lost the fight, you say. It's over. You've won, you tell Red Windbreaker.

Someone jumps you from behind. Arms snake around you, wrapping you in a bear hug.

You are trapped.

Red Windbreaker comes at you now. Your heart is beating against your chest like a bird in too small a cage. You reel your head back. Your skull crashes into someone's nose. Red Windbreaker is closer now. You duck out of the way. Someone else comes out of the crowd. He has blond hair, his complexion ruddy. You figure that he is another one of Red Windbreaker's pals.

His name is Stephen McGrath.

He reaches for you. You buck away like a fish on a hook. More are coming at you. You panic. Stephen McGrath puts his hands on your shoulders. You try to break free. You spin frantically.

That is when you reach out and grab his neck.

Did you lunge at him? Did he pull you or did you push him? You don't know. Did one of you lose your footing on the sidewalk? Was the ice to blame? You will flash back to this moment countless times, but the answer will never be clear.

Either way, you both fall.

Both of your hands are still on his neck. On his throat. You don't let go.

5

You land with a thud. The back of Stephen McGrath's skull hits the sidewalk curb. There is a sound, an awful hell-spawned crack, something wet and too hollow and unlike anything you have heard before.

The sound marks the end of life as you know it.

You will always remember it. That awful sound. It will never leave you.

Everything stops. You stare down. Stephen McGrath's eyes are open and unblinking. But you know already. You know by the way his body went suddenly slack. You know by that awful hell-spawned crack.

People scatter. You do not move. You do not move for a very long time.

It happens fast then. Campus security arrives. Then the police. You tell them what happened. Your parents hire a hotshot lawyer from New York City. She tells you to plead self-defense. You do.

And you keep hearing that awful sound.

The prosecutor scoffs. Ladies and gentlemen of the jury, he says, the defendant happened to slip with his hands wrapped around Stephen McGrath's throat? Does he really expect us to believe that?

The trial does not go well.

Nothing matters to you. You once cared about grades and playing time. How pathetic. Friends, girls, pecking order, parties, getting ahead, all that stuff. They are vapors. They have been replaced by the awful sound of that skull cracking against stone.

At the trial, you hear your parents cry, yes, but it is the faces of Sonya and Clark McGrath, the victim's parents, that will haunt you. Sonya McGrath glares at you throughout the proceedings. She dares you to meet her eye.

You can't.

You try to hear the jury announce the verdict, but those other sounds get in the way. The sounds never cease, never let up, even when the judge looks down sternly and sentences you. The press is watching. You will not be sent to a soft white-boy country-club prison. Not now. Not during an election year.

Your mother faints. Your father tries to be strong. Your sister runs out of the courtroom. Your brother, Bernie, stands frozen.

You are put in handcuffs and taken away. Your upbringing does little to prepare you for what lies ahead. You have watched TV and have heard all the tales of prison rape. That does not happen – no sexual assault – but you are beaten with fists during your first week. You make the mistake of identifying who did it. You get beaten twice more and spend three weeks in the infirmary. Years later, you will still sometimes find blood in your urine, a souvenir from a blow to the kidney.

You live in constant fear. When you are let back into the general population, you learn that the only way you can survive is to join a bizarre offshoot of the Aryan Nation. They do not have big ideas or a grandiose vision of what America should be like. They pretty much just love to hate.

Six months into your incarceration your father dies of a heart attack. You know that it's your fault. You want to cry, but you can't.

You spend four years in prison. Four years – the same amount of time most students spend in college. You are just shy of your twenty-fifth birthday. They say you've changed, but you're not really sure.

When you walk out, you step tentatively. As if the ground below your feet might give. As if the earth might simply cave in on you at any time.

7

In some ways you will always walk like that.

Your brother, Bernie, is at the gate to meet you. Bernie just got married. His wife, Marsha, is pregnant with their first child. He puts his arms around you. You can almost feel the last four years shed away. Your brother makes a joke. You laugh, really laugh, for the first time in so long.

You were wrong before – your life did not end on that cold night in Amherst. Your brother will help you find normalcy. You will even meet a beautiful woman down the road. Her name is Olivia. She will make you enormously happy.

You will marry her.

One day – nine years after you walk through those gates – you will learn that your beautiful wife is pregnant. You decide to buy camera phones to stay in constant touch. While you're at work, that phone rings.

Your name is Matt Hunter. The phone rings a second time. And then you answer it. . . .

nine years later

1

The doorbell jangled Kimmy Dale out of her dreamless sleep.

She stirred in her bed, groaned, checked the digital clock next to her bed.

11:47 a.m.

Despite it being solidly midday, the trailer remained night-dark. That was how Kimmy liked it. She worked nights and was a light sleeper. Back in her Vegas head-lining days it had taken years of testing shades, blinds, curtains, shutters, sleeping blindfolds, before she found a combination that could truly keep the branding-iron Nevada sun from niggling at her slumber. The Reno rays were less relentless, but they still searched and exploited even the smallest sliver.

Kimmy sat up in her king-size bed. The television, a no-name model she'd bought used when a local motel finally decided to upgrade, was still on with the volume off. The images floated ghostly in some distant world. She slept alone right now, but that was a condition in constant flux. There was a time when each visitor, each prospective mate, brought hope with them to this bed, brought a this-could-be-the-one optimism that, in hind-sight, Kimmy realized, bordered on the delusional.

There was no such hope anymore.

She rose slowly. The swelling on her chest from her most recent cosmetic surgery ached with the movement. It was her third procedure in the area, and she wasn't a kid anymore. She hadn't wanted to do it, but Chally, who thought he had an eye for such things, had insisted. Her tips were getting low. Her popularity was waning. So she agreed. But the skin in that area had become too stretched out from past surgical abuse. When Kimmy laid on her back, the damn things fell to the side and looked like fish eyes.

The doorbell rang again.

Kimmy looked down at her ebony legs. Thirty-five years old, never had a baby, but the varicose veins were growing like feeding worms. Too many years on her feet. Chally would want those worked on too. She was still in shape, still had a pretty great figure and terrific ass, but hey, thirty-five is not eighteen. There was some cellulite. And those veins. Like a damn relief map.

She stuck a cigarette in her mouth. The book of matches came from her current place of employment, a strip joint called the Eager Beaver. She had once been a headliner in Vegas, going by the stage name Black Magic. She did not long for those days. She did not, in truth, long for any days.

Kimmy Dale threw on a robe and opened her bedroom door. The front room had no sun protection. The glare assaulted her. She shielded her eyes and blinked. Kimmy did not have a lot of visitors – she never tricked at home – and figured that it was probably a Jehovah's Witness. Unlike pretty much everybody else in the free world, Kimmy did not mind their periodic intrusions. She always invited the religiously rapt into her home and listened carefully, envious that they had found something, wishing she could fall for their line of bull. As with the men in her life, she hoped that this one would be different, that this one would be able to convince her and she'd be able to buy into it.

She opened the door without asking who it was.

'Are you Kimmy Dale?'

The girl at the door was young. Eighteen, twenty, something like that. Nope, not a Jehovah's Witness. Didn't have that scooped-out-brain smile. For a moment Kimmy wondered if she was one of Chally's recruits, but that wasn't it. The girl wasn't ugly or anything, but she wasn't for Chally. Chally liked flash and glitter.

'Who are you?' Kimmy asked.

'That's not important.'

'Excuse me?'

The girl lowered her eyes and bit on her lower lip. Kimmy saw something distantly familiar in the gesture and felt a small ripple in her chest.

The girl said, 'You knew my mother.'

Kimmy fiddled with the cigarette. 'I know lots of mothers.'

'My mother,' the girl said, 'was Candace Potter.'

Kimmy winced when she said that. It was north of ninety degrees, but she suddenly tightened her robe.

'Can I come in?'

Did Kimmy say yes? She couldn't say. She stepped to the side, and the girl pushed her way past.

Kimmy said, 'I don't understand.'

'Candace Potter was my mother. She put me up for adoption the day I was born.'

Kimmy tried to keep her bearings. She closed the trailer door. 'You want something to drink?'

'No, thank you.'

The two women looked at each other. Kimmy crossed her arms.

'Not sure what you want here,' she said.

The girl spoke as if she'd been rehearsing. 'Two years ago I learned that I was adopted. I love my adopted family, so I don't want you to get the wrong idea. I have two sisters and wonderful parents. They've been very good to me. This isn't about them. It's just that . . . when you find out something like this, you need to know.'

Kimmy nodded, though she wasn't sure why.

'So I started digging for information. It wasn't easy. But there are groups who help adopted kids find their birth parents.'

Kimmy plucked the cigarette out of her mouth. Her hand was shaking. 'But you know that Candi – I mean, your mother – Candace . . .'

'. . . is dead. Yes, I know. She was murdered. I found out last week.'

Kimmy's legs started to feel a little rubbery. She sat. Memories rushed back in and they stung.

Candace Potter. Known as 'Candi Cane' in the clubs.

'What do you want from me?' Kimmy asked.

'I spoke to the officer who investigated her murder. His name is Max Darrow. Do you remember him?'

Oh, yes, she remembered good ol' Max. Knew him even before the murder. At first Detective Max Darrow had barely gone through the motions. Talk about low priority. Dead stripper, no family. Another dying cactus on the landscape, that was all Candi was to Darrow. Kimmy had gotten involved, traded favors for favors. Way of the world.

'Yeah,' Kimmy said, 'I remember him.'

'He's retired now. Max Darrow, I mean. He says they know who killed her, but they don't know where he is.'

Kimmy felt the tears coming to her eyes. 'It was a long time ago.'

'You and my mom were friends?'

Kimmy managed to nod. She still remembered it all, of course. Candi had been more than a friend to her. In this life you don't find too many people you can truly count on. Candi had been one – maybe the only one since Mama died when Kimmy was twelve. They had been inseparable, Kimmy and this white chick, sometimes calling themselves, professionally at least, Pic and Sayers from the old movie *Brian's Song*. And then, like in the movie, the white friend died.

'Was she a prostitute?' the girl asked.

Kimmy shook her head and told a lie that felt like truth. 'Never.'

'But she stripped.'

Kimmy said nothing.

'I'm not judging her.'

'What do you want then?'

'I want to know about my mother.'

'It doesn't make any difference now.'

'It does to me.'

Kimmy remembered when she first heard the news. She'd been onstage out near Tahoe doing a slow number for the lunch crowd, the biggest group of losers in the history of mankind, men with dirt on their boots and holes in their hearts that staring at naked women only made bigger. She hadn't seen Candi for three days running, but then again Kimmy had been on the road. Up there, on that stage, that was where she first overheard the rumors. She knew something bad had gone down. She'd just prayed it hadn't involved Candi.

But it had.

'Your mother had a hard life,' Kimmy said.

The girl sat rapt.

'Candi thought we'd find a way out, you know? At

first she figured it'd be a guy at the club. They'd find us and take us away, but that's crap. Some of the girls try that. It never works. The guy wants some fantasy, not you. Your mother learned that pretty quick. She was a dreamer but with a purpose.'

Kimmy stopped, looked off.

'And?' the girl prompted.

'And then that bastard squashed her like she was a bug.'

The girl shifted in her chair. 'Detective Darrow said his name was Clyde Rangor?'

Kimmy nodded.

'He also mentioned a woman named Emma Lemay? Wasn't she his partner?'

'In some things, yeah. But I don't know the details.'

Kimmy did not cry when she first heard the news. She was beyond that. But she had come forward. She risked everything, telling that damn Darrow what she knew.

Thing is, you don't take too many stands in this life. But Kimmy would not betray Candi, even then, even when it was too late to help. Because when Candi died, so did the best parts of Kimmy.

So she talked to the cops, especially Max Darrow. Whoever did this – and yeah, she was sure it was Clyde and Emma – could hurt her or kill her, but she wouldn't back down.

In the end, Clyde and Emma had not confronted her. They ran instead.

That was ten years ago now.

The girl asked, 'Did you know about me?'

Kimmy nodded slowly. 'Your mother told me – but only once. It hurt her too much to talk about it. You have to understand. Candi was young when it happened. Fifteen, sixteen years old. They took you away the moment

16

you popped out. She never even knew if you were a boy or girl.'

The silence hung heavy. Kimmy wished that the girl would leave.

'What do you think happened to him? Clyde Rangor, I mean.'

'Probably dead,' she said, though Kimmy didn't believe it. Cockroaches like Clyde don't die. They just burrow back in and cause more hurt.

'I want to find him,' the girl said.

Kimmy looked up at her.

'I want to find my mother's killer and bring him to justice. I'm not rich, but I have some money.'

They were both quiet for a moment. The air felt heavy and sticky. Kimmy wondered how to put this.

'Can I tell you something?' she began.

'Of course.'

'Your mother tried to stand up to it all.'

'Up to what?'

Kimmy pressed on. 'Most of the girls, they surrender. You see? Your mother never did. She wouldn't bend. She dreamed. But she could never win.'

'I don't understand.'

'Are you happy, child?'

'Yes.'

'You still in school?'

'I'm starting college.'

'College,' Kimmy said in a dreamy voice. Then: 'You.'

'What about me?'

'See, you're your mother's win.'

The girl said nothing.

'Candi – your mother – wouldn't want you mixed up in this. Do you understand?'

'I guess I do.'

'Hold on a second.' Kimmy opened her drawer. It was there, of course. She didn't have it out anymore, but the photograph was right on top. She and Candi smiling out at the world. Pic and Sayers. Kimmy looked at her own image and realized that the young girl they'd called Black Magic was a stranger, that Clyde Rangor might as well have pummeled her body into oblivion too.

'Take this,' she said.

The girl held the picture as if it were porcelain.

'She was beautiful,' the girl whispered.

'Very.'

'She looks happy.'

'She wasn't. But she would be today.'

The girl put her chin up. 'I don't know if I can stay away from this.'

Then maybe, Kimmy thought, you are more like your mother than you know.

They hugged then, made promises of staying in touch. When the girl was gone, Kimmy got dressed. She drove to the florist and asked for a dozen tulips. Tulips had been Candi's favorite. She took the four-hour trip to the graveyard and knelt by her friend's grave. There was no one else around. Kimmy dusted off the tiny headstone. She had paid for the plot and stone herself. No potter's grave for Candi.

'Your daughter came by today,' she said out loud.

There was a slight breeze. Kimmy closed her eyes and listened. She thought that she could hear Candi's voice, silenced so long, beg her to keep her daughter safe.

And there, with the hot Nevada sun pounding on her skin, Kimmy promised that she would.

2

'A camera phone,' Matt Hunter muttered with a shake of his head.

He looked up for divine guidance, but the only thing looking back was an enormous beer bottle.

The bottle was a familiar sight, one Matt saw every time he stepped out of his sagging two-family with the shedding paint job. With its crown 185 feet in the air, the famed bottle dominated the skyline. Pabst Blue Ribbon used to have a brewery here, but they abandoned it in 1985. Years ago, the bottle had been a glorious water tower with copper-plated steel plates, glossy enamel, and a gold stopper. At night spotlights would illuminate the bottle so that Jerseyites could see it from miles around.

But no more. Now the color looked beer-bottle brown but it was really rust red. The bottle's label was long gone. Following its lead, the once-robust neighborhood around it had not so much fallen apart as slowly disintegrated. Nobody had worked in the brewery for twenty years. From the eroding ruins, one would think it would have been much longer.

Matt stopped on the top step of their stoop. Olivia, the love of his life, did not. The car keys jangled in her hand.

'I don't think we should,' he said.

Olivia did not break stride. 'Come on. It'll be fun.'

'A phone should be a phone,' Matt said. 'A camera should be a camera.'

'Oh, that's deep.'

'One gizmo doing both . . . it's a perversion.'

'Your area of expertise,' Olivia said.

'Ha, ha. You don't see the danger?'

'Er, nope.'

'A camera and a phone in one' – Matt stopped, searching for how to continue – 'it's, I don't know, it's interspecies breeding when you think about it, like one of those B-movie experiments that grows out of control and destroys all in its path.'

Olivia just stared at him. 'You're so weird.'

'I'm not sure we should get camera phones, that's all.'

She hit the remote and the car doors unlocked. She reached for the door handle. Matt hesitated.

Olivia looked at him.

'What?' he asked.

'If we both had camera phones,' Olivia said, 'I could send you nudies when you're at work.'

Matt opened the door. 'Verizon or Sprint?'

Olivia gave him a smile that made his chest thrum. 'I love you, you know.'

'I love you too.'

They were both inside the car. She turned to him. He could see the concern and it almost made him turn away. 'It's going to be okay,' Olivia said. 'You know that, right?'

He nodded and feigned a smile. Olivia wouldn't buy it, but the effort would count toward something.

'Olivia?' he said.

'Yes?'

'Tell me more about the nudies.'

She punched his arm.

But Matt's unease returned the moment he entered the Sprint store and started hearing about the two-year commitment. The salesman's smile looked somehow satanic, like the devil in one of those movies where a naïve guy sells his soul. When the salesman whipped out a map of the United States – the 'nonroaming' areas, he informed them, were in bright red – Matt started to back away.

As for Olivia, there was simply no quelling her excitement, but then again his wife had a natural lean toward the enthusiastic. She was one of those rare people who find joy in things both large and small, one of those traits that demonstrates, certainly in their case, that opposites do attract.

The salesman kept jabbering. Matt tuned him out, but Olivia gave the man her full attention. She asked a question or two, just out of formality, but the salesman knew that this one was not only hooked, lined, and sinkered but fried up and halfway down the gullet.

'Let me just get the paperwork ready,' Hades said, slinking away.

Olivia gripped Matt's arm, her face beaming. 'Isn't this fun?'

Matt made a face.

'What?'

'Did you really use the word "nudie"?'

She laughed and leaned her head against his shoulder.

Of course Olivia's giddiness – and nonstop beaming – was due to much more than the changing of their mobile phone service. Purchasing the camera phones was merely a symbol, a signpost, of what was to come.

A baby.

Two days ago, Olivia had taken a home pregnancy test and, in a move Matt found oddly loaded with religious significance, a red cross finally appeared on the white stick. He was stunned silent. They had been trying to have a child for a year – pretty much since they first got married. The stress of continuous failure had turned what had always been a rather spontaneous if not downright magical experience into well-orchestrated chores of temperature taking, calendar markings, prolonged abstinence, concentrated ardor.

Now that was behind them. It was early, he warned her. Let's not get ahead of ourselves. But Olivia had a glow that could not be denied. Her positive mood was a force, a storm, a tide. Matt had no chance against it.

That was why they were here.

Camera phones, Olivia had stressed, would allow the soon-to-be threesome to share family life in a way their parents' generation could never have envisioned. Thanks to the camera phone, neither of them would miss out on their child's life-defining or even mundane moments – the first step, the first words, the average play-date, what-have-you.

That, at least, was the plan.

An hour later, when they returned to their half of the two-family home, Olivia gave him a quick kiss and started up the stairs.

'Hey,' Matt called after her, holding up his new phone and arching an eyebrow. 'Want to try out the, uh, video feature?'

'The video only lasts fifteen seconds.'

'Fifteen seconds.' He considered that, shrugged, and said, 'So we'll extend foreplay.'

Olivia understandably groaned.

They lived in what most would consider a seedy area, in the strangely comforting shadow of the giant beer bottle of Irvington. When he was fresh out of prison,

22

Matt had felt he deserved no better (which worked neatly because he could afford little better) and despite protestations from family, he began renting space nine years ago. Irvington is a tired city with a large African-American population, probably north of eighty percent. Some might reach the obvious conclusion about guilt over what he'd had to be like in prison. Matt knew that such things were never so simple, but he had no better explanation other than he couldn't yet return to the suburbs. The change would have been too fast, the land equivalent of the bends.

Either way, this neighborhood – the Shell gas station, the old hardware store, the deli on the corner, the winos on the cracked sidewalk, the cut-throughs to Newark Airport, the tavern hidden near the old Pabst brewery – had become home.

When Olivia relocated from Virginia, he figured that she'd insist on moving to a better neighborhood. She was used to, he knew, if not better, definitely different. Olivia grew up in the small hick town of Northways, Virginia. When Olivia was a toddler, her mother ran off. Her father raised her alone.

On the elderly side for a new dad – her father was fifty-one when Olivia was born – Joshua Murray worked hard to make a home for him and his young daughter. Joshua was the town doctor of Northways – a general practitioner who worked on everything from six-year-old Mary Kate Johnson's appendix to Old Man Riteman's gout.

Joshua was, according to Olivia, a kind man, a gentle and wonderful father who doted on his only true relative. There was just the two of them, father and daughter, living in a brick town house off Main Street. Dad's medical office was attached, on the right side off the driveway. Most days, Olivia would sprint home after school so that she could help out with the patients. She would cheer up scared kids or gab with Cassie, the long-time receptionist/nurse. Cassie was a 'sorta nanny' too. If her father was too busy, Cassie cooked dinner and helped Olivia with her homework. For her part, Olivia worshipped her father. Her dream – and yes, she thought now that it sounded hopelessly naïve – had been to become a doctor and work with her father.

But during Olivia's senior year of college, everything changed. Her father, the only family Olivia had ever known, died of lung cancer. The news took Olivia's legs out from under her. The old ambition of going to medical school – following in her father's footsteps – died with him. Olivia broke off her engagement to her college sweetheart, a premed named Doug, and moved back to the old house in Northways. But living there without her father was too painful. She ended up selling the house and moving to an apartment complex in Charlottesville. She took a job with a computer software company that required a fair amount of travel, which was, in part, how she and Matt rekindled their previously too-brief relationship.

Irvington, New Jersey, was a far cry from either Northways or Charlottesville, Virginia, but Olivia surprised him. She wanted them to stay in this place, seedy as it was, so that they could save the money for the now-under-contract dream house.

Three days after they bought the camera phones, Olivia came home and headed straight upstairs. Matt poured a glass of lime-flavored seltzer and grabbed a few of those cigar-shaped pretzels. Five minutes later he followed her. Olivia wasn't in the bedroom. He checked the small office. She was on the computer. Her back was to him.

'Olivia?'

She turned to him and smiled. Matt had always disdained that old cliché about a smile lighting up a room, but Olivia could actually do that – had that whole 'turn the world on with her smile' thing going on. Her smile was contagious. It was a startling catalyst, adding color and texture to his life, altering everything in a room.

'What are you thinking?' Olivia asked him.

'That you're smoking hot.'

'Even pregnant?'

'Especially pregnant.'

Olivia hit a button, and the screen vanished. She stood and gently kissed his cheek. 'I have to pack.'

Olivia was heading to Boston on a business trip.

'What time is your flight?' he asked.

'I think I'm going to drive.'

'Why?'

'A friend of mine miscarried after a plane ride. I just don't want to chance it. Oh, and I'm going to see Dr. Haddon tomorrow morning before I go. He wants to reconfirm the test and make sure everything is all right.'

'You want me to go?'

She shook her head. 'You have work. Come next time, when they do a sonogram.'

'Okay.'

Olivia kissed him again, her lips lingering. 'Hey,' she whispered. 'You happy?'

He was going to crack a joke, make another double entendre. But he didn't. He looked straight into those eyes and said, 'Very.'

Olivia moved back, still holding him steady with that smile. 'I better pack.'

Matt watched her walk away. He stayed in the doorway for another moment. There was a lightness in his chest. He was indeed happy, which scared the hell out of him. The good is fragile. You learn that when you kill a boy. You learn that when you spend four years in a maximum-security facility.

The good is so flimsy, so tenuous, that it can be destroyed with a gentle puff.

Or the sound of a phone.

Matt was at work when the camera phone vibrated.

He glanced at the caller ID and saw that it was Olivia. Matt still sat at his old partner desk, the kind where two people face each other, though the other side had been empty for three years now. His brother, Bernie, had bought the desk when Matt got out of prison. Before what the family euphemistically called 'the slip,' Bernie had big ideas for the two of them, the Hunter Brothers. He wanted nothing to change now. Matt would put those years behind him. The slip had been a bump in the road, nothing more, and now the Hunter Brothers were back on track.

Bernie was so convincing that Matt almost started to believe it.

The brothers shared that desk for six years. They practiced law in this very room – Bernie lucrative corporate while Matt, barred from being a real attorney because he'd been a convicted felon, handled the direct opposite, neither lucrative nor corporate. Bernie's law partners found the arrangement odd, but privacy was something neither brother craved. They had shared a bedroom for their entire childhood, Bernie on the top bunk, a voice from above in the dark. Both longed for those days again – or at least, Matt did. He was never comfortable alone. He was comfortable with Bernie in the room.

For six years.

Matt put both palms on the mahogany top. He should have gotten rid of the desk by now. Bernie's side had not been touched in three years, but sometimes Matt still looked across and expected to see him.

The camera phone vibrated again.

One moment Bernie had it all – a terrific wife, two terrific boys, the big house in the burbs, partnership in a big law firm, good health, loved by everyone – the next his family was throwing dirt on his grave and trying to make sense of what happened. A brain aneurysm, the doctor said. You walk around with it for years and then, bam, it ends your life.

The phone was on 'Vibrate-Ring.' The vibrate ended and the ringer started playing the old TV *Batman* song, the one with the clever lyrics that basically consisted of going nah-nah-nah for a while and then shouting 'Batman!'

Matt pulled the new camera phone off his belt.

His finger hovered over the answer button. This was sort of weird. Olivia, despite being in the computer business, was terrible with all things technical. She'd rarely used the phone and when she did, well, she knew Matt was at the office. She'd call him on his landline.

Matt pressed down on the answer button, but the message appeared telling him that a photograph was 'incoming.' This, too, was curious. For all her initial excitement, Olivia had not yet learned how to use the camera feature.

His intercom sounded.

Rolanda – Matt would call her a secretary or assistant but then she'd hurt him – cleared her throat. 'Matt?'

'Yes.'

'Marsha is on line two.'

Still looking at the screen, Matt picked up the office phone to talk to his sister-in-law, Bernie's widow.

'Hey,' he said.

'Hey,' Marsha said. 'Is Olivia still in Boston?'

'Yep. In fact, right now, I think she's sending me a photo on our new cell phone.'

'Oh.' There was a brief pause. 'Are you still coming out today?'

In another move signaling familyhood, Matt and Olivia were closing on a house not far from Marsha and the boys. The house was located in Livingston, the town where Bernie and Matt grew up.

Matt had questioned the wisdom of returning. People had long memories. No matter how many years passed, he would always be the subject of whispers and innuendo. On the one hand, Matt was long past caring about that petty stuff. On the other, he worried about Olivia and about his upcoming child. The curse of the father visited upon the son and all that.

But Olivia understood the risks. This was what she wanted.

More than that, the somewhat high-strung Marsha had – he wondered what euphemism to use here – issues. There had been a brief breakdown a year after Bernie's sudden death. Marsha had 'gone to rest' – another euphemism – for two weeks while Matt moved in and took care of the boys. Marsha was fine now – that was what everyone said – but Matt still liked the idea of staying close.

Today was the physical inspection of the new house. 'I should be out in a little while. Why, what's up?'

'Could you stop by?'

'Stop by your place?'

'Yes.'

'Sure.'

'If it's a bad time . . .'

'No, of course not.'

Marsha was a beautiful woman with an oval face that sometimes looked sad-sack, and a nervous upward glance as if making sure the black cloud was in place. That was a physical thing, of course, no more a true reflection on her personality than being short or scarred.

'Everything all right?' Matt asked.

'Yeah, I'm fine. It's no big deal. It's just . . . Could you take the kids for a couple of hours? I got a school thing and Kyra's going to be out tonight.'

'You want me to take them out for dinner?'

'That would be great. But no McDonald's, okay?'

'Chinese?'

'Perfect,' she said.

'Cool, I'm there.'

'Thanks.'

The image started coming in on the camera phone.

'I'll see you later,' he said.

She said good-bye and hung up.

Matt turned his attention back to the cell phone. He squinted at the screen. It was tiny. Maybe an inch, no more than two. The sun was bright that day. The curtain was open. The glare made it harder to see. Matt cupped his hand around the tiny display and hunched his body so as to provide shade. It worked somewhat.

A man appeared on the screen.

Again it was hard to make out details. He looked in his mid-thirties – Matt's age – and had really dark hair, almost blue. He wore a red button-down shirt. His hand was up as though waving. He was in a room with white walls and a gray-sky window. The man had a smirk on his face – one of those knowing, I'm-better-than-you smirks. Matt stared at the man. Their eyes met and Matt could have sworn he saw something mocking in them.

Matt did not know the man.

He did not know why his wife would take the man's photograph.

The screen went black. Matt did not move. That seashell rush stayed in his ears. He could still hear other sounds – a distant fax machine, low voices, the traffic outside – but it was as though through a filter.

'Matt?'

It was Rolanda Garfield, said assistant/secretary. The law firm had not been thrilled when Matt hired her. Rolanda was a tad too 'street' for the stuffed shirts at Carter Sturgis. But he'd insisted. She had been one of Matt's first clients and one of his painfully few victories.

During his stint in prison, Matt managed to accrue enough credits to get his BA. The law degree came not long after his release. Bernie, a powerhouse at his uber-Newark law firm of Carter Sturgis, figured that he'd be able to convince the bar to make an exception and let his ex-con brother in.

He had been wrong.

But Bernie was not easily discouraged. He then persuaded his partners to take Matt in as a 'paralegal,' a wonderful all-encompassing term that, for the most part, seemed to mean 'scut work.'

The partners at Carter Sturgis didn't like it, at first. No surprise, of course. An ex-con at their white-shoe law firm? That simply wouldn't do. But Bernie appealed to their purported humanity: Matt would be good for public relations. He would show that the firm had heart and believed in second chances, at least in theoretical spin. He was smart. He would be an asset. More to the point, Matt could take on the large bulk of the firm's pro bono cases, freeing the partners to gouge the deep pockets without the distraction of the underclass.

The two closers: Matt would work cheap – what choice did he have? And Brother Bernie, a major-league rainmaker, would walk if they didn't agree.

The partners considered the scenario: Maybe do good *and* help yourself? It was the kind of logic upon which charities are built.

Matt's eyes stayed on the blank phone screen. His pulse did a little two-step. Who, he wondered, is that guy with the blue-black hair?

Rolanda put her hands on her hips. 'Earth to doofus,' she said.

'What?' Matt snapped out of it.

'You okay?'

'Me? I'm fine.'

Rolanda gave him a funny look.

The camera phone vibrated again. Rolanda stood with her arms crossed. Matt looked back at her. She did not get the hint. She rarely did. The phone vibrated again and then the *Batman* theme started up.

'Aren't you going to answer that?' Rolanda said.

He glanced down at the phone. The caller ID blinked out his wife's phone number again.

'Yo, Batman.'

'I'm on it,' Matt said.

His thumb touched on the green send button, lingering there for a moment before it pressed down. The screen lit up anew.

A video appeared now.

The technology was improving, but the shaky video display usually had a quality two steps below the Zapruder film. For a second or two, Matt had trouble focusing in on what was happening. The video would not last long, Matt knew. Ten, fifteen seconds tops.

It was a room. He could see that. The camera panned past a television on a console. There was a painting on the wall – Matt couldn't tell of what – but the overall impression led him to conclude that it was a hotel room. The camera stopped on the bathroom door.

And then a woman appeared.

Her hair was platinum blonde. She wore dark sunglasses and a slinky blue dress. Matt frowned.

What the hell was this?

The woman stood for a moment. Matt had the impression she did not know the camera was on her. The lens moved with her. There was a flash of light, sun bursting in through the window, and then everything came back into focus.

When the woman walked toward the bed, he stopped breathing.

Matt recognized the walk.

He also recognized the way she sat on the bed, the tentative smile that followed, the way her chin tilted up, the way she crossed her legs.

He did not move.

From across the room he heard Rolanda's voice, softer now: 'Matt?'

He ignored her. The camera was put down now, probably on a bureau. It was still aiming at the bed. A man walked toward the platinum blonde. Matt could only see the man's back. He was wearing a red shirt and had blue-black hair. His approach blocked the view of the woman. And the bed.

Matt's eyes started to blur. He blinked them back into focus. The LCD screen on the camera started to darken. The images flickered and disappeared and Matt was left sitting there, Rolanda staring at him curiously, the photographs on his brother's side of the desk still in place, and he was sure – well, pretty sure, the screen was only an inch or two, right? – that the woman in the strange hotel room, the woman in the slinky dress on the bed, that she was wearing a platinum-blonde wig and that she was really a brunette and that her name was Olivia and she was his wife.

3

Newark, New Jersey
June 22

Essex County homicide investigator Loren Muse sat in her boss's office.

'Wait a second,' she said. 'Are you telling me that the nun had breast implants?'

Ed Steinberg, the Essex County prosecutor, sat behind his desk rubbing his bowling-ball gut. He had that kind of build that from the back you wouldn't even know he was heavy, just that he had a flat ass. He leaned back and put his hands behind his head. The shirt was yellow under the armpits. 'So it appears, yeah.'

'But she died of natural causes?' Loren said.

'That's what we thought.'

'You don't think that anymore?'

'I don't think anything anymore,' Steinberg said.

'I could make a crack here, boss.'

'But you won't.' Steinberg sighed and put on his reading glasses. 'Sister Mary Rose, a tenth-grade social studies teacher, was found dead in her room at the convent. No signs of struggle, no wounds, she's sixty-two years old. Apparently a standard death – heart, stroke, something like that. Nothing suspicious.'

'But?' Loren added.

'But there's been a new development.'

'I think the word is "augmentation".'

34

'Stop it, you're killing me.'

Loren turned both palms up. 'I still don't see why I'm here.'

'How about that you're the greatest homicide investigator in the naked, uh, county?'

Loren made a face.

'Yeah, didn't think that'd fly. This nun' – Steinberg lowered the reading glasses again – 'taught at St. Margaret's High.' He looked at her.

'So?'

'So you were a student there, right?'

'And again I say: So?'

'So the Mother Superior has some juice with the brass. She requested you.'

'Mother Katherine?'

He checked the sheet. 'That's her name.'

'You're kidding, right?'

'Nope. She called in a favor. Requested you by name.'

Loren shook her head.

'You know her, I assume?'

'Mother Katherine? Only because I was constantly being sent to her office.'

'Wait, you weren't an easy kid?' Steinberg put his hand to his heart. 'Tattoo me shocked.'

'I still don't see why she'd want me.'

'Maybe she thought you'd be discreet.'

'I hated that place.'

'Why?'

'You didn't go to Catholic school, did you?'

He lifted his nameplate on his desk and pointed to the letters one at a time. 'Steinberg,' he read to her slowly. 'Note the Stein. Note the Berg. See those names much in church?'

Loren nodded. 'Right, then it'd be like explaining music

to the deaf. What prosecutor will I be reporting to?'
'Me.'
That surprised her. 'Directly?'
'Directly and only. Nobody else is on this, understood?'
She nodded. 'Understood.'
'You ready then?'
'Ready for what?'
'Mother Katherine.'
'What about her?'
Steinberg stood and sauntered around his desk. 'She's
in the next room. She wants to talk to you privately.'

When Loren Muse was a student at St. Margaret's School
for Girls, Mother Katherine was twelve feet tall and
approximately one hundred years old. The years had
shrunk her down and reversed the aging process – but
not by a lot. Mother Katherine had worn the full habit
when Loren was at St. Margaret's. Now she was decked
out in something undeniably pious, though far more
casual. The clerical answer to Banana Republic, Loren
guessed.

Steinberg said, 'I'll leave you two alone.'

Mother Katherine was standing, her hands folded in
preprayer position. The door closed. Neither of them
said anything. Loren knew this technique. She would not
talk first.

As a sophomore at Livingston High School, Loren
had been labeled a 'problem student' and sent to St. Margaret's. Loren was a petite thing back then, just five feet
tall, and she hadn't grown much in the ensuing years.
The other investigators, all males and oh so clever, called
her Squirt.

Investigators. You get them started, they'll shred you
with the cutting lines.

But Loren hadn't always been one of the so-called troubled youth. When she was in elementary school, she was that tiny tomboy, that spunky spark plug of a girl who kicked ass in kickball and would sooner die than don anything in the pink family. Her father worked a variety of blue-collar jobs, mostly involving trucking. He was a sweet, quiet man who made the mistake of falling for a woman far too beautiful for him.

The Muse clan lived in the Coventry section of Livingston, New Jersey, a slice of suburbia well beyond their social and economic means. Loren's mother, the ravishing and demanding Mrs. Muse, had insisted because, dammit, she deserved it. No one – but no one – was going to look down on Carmen Muse.

She pushed Loren's father, demanding he work harder, take out more loans, find a way to keep up, until – exactly two days after Loren turned fourteen years old – Dad blew his brains out in their detached two-car garage.

In hindsight her father was probably bipolar. She understood that now. There was a chemical imbalance in his brain. A man kills himself – it's not fair to blame others. But Loren did. She blamed her mother. She wondered what her sweet, quiet father's life would have been like had he married someone less high maintenance than Carmen Valos of Bayonne.

Young Loren took the tragedy as one might expect: She rebelled like mad. She drank, smoked, hung out with the wrong crowd, slept around. It was, Loren knew, grossly unfair that boys with multiple sex partners are revered while girls who do the same are dumb sluts. But the truth was – and Loren hated to admit this – for all the comforting feminist rationalizations, Loren knew that her level of promiscuity was adversely (though directly) related to her self-esteem. That is, when her self-worth was low, her, uh, easiness factor rose. Men didn't seem to suffer the same fate, or if they did, they hid it better.

Mother Katherine broke the stalemate. 'It's nice to see you, Loren.'

'Same here,' Loren said in a tentative voice that was so not like her. Gee, what next? Would she start biting her fingernails again? 'Prosecutor Steinberg said you wanted to talk to me?'

'Should we sit?'

Loren shrugged a suit-yourself. They both sat. Loren folded her arms and slid low in her chair. She crossed her feet. It occurred to her that she had gum in her mouth. Mother Katherine's face pinched up in disapproval. Not to be cowed, Loren picked up the pace so that the discreet chew turned into something more like a bovine mastication.

'Do you want to tell me what's going on?'

'We have a delicate situation here,' Mother Katherine began. 'It requires . . .' She looked up as if asking the Big Guy for a little assistance.

'Delicacy?' Loren replied.

'Yes. Delicacy.'

'Okay,' Loren said, dragging out the word. 'This is about the nun with the boob job, right?'

Mother Katherine closed her eyes, opened them again. 'It is. But I think you're missing the point.'

'Which is?'

'We had a wonderful teacher pass away.'

'That would be Sister Mary Rose.' Thinking: Our Lady of the Cleavage.

'Yes.'

'Do you think she died of natural causes?' Loren asked.

'I do.'

'So?'

38

'This is very tough to talk about.'

'I'd like to help.'

'You were a good girl, Loren.'

'No, I was a pain in the ass.'

Mother Katherine smothered a smile. 'Well, yes, that too.'

Loren returned the smile.

'There are different kinds of troublemakers,' Mother Katherine said. 'You were rebellious, yes, but you always had a good heart. You were never cruel to others. That, for me, has always been the key. You often got in trouble because you were sticking up for someone weaker.'

Loren leaned forward and surprised herself: She took the nun's hand. Mother Katherine too seemed startled by the gesture. Her blue eyes looked into Loren's.

'Promise me you will keep what I'm about to tell you to yourself,' Mother Katherine said. 'It's very important. In this climate especially. Even the whiff of scandal –'

'I won't cover anything up.'

'Nor would I want you to,' she said, now giving her the theologically offended tone. 'We need to get to the truth. I seriously considered the idea of just' – she waved her hand – 'of just letting this go. Sister Mary Rose would have been buried quietly and that would have been the end of it.'

Loren kept her hand on the nun's. The older woman's hand was dark, like it was made of balsam wood. 'I'll do my best.'

'You must understand. Sister Mary Rose was one of our best teachers.'

'She taught social studies?'

'Yes.'

Loren searched the memory banks. 'I don't remember her.'

'She joined us after you graduated.'

'How long had she been at St. Margaret's?'

'Seven years. And let me tell you something. The woman was a saint. I know the word is overused, but there is no other way to describe her. Sister Mary Rose never asked for glory. She had no ego. She just wanted to do what was right.'

Mother Katherine took back her hand. Loren leaned back and recrossed her legs. 'Go on.'

'When we – by we, I mean two sisters and myself – when we found her in the morning, Sister Mary Rose was in her nightclothes. She, like many of us, was a very modest woman.'

Loren nodded, trying to encourage.

'We were upset, of course. She had stopped breathing. We tried mouth-to-mouth and chest compressions. A local policeman had recently visited to teach the children about lifesaving techniques. So we tried it. I was the one who did the chest compressions and. . . .' Her voice trailed off.

'. . . And that was when you realized that Sister Mary Rose had breast implants?'

Mother Katherine nodded.

'Did you mention this to the other sisters?'

'Oh, no. Of course not.'

Loren shrugged. 'I don't really understand the problem,' she said.

'You don't?'

'Sister Mary Rose probably had a life before she became a nun. Who knows what it was like?'

'That's just it,' Mother Katherine said. 'She didn't.'

'I'm not sure I follow.'

'Sister Mary Rose came to us from a very conservative parish in Oregon. She was orphaned and joined the convent when she was fifteen years old.'

Loren considered that. 'So you had no idea that . . . ?' She made halfhearted back-and-forth gestures in front of her own chest.

'Absolutely no idea.'

'How do you explain it then?'

'I think' – Mother Katherine bit her lip – 'I think Sister Mary Rose came to us under false pretenses.'

'What sort of false pretenses?'

'I don't know.' Mother Katherine looked up at her expectantly.

'And,' Loren said, 'that's where I come in?'

'Well, yes.'

'You want me to find out what her deal was.'

'Yes.'

'Discreetly.'

'That would be my hope, Loren. But we need to find the truth.'

'Even if it's ugly?'

'Especially if it's ugly.' Mother Katherine rose. 'That's what you do with the ugly of this world. You pull it into God's light.'

'Yeah,' Loren said. 'Into the light.'

'You're not a believer anymore, are you, Loren?'

'I never was.'

'Oh, I don't know about that.' Loren stood, but Mother Katherine still towered over her. Yep, Loren thought, twelve feet tall. 'Will you help me?'

'You know I will.'

4

Seconds passed. Matt Hunter guessed it was seconds. He stared at the phone and waited. Nothing happened. His mind was in deep freeze. It came out and when it did, he longed for the deep freeze to return.

The phone. He turned it over in his hand, studying it as if he'd never seen it before. The screen, he reminded himself, was small. The images were jerky. The tint and color were off. The glare had also been a problem.

He nodded to himself. Keep going.

Olivia was not a platinum blonde.

Good. More, more . . .

He knew her. He loved her. He was not the best catch. He was an ex-con with few bright prospects. He had a tendency to withdraw emotionally. He did not love or trust easily. Olivia, on the other hand, had it all. She was beautiful. She was smart, had graduated summa cum laude from the University of Virginia. She even had some money her father left her.

This wasn't helping.

Yes. Yes, it was because, despite all that, Olivia had still chosen him – the ex-con with zero prospects. She had been the first woman he'd told about his past. No other had hung around long enough for it to become an issue.

Her reaction?

Well, it hadn't been all flowers. Olivia's smile – that drop-you-to-your-knees pow – had dimmed for a moment. Matt wanted to stop right there. He wanted to walk away because there was no way he could handle being responsible for dimming, even for a brief moment, that smile. But the flicker hadn't lasted long. The beam soon returned to full wattage. Matt had bitten down on his lip in relief. Olivia had reached across the table and taken his hand and, in a sense, had never let it go.

But now, as Matt sat here, he remembered those first tentative steps when he left the prison, the careful ones he took when he blinked his eyes and stepped through the gate, that feeling – that feeling that has never totally left him – that the thin ice beneath him could crack at any time and plunge him into the freezing water.

How does he explain what he just saw?

Matt understood human nature. Check that. He understood subhuman nature. He had seen the Fates curse him and his family enough to come up with an explanation or, if you will, an anti-explanation for all that goes wrong: In sum, there is no explanation.

The world is neither cruel nor joyous. It is simply random, full of particles hurtling, chemicals mixing and reacting. There is no real order. There is no preordained cursing of the evil and protecting of the righteous.

Chaos, baby. It's all about chaos.

And in the swirl of all that chaos, Matt had only one thing – Olivia.

But as he sat in his office, eyes still on that phone, his mind wouldn't let it go. Now, right now, at this very second . . . what was Olivia doing in that hotel room?

He closed his eyes and sought a way out.

Maybe it wasn't her.

Again: the screen, it was small. The video, it was jerky. Matt kept going with that, running similar rationalizations up the flagpole, hoping one would fly.

None did.

There was a sinking feeling in his chest.

Images flooded in. Matt tried to battle them, but they were overwhelming. The guy's blue-black hair. That damned knowing smirk. He thought about the way Olivia would lean back when they made love, biting her lower lip, her eyes half closed, the tendons in her neck growing taut. He imagined sounds too. Small groans at first. Then cries of ecstasy . . .

Stop it.

He looked up and found Rolanda still staring at him.

'Was there something you wanted?' he asked.

'There was.'

'And?'

'I've been standing here so long, I forget.'

Rolanda shrugged, spun, left the office. She did not close the door behind her.

Matt stood and moved to the window. He looked down at a photograph of Bernie's sons in full soccer gear. Bernie and Marsha had used this picture for their Christmas card three years ago. The frame was one of those faux bronze numbers you get at Rite-Aid or a similar drugstore-cum-frame store. In the photograph Bernie's boys, Paul and Ethan, were five and three and smiled like it. They don't smile like that anymore. They were good kids, well-adjusted and all, but there was still an inescapable, underlying sadness. When you looked closely, the smiles were more cautious now, a wince in the eye, a fear of what else might be taken from them.

So what to do now?

The obvious, he decided. Call Olivia back. See what's what.

It sounded rational on one level and ridiculous on another. What did he really think would happen here? Would the first sound he heard be his wife breathing heavily, a man's laughter in the background? Or did he think Olivia would answer with her usual sunny voice and then – what? – he'd say, 'Hi, hon, say, what's up with the motel?' – in his mind's eye it was no longer a hotel room, but now a dingy no-tell motel, changing the *h* to an *m* adding a whole new significance – 'and the platinum wig and the smirking guy with the blue-black hair?'

That didn't sound right.

He was letting his imagination run away with him. There was a logical explanation for all this. Maybe he couldn't see it yet, but that didn't mean it wasn't there. Matt remembered watching those TV specials about how magicians did their tricks. You watched the trick and you couldn't fathom the answer and once they showed it to you, you wondered how you could have been so stupid to miss it the first time. That was what this was like.

Seeing no other option, Matt decided to call.

Olivia's cell was programmed into his speed dial in the number one spot. He pressed down on the button and held it. The phone began to ring. He stared out the window and saw the city of Newark. His feelings for this city were, as always, mixed. You see the potential, the vibrancy, but mostly you see the decay and shake your head. For some reason he flashed back to the day Duff had visited him in prison. Duff had started bawling, his face red, looking so like a child. Matt could only watch. There was nothing to say.

The phone rang six times before going into Olivia's voice mail. The sound of his wife's animated voice, so familiar, so . . . *his*, made his heart stutter. He waited patiently for Olivia to finish. Then the beep sounded.

'Hey, it's me,' he said. He could hear the tautness in his tone and fought against it. 'Could you give me a call when you have a second?' He paused. He usually ended with a perfunctory 'love you,' but this time he hit the end button without adding what had always come so naturally.

He kept looking out the window. In prison what eventually got to him was not the brutality or the repulsion. Just the opposite. It was when those things became the norm. After a while Matt started to like his brothers in the Aryan Nation – actually enjoyed their company. It was a perverse offshoot of the Stockholm syndrome. Survival is the thing. The mind will twist to survive. Anything can become normal. That was what made Matt pause.

He thought about Olivia's laugh. How it took him away from all that. He wondered now if that laugh was real or just another cruel mirage, something to mock him with kindness.

Then Matt did something truly strange.

He held the camera phone out in front of him, arm's distance, and snapped a picture of himself. He didn't smile. He just looked into the lens. The photograph was on the little screen now. He looked at his own face and was not sure what he saw.

He pressed her phone number and sent the picture to Olivia.

5

Two hours passed. Olivia did not call back.

Matt spent those two hours with Ike Kier, a pampered senior partner who wore his gray hair too long and slicked back. He came from a wealthy family. He knew how to network and not much else, but sometimes that was enough. He owned a Viper and two Harley-Davidsons. His nickname around the office was Midlife, short for Midlife Crisis.

Midlife was bright enough to know that he was not that bright. He thus used Matt a lot. Matt, he knew, was willing to do most of the heavy lifting and stay behind the scenes. This allowed Midlife to maintain the big corporate client relationship and look good. Matt cared, he guessed, but not enough to do anything about it.

Corporate fraud may not be good for America, but it was damned profitable for the white-shoe, white-collar law firm of Carter Sturgis. Right now they were discussing the case of Mike Sterman, the CEO of a big pharmaceutical company called Pentacol, who'd been charged with, among other things, cooking the books to manipulate stock prices.

'In sum,' Midlife said, giving the room his best you-the-jury baritone, 'our defense will be . . . ?' He looked to Matt for the answer.

'Blame the other guy,' Matt said.

'Which other guy?'

'Yes.'

'Huh?'

'We blame whoever we can,' Matt said. 'The CFO' – Sterman's brother-in-law and former best friend – 'the COO, the C Choose-Your-Favorite-Two-Letter Combination, the accounting firm, the banks, the board, the lower-level employees. We claim some of them are crooks. We claim some of them made honest mistakes that steamrolled.'

'Isn't that contradictory?' Midlife asked, folding his hands and lowering his eyebrows. 'Claiming both malice and mistakes?' He stopped, looked up, smiled, nodded. Malice and mistakes. Midlife liked the way that sounded.

'We're looking to confuse,' Matt said. 'You blame enough people, nothing sticks. The jury ends up knowing something went wrong, but you don't know where to place the blame. We throw facts and figures at them. We bring up every possible mistake, every uncrossed *t* and undotted *i*. We act like every discrepancy is a huge deal, even if it's not. We question everything. We are skeptical of everyone.'

'And what about the bar mitzvah?'

Sterman had thrown his son a two-million-dollar bar mitzvah, featuring a chartered plane to Bermuda where both Beyoncé and Ja Rule performed. The videotape – actually, it was a surround-sound DVD – was going to be shown to the jury.

'A legitimate business expense,' Matt said.

'Come again?'

'Look who was there. Executives from the big drug chains. Top buyers. Government officials from the FDA who approve drugs and give out grants. Doctors, researchers, whatever. Our client was wining and dining clients – a legit American business practice since before

48

the Boston Tea Party. What he did was for the good of the company.'

'And the fact that the party was for his son's bar mitzvah?'

Matt shrugged. 'It works in his favor, actually. Sterman was being brilliant.'

Midlife made a face.

'Think about it. If Sterman had said, 'I'm throwing a big party to win over important clients,' well, that wouldn't have helped him develop the relationships he was looking for. So Sterman, that sly genius, went with something more subtle. He invites his business associates to his son's bar mitzvah. They are caught off guard now. They find it sweet, this family guy inviting them to something personal rather than hitting them up in some stuffy business venue. Sterman, like any brilliant CEO, was creative in his approach.'

Midlife arched an eyebrow and nodded slowly. 'Oh, I like that.'

Matt had figured as much. He checked his cell phone, making sure it was still powered up. It was. He checked to see if there were any messages or missed calls. There were none.

Midlife rose. 'We'll do more prep tomorrow?'

'Sure,' Matt said.

He left. Rolanda stuck her head in the door. She looked down the hall in the direction of Midlife, faked sticking a finger down her throat, and made a gagging noise. Matt checked the time. Time to get moving.

He hurried out to the firm's parking lot. His gaze wandered, focusing on nothing and everything. Tommy, the parking lot attendant, waved to him. Still dazed, Matt may have waved back. His spot was in the back, under the dripping pipes. The world was about the pecking order, he knew, even in parking lots.

Someone was cleaning a green Jag belonging to one of the founding partners. Matt turned. One of Midlife's Harleys was there, covered by a see-through tarp. There was a tipped-over shopping cart. Three of the four wheels had been ripped off the cart. What would someone want with three shopping-cart wheels?

Matt's eyes drifted over the cars on the street, mostly gypsy cabs, and noticed a gray Ford Taurus because the license plate was MLH-472, and Matt's own initials were MKH, pretty close, and things like that were distractions.

But once in his car – once alone with his thoughts – something new started gnawing at him.

Okay, he thought, trying his best to stay rational. Let's assume the worst – that what he saw on the camera phone were the opening moments of a tryst of some kind.

Why would Olivia send it to him?

What would be the point? Did she want to get caught? Was this a cry for help?

That didn't really add up.

But then he realized something else: Olivia hadn't sent it.

It had come from her phone, yes, but she – assuming that was Olivia with the platinum wig – didn't seem to realize that the camera was on her. He remembered thinking that. She was the subject of the film – the filmee, if you will, not the filmer.

So who sent it? Was it Mr. Blue-Black Hair? If so, then who snapped the first picture, the one of Blue-Black? Had he taken it himself?

Answer: No.

Blue-Black had his palm up as if waving. Matt remembered the backside of a ring on his finger – or what he thought was a ring. He really wasn't up for looking at the picture again. But he thought about it. Could that have been a wedding band? No, the ring was on the right hand.

Either way, who had taken Blue-Black's picture?

Olivia?

Why would she send it to him? Or was the picture sent to him inadvertently? Like maybe someone hit the wrong number on the speed dial?

It seemed unlikely.

Was there a third person in the room?

Matt couldn't see it. He mulled it over some more, but nothing came together. Both calls had originated from his wife's phone. Got that. But if she was having an affair, why would she want him to know?

Answer – and yes, his reasoning was getting circular – she wouldn't.

So who would?

Matt thought again of the cocky smirk on Blue-Black's face. And his stomach roiled. When he was younger, he used to feel too much. Strange to imagine it now, but Matt had been too sensitive. He'd cry when he lost a basketball game, even a pickup game. Any slight would stay with him for weeks. All of that changed the night Stephen McGrath died. If prison teaches you one thing, it's how to deaden yourself. You show nothing. Ever. You never allow yourself anything, even an emotion, because it will either be exploited or taken away. Matt tried that now. He tried to deaden the sinking feeling in the pit of his belly.

He couldn't do it.

The images were back now, terrible ones blended in with achingly wonderful memories, the memories hurting most of all. He remembered a weekend he and Olivia had spent at a Victorian B&B in Lenox, Massachusetts.

He remembered spreading pillows and blankets in front of the fireplace in the room and opening a bottle of wine. He remembered the way Olivia held the stem of the glass, the way she looked at him, the way the world, the past, his tentative, fearful steps all faded away, the way the fire reflected off her green eyes, and then he would think of her like that with another man.

A new thought hit him then – one so awful, so unbearable he nearly lost control of his car:

Olivia was pregnant.

The light turned red. Matt almost drove through it. He slammed on the brakes at the last moment. A pedestrian, already starting across the street, jumped back and waved his fist at him. Matt kept both hands on the wheel.

Olivia had taken a long time to conceive.

They were both in their mid-thirties and in Olivia's mind the clock was ticking. She so badly wanted to start a family. For a long time their attempts at conception hadn't gone well. Matt had started to wonder – and not just idly – if the fault lay with him. He had taken some pretty good beatings in prison. During his third week there, four men had pinned him down and spread-eagled his legs while a fifth kicked him hard in the groin. He had nearly passed out from the pain.

Now suddenly Olivia was pregnant.

He wanted to shut down his brain, but it wouldn't happen. Rage started to seep in. It was better, he thought, than the hurt, than the awful gut-wrenching ache of having something he cherished ripped away from him again.

He had to find her. He had to find her now.

Olivia was in Boston, a five-hour journey from where he now was. Screw the house inspection. Just drive up, have it out with her now.

Where was she staying?

He thought about that. Had she told him? He couldn't remember. That was another thing about having cell phones. You don't worry so much about things like that. What difference did it make if she was staying at the Marriott or the Hilton? She was on a business trip. She would be moving about, out at meetings and dinners, rarely in her room.

Easiest, of course, to reach her by cell phone.

So now what?

He had no idea where she was staying. And even if he did, wouldn't it make more sense to call first? For all he knew, that might not even be her hotel room he'd seen on the camera phone. It might have belonged to Blue-Black Hair. And suppose he did know the hotel. Suppose he did show up and pounded on the door and then, what, Olivia would open it in a negligee with Blue-Black standing behind her, a towel wrapped around his waist? Then what would Matt do? Beat the crap out of him? Point and shout 'Aha!'?

He tried calling her on the camera phone again. Still no answer. He didn't leave another message.

Why hadn't Olivia told him where she was staying?

Pretty obvious now, isn't it, Matt ol' boy?

The red curtain came down over his eyes.

Enough.

He tried her office, but the call went directly into her voice mail: *'Hi, this is Olivia Hunter. I'll be out of the office until Friday. If this is important, you can reach my assistant, Jamie Suh, by pressing her extension, six-four-four –'*

That was what Matt did. Jamie answered on the third ring.

'Olivia Hunter's line.'

'Hey, Jamie, it's Matt.'

'Hi, Matt.'

He kept his hands on the wheel and talked using a hands-free, which always felt weird – like you're a crazy person chatting with an imaginary friend. When you talk on a phone, you should be holding one. 'Just got a quick question for you.'

'Shoot.'

'Do you know what hotel Olivia's staying in?'

There was no reply.

'Jamie?'

'I'm here,' she said. 'Uh, I can look it up, if you want to hold on. But why don't you just call her cell? That's the number she left if any client had an emergency.'

He was not sure how to reply to that without sounding somehow desperate. If he told her he had tried that and got the message, Jamie Suh would wonder why he couldn't simply wait for her to reply. He wracked his brain for something that sounded plausible.

'Yeah, I know,' he said. 'But I want to send her flowers. You know, as a surprise.'

'Oh, I see.' There was little enthusiasm in her voice. 'Is it a special occasion?'

'No.' Then he added extra-lamely: 'But hey, the honeymoon is still on.' He laughed at his own pitiful line. Not surprisingly, Jamie did not.

There was a long silence.

'You still there?' Matt said.

'Yes.'

'Could you tell me where she's staying?'

'I'm looking it up now.' There was the tapping sound of her fingers on a keyboard. Then: 'Matt?'

'Yes.'

'I have another call coming in. Can I call you back when I find it?'

'Sure,' he said, not liking this at all. He gave her his cell phone number and hung up.

What the hell was going on?

His phone vibrated again. He checked the number. It was the office. Rolanda didn't bother with hellos.

'Problem,' she said. 'Where are you?'

'Just hitting seventy-eight.'

'Turn around. Washington Street. Eva is getting evicted.'

He swore under his breath. 'Who?'

'Pastor Jill is over there with those two beefy sons of hers. They threatened Eva.'

Pastor Jill. A woman who got her religious degree online and sets up 'charities' where the youth can stay with her as long as they cough up enough in food stamps. The scams run on the poor are beyond reprehensible. Matt veered the car to the right.

'On my way,' he said.

Ten minutes later he pulled to a stop on Washington Street. The neighborhood was near Branch Brook Park. As a kid Matt used to play tennis here. He played competitively for a while, his parents schlepping him to tournaments in Port Washington every other weekend. He was even ranked in the boys' fourteen-and-under division. But the family stopped coming to Branch Brook way before that. Matt never understood what happened to Newark. It had been a thriving, wonderful community. The wealthier eventually moved out during the suburban migration of the fifties and sixties. That was natural, of course. It happened everywhere. But Newark was abandoned. Those who left – even those who traveled just a few miles away – never looked back. Part of that was the riots in the late sixties. Part of that was simple racism. But there was something more here, something worse, and Matt didn't know exactly what it was.

He got out of the car. The neighborhood was predominantly African American. So were most of his clients. Matt wondered about that. During his prison stint, he heard the 'n'-word more often than any other. He had said it himself, to fit in at first, but it became less repulsive as time went on, which of course was the most repulsive thing of all.

In the end he'd been forced to betray what he had always believed in, the liberal suburban lie about skin color not mattering. In prison, skin color was all that mattered. Out here, in a whole different way, it mattered just as much.

His gaze glided over the scenery. It got snagged on an interesting chunk of graffiti. On a wall of chipped brick, someone had spray-painted two words in four-foot-high letters:

BITCHES LIE!

Normally Matt would not stop and study something like this. Today he did. The letters were red and slanted. Even if you couldn't read, you could feel the rage here. Matt wondered about the creator – what inspired him to write this. He wondered if this act of vandalism had diluted the creator's wrath – or been the first step toward greater destruction.

He walked toward Eva's building. Pastor Jill's car, a fully loaded Mercedes 560, was there. One of her sons stood guard with his arms crossed, his face set on scowl. Matt's eyes started their sweep again. The neighbors were out and about. One small child of maybe two sat atop an old lawn mower. His mother was using it as a stroller. She muttered to herself and looked strung out. People stared at Matt – a white man was not unfamiliar here but still a curiosity.

Pastor Jill's sons glared as he approached. The street

went quiet, like in a Western. The people were ready for a showdown.

Matt said, 'How are you doing?'

The brothers might have been twins. One kept up the stare. The other started loading Eva's belongings into the trunk. Matt did not blink. He kept smiling and walking.

'I'd like you to stop that now.'

Crossed-Tree-Trunk-Arms said, 'Who are you?'

Pastor Jill came out. She looked over at Matt and scowled too.

'You can't throw her out,' Matt said.

Pastor Jill gave him the high-and-mighty. 'I own this residence.'

'No, the state owns it. You claim it's charitable housing for the city's youths.'

'Eva didn't follow the rules.'

'What rules are those?'

'We are a religious institution. We have a strict moral code here. Eva here broke it.'

'How?'

Pastor Jill smiled. 'I'm not sure that's any of your concern. May I ask your name?'

Her two sons exchanged a glance. One put down Eva's stuff. They turned toward him.

Matt pointed at Pastor Jill's Mercedes. 'Sweet wheels.'

The brothers frowned and strolled toward him. One cracked his neck as he strutted. The other opened and closed fists. Matt felt his blood hum. Strangely enough the death of Stephen McGrath – the 'slip' – hadn't made him fearful of violence. Perhaps if he had been more aggressive that night, not less . . . but that wasn't what mattered now. He had learned a valuable lesson about physical confrontations: You can predict nothing. Sure, whoever lands the first blow usually wins. The bigger man was usually victorious too. But once it got going, once the red tornado took hold of the combatants, anything could happen.

The Neck Cracker said, 'Who are you?' again.

Matt would not risk it. He sighed and took out his camera phone. 'I'm Bob Smiley, Channel Nine News.'

That stopped them.

He pointed the camera in their direction and pretended to turn it on. 'If you don't mind, I'm going to film what you're doing here. The Channel Nine News van will be here for clearer shots in three minutes.'

The brothers looked back at their mother. Pastor Jill's face broke into a beatific albeit phony smile.

'We're helping Eva move,' she said. 'To better quarters.'

'Uh huh.'

'But if she'd rather just stay here . . .'

'She'd rather stay here,' Matt said.

'Milo, move her things back into the apartment.'

Milo, the Neck Cracker, gave Matt the fish eye. Matt held up the camera. 'Hold that pose, Milo.' Milo and Fist Flex started to take the stuff out of the van. Pastor Jill hurried to her Mercedes and waited in the back. Eva looked down at Matt from the window and mouthed a thank-you. Matt nodded and turned away.

It was then, turning away, not really looking at anything, that Matt saw the gray Ford Taurus.

The car was idling about thirty yards behind him. Matt froze. Gray Ford Tauruses were plentiful, of course, perhaps the most popular car in the country. Seeing two in a day would hardly be uncommon. Matt figured that there was probably another Ford Taurus on this very block. Maybe two or three. And he would not be surprised to learn that another one might even be gray.

But would it have a license plate that started with MLH, so close to his own initials of MKH?

His eyes stayed glued to the license plate.

MLH-472.

The same car he'd seen outside his office.

Matt tried to keep his breathing even. It could, he knew, be nothing more than a coincidence. Taking a step back, that was indeed a strong possibility. A person could see the same car twice in a day. He was only, what, half a mile away from his office. This was a fairly congested neighborhood. There was no big shock here.

On a normal day – check that: On pretty much *any* other day – Matt would have let that logic win him over.

But not today. He hesitated, but not for very long. Then he headed toward the car.

'Hey,' Milo shouted, 'where you going?'

'Just keep unloading, big man.'

Matt hadn't moved five steps when the front wheels of the Ford Taurus started to angle themselves to move out of the spot. Matt hurried his pace.

Without warning, the Taurus jumped forward and cut across the street. The white taillights came on and the car jerked back. Matt realized that the driver planned on making a K turn. The driver hit the brake and turned the steering wheel hard and fast. Matt was only a few feet from the back window.

Matt yelled, 'Wait!' – as if that would do any good – and broke into a sprint. He leapt in front of the car.

Bad move.

The Taurus's tire grabbed gravel, made a little shriek, and shot toward him.

There was no slowdown, no hesitation. Matt jumped to the side. The Taurus accelerated. Matt was off the ground now, horizontal. The bumper clipped his ankle.

A burst of pain exploded through the bone. The momentum swung Matt around in midair. He landed face-first and tucked into a roll. He ended up on his back.

For a few moments Matt lay there blinking into the sunlight. People gathered around him. 'You all right?' someone asked. He nodded and sat up. He checked his ankle. Bruised hard but no break. Someone helped him to his feet.

The whole thing – from the moment he saw the car to the moment it tried to run him down – had maybe taken five, maybe ten seconds. Certainly no more. Matt stared off.

Someone had been – at the very least – following him.

He checked his pocket. The cell phone was still there. He limped back toward Eva's apartment. Pastor Jill and her sons were gone. He checked to make sure Eva was okay. Then he got into his own car and took a deep breath. He thought about what to do and realized that the first step was fairly obvious.

He dialed her private line number. When Cingle answered, he asked, 'You in your office?'

'Yup,' Cingle said.

'I'll be there in five minutes.'

6

As soon as county homicide investigator Loren Muse opened her apartment door, the waft of cigarette smoke attacked. Loren let it. She stood there and sucked in a deep breath.

Her garden apartment was on Morris Avenue in Union, New Jersey. She never understood the term 'garden.' The place was a pit – all brick, no personality, and nothing resembling green. This was New Jersey's version of purgatory, a way station, the place people stayed on the way up or down economic and social ladders. Young couples lived here until they could afford the house. Unlucky pensioners returned here after the kids flew the coop.

And, of course, single women on the verge of old-maidhood who worked too hard and entertained too little – they ended up here too.

Loren was thirty-four years old, a serial dater who, to quote her cigarette-toting mother who was currently on the couch, 'never closed the sale.' The cop-thing worked liked that. It initially attracted men and then sent them scurrying when the commitment-aka-expiration date approached. She was currently dating a guy named Pete whom her mother labeled a 'total loser,' and Loren had trouble arguing with that assessment.

Her two cats, Oscar and Felix, were nowhere in sight, but that was normal. Her mother, the lovely Carmen Valos Muse Brewster Whatever, lay sprawled on the couch watching *Jeopardy!* She watched the show nearly every day and had never gotten a question right.

'Hey,' Loren said.

'This place is a pigsty,' her mother said.

'Then clean it. Or better yet, move out.'

Carmen had recently split with Husband Four. Her mother was a good-looking woman – far better looking than the plain daughter who'd taken after her suicidal father. Still sexy, though now it was in a sort of sloppy-seconds way. Her looks were starting to droop, but she still landed better dates than Loren. Men loved Carmen Valos Muse Etcetera.

Carmen turned back to the television and took another deep puff of the cigarette.

Loren said, 'I told you a thousand times not to smoke in here.'

'You smoke.'

'No, Ma, I quit.'

Carmen turned the big browns in her direction, blinking seductively out of habit. 'You quit?'

'Yes.'

'Oh, come on. Two months? That's not quitting.'

'It's five months.'

'Still. Didn't you smoke in here?'

'So?'

'So what's the big deal? It's not like the smell is gone or anything. It's not like this is one of those fancy no-smoking hotel rooms. Right?'

Her mother gave her the familiar judgmental eye, sizing Loren up the way she always did and finding her wanting the way she always did. Loren waited for the inevitable 'just trying to help' beauty tip: Your hair could use some shape, you should wear something clingier, why do you have to look like a boy, have you seen the new push-up bras at Victoria's Secret, would a little makeup kill you, short girls should never go out without heels . . .

Carmen's mouth opened and the phone rang.

'Hold that thought,' Loren said.

She picked up the receiver.

'Yo, Squirt, it's *moi*.'

'*Moi*' was Eldon Teak, a sixty-two-year-old Caucasian grandfather who only listened to rap music. Eldon was also the Essex County medical examiner.

'What's up, Eldon?'

'You catch the Stacked Nun case?'

'That's what you're calling it?'

'Until we come up with something funnier. I liked Our Lady with the Valley or Mount Saint Mountains, but no one else did.'

She gently rubbed her eyes with an index finger and thumb. 'You got something for me?'

'I do.'

'Like?'

'Like the death wasn't accidental.'

'She was murdered?'

'Yup. Pillow over the face.'

'God, how the hell did they miss that?'

'How the hell did who miss that?'

'Wasn't she originally listed as death by natural causes?'

'Yes.'

'Well, Eldon, see, that's what I mean when I say, how the hell did they miss that?'

'And I asked you who you meant.'

'Whoever originally examined her.'

'No one originally examined her. That's the point.'

'Why not?'

'You're kidding, right?'

'No. I mean, shouldn't that have shown up right away?'

'You watch too much TV. Every day zillions of people die, right? Wife finds the husband dead on the floor. You think we do an autopsy? You think we check to see if it's murder? Most of the time cops don't even come in. My old man croaked, what, ten years ago. My mom called the funeral home, a doc declares him dead, they pick him up. That's how it normally works, you know that. So here a nun dies, looks like natural causes to anyone who doesn't know exactly what to look for. I would have never gotten her on the table if your Mother Superior doesn't say something.'

'You sure it was a pillow?'

'Yup. Pillow in her room, matter of fact. Plenty of fibers in the throat.'

'How about under her fingernails?'

'They're clean.'

'Isn't that unusual?'

'Depends.'

Loren shook her head, tried to put it together. 'You have an ID?'

'An ID on what?'

'On the victim?'

'I thought she was Sister Silicon or something. What do we need an ID for?'

Loren checked her watch. 'How much longer are you in the office?'

'Another two hours,' Eldon Teak said.

'I'm on my way.'

7

Here is how you find your soul mate.

It is spring break your freshman year of college. Most of your friends head down to Daytona Beach, but your high school bud Rick has a mother in the travel business. She gets you super-low rates to Vegas, so you and six friends go for a five-night stay at the Flamingo Hotel.

On the last night, you head to a nightclub at Caesars Palace because you hear it's supposed to be a great hangout for coeds on vacation. The nightclub, no surprise, is noisy and crowded. There is too much neon. It is not your scene. You are with your friends, trying to hear them over the loud crush of music, when you look across the bar.

That is when you see Olivia for the first time.

No, the music doesn't stop or segue to angelic harps. But something happens to you. You look at her and feel it in your chest, a warm twang, and you can see that she feels it too.

You are normally shy, not good with approaches, but tonight you can do no wrong. You make your way over to her and introduce yourself. We all have special nights like this, you think. You're at a party and you see a beautiful girl and she's looking at you and you start talking and you just click in a way that makes you think about lifetimes instead of one-nights.

You talk to her. You talk for hours. She looks at you as if you're the only person in the world. You go somewhere quieter. You kiss her. She responds. You start to make out. You make out all night and have no real desire to push it any further. You hold her. You talk some more. You love her laugh. You love her face. You love everything about her.

You fall asleep in each other's arms, fully clothed, and you wonder if you will ever be this happy again. Her hair smells like lilacs and berries. You will never forget that smell.

You'd do anything to make this last, but you know it won't. These sorts of interactions aren't built for the long term. You have a life, and Olivia has a 'serious' boyfriend, a fiancé really, back home. This isn't about that. It is about the two of you, your own world, for just too brief a time. You pack a small life span into that night, a complete cycle of courtship, relationship, breakup into those few hours.

In the end, you will go back to your life and she'll go back to hers.

You don't bother trading phone numbers – neither one of you wants to pretend like that – but she takes you to the airport and you passionately kiss good-bye. Her eyes are wet when you release her. You return to school.

You go on, of course, but you never quite forget her or that night or the way it felt to kiss her or the smell of her hair. She stays with you. You think of her. Not every day, maybe not even every week. But she's there. The memory is something you take out every now and then, when you're feeling alone, and you don't know if it comforts or stings.

You wonder if she ever does the same.

Eleven years pass. You don't see her in all that time.

You are no longer the same person, of course. The death of Stephen McGrath had set you off the rails. You have spent time in prison. But you're free now. Your life has been given back to you, you guess. You work at the Carter Sturgis law firm.

One day you sign onto the computer and Google her name.

You know it is stupid and immature. You realize that she probably married the fiancé, has three or four kids by now, maybe taken her husband's name. But this is harmless. You will take it no further. You are simply curious.

There are several Olivia Murrays.

You search a little deeper and find one that might be her. This Olivia Murray is the sales director for DataBetter, a consulting business that designs computer systems for small-to-midsize companies. DataBetter's Web site has employee biographies. Hers is brief but it does mention that she is a graduate of the University of Virginia. That was where your Olivia Murray was going when you met all those years ago.

You try to forget about it.

You are not one who believes in fate or kismet – just the opposite – but six months later, the partners at Carter Sturgis decide that the firm's computer system needs to be overhauled. Midlife knows that you learned about computer programming during your tenure in prison. He suggests that you be on the committee to develop a new office network. You suggest several firms come in and make bids.

One of those firms is DataBetter.

Two people from DataBetter arrive at the offices of Carter Sturgis. You are in a panic. In the end, you fake an emergency and don't attend the presentation. That would be too much – showing up like that. You let the other three men on the committee handle the interview. You stay in your office. Your leg shakes. You bite your nails. You feel like an idiot.

At noon, there is a knock on your office door.

You turn and Olivia is there.

You recognize her right away. It hits you like a physical blow. The warm twang is back. You can barely speak. You look at her left hand. At her ring finger.

There is nothing there.

Olivia smiles and tells you that she's here at Carter Sturgis doing a presentation. You try to nod. Her company is bidding to set up the firm's computer systems, she says. She spotted your name on the list of people who were supposed to be at the meeting and wondered if you were the same Matt Hunter she met all those years ago.

Still stunned, you ask her if she wants to grab a cup of coffee. She hesitates but says yes. When you rise and walk past her, you smell her hair. The lilacs and berries are still there, and you worry that your eyes will well up.

You both gloss over the phony catch-up preliminaries, which, of course, works well for you. Over the years she has thought about you too, you find out. The fiancé is long gone. She has never been married.

Your heart soars even as you shake your head. You know that this is all too impossible. Neither of you believes in concepts like love at first sight.

But there you are.

In the weeks that follow you learn what true love is. She teaches it to you. You eventually tell her the truth about your past. She gets over it. You get married. She becomes pregnant. You are happy. You both celebrate the news by buying matching camera phones.

And then, one day, you get a call and see the woman you met during that long-ago spring break – the only woman you ever loved – in a hotel room with another man.

*

Why the hell would someone be following him?

Matt kept his hands steady on the wheel as his head spun with possibilities. He sorted through them. Nothing stuck.

He needed help, big-time. And that meant visiting Cingle.

He was going to be late for his appointment with the home inspector. He didn't much care. Suddenly the future he had allowed himself to imagine – house, picket fence, the always-beautiful Olivia, the 2.4 kids, the Lab retriever – seemed frighteningly unrealistic. More fooling himself, he guessed. A convicted murderer returning to the suburbs he grew up in and raising the ideal family – it suddenly sounded like a bad sitcom pitch.

Matt called Marsha, his sister-in-law, to tell her he wouldn't get out there until later, but her machine picked up. He left a message and pulled into the lot.

Housed in a building of sleek glass not far from Matt's office is MVD – Most Valuable Detection, a large private-eye firm Carter Sturgis uses. By and large Matt was not a huge fan of private detectives. In fiction they were pretty cool dudes. In reality they were, at best, retired (emphasis on the 'tired') cops and at worst, guys who couldn't become cops and thus are that dangerous creation known as the 'cop wannabe.' Matt had seen plenty of wannabes working as prison guards. The mixture of failure and imagined testosterone produced volatile and often ugly consequences.

Matt sat in the office of one of the exceptions to this rule – the lovely and controversial Ms. Cingle Shaker. Matt didn't think that was her real name, but it was the one she used professionally. Cingle was six feet tall with blue eyes and honey-colored hair. Her face was fairly attractive. Her body caused heart arrhythmia – a total, no-let-up traffic-stopper. Even Olivia said 'Wow' when she met her. Rumor had it that Cingle had been a Rockette at Radio City Music Hall, but that the other girls complained that she ruined their 'symmetry.' Matt did not doubt it.

Cingle had her feet up on her desk. She had on cowboy boots that added another two inches to her height and dark jeans that fit like leggings. Up top, she wore a black turtleneck that on some women would be considered clingy but on Cingle could legitimately draw a citation for indecency.

'It was a New Jersey plate,' Matt told her for the third time. 'MLH-472.'

Cingle hadn't moved. She rested her chin in the L made by her thumb and index finger. She stared at him.

'What?' Matt said.

'What client am I supposed to bill for this?'

'No client,' he said. 'You bill me.'

'This is for you then.'

'Yes.'

'Hmm.' Cingle dropped her feet to the floor, stretched back, smiled. 'So this is personal?'

'Man,' Matt said, 'you are good. I tell you to bill *me*, that it's for *me*, and bang, you figure out that it's personal.'

'Years of detecting, Hunter. Don't be intimidated.'

Matt tried to force up a smile.

She kept her eyes on him. 'Want to hear one of the ten rules from the Cingle Shaker Book of Detection?'

'No, not really.'

'Rule Six: When a man asks you to look up a license plate for personal reasons, it can be only one of two things. One' – Cingle raised a finger – 'he thinks his wife is cheating and he wants to know who with.'

'And two?'

'There's no two. I lied. There's only one.'

'That's not it.'

Cingle shook her head.

'What?'

'Ex-cons usually lie better.'

He let that one alone.

'Okay, so let's say I believe you. Why, pray tell, do we want me to trace this down?'

'It's personal. Remember? Bill *me*, for *me*, personal?'

Cingle stood up, waaay up, and put her hands on her hips. She glared down at him. Unlike Olivia, Matt did not say 'Wow' out loud, but maybe he thought it.

'Think of me as your religious advisor,' she said. 'Confession is good for the soul, you know.'

'Yeah,' Matt said. 'Religion. That's what comes to mind.' He sat up. 'Will you just do this for me?'

'Okeydokey.' She stared at him another beat. Matt did not cringe. Cingle sat back down and threw her feet back on the desk. 'The standing up with the hands on the hips. That usually weakens a guy.'

'I'm stone.'

'Well, yes, that's part of it.'

'Ha, ha.'

She gave him the curious look again. 'You love Olivia, right?'

'I'm not getting into this with you, Cingle.'

'You don't have to answer. I've seen you with her. And her with you.'

'So you know then.'

She sighed. 'Give me the plate number again.'

He did. This time Cingle wrote it down.

'Shouldn't take more than an hour. I'll call you on your cell.'

'Thanks.' He started for the door.

'Matt?'

He turned back toward her.

'I've had some experience in stuff like this.'

'I'm sure.'

'Opening this door.' Cingle held up the slip of paper with the license plate. 'It's kinda like trying to break up a fight. Once you jump in, you don't know what could happen.'

'Gee, Cingle, that's pretty subtle.'

She spread her arms. 'Subtlety ended for me the day I hit puberty.'

'Just do this for me, okay?'

'I will.'

'Thank you.'

'But' – she put up her index finger – 'should you feel the need to take it further, I want you to promise to let me help.'

'I won't take it further,' he said, and the look on her face told him all he needed to know about how much she believed him.

Matt was just entering his old hometown of Livingston when his cell phone rang again. It was Jamie Suh, Olivia's assistant, finally calling back. 'Sorry, Matt, I can't find a hotel contact.'

'How can that be?' he snapped without thinking.

There was too long a pause.

He tried to backtrack. 'I mean, doesn't she usually leave one? Suppose there was an emergency.'

'She has her cell phone.'

He didn't know what to say.

'And most of the time,' Jamie went on, 'I book the hotel for her.'

'You didn't this time?'

'No.' Then she hurriedly added: 'But that's not unusual or anything. Olivia does it herself sometimes too.'

He didn't know what to make of that. 'Have you heard from her today?'

'She called in this morning.'

'Did she say where she was going to be?'

There was another pause. Matt knew that his behavior would be considered beyond the scope of normal husbandly curiosity, but he figured it was worth the risk.

'She just said she had some meetings. Nothing specific.'

'Okay, if she calls back –'

'I'll tell her you're looking for her.'

Then Jamie hung up.

Another memory struck him. He and Olivia had a huge fight, one of those no-holds-barred verbal brawls where you know you're wrong and you just keep pushing. She ran out in tears and didn't call for two days. Two full days. He would call, she wouldn't answer. He searched, but he couldn't find her. It punched a huge hole in his heart. That was what he remembered right now. The idea that she would never come back to him hurt so much he could barely breathe.

The home inspector was just finishing up when he arrived at the house. Nine years ago Matt walked out of jail after serving four years for killing a man. Now, incredible as it might seem, he was on the verge of buying a home, sharing it with the woman he loved, raising a child.

He shook his head.

The house was part of a suburban tract built in 1965. Like most of Livingston, the area used to be a farm. All the houses were pretty much the same, but if that discouraged Olivia, she hid it pretty well. She'd stared at the house with a nearly religious fervor and whispered, 'It's perfect.' Her enthusiasm had swept away any doubts he'd had about moving back.

Matt stood on what would soon be his front yard and tried to imagine himself living here. It felt odd. He didn't belong here anymore. He had known that until, well, until Olivia. Now he was back.

Behind him a police cruiser pulled up. Two men got out. The first one was in uniform. He was young and in shape. He gave Matt the cop squint. The second man was in plainclothes.

'Hey, Matt,' the man in the brown suit called out. 'Long time, no see.'

It had been a long time, since Livingston High at least, but he recognized Lance Banner right away.

'Hi, Lance.'

Both men slammed their doors closed as if they'd coordinated the move. The uniform crossed his arms and remained silent. Lance moved toward Matt.

'You know,' Lance said, 'I live on this street.'

'That a fact.'

'It is.'

Matt said nothing.

'I'm a detective on the force now.'

'Congrats.'

'Thanks.'

How long had he known Lance Banner? Since second grade, at least. They were never friends, never enemies. They played on the same Little League team for three years running. They shared a gym class in eighth grade and a study hall junior year of high school. Livingston High School had been big – six hundred kids per grade. They'd simply traveled in different circles.

'How's it been going for you?' Lance asked.

'Super.'

The home inspector stepped outside. He had a clipboard. Lance said, 'How's it look, Harold?'

Harold looked up from his clipboard and nodded. 'Pretty solid, Lance.'

'You sure?'

Something in his tone made Harold take a step back. Lance looked back at Matt.

'We have a nice neighborhood here.'

'It's why we picked it.'

'You really think it's a good idea, Matt?'

'What's that, Lance?'

'Moving back.'

'Done my time.'

'And you think that's the end of it?'

Matt didn't say anything.

'That boy you killed. He's still dead, isn't he?'

'Lance?'

'I'm Detective Banner now,' he said.

'Detective Banner, I'm going inside now.'

'I read all about your case. I even called a couple of cop buddies, got the whole scoop on what happened.'

Matt looked at him. The man had gray flecks in his eyes. He had put on weight. His fingers kept itching and Matt didn't like the way he smiled at him. Lance Banner's family had worked this land as farmers. His grandfather or maybe it was his great-grandfather had sold the land for a song. The Banners still considered Livingston their town. They were the soil here. The father drank too much. So did Lance's two dull brothers. Lance, on the other hand, always hit Matt as being pretty sharp.

'Then you know it was an accident,' Matt said.

Lance Banner nodded slowly. 'Could be.'

75

'So why the hard time, Lance?'

'Because you're an ex-con.'

'You think I should have gone to prison?'

'Tough call,' he said, rubbing his chin. 'But from what I read, I think you got a bad break.'

'So?'

'So you did. Go to prison, I mean.'

'I don't understand.'

'Society wants to peddle that rehabilitation crap on the public, hey, that's fine with me. But I' – he pointed to himself – 'know better. And you' – he turned the finger toward Matt – 'know better.'

Matt said nothing.

'You may have gone into that place an okay guy. But you want to tell me you're the same man now?'

Matt knew that there was no right answer to that one. He turned and started toward the door.

Lance said, 'Maybe your home inspector will find something. Give you a way to back out.'

Matt went inside and finished up with the inspector. There were several issues – some pipe problem, one overloaded breaker – but they were all small. He and Harold finished up, and Matt started for Marsha's house.

He pulled into the tree-lined street where his nephews and sister-in-law – was she still considered a sister-in-law after your brother died? 'Ex' certainly didn't sound right – resided. The boys, Paul and Ethan, were on the front lawn rolling in the leaves. Their babysitter, Kyra, was with them. Kyra Walsh was a recent freshman-transfer taking summer classes at William Paterson University. She rented a room above Marsha's garage. Kyra had come highly recommended from someone at Marsha's church, and while Matt had been initially skeptical of the whole idea of a live-in babysitter (nonetheless a college student) it seemed to be working great. Kyra ended up being a pretty terrific kid, a fresh-faced burst of needed sunshine from one of the 'I' states in the Midwest, he could never remember which one.

Matt stepped out of the car. Kyra shaded her eyes with one hand and waved with the other. She smiled as only the young can. 'Hi, Matt.'

'Hey, Kyra.'

The boys heard his voice and turned their heads like dogs hearing their owner rummaging for treats. They sprinted at him, calling, 'Uncle Matt! Uncle Matt!'

Matt felt a sudden lightness in his chest. A smile played with the corner of his lips as the boys rushed him. Ethan grabbed hold of Matt's right leg. Paul aimed for the midsection.

'McNabb back to pass,' Matt said, doing his best Greg Gumbel impression. 'Look out! Strahan breaks through the line and has a leg . . .'

Paul stopped. 'I want to be Strahan!' he demanded.

Ethan would have none of that. 'No, I want to be Strahan!'

'Hey, you both can be Strahan,' Matt said.

The two youngsters squinted at their uncle as if he were the slow kid sitting in the back. 'You can't have two Michael Strahans,' Paul said.

'Yeah,' his brother chimed in.

Then they lowered their shoulders and hit him again. Matt performed a near Pacino-esque performance of a quarterback about to be sacked. He stutter-stepped, he looked desperately for imaginary receivers, he pump-faked a pass with his invisible football, and ultimately he went down in a slow-motion heap.

'Woo-hoo!' The boys stood, high-fived each other, bumped chests. Matt groaned into a sitting position.

Kyra was smothering a giggle.

Paul and Ethan were still doing a celebration dance when Marsha appeared at the door. She looked, Matt thought, very nice. She wore a dress and makeup. Her hair had that carefully mussed thing going on. The car keys were already jiggling in her hand.

When Bernie died, Matt and Marsha had both been so devastated, so desperate, that they tried to knit something together where Matt could maybe take over as husband and father.

It was a disaster.

Matt and Marsha had waited a proper amount of time – six months – and then one night, without discussing it but knowing what was about to happen, they both got drunk. Marsha made the first move. She kissed him, kissed him hard, and then she started to sob. That had been the end.

Before 'the slip,' Matt's family had been strangely blessed or maybe just blessedly naïve. Matt had been twenty years old and all four of his grandparents were alive and in good health – two in Miami, two in Scottsdale. Tragedy had visited other families, but the Hunters had been left alone. The slip changed all that. It left them ill prepared for what followed.

Tragedy sort of works this way: Once it snakes its way in, it cuts down all your defenses and allows its brethren easy access to feed. Three of his four grandparents died during Matt's stint in prison. The burden killed his father and sapped his mother. Mom fled to Florida. Their sister ran west to Seattle. Bernie had the aneurysm.

Just like that, they were all gone.

Matt stood up. He waved to Marsha. She waved back. Kyra said, 'Is it okay if I go?'

Marsha nodded. 'Thanks, Kyra.'

'No problem.' Kyra slipped on the backpack. 'Bye, Matt.'

'Bye, kiddo.'

Matt's cell phone rang. The caller ID told him it was Cingle Shaker. He signaled to Marsha that he needed to take it. She gestured for him to go ahead. Matt moved toward the curb and picked it up.

'Hello.'

'Got some info on the license plate,' Cingle said.

'Go ahead.'

'It's a rental. Avis at Newark Airport.'

'So does that mean it's a dead end?'

'For most private investigators, most definitely. But you're dealing with a near legend in the business.'

'Near?'

'I'm trying to be modest.'

'Doesn't work on you, Cingle.'

'Yeah, but the effort is there. I called a contact at the airport. He ran it down for me. The car was rented by one Charles Talley. You know him?'

'No.'

'I figured the name might mean something to you.'

'It doesn't.'

'You want me to check this Talley guy out?'

'Yes.'

'Call you back.'

She hung up. Matt started to lower the phone when he spotted the same police cruiser turning onto the block. It slowed as it passed Marsha's house. The uniformed cop who'd been with Lance eyed him. Matt eyed him back and felt his face flush.

Paul and Ethan stood and watched the cruiser. Matt turned back to Marsha. She saw it too. He tried to smile and wave it off. Marsha frowned.

That was when his phone rang again.

Still watching Marsha, Matt put the phone to his ear without checking the caller ID.

'Hello,' he said.

'Hi, hon, how was your day?'

It was Olivia.

8

Television shows, Loren knew, had convinced people that cops commonly meet with medical examiners in a morgue over a corpse. In reality that pretty much never happens. Loren was grateful for that. She was not squeamish or any of that, but she wanted death to be a constant shock to her. She didn't make jokes at the scene. She didn't try to block or use other defense mechanisms to look past it. For Loren a morgue is too matter-of-fact, too casual, too mundane about murder.

Loren was about to open Eldon's office door when Trevor Wine, a fellow homicide investigator, stepped out. Trevor was overweight and old-school. He tolerated Loren as one might a cute pet that sometimes pees on the good carpet.

'Hey, Squirt,' he said to her.

'You catch a homicide?'

'Yup.' Trevor Wine pulled up his belt. He had that weird kind of fat where you can never get the waist to perch and stay. 'Gunshot victim. Two to the head at close range.'

'Robbery, gang, what?'

'Maybe a robbery, definitely not a gang. The vic was a retired white guy.'

'Where did you find the body?'

'Near the Hebrew cemetery off Fourteenth Avenue. We think he's a tourist.'

'A tourist in that neighborhood?' Loren made a face. 'What's there to see?'

Trevor faked a laugh and put a meaty hand on her shoulder. 'I'll let you know when I know.' He didn't add 'little lady' but he might as well have. 'See you later, Squirt.'

'Yeah, later.'

He moved away. Loren opened the door.

Eldon sat at his desk. He wore a pair of clean scrubs. Eldon always wore scrubs. His office had absolutely no personality or color. When Eldon first took the job he wanted to change that, but when people came into this room to hear the details of the death, they wanted nothing stimulating any of the senses. So Eldon shifted the décor into neutral.

'Here,' Eldon said, 'catch.'

He tossed her something. Instinctively Loren caught it. It was a plastic bag, filmy and yellow. There was some sort of gel inside it. Eldon held a matching bag in his hand.

'Is this . . . ?'

Eldon nodded. 'A well-used and thus well-soiled breast implant.'

'Can I just say for the record, "Eeuw"?'

'You may.'

Loren held the bag up to the light and frowned. 'I thought implants were clear.'

'They start off that way – at least the saline ones.'

'These aren't saline?'

'Nope. Silicone. And they've been marinating in bosom for well over a decade.'

Loren tried not to make a face. There was some sort of gel inside them. Eldon arched an eyebrow and started to knead the implant.

'Cut that out.'

He shrugged. 'Anyway, these belong to your Sister of the Immaculate Hooters.'

'And you're showing them to me because . . . ?'

'Because they offer us clues.'

'I'm listening.'

'First off, they're silicone.'

'So you said.'

'Remember, what, five, ten years ago when they had the big cancer scare?'

'The implants were leaking.'

'Right. So the companies were forced to move to saline.'

'Aren't some people moving back now to silicone?'

'Yes, but the point remains: These are old. Very old. Well over a decade.'

She nodded. 'Okay, good, that's a start.'

'There's more.' Eldon took out a magnifying glass. He flipped one of the implants over. 'See this here?'

Loren took the magnifying glass. 'It's a tag.'

'See that number over on the bottom?'

'Yes.'

'That's the serial number. This is true with pretty much any surgical implant – knees, hips, breasts, pacemaker, whatever. The device has to have a serial number.'

Loren nodded. 'And the manufacturer keeps records.'

'Exactly.'

'So if we call the manufacturer and give them the serial number . . .'

'We learn the real name of Mother with the Superiors.'

Loren looked up. 'Thanks.'

'There's a problem.'

She sat back.

'The company that made the implants was named SurgiCo. They went under eight years ago.'

'And their records?'

Eldon shrugged. 'We're trying to look into it. Look, it's late. We won't get anything tonight. I'm hoping to find out what happened to the records in the morning.'

'Okay. Anything else?'

'You asked why there were no fibers under her finger-nails.'

'Yes.'

'We're still running a full tox report. It could be that she was drugged, but I don't think that was it.'

'You have another theory.'

'I do.'

'What's that?'

Eldon leaned back and crossed his legs. He turned to the side and stared at the wall. 'There was slight bruising along both inner biceps.'

Loren's eyes narrowed. 'I'm not following.'

'If a man were very strong and, uh, knowledgeable, he could sneak up on a sleeping woman,' he began, his voice almost singsong, as if he were talking to a child. 'He might flip the woman onto her back – or maybe she slept that way. He'd straddle her chest, pin her arms down with his knees – that, if he was careful and professional, could be done so as to leave very little bruising – and then he'd smother her with a pillow.'

The room dropped ten degrees. Loren's voice was barely a whisper. 'You think that's what happened here?'

'We have to wait for the full tox,' Eldon said, turning away from the wall and looking directly at her. 'But yeah. Yeah, I think that's what happened here.'

She said nothing.

'There's one more thing that backs my theory up. It could help us.' Eldon put a photograph on the desk. A headshot of the nun. Her eyes were closed as if she were expecting a facial. She'd been in her early sixties, but the lines had all been smoothed away in death. 'You know anything about fingerprints on the skin?'

'Just that they're hard to pick up.'

'Nearly impossible, if you don't catch the corpse right away. Most of the major studies are telling us to try to pick up the fingerprints at the crime scene if possible. At a minimum the lab guys should make sure the body is glue fumed right away to preserve the prints before the vic is packed away.'

Forensic detail was not Loren's forte. 'Uh huh.'

'Well, it was too late for that with our Dying Nun here.' He looked up. 'Get it? Dying Nun instead of Flying Nun?'

'It's like I'm hanging with Chris Rock here. Go on.'

'Right, so I'm trying something experimental. We got lucky that the corpse wasn't refrigerated. The condensation that builds up on the skin throws the whole thing out of whack. Anyway, I thought about going with the polyethylene terephthalate semirigid sheet. That's the one we use based on the fact that static electricity attracts dust particles – '

'Whoa.' Loren held up her palm in the classic stop gesture. 'Let's skip the CSI casting call. Did you get prints off the body?'

'Yes and no. I found smudges on both temples, one looks like a thumb, the other might be a ring finger.'

'On her temples?'

Eldon nodded. He took off his glasses, gave them a wipe down, put them back on the end of his nose, pushed up. 'I think the perp grabbed her face with one hand. Palmed it like a basketball player – with the heel of his hand on her nose.'

'Jesus.'

'Yeah. Then I think he pushed her head down as he climbed on top.'

'But the fingerprints. Can you get any kind of ID off them?'

'Doubtful. We have partials at best. It'll never be enough for court, but there's this new software that helps you, I don't know, fill in the blanks, if you will. If you find somebody, I might get enough to confirm or eliminate.'

'That might help.'

He stood. 'I'll get on it now. Probably take a day, maybe two. I'll let you know when I have more.'

'Okay,' Loren said. 'Anything else?'

It was like a shadow fell over his face.

'Eldon?'

'Yeah,' he said. 'There's something else.'

'I don't like the way you said that.'

'I don't like saying it, believe me. But I think whoever did this did more than just smother her.'

'What do you mean?'

'You know anything about stun guns?'

'Some.'

'I think they used one.' He swallowed. 'In her.'

'When you say "in her," do you mean –'

'I mean exactly what you think,' he said, interrupting her. 'Hey, I'm a product of Catholic school too, okay?'

'Are there burn marks?'

'Faint. But if you know what you're doing – and especially in an area that sensitive – you really shouldn't leave them. It was also a one-prong stunner, if that helps. Most, like the police-issue stun guns, have two prongs. I'm still running tests, but my guess is, she died in a lot of pain.'

Loren closed her eyes.

'Hey, Squirt?'

'What?'

'Do me a favor,' Eldon said. 'Nail this son of a bitch, will ya?'

9

Olivia said, 'Hi, hon, how was your day?'

Matt just held the phone.

'Matt?'

'I'm here,' he said.

The police cruiser was gone now. Matt looked behind him. Marsha stood on the front step with her hands on her hips. Paul was chasing Ethan, both of them shrieking with laughter.

'So,' Olivia said, as if it were just another day, 'where are you?'

'At Marsha's.'

'Everything okay?'

'I'm just taking the boys out to dinner.'

'Not McDonald's again. Those fries are so unhealthy.'

'Right.'

Tentative steps. The ground giving way. Matt held the phone, thinking: *You don't just jump up and scream, 'Aha, caught ya!'*

'So anything going on?' Olivia asked.

'Not much,' he said. Kyra was getting in her car. She gave him a big smile and waved good-bye. He gestured back with his chin. 'I called you before,' Matt said with as much nonchalance as he could muster.

'You did?'

'Yes.'

'When?'

'Around noon.'

'Really?'

'No, I'm making it up. Yes, really.'

'Well, that's weird.'

'Why?'

'I didn't hear the phone ring.'

'Maybe you were out of range,' he tried, giving her an out.

'Maybe,' she said slowly.

'I left a message.'

'Hold on.' There was a pause. 'Wait, it says here "three missed calls."'

'That would be me.'

'I'm sorry, honey. I know this sounds ridiculous but I still get confused about how to retrieve messages. My old phone's code was six-seven-six and then I hit a star, but I don't think that works on this one.'

'It doesn't,' Matt said. 'Your new code is the last four digits of your phone number and then you hit the pound key.'

'Oh, right. I usually just check the missed calls log.'

Matt closed his eyes. He could not believe how inane and ordinary this all felt.

'Where have you been?' he asked.

'What?'

'When I called. Where were you?'

'Oh, I was at a seminar.'

'Where?'

'What do you mean, where? I'm in Boston.'

'What was it on?'

'Some new surfing tool to guard against employees using the Web for personal use. You can't imagine the amount of work hours lost on the Internet.'

'Uh huh.'

'Listen, I have to run. I'm meeting some people for dinner.'

'Anyone I know?'

'Nope, no one you know.' Olivia sighed with a little too much flair. 'Check that: No one you'd even *want* to know.'

'Boring?'

'Very.'

'What hotel are you staying at?'

'Didn't I tell you?'

'No.'

'The Ritz. But I'll be in and out. You're better off getting me on the cell phone.'

'Olivia?'

'Oh,' she said. 'Hold up a second.'

There was a long pause. Marsha crossed the lawn, approaching him. She signaled to her car, asking if it was okay if she took off. He waved that it was fine. Ethan and Paul, tired of running around in circles, headed toward him. Ethan grabbed his right leg, Paul his left. Matt made a face and pointed to the phone, as if they'd get the meaning that he was otherwise occupied. They didn't.

Olivia said, 'There's a picture on my phone. Which button do I press again?'

'The one on the right side.'

'Hold on. Here it comes.' Then: 'Hey, it's you. Dang, I married a handsome devil.'

Matt couldn't help but smile – and that just made it hurt more. He loved her. He could try to soften the blow, but there was no way he could escape it. 'It would be wrong for me to argue with you,' he said.

'Not your best smile though. Heck, no smile at all. And next time, take your shirt off.'

'You too,' he said.

She laughed but it wasn't as let-go as usual.

'Better yet' – Matt added and then the next words:

were they planned? – 'why not wear a platinum-blonde wig?'

Silence.

This time he broke it. 'Olivia?'

'I'm here.'

'Before. When I called you.'

'Yes?'

'I was calling you back.'

As if sensing the tenseness, the boys let go of his legs. Paul tilted his head at Ethan.

'But I didn't call you,' Olivia said.

'Yes, you did. I mean, I got a call from your phone.'

'When?'

'Right before I called.'

'I don't understand.'

'There was a picture on the line. Of a man with dark hair. And then there was a video.'

'A video?'

'You were in a room. At least it looked like you. Except you were wearing a platinum-blonde wig.'

More silence. Then: 'I don't know what you're talking about.'

Did he believe her? He so wanted to, so wanted to just drop it . . .

'Earlier today,' he said, 'right before I left you that message, I got a call from your cell phone. It was a camera call –'

'No, I understand that, but . . .'

'But what?'

'Oh, wait,' Olivia said. 'That might explain something.'

Paul and Ethan had started running in dizzying circles again. They were out of control and a little too close to the street. Matt put his hand over the mouthpiece and called them back.

'Explain what?' he asked.

'I think . . . well, I don't really understand why I didn't get your first call. I'm in range. I looked on the missed calls log and you know what? Jamie called too. I never heard that one either.'

'So?'

'So I'm thinking. The guys at these seminars. They're all jokers. Maybe one of them played a prank.'

'A prank.'

'Okay, during this seminar? I fell asleep. It was boring as hell. When I woke up, my purse had been moved. Not a lot. But now that I think about it, it was definitely moved. I didn't think much about it at the time.'

'And now you think . . . ?'

'That, yeah, they took it and did something with it and then put it back. I don't know, I guess that's crazy too.'

Matt didn't know what to make of this, but Olivia's tone did not ring true. 'When are you coming home?'

'Friday.'

He switched hands. 'I'll come up.'

'Don't you have work?'

'Nothing that can't keep.'

'But,' she said, and her voice dropped a little, 'isn't tomorrow your, uh, Thursday at the museum?'

He had almost forgotten about it.

'You can't miss that.'

In three years he never had. For a long time Matt had told no one about his every-other-Thursday rendezvous at the museum. People would never understand. There was a bond there, a draw built on necessity and secrecy. It was hard to say more. Those meetings were simply too important.

But he still said, 'I can put it off.'

'You shouldn't, Matt. You know that.'

'I can fly up right now –'

'There's no need. I'll be home the day after tomorrow.'

'I don't want to wait.'

'I'm crazy busy with stuff here anyway. Look, I have to go. We'll talk about this later, okay?'

'Olivia?'

'Friday,' she said. 'I love you.'

And then she hung up.

10

'Uncle Matt?'

Paul and Ethan were safely ensconced in the backseat. It had taken Matt the better part of fifteen minutes to secure the car booster seats into place. Who the hell had designed these things – NASA?

'What's up, partner?'

'You know what McDonald's has right now?'

'I already told you. We're not going to McDonald's.'

'Oh, I know. I'm just saying.'

'Uh huh.'

'You know what McDonald's has right now?'

'No,' Matt said.

'You know the new *Shrek* movie?'

'Yes.'

'They got *Shrek* toys,' Paul said.

'He means McDonald's does,' Ethan chipped in.

'Is that a fact?'

'And they're free.'

'They're not free,' Matt said.

'They are so. It's in the Happy Meal.'

'Which are overpriced.'

'Overwhat?'

'We're not going to McDonald's.'

'Oh, we know.'

'We were just saying.'

'They got free toys, is all.'

'From the new *Shrek* movie.'

'Remember when we saw the first *Shrek* movie, Uncle Matt?'

'I remember,' he said.

'I like Donkey,' Ethan said.

'Me too,' Matt agreed.

'Donkey is the toy this week.'

'We're not going to McDonald's.'

'I'm just saying.'

' 'Cause Chinese is good too,' Paul said.

'Even though they don't got toys.'

'Yeah, I like spare ribs.'

'And dim sum.'

'Mom likes the string beans.'

'Ugh. You don't like string beans, do you, Uncle Matt?'

'They're good for you,' Matt said.

Ethan turned to his brother. 'That means no.'

Matt smiled, tried to push away the day. Paul and Ethan were good for that.

They arrived at Cathay, an old-fashioned Chinese restaurant with the retro classics like chow mein and egg foo young, cracked vinyl booths, and a grumpy old woman at the front counter who watched you eat as if fearing you'd pocket the utensils.

The food was greasy, but that was as it should be. The boys ate a ton. At McDonald's, they picked. They managed maybe half a burger and a dozen fries. Here they cleaned the plate. Chinese restaurants would be well served by handing out movie tie-in toys.

Ethan, as always, was animated. Paul was a bit more reserved. They had been raised in pretty much the exact manner, the same gene pool, and yet they couldn't be more different. Ethan was the cutup. He never sat still. He was messy and lively and shunned affection. When

Paul colored, he always stayed in the lines. He got frustrated when he made a mistake. He was thoughtful, a good athlete, and liked to cuddle.

Nature waaay over nurture.

They stopped at Dairy Queen on the ride home. Ethan ended up wearing more soft vanilla than he consumed. When he pulled into the driveway Matt was surprised to see that Marsha wasn't back yet. He took them inside – he had a key – and gave them a bath. It was eight o'clock.

Matt put on an episode of *The Fairly OddParents*, which was pretty funny on an adult level, and then convinced the boys using negotiating skills picked up in legal pleadings across the state to get into bed. Ethan was afraid of the dark, so Matt turned on the SpongeBob night-light.

Matt checked his watch. Eight thirty. He didn't mind staying later, but he was getting a little worried.

He headed into the kitchen. The latest works of art by Paul and Ethan hung on the refrigerator by magnets. There were photographs, too, in acrylic frames that never seemed to hold the photos in place. Most were halfway slipping out. Matt carefully slid the images back where they belonged.

Near the top of the fridge, too high for the children to reach (if not see?) there were two photographs of Bernie. Matt stopped and stared at his brother. After a while he turned away and picked up the kitchen phone. He dialed Marsha's cell.

Marsha had caller ID and answered, 'Matt? I was just about to call you.'

'Hey.'

'Are you at the house?'

'We are. And the boys are bathed and in bed.'

'Wow, you're good.'

'I thank you.'

'No, I thank you.'

No one spoke for a moment.

Matt asked, 'Do you need me to stay awhile?'

'If it's okay.'

'No problem. Olivia's still in Boston.'

'Thank you,' she said, and there was something in her voice.

He switched ears. 'Uh, what time do you think you'll be getting –'

'Matt?'

'Yes.'

'I lied to you before.'

He said nothing.

'I didn't have a school meeting.'

He waited.

'I'm out on a date.'

Not sure what to say to that, Matt went with the reliable 'Oh.'

'I should have told you before.' She lowered her voice. 'It's not a first date either.'

His eyes found his brother's in the photograph on the refrigerator. 'Uh huh.'

'I've been seeing someone. It's been almost two months now. The boys don't know anything about it, of course.'

'You don't have to explain to me.'

'Yeah, Matt. Yeah, I do.'

He said nothing.

'Matt?'

'I'm here.'

'Would you mind spending the night?'

He closed his eyes. 'No,' he said. 'I don't mind at all.'

'I'll be home before the boys wake up.'

'Okay.'

He heard a sniffle then. She was crying.

'It's okay, Marsha.'

'Really?'

'Yeah,' he said. 'I'll see you in the morning.'

'I love you, Matt.'

'I love you too.'

He hung up the phone. It was a good thing, Marsha going out. It was a very good thing. But his eyes drifted back toward his brother. Unfair and wrong as it was, Matt couldn't help but think that his brother had never seemed more gone.

11

Everyone seems to have this terrifying dream where you are suddenly about to take the final exam in a class you haven't attended all semester. Matt did not. Instead, in a strangely similar vein, he dreamed that he was back in prison. He had no idea what he'd done to get back there. There was no memory of a crime or a trial, just the sense that he had somehow messed up and that this time he would never get out.

He'd wake up with a start. He'd be sweating. There'd be tears in his eyes. His body would quake.

Olivia had grown used to it. She would wrap her arms around him and whisper that it was okay, that nothing could hurt him anymore. She had bad dreams of her own, his lovely wife, but she never seemed to need or want that sort of comfort.

He slept on the couch in the den. The upstairs guest room had a pullout queen-size bed that somehow felt too big when he was sleeping alone. Now, as he stared up in the dark, feeling more alone than he had since Olivia walked into his office, Matt actually feared sleep. He kept his eyes open. At four in the morning Marsha's car pulled into the driveway.

When he heard the key in the door, Matt closed his eyes and pretended to be asleep on the couch. Marsha tiptoed over and kissed him on the forehead. The smell of shampoo and soap wafted from her. She had showered, wherever she had been. He wondered if she had showered alone. He wondered why he cared.

She moved into the kitchen. Still feigning sleep, Matt slowly opened one eye. Marsha was making lunch for the boys. She spread jelly with a too-practiced hand. There were tears on her cheek. Matt kept still. He let her finish in peace and listened to her gentle footsteps pad up the stairs.

At 7 a.m., Cingle called him.

'I tried your home number,' she said. 'You weren't there.'

'I'm at my sister-in-law's.'

'Oh.'

'Just babysitting my nephews.'

'Did I ask?'

He rubbed his face. 'So what's up?'

'You coming into the office?'

'Yeah, a little later. Why?'

'I found your follower, Charles Talley.'

He sat all the way up. 'Where?'

'Let's talk about this in person, okay?'

'Why?'

'I need to do a little more research.'

'On what?'

'On Charles Talley. I'll meet you at your office at noon, okay?'

He had his Thursday rendezvous at the museum anyway. 'Yeah, okay.'

'And Matt?'

'What?'

'You said this was personal? Whatever it is with Talley?'

'Yes.'

'Then you're in deep doo-doo.'

Matt was a member of the Newark Museum. He flashed his membership card but there was no need. The guards at the door knew him by now. He nodded and entered. Very few people roamed the hall this time of the morning. Matt headed to the art gallery in the west wing. He passed the museum's newest piece, a colorful canvas by Wosene Worke Kosrof, and took the steps to the second floor.

She was the only one there.

He could see her way down at the end of the corridor. She was standing where she always stood – in front of the painting by Edward Hopper. Her head was tilted ever so slightly to the left. She was a very attractive woman, nearing sixty, almost six feet tall, high cheekbones, the kind of blonde hair only the wealthy seem to possess. As always she looked smart and tailored and polished.

Her name was Sonya McGrath. She was the mother of Stephen McGrath, the boy Matt had killed.

Sonya always waited by the Hopper. The painting was called *Sheridan Theater* and managed to catch pure desolation and despair in a picture of a movie theater. It was amazing. There were famous images depicting the ravages of war, of death, of destruction, but there was something in this seemingly simple Hopper, something in this near-empty theater balcony that spoke to both of them in ways no other image ever had.

Sonya McGrath heard him approach but she didn't turn away from the picture. Matt passed Stan, the security guard who always worked this floor on Thursday mornings. They exchanged a quick smile and nod. Matt wondered what Stan must think of his quiet trysts with this attractive older woman.

He stood next to her and looked at the Hopper. It worked like a bizarre mirror. He saw them as the two isolated figures – he Hopper's usher, she the lone patron. For a long time they didn't speak. Matt glanced at Sonya McGrath's profile. He had seen a photograph of her in the paper once, the Sunday *New York Times* Style section. Sonya McGrath was something of a socialite. In the photograph, her smile dazzled. He had never seen that smile in person – wondered, in fact, if it could exist anywhere but on film.

'You don't look so good,' Sonya said.

She was not looking at him – had not, as far as he could tell, yet glanced his way – but he nodded anyway. Sonya faced him full.

Their relationship – though the term 'relationship' didn't seem to capture it – began a few years after Matt got out of prison. His phone would ring, he would pick it up, and there would be no one there. No hang-up. No words. Matt thought that maybe he could hear breathing, but mostly there was pure silence.

Somehow Matt knew who was on the other end.

The fifth time she called, Matt took several deep breaths before working up the courage to speak. 'I'm sorry,' he said.

There was a long silence. Then Sonya replied, 'Tell me what really happened.'

'I did. In court.'

'Tell me again. Everything.'

He tried. He took a long time. She stayed silent. When he finished she hung up.

The next day she called again. 'I want to tell you about my son,' she said without preamble.

And she did.

Matt now knew more than he really wanted to know about Stephen McGrath. He was no longer merely a kid who stepped into a fight, the log jammed onto the track that sent Matt Hunter's life off the rails. McGrath had two younger sisters who adored him. He loved playing guitar. He was a little hippy-ish – he got that, Sonya said with a trace of a laugh, from his mother. He was a great listener, that was what his friends always said. If they had a problem, they went to Stephen. He never needed to be the center of attention. He was content on the sidelines. He would laugh at your joke. He had gotten in trouble only once in his life – the police caught him and some buddies drinking behind the high school – but he had never gotten into a fight, not even as a kid, and seemed deathly afraid of physical violence.

During that same phone call, Sonya asked him, 'Did you know that Stephen didn't know any of the boys in the fight?'

'Yes.'

She started to cry then. 'So why did he step in?'

'I don't know.'

They first met in person here at the Newark Museum three years ago. They had coffee and barely spoke. A few months later, they stayed for lunch. It became a steady thing, every other Thursday morning in front of the Hopper. Neither of them had ever missed one.

At first they told no one. Sonya's husband and daughters would never understand. Of course neither of them understood it either. Matt could never explain why these meetings meant so much to him. Most would assume that he did it purely out of guilt, that he did it for her or for redemption or something like that. But that wasn't the case at all.

For two hours – that's how long their meetings lasted – Matt felt strangely free because he ached and hurt and felt. He didn't know what she got out of it, but he assumed that it was something similar. They talked about that night. They talked about their lives. They talked about the tentative steps, the feeling that the ground could give way at any time. Sonya never said, 'I forgive you.' She never said that it wasn't his fault, that it was an accident, that he served his time.

Sonya started down the corridor. Matt stared at the painting another second or two and then followed. They moved back downstairs and into the museum's atrium. They grabbed coffee and sat at their usual table.

'So,' she said. 'Tell me what's going on.'

She didn't say this to be polite or as an icebreaker. This was not about how-are-you-fine-and-you? Matt told her everything. He told this woman, Sonya McGrath, things he told no one else. He never lied to her, never fudged or edited.

When he was done, Sonya asked, 'Do you think Olivia is having an affair?'

'The evidence seems pretty clear.'

'But?'

'But I've learned that evidence rarely gives you the full picture.'

Sonya nodded. 'You should call her again,' she said.

'I did.'

'Try the hotel.'

'I did.'

'Not there?'

'She wasn't registered.'

'There are two Ritz-Carltons in Boston.'

'I tried them both.'

'Ah.' She sat back and put her hand on her chin. 'So you know that, in some way, Olivia is not being truthful.'

'Yes.'

Sonya considered that. She had never met Olivia, but she knew more about Matt's relationship with her than anyone. She looked off.

'What?' he said.

'I'm just trying to find a plausible reason for her behavior.'

'And?'

'And so far I've come up with nothing.' She shrugged and took a sip of her coffee. 'I've always found your relationship with Olivia an oddity.'

'How so?'

'The way you hooked up ten years after a one-night stand.'

'It wasn't a one-night stand. We didn't sleep together.'

'Which may be the point.'

'I don't get what you mean.'

'If you slept together, well, the spell might have been broken. People claim that making love is the most intimate thing in the world. In truth, it's probably the opposite.'

He waited.

'Well, this is an odd coincidence,' she said.

'Why's that?'

'Clark is having an affair.'

Matt didn't ask her if she was sure or how she knew. He simply said, 'I'm sorry.'

'It's not what you think.'

He said nothing.

'It has nothing to do with what happened to our son.'

Matt tried to nod.

'We like to blame Stephen's death for all our problems. He's become our big life's-not-fair card. But the reason behind Clark's affair is far more basic.'

'That being?'

'He's horny.'

She smiled. Matt tried to smile back.

'Oh, did I mention that she's young? The girl Clark is sleeping with?'

'No.'

'Thirty-two. We have a daughter that age.'

'I'm sorry,' Matt said again.

'Don't be. It's the flip side of what we said before. About intimacy and sex.'

'How so?'

'The truth is, like most women my age, I have very little interest in sex. Yes, I know *Cosmo* and the like will tell you differently, what with all that nonsense about men peaking at nineteen and women in their thirties. But in reality, men are always hornier. Period. To me sex no longer has anything to do with intimacy. Clark, on the other hand, needs it. So that's all she is to him, this young girl. Sex. A release. A physical need.'

'And that doesn't bother you?'

'It's not about me.'

Matt said nothing.

'When you think about it, it's simple: Clark needs something that I have no interest in providing. So he goes elsewhere.' Sonya saw the look on his face. She sighed, put her hands on her thighs. 'Let me give you an example. If Clark loved, say, poker and I didn't want to play . . .'

'Come on, Sonya. That's not the same thing.'

'Oh, but isn't it?'

'Sex and poker?'

'Okay, fine, let's keep it on the physically pleasing. A professional massage. Clark gets rubdowns at his club every week from a masseur named Gary –'

'That's not the same thing either.'

'But don't you see? It is. Sex with this girl isn't about intimacy. It's just a physical thing. Like a back rub or a handshake. So shouldn't it be okay with me?'

Sonya looked up at him and waited.

'It wouldn't be okay with me,' Matt said.

There was a small smile on her lips. Sonya liked mind games. She liked a challenge. He wondered if she meant what she said or if she was merely testing him. 'So what are you going to do?' she asked him.

'Olivia comes home tomorrow.'

'You think you can wait till then?'

'I'm going to try.'

Her eyes stayed on him.

'What?' he asked.

'We can't escape it, can we? I thought . . .' She stopped.

'You thought what?'

Their eyes locked. 'I know it's a terrible cliché, but it all felt like a nightmare. The news about Stephen. The trial. I kept expecting to wake up and find it was all some cruel joke, that everything was okay.'

He'd felt the same way. He was stuck in a bad dream, waiting for the *Candid Camera* climax when Stephen would show up unharmed and smiling.

'But now the world feels like the opposite, doesn't it, Matt?'

He nodded.

'Instead of believing the bad is a nightmare from which you'll awaken,' she went on, 'you think it's the good that's an illusion. And that's what this call on your camera phone did. It woke you from the good dream.'

He could not speak.

'I know that I'll never get past what happened,' Sonya McGrath said. 'It's simply not possible. But I thought . . . I hoped maybe you could.'

Matt waited for her to say more. She did not. She rose suddenly, as if she had said too much. They headed together for the exit. Sonya kissed him on the cheek and when they hugged, they both held on longer than usual. He could, as always, feel the devastation emanating from her. Stephen's death was there, in every moment, in every gesture. He sat with them, their forever companion.

'If you need me,' she whispered, 'you call. Anytime.'

'I will.'

He watched her walk away. He thought about what she had said, about the fine line between the good dreams and the bad, and then, when she finally disappeared around the corner, he turned away.

12

When Matt reached Rolanda's desk, she said, 'Cingle's waiting in your office.'

'Thanks.'

'Midlife wants me to buzz him the very second you arrive.' Rolanda looked up. 'Have you arrived yet?'

'Give me five.'

She turned back to the computer terminal and started typing. Matt entered. Cingle Shaker was standing looking at the window. 'Nice view,' she said.

'You think?'

'Nah. That's just my idea of small talk.'

'You're very good at it,' he said.

'I thought you were just a paralegal.'

'I am.'

'So why the fancy digs?'

'It was my brother's.'

'So?'

'So Bernie was a big rainmaker here.'

'So?' Cingle turned toward him. 'I don't want to sound cold, but he's dead.'

'I think you were being hard on yourself before. You really are good at this small talk stuff.'

'No, I mean, he's been dead for, what, three years now? I can't believe they let an ex-con paralegal keep a space like this.'

He smiled. 'I knew what you meant.'

'So what gives?'

'Maybe they're being respectful to my brother's memory.'

'Attorneys?' Cingle made a face. 'Please.'

'Actually,' he said, 'I think they like having me around.'

'Because you're such a nice guy?'

'Because of the ex-con angle. I'm a fun oddity.'

Cingle nodded. 'Kinda like having a lesbian couple at your hoity-toity soiree.'

'Something like that, but even more exotic. It's funny. In some ways I'm the ultimate curiosity. Whenever they're drunk, they all ask me, on the sly, of course, what it's really like for a guy like them to go to the' – he made quote marks with his fingers – 'Big House.'

'You're like a local celebrity.'

'In a bizarre way, yeah.'

'And that's why they don't throw you out of the office?'

He shrugged.

'They might also be afraid of you,' Cingle said. 'You already killed one man with your bare hands.'

He sighed and took his seat. Cingle took hers.

'Sorry,' she said.

He waved her off. 'What's up?'

Cingle crossed her long legs. It was for effect, he knew that, but he wondered if it had become something of an unconscious move on her part. 'So tell me,' she said. 'Why did you want the license plate traced?'

He spread his hands. 'Do we really have to go through the meaning of 'personal' again?'

'Only if you want me to tell you what I know.'

'So you're resorting to blackmail now?'

But he could see that she was serious.

'I think he was following me,' Matt said.

'Why do you think that?'

'Why do you think? I went a few places, his car was there.'

'And you just happened to pick up on that?'

'His license plate was close to my initials.'

'Excuse me?'

Matt explained about the license plate, about the three letters being similar to his own initials, about the way the car raced off when he approached. Cingle listened without moving.

When Matt finished, Cingle asked, 'So why is Charles Talley following you, Matt?'

'I don't know.'

'No idea at all?'

He did not repeat himself. He knew all about men who doth protest too much. Silence was the best response here.

'Talley has a record.'

Matt was tempted to say 'So do I,' but he knew better. Having a record – a record worth Cingle's attention – meant something. The fact that it didn't in Matt's case only proved the rule by the exception. Matt didn't like thinking that way – hadn't Lance Banner used that same prejudice? – but you'd be hard-pressed to argue with the reality.

'Assault,' Cingle said. 'He used brass knuckles. Didn't kill the poor bastard but scrambled his brains to the point where it would have been more merciful if he had.'

Matt thought about that, tried to make it fit. 'How long did he get?'

'Eight years.'

'Long time.'

'Not his first charge. And Talley was far from a model prisoner.'

Matt tried to put it together. Why would this guy be following him?

'Do you want to see what he looks like?' Cingle asked.

'You have a picture?'

'His mug shot, yeah.'

Cingle wore a blue blazer with jeans. She reached into the inner jacket pocket, plucked out the photographs, and sent Matt's world spinning all over again.

How the . . . ?

He knew that her eyes were on him, gauging his reaction, but he couldn't help it. When he saw the two mug shots – the classic front view and turn-to-the-side profile – he nearly gasped out loud. His hands gripped the desk. It felt as though he were in free fall.

'So you recognize him,' Cingle said.

He did. The same smirk. The same blue-black hair. Charles Talley was the man from the camera phone.

13

Loren Muse walked through a time machine.

Revisiting St. Margaret's, her high school alma mater, the clichés applied: The corridors seemed tighter, the ceilings seemed lower, the lockers seemed smaller, the teachers shorter. But others things, the important stuff, did not change too much. Loren fell into a time portal as she entered. She felt the high school tingle in her belly, the constant state of insecurity, the need for both approval and rebellion churned inside of her.

She knocked on Mother Katherine's door.

'Come in.'

There was a young girl sitting in the office. She wore the same school uniform that Loren had so many years ago, the white blouse and tartan skirt. God, she'd hated that. The girl had her head down, clearly post-Mother Katherine berate. Her stringy hair hung down in front of her face like a beaded curtain.

Mother Katherine said, 'You may go now, Carla.'

Shoulders slumped, head still lowered, Carla slinked off. Loren nodded as she passed, as if to say, I feel for ya, sister. Carla did not meet her eye. She closed the door behind her.

Mother Katherine watched all of this with a look both bemused and disheartened, as though she could read Loren's mind. There were stacks of bracelets, all different colors, on her desk. When Loren pointed to them, the bemusement vanished.

'Those bracelets belong to Carla?' Loren asked.

'Yes.'

A dress code violation, Loren thought, fighting off the desire to shake her head. Man, this place will never change.

'You haven't heard about this?' Mother Katherine asked.

'Heard about what?'

'The bracelet' – she took a deep breath – 'game.'

Loren shrugged.

Mother Katherine closed her eyes. 'It's a recent . . . the word would be fad, I believe.'

'Uh huh.'

'The different bracelets . . . I don't even know how to say this . . . the different colors represent certain acts of a sexual nature. The black one, for example, is supposed to be . . . uh, for one thing. Then the red one . . .'

Loren held her hand up. 'I think I get the picture. So the girls wear them as some kind of, I don't know, level of achievement?'

'Worse.'

Loren waited.

'You're not here about this.'

'Tell me anyway.'

'Girls like Carla wear the bracelets around the boys. If the boy can grab the bracelet off the girl's arm, she must then, well, perform the act that corresponds with the bracelet color.'

'Please tell me you're kidding.'

Mother Katherine gave her a look as heavy as the ages.

'How old is Carla?' Loren asked.

'Sixteen.' Mother Katherine pointed to another set of bracelets as if afraid to touch them. 'But I took this set off an eighth grader.'

There was nothing to say to that.

Mother Katherine reached behind her. 'Here are the phone logs you requested.'

The building still had that chalk-dust musk Loren had always associated, until just now, with a certain sort of adolescent naïveté. Mother Katherine handed her a small stack of papers.

'Eighteen of us share three phones,' Mother Katherine said.

'Six of you to a phone, then?'

Mother Katherine smiled. 'And they say we don't teach math anymore.'

Loren looked at Christ on the cross behind the Mother Superior's head. She remembered an old joke, one she heard when she first got here. A boy is getting all Ds and Fs in math so his parents send him to Catholic school. On his first report card, his parents are shocked to see their son getting straight As. When his parents ask him why, he says, 'Well, when I went into the chapel and saw that guy nailed to a plus sign, I knew they were serious.'

Mother Katherine cleared her throat. 'May I ask a question?'

'Shoot.'

'Do they know how Sister Mary Rose died?'

'They're still running tests.'

Mother Katherine waited.

'That's all I can tell you right now.'

'I understand.'

Now it was Loren who waited. When Mother Katherine turned away, Loren said, 'You know more than you're saying.'

'About?'

'About Sister Mary Rose. About what happened to her.'

'Have you learned her identity yet?'

'No. But we will. Before the end of the day, I'd bet.'

Mother Katherine straightened her back. 'That would be a good start.'

'And there's nothing else you want to tell me?'

'That's correct, Loren.'

Loren waited a beat. The old woman was . . . lying would be too strong a word. But Loren could smell evasion. 'Did you go through these calls, Mother?'

'I did. I had the five sisters who shared the phone with her go through them too. Most were to family members, of course. They called siblings, parents, some friends. There were some to local businesses. They order pizza sometimes. Chinese food.'

'I thought nuns had to eat, uh, convent food.'

'You thought wrong.'

'Fair enough,' Loren said. 'Any numbers that stuck out?'

'Just one.'

Mother Katherine's reading glasses dangled from a chain. She slid them onto the end of her nose and beckoned for the sheets. Loren handed them back to her. She studied the first page, licked her finger, moved to the second. She took out a pen and circled something.

'Here.'

She gave the sheet back to Loren. The number had a 973 area code. That would put it in New Jersey, no more than thirty miles from here. The call had been made three weeks ago. It lasted six minutes.

Probably nothing.

Loren spotted the computer on the credenza behind Mother Katherine's desk. It was weird to think about, the Mother Superior surfing the Web, but it truly seemed as though there were very few holdouts anymore.

'May I borrow your computer?' Loren asked.

'Of course.'

Loren tried a simple Google search on the phone number. Nothing.

'Are you looking up the number?' Mother Katherine asked.

'I am.'

'According to the link on the Verizon Web page, the number is unlisted.'

Loren looked back at her. 'You tried already?'

'I looked up all the numbers.'

'I see,' Loren said.

'Just to be certain nothing was overlooked.'

'That was very thorough of you.'

Mother Katherine nodded, kept her head high. 'I assume that you have sources to track down unlisted numbers.'

'I do.'

'Would you like to see Sister Mary Rose's quarters now?'

'Yes.'

The room was pretty much what you'd expect – small, stark, white walls of swirling concrete, one large cross above a single bed, one window. Very dormitory. The room had all the warmth and individuality of a Motel Six. There was almost nothing of a personal nature, nothing that told you anything about the room's inhabitant, almost as if that were Sister Mary Rose's goal.

'The crime-scene technicians will be here in about an hour,' Loren said. 'They'll need to dust for prints, check for hairs, that kind of thing.'

Mother Katherine's hand went slowly to her mouth. 'Then you do think Sister Mary Rose was . . . ?'

'Don't read into it, okay?'

Her cell phone trilled. Loren picked it up. It was Eldon Teak.

'Yo, sweetums, you coming by today?' he asked.

'In an hour,' she said. 'Why, what's up?'

'I found the current owner of our silicone breast manufacturer. SurgiCo is now part of the Lockwood Corporation.'

'The huge one in Wilmington?'

'Somewhere in Delaware, yeah.'

'Did you give them a call?'

'Yes.'

'And?'

'And it did not go well.'

'How's that?'

'I told them we had a dead body, a serial number on a breast implant, and that we needed an ID.'

'And?'

'They won't release the information.'

'Why not?'

'I don't know. They blathered on and on and used the term "medical privacy" a whole lot.'

'That's bullsh –' Mother Katherine's lips pursed. Loren caught herself. 'I'll get a court order.'

'They're a big company.'

'They'll cave on this. They just want legal protection.'

'It'll take time.'

She thought about that. Eldon had a point. The Lockwood Corporation was out of state. She'd probably need a federal court judge to issue a subpoena.

'Something else,' Eldon said.

'What?'

'At first they seemed to have no problem with any of it. I called down, spoke to someone, she was going to look up the serial number for me. I'm not saying it's routine, but it really shouldn't be a big issue.'

'But?'

'But then some lawyer with a bigwig-sounding name called back and gave me a very terse no.'

Loren thought about it. 'Wilmington's only, what, two hours from here?'

'The way you drive, maybe fifteen minutes.'

'I'm thinking of testing out that theory. You have the name of Mr. Bigwig Lawyer?'

'I got it here somewhere. Oh, wait, yes, Randal Horne of Horne, Buckman and Pierce.'

'Call Mr. Horne. Tell him I'm driving down to serve his ass a subpoena.'

'You don't have a subpoena.'

'You don't know that.'

'Oh, right.'

She hung up and placed another call. A woman answered the phone. Loren said, 'I need an unlisted number looked up.'

'Name and badge number, please.'

Loren gave it. Then she read the unlisted phone number Sister Mary Rose had called.

'Please hold,' the woman said.

Mother Katherine pretended to be busy. She looked in the air, then across the room. She fiddled with her prayer beads. Through the phone Loren heard fingers clacking a keyboard. Then: 'Do you have a pen?'

Loren grabbed a stubby golf pencil from her pocket. She took a gas receipt and flipped it over. 'Go ahead.'

'The number you requested is listed to a Marsha Hunter at Thirty-eight Darby Terrace, Livingston, New Jersey.'

14

'Matt?'

He stared at the mug shots of Charles Talley. That same damn knowing smirk, the one he'd seen in that picture on his cell phone. Matt had the falling sensation again, but he held on.

Cingle said, 'You know him, don't you?'

'I need you to do me a favor,' he said.

'I don't do favors. This is my job. You're being billed for this, you know.'

'Even better.' He looked up at Cingle. 'I want you to find me everything you can on Charles Talley. I mean, everything.'

'And what would I be looking for?'

Good question. Matt wondered how to play it.

'Just tell me,' Cingle said.

Matt took out his cell phone. He hesitated, but really, what was the point in trying to keep it a secret anymore? He flipped it open, hit the camera function, and pressed the back arrow until the photograph of Charles Talley, the one taken in that hotel room, came up. It was the same man, no question. He stared at it for a moment.

'Matt?'

His words were slow, deliberate. 'Yesterday I got a call from Olivia's camera phone.' He handed it to her. 'This was on it.'

Cingle reached for the camera phone. Her eyes found the screen. Matt watched them widen in surprise. Her eyes shifted back and forth between the mug shots and the image on the small display. Finally she looked up at him.

'What the hell is this?'

'Hit the forward button,' he said.

'The one on the right here?'

'Yes. It'll take you to the video that came in right after the picture.'

Cingle's face was a mask of concentration. When the video finished she said, 'If I hit this replay button, will it run again?'

'Yes.'

Cingle did. She played the short video two more times. When she was done, Cingle carefully put the camera on the desktop. 'You have an explanation for this?' she asked.

'Nope.'

Cingle thought about it. 'I've only met Olivia once.'

'I know.'

'I can't tell if that was her or not.'

'I think it is.'

'Think?'

'It's hard to make out the face.'

Cingle gnawed on her lower lip. She reached behind, grabbed her purse, started rummaging through it.

'What?' he asked.

'You're not the only one who's technically savvy,' Cingle said.

She pulled out a small handheld computer, not much bigger than Matt's phone.

'A Palm Pilot?'

'A high-end pocket PC,' she corrected. Cingle pulled out a cord. She plugged one end into the phone, one end into the pocket PC. 'You mind if I download the picture and video?'

'Why?'

'I'll take them back to the office. We have all kinds of software to blow the images up frame by frame, enhance them, make a solid analysis.'

'This stays between us.'

'Understood.' Two minutes later, the pictures were downloaded. Cingle handed the phone back to Matt. 'One more thing.'

'I'm listening.'

'Learning all we can about our friend Charles Talley may not get us what we need.' She leaned forward. 'We need to start drawing lines. We need to find a connection between Talley and . . .'

'Olivia,' he finished for her.

'Yes.'

'You want to investigate my wife.'

She sat back, recrossed the legs. 'If this was just a run-of-the-mill hot-sheet affair, it would probably be unnecessary. I mean, maybe they just met. Maybe they hooked up at a bar, I don't know. But Talley is tailing you. He's also sending you pictures, throwing it in your face.'

'Meaning?'

'Meaning there's something more here,' Cingle said. 'Let me ask you something and don't take offense, okay?'

'Okay.'

She shifted in her chair. Her every move, intentional or not, came across as a double entendre. 'What do you really know about Olivia? Her background, I mean.'

'I know everything – where she's from, where she went to school –'

'How about family?'

'Her mother ran off when she was a baby. Her father died when she was twenty-one.'

122

'Siblings?'

'None.'

'So her father raised her alone?'

'Basically. So?'

Cingle kept going. 'Where did she grow up?'

'Northways, Virginia.'

Cingle wrote it down. 'She went to college there, right?'

Matt nodded. 'She went to UVA.'

'What else?'

'What do you mean, what else? What else is there? She's worked for DataBetter Associates for eight years. Her favorite color is blue. She has green eyes. She reads more than any human being I know. Her guilty pleasure is corny Hallmark movies. And – at the risk of making you vomit – when I wake up and Olivia is next to me, I know, *know,* that there is no luckier man on the planet. You writing this down?'

The door to his office burst open. They both turned toward it. Midlife stepped in. 'Oh, sorry, didn't mean to interrupt.'

'No, that's okay,' Matt said.

Midlife looked at his watch, making a full production out of it. 'I really need to go over the Sterman case with you.'

Matt nodded. 'I was just about to call you anyway.'

They both looked at Cingle. She rose. Midlife unconsciously adjusted his tie and patted his hair.

'Ike Kier,' he said, sticking out his hand.

'Yeah,' Cingle said, managing not to roll her eyes. 'Charmed.' She looked at Matt. 'We'll talk.'

'Thank you.'

She looked at him a second longer than necessary and spun toward the door. Midlife moved out of her wake.

After she left, Midlife took her seat, whistled, and said, 'Who in heaven is that?'

'Cingle Shaker. She works for MVD.'

'You mean she's a private dick?'

Midlife laughed at his own joke. When Matt didn't join in, he segued it into a cough and crossed his legs. His gray hair was neatly parted. Gray hair works on lawyers – a full head of it anyway. It gave them a certain gravitas with jurors.

Matt opened his desk drawer and pulled out the Sterman file. The two talked for three hours about the case, about the prelim, about what the DA might offer. They had just about talked themselves out when Matt's camera phone rang. He checked the caller ID. The screen spelled out: 'Unavailable.' Matt put the phone to his ear.

'Hello?'

'Hey.' It was a man whispering. 'Guess what I'm doing to your wife right now?'

15

For Loren Muse, there was no escaping déjà vu today.

She pulled up to the home of Marsha Hunter at 38 Darby Terrace in Livingston, New Jersey. Livingston had been Loren's hometown. Growing up, she'd decided, was never easy. Adolescence is a war zone, no matter where you live. Comfortable towns like Livingston are supposed to cushion the blows. For those who belonged, maybe it did. For Loren, this was where she lived when her father decided that he really, truly did not belong anywhere, not even with his daughter.

Livingston had all the trappings: great schools, great sports programs, great Kiwanis Club, great PTA, great high school productions. When Loren grew up here, the Jewish kids dominated the honor roll. Now it was the Asians and Indians, the next generation of immigrants, the new hungry ones. It was that kind of place. You come out here, you buy the house, you pay the taxes, you get the American dream.

But you know what they say: Be careful what you wish for.

She knocked on the door to Marsha Hunter's home. Loren hadn't figured the connection between this single mom, a rarity in Livingston, and Sister Mary Rose – other than a six-minute phone call. She probably should have done some checking first, a little background work, but there was no time. So here she stood, on the front stoop in the bright sunshine, when the door opened.

'Marsha Hunter?'

The woman, attractive in a plain way, nodded. 'Yes, that's right.'

Loren held up her identification. 'I'm Investigator Loren Muse from the Essex County prosecutor's office. I'd like a moment of your time.'

Marsha Hunter blinked, confused. 'What's this about?'

Loren tried a disarming smile. 'Could I come in a moment?'

'Oh, yes. Of course.'

She stepped back. Loren entered the home and whammo, another hit of déjà vu. Such a sameness to the interiors. In here it could be any year between 1964 and now. There was no change. The television might be fancier, the carpet a little less plush, the colors more muted, but that feeling of falling back into her old bizarro-kid-world dimension still hung in the air.

She checked the walls, looking for a cross or Madonna or some hint of Catholicism, something that might easily explain the phone call from the faux Sister Mary Rose. There was nothing hinting at any religion. Loren noticed a folded sheet and blanket on the edge of the couch, as if someone had recently slept there.

There was a young woman in the room, maybe twenty years old, and two boys no more than eight or nine. 'Paul, Ethan,' their mother said, 'this is Investigator Muse.' The well-trained boys dutifully shook Loren's hands, both going so far as to make eye contact.

The smaller one – Ethan, she thought – said, 'Are you a policeman?'

'Woman,' Loren replied automatically. 'And the answer is, sorta. I'm an investigator in the county prosecutor's office. That's like being a police officer.'

'You got a gun?'

126

'Ethan,' Marsha said.

Loren would have responded, would have shown it to him, but she knew that some mothers freaked about things like that. Loren understood it – anything to prevent Precious from understanding violence – but the gun-denial step was a woefully inadequate long-term tactic.

'And this is Kyra Sloan,' Marsha Hunter said. 'She helps me look after the kids.'

The young woman named Kyra waved from across the room, picking up some kind of toy. Loren waved back.

'Kyra, do you mind taking the boys outside for a little while?'

'Sure.' Kyra turned to the boys. 'How about a game of Wiffle ball, guys?'

'I'm up first!'

'No, you were up first last time! It's my turn!'

They headed outside, still debating the batting order. Marsha turned toward Loren. 'Is something wrong?'

'No, not at all.'

'So why are you here?'

'This is just a routine follow-up to an ongoing investigation.' It was a lot of vague malarkey, but Loren had found this particular brand fairly efficient.

'What investigation?'

'Mrs. Hunter –'

'Please. Call me Marsha.'

'Fine, sorry. Marsha, are you Catholic?'

'Excuse me?'

'I don't mean to pry. This isn't really a religious question. I'm just trying to see if you're in any way associated with St. Margaret's parish in East Orange.'

'St. Margaret's?'

'Yes. Are you a member?'

'No. We're with St. Philomena's in Livingston. Why would you ask that?'

'Are you associated in any way with St. Margaret's?'

'No.' Then: 'What do you mean associated?'

Loren kept going, not wanting to lose the rhythm. 'Do you know anybody attending the school?'

'St. Margaret's? No, I don't think so.'

'Do you know any of the teachers there?'

'I don't think so.'

'How about Sister Mary Rose?'

'Who?'

'Do you know any of the nuns at St. Margaret's?'

'No. I know several at St. Phil's, but no Sister Mary Rose.'

'So the name Sister Mary Rose means nothing to you?'

'Nothing at all. What is this about?'

Loren kept her eyes on the woman's face, searching for a mythical 'tell.' Nothing was showing up, but that didn't mean much.

'Do you and your children live here alone?'

'Yes. Well, Kyra has a room above the garage, but she's from out of state.'

'But she lives here?'

'She rents a room and helps out. She's taking classes at William Paterson University.'

'Are you divorced?'

'A widow.'

Something in the way Marsha Hunter said it made a piece or two tumble into place. Not all of them by any means. Not even enough yet. Loren almost kicked herself. She should have done some background work.

Marsha crossed her arms. 'What is this about anyway?'

'A Sister Mary Rose recently passed away.'

'And she worked at this school?'

'Yes, she was a teacher. At St. Margaret's.'

'I still don't see how –'

'When we were going through the phone logs, we found a call she'd made that we couldn't quite explain.'

'She called here?'

'Yes.'

Marsha Hunter looked perplexed. 'When?'

'Three weeks ago. June second to be exact.'

Marsha shook her head. 'It could have been a wrong number.'

'For six minutes?'

That made Marsha pause. 'What day again?'

'June second. Eight p.m.'

'I can check my calendar, if you'd like.'

'I'd like that very much, thank you.'

'It's upstairs. I'll be right back. But I'm sure none of us talked to this sister.'

'None of us?'

'Excuse me?'

'You said, 'us.' Who did you mean?'

'I don't know. Anyone in the house, I guess.'

Loren didn't comment on that. 'Do you mind if I ask your baby-sitter a few questions?'

Marsha Hunter hesitated. 'I guess that wouldn't be a problem.' She forced up a smile. 'But the boys will throw a fit if you use the word 'baby' in front of them.'

'Understood.'

'I'll be right back.'

Loren headed through the kitchen toward the back door. She glanced out the window. Kyra was pitching underhand to Ethan. He swung wildly and missed. Kyra took a step in closer and bent lower and pitched again. This time, Ethan made contact.

Loren turned away. She was almost at the back door when something made her pull up.

The refrigerator.

Loren wasn't married, didn't have kids, didn't grow up in one of those sweet happy homes, but if there was anything more Americana – more family – than the front of a refrigerator she did not know what it was. Her friends had refrigerators like this. She didn't, and she realized how pitiful that was. Loren had two cats and no real family, unless you wanted to count her melodramatic and self-involved mother.

But in most American homes, if you wanted to find the personal, this – your refrigerator front – was where you looked. There was kid artwork. There were essays from school, all adorned with stars for mediocrity that passed for excellence. There were preprinted birthday invitations, one to a party at something called the Little Gym, the other to the East Hanover bowling alley. There were forms for class trips, child vaccinations, a soccer league.

And, of course, there were family snapshots.

Loren had been an only child and no matter how often she saw them – this magnetized swirl of smiles – it always seemed slightly unreal to her, like she was watching a bad TV show or reading a corny greeting card.

Loren stepped toward the photograph that had caught her eye. More pieces started to pour into place now.

How could she have missed this?

She should have put it together right away. Hunter. The name wasn't rare but it wasn't overly common either. Her eyes scanned the other pictures, but they kept coming back to the first one, the one on the left taken at what looked like a baseball game. Loren was still staring at the picture when Marsha returned.

'Is everything okay, Inspector Muse?'

Loren startled up at the voice. She tried to conjure up the details, but only a sketch came to mind. 'Did you find your calendar?'

'There's nothing there. I really don't remember where I was that day.'

Loren nodded and turned back to the refrigerator. 'This man' – she pointed and looked back at Marsha – 'this is Matt Hunter, right?'

Marsha's face closed like a metal gate.

'Mrs. Hunter?'

'What do you want?'

There had been hints of warmth before. There were none now.

'I knew him,' Loren said. 'A long time ago.'

Nothing.

'In elementary school. We both went to Burnet Hill.'

Marsha crossed her arms. She was having none of it.

'How are you two related?'

'He's my brother-in-law,' Marsha said. 'And a good man.'

Right, sure, Loren thought. *A real prince.* She'd read about the manslaughter conviction. Matt Hunter had served time at a max-security facility. Serious hard time, as she recalled. She remembered the folded blanket and sheets on the couch.

'Does Matt visit here a lot? I mean, he's the boys' uncle and all.'

'Inspector Muse?'

'Yes?'

'I'd like you to leave now.'

'Why's that?'

'Matt Hunter is not a criminal. What happened was an accident. He has more than paid for it.'

Loren kept quiet, hoping she'd go on. She didn't. After a few moments she realized that this line of questioning would probably not take her anywhere. Better to try a less defensive route.

'I liked him,' Loren said.

'Excuse me?'

'When we were kids. He was nice.'

That was true enough. Matt Hunter had been a pretty good guy, another Livingston wanna-fit-in who probably shouldn't have tried so hard.

'I'll leave now,' Loren said.

'Thank you.'

'If you learn anything about that phone call on June second –'

'I'll let you know.'

'Do you mind if I speak to your sitter on the way out?'

Marsha sighed, shrugged.

'Thank you.' Loren reached for the door.

Marsha called out, 'Can I ask you something?'

Loren faced her.

'Was this nun murdered?'

'Why would you ask that?'

Marsha shrugged again. 'It's a natural question, I guess. Why else would you be here?'

'I can't discuss details with you. I'm sorry.'

Marsha said nothing. Loren opened the door and headed into the yard. The sun was still high, the long days of June. The boys ran and played with such wonderful abandonment. Adults could never play like that. Never in a million years. Loren remembered her tomboy youth, the days when you could play Running Bases for hours and never, not for a second, be bored. She wondered if Marsha Hunter ever did that, ever came out and played Running Bases with her sons, and thinking about that Loren felt another pang.

No time for that now.

Marsha would be watching from the kitchen window. Loren needed to do this fast. She approached the girl – what was her name? Kylie, Kyra? Kelsey? – and waved.

'Hi.'

The girl cupped her hands over her eyes and blinked. She was pretty enough, with blonde highlights that you can only find in youth or a bottle. 'Hi.'

Loren didn't waste time with preamble. 'Does Matt Hunter come over a lot?'

'Matt? Sure.'

The girl had answered without hesitation. Loren muffled a smile. Ah, youth.

'How often?'

Kyra – that was definitely the name – shifted now, slightly more wary, but she was still young. As long as Loren remained the authority figure, she'd talk. 'I don't know. Few times a week, I guess.'

'Good guy?'

'What?'

'Matt Hunter. Is he a good guy?'

Kyra gave a huge smile. 'He's great.'

'Good with the kids?'

'The best.'

Loren nodded, feigning disinterest. 'Was he here last night?' she asked as casually as she could.

But now Kyra cocked her head to the side. 'Didn't you ask Mrs. Hunter these questions?'

'I'm just reconfirming. He was here, right?'

'Yeah.'

'All night?'

'I was in the city with some friends. I don't know.'

'There were sheets on the couch. Who stayed on it?'

She gave a shrug. 'I guess it was Matt.'

Loren risked a glance behind her. Marsha Hunter disappeared from the window. She'd be moving toward the back door now. The girl would not remember June 2. Loren had enough for now, though she didn't have a clue what it meant.

'Do you know where Matt lives?'

'In Irvington, I think.'

The back door opened. Enough, Loren thought. Finding Matt Hunter shouldn't be a problem. She smiled and started away then, trying not to give Marsha a reason to call and warn her brother-in-law. She tried to walk away as casually as possible. She waved a good-bye at Marsha. Marsha's return wave was slow.

Loren hit the driveway and headed toward her car, but another face from her distant past – wow, this case was turning into a bad episode of *Loren Muse, This Is Your Life* – stood by her car. He leaned against the hood, a cigarette dangling from his lips.

'Hey, Loren.'

'As I live and breathe,' she said. 'Detective Lance Banner.'

'In the flesh.' He tossed the cigarette onto the ground and stomped on it.

She pointed to the stub. 'I may write you up for that.'

'I thought you were county homicide.'

'Cigarettes kill. Don't you read the carton?'

Lance Banner gave her a crooked smile. His car, an obvious unmarked police vehicle, was parked across the street. 'Been a long time.'

'That firearm safety convention in Trenton,' Loren said. 'What, six, seven years ago?'

'Something like that.' He folded his arms, kept leaning against her hood. 'You here on official business?'

'I am.'

'It involve a former school chum of ours?'

'It might.'

'Wanna tell me about it?'

'Wanna tell me why you're here?'

'I live near here.'

'So?'

'So I spotted a county vehicle. Figured I might be able to be of some assistance.'

'How's that?'

'Matt Hunter wants to move back to town,' Lance said. 'He's closing on a house not far from here.'

Loren said nothing.

'Does that work into your case?'

'I don't see how.'

Lance smiled and opened the car door. 'Why don't you tell me what's going on? Maybe we can figure out how together.'

16

'Hey, guess what I'm doing to your wife right now?'

Matt held the phone to his ear.

The man whispered, 'Matt? You still there?'

Matt said nothing.

'Yo, Matt, did you tattle on me? I mean, did you tell the wife about me sending you those pictures?'

He couldn't move.

'Because Olivia is being much more protective with her phone. Oh, she won't stop doing me. That ain't gonna happen. She's addicted, you know what I'm saying?'

Matt's eyes closed.

'But all of a sudden she says she wants to be more careful. So I'm wondering, you know, guy to guy here, did you say something? Let her in on our little secret?'

Matt's hand clamped down so hard he thought the phone might crack in his hand. He tried to take in deep breaths, but his chest kept hitching up. He found his voice and said, 'When I find you, Charles Talley, I'm going to rip off your head and crap down your neck.'

Silence.

'You still there, Charles?'

The voice on the phone was a whisper. 'Gotta run. She's coming back.'

And then he was gone.

Matt told Rolanda to cancel his afternoon appointments.

'You don't have any appointments,' she said.

'Don't be a wiseass.'

'You want to tell me what's wrong?'

'Later.'

He started home. The camera phone was still in his hand. He waited until he pulled up to their place off Main Street in Irvington. The already-sparse grass had pretty much died in the recent drought – there had been no rainfall on the East Coast for three weeks. In suburbs like Livingston, the lushness of one's lawn is taken seriously. Banning it, sitting by idly as one's green deadened to brown, was worthy of a good neighborly teeth-gnashing over the new Weber Genesis Gold B backyard grill. Here, in Irvington, nobody cared.

Lawns were a rich man's game.

Matt and Olivia lived in a declining two-family held together by aluminum siding. They had the right side of the dwelling; the Owens, an African-American family of five, had the left. Both sides had two bedrooms and one and a half baths.

He took the stoop two steps at a time. When he got inside he hit the speed-dial-one spot for Olivia. It went into her voice mail again. He wasn't surprised. He waited for the beep.

'I know you're not at the Ritz,' Matt said. 'I know it was you in the blonde wig. I know it wasn't a big joke. I even know about Charles Talley. So call me and explain.'

He hung up and looked out the window. There was a Shell gas station on the corner. He watched it. His breaths were coming in shallow gulps. He tried to slow them down. He grabbed a suitcase from the closet, threw it on the bed, started stuffing his clothes into it.

He stopped. Packing a suitcase. A stupid and histrionic move. Cut it out.

Olivia would be home tomorrow.

And if she wasn't?

No use thinking about it. She would be home. It would all come together, one way or the other, in a few hours.

But he was no longer above snooping. He started in Olivia's drawers. He barely hated himself for doing it. That voice on the phone had set him off. Best-case scenario now: Olivia was hiding something from him. He might as well find out what.

But he found nothing.

Not in the drawers, not in the closets. He thought about other possible hiding spots when he remembered something.

The computer.

He headed upstairs and hit the power switch. The computer booted up, came to life. It seemed to take an inordinate amount of time. Matt's right leg started shaking up and down. He put his palm on the knee to slow it down.

They'd finally gotten a cable modem – dial-ups going the way of the Betamax – and he was on the Web in seconds. He knew Olivia's password, though he had never dreamed of using it like this. He logged onto her e-mail and scanned the messages. The new stuff held no surprises. He tried the old mail.

The directory was empty.

He tried looking under her 'Sent Mail' folder. Same thing – everything had been deleted. He tried the section called 'Deleted Mail.' It too had been cleaned out. He checked through the browser's 'History,' hoping to see where Olivia had last surfed. That, too, had been erased.

Matt sat back and drew an obvious conclusion: Olivia had been covering her tracks. And the obvious follow-up question was: Why?

There was one more area to check: the cookies.

People often erased their surfing history or their mailbox, but the cookies were something different. If Olivia had wiped out the cookies, Matt would automatically know something had gone awry. His Yahoo! home page wouldn't automatically come up, for instance. Amazon wouldn't know who he was. A person trying to cover their tracks would not want that.

Clearing out the cookies would be too noticeable.

He went through Explorer and found the folder that held the Web's cookies. There were tons of them. He clicked the date button, thereby putting them in date order, the most recent at the top. His eyes ran down them. Most of them he recognized – Google, OfficeMax, Shutterfly – but there were two unfamiliar domains. He wrote them down, minimized the Explorer window, went back to the Web.

He typed in the first address and hit return. It was for the *Nevada Sun News* – a newspaper that required you to sign up in order to access the archives. The paper's home office was in Las Vegas. He checked the 'personal profile.' Olivia had signed up using a fake name and e-mail address. No surprise there. They both did that, to prevent spam and protect privacy.

But what had she been looking up?

There was no way to tell.

Strange, maybe, but the second Web address was far more so.

It took a while for the Web to recognize what he'd typed in. The address bounced from one spot to another before finally landing on something called:

Stripper-Fandom.com.

Matt frowned. There was a warning on the home page that nobody under the age of eighteen should continue.

That didn't bode well. He clicked the enter icon. The pictures that appeared were, as one might expect, provocative. Stripper-Fandom was an 'appreciation' site for . . .
. . . for female strippers?

Matt shook his head. There were countless thumbnails of topless women. He clicked one. There were biographies listed for each girl:

Bunny's career as an exotic dancer started in Atlantic City, but with her impressive dance moves and slinky costumes, she quickly rose to stardom and moved to Vegas. 'I love it out here! And I love rich men!' Bunny's specialty is wearing bunny ears and doing a hop-dance using the pole . . .

Matt clicked the link. An e-mail address came up, in case you wanted to write Bunny and request rates for a 'private audience.' It actually said that – private audience. Like Bunny was the pope.

What the hell was going on here?

Matt searched through the stripper fan site until he could take no more. Nothing jumped out at him. Nothing fell into place. He just felt more confused. Maybe the site meant nothing at all. Most of the strippers were from the Vegas area. Maybe Olivia had gotten there by clicking an advertising link at that Nevada newspaper. Maybe the link wasn't even marked as a stripper site and just led there.

But why was she on a Nevada newspaper site in the first place? Why had she erased all her e-mails?

No answer.

Matt thought about Charles Talley. He Googled the name. Nothing interesting came up. He shut down the browser and moved back downstairs, that whisper from the phone call still echoing in his head, shredding all reason:

'Hey, guess what I'm doing to your wife right now?'

Time to get some air. Air and something more potent.

He headed outside and started for South Orange Avenue. From the Garden State Parkway, you couldn't miss the giant brown beer bottle rising up and dominating the skyline. But when you traveled this section of the GSP, the other thing you noticed – maybe even more than the old water tank – was the sprawling cemetery on both sides of the road. The parkway cut smack through the middle of a burial ground. You were encased left and right by unending rows of weather-beaten gravestones. But the effect of driving through was not so much splitting a cemetery in half as much as zipping it together, of making something whole. And there, in the not-so-far distance, this strange giant beer bottle stood, high in the air, a silent sentinel guarding or maybe mocking the buried inhabitants.

The damage to the brewery was somewhat mystifying. Every window was only partially broken, not fully smashed, as if someone had taken the time to throw one rock and only one rock at every single window in the twelve-story structure. Shards lay everywhere. Every opening was a yawning, jangled threat. The combination of erosion and pride, the strong skeleton against the missing-teeth shattered-eye look from the broken glass, gave the place a strange downtrodden-warrior bearing.

Soon they would tear the old factory down and build an upscale mall. Just what Jersey needed, he thought – another mall.

Matt turned down the alley and headed for the faded red door. The tavern did not have a name on it. There was one window with a Pabst Blue Ribbon neon sign in it. Like the brewery – like this city? – the sign no longer lit up.

Matt opened the door, forcing sunlight into a place bathed in darkness. The men – there was only one woman here right now and she'd hit you if you called her a lady – blinked like bats who'd had a flashlight shined on them. There was no jukebox playing, no music at all. The conversations were kept as low as the lights.

Mel was still behind the bar. Matt hadn't been here in, what, two, three years at least, but Mel still knew him by name. The tavern was a classic dive. You see them everywhere across the United States. Men – mostly, anyway – finishing up whatever job they grinded out were now looking to get a buzz on. If that included some boasting or banter, so be it, but places like this were much more about inebriation than consolation or conversation.

Before his stint in prison Matt would have never gone into a dump like Mel's. He now liked rougher spots. He was not sure why. The men in here were big with undefined muscle. They wore flannel shirts in the fall and winter, and bowling-gut-emphasizing T-shirts in the spring and summer. They wore jeans year-round. There weren't many fights in here, but you didn't walk in a place like this unless you knew how to use your fists.

Matt took a seat on a stool. Mel nodded at him. 'Beer?'

'Vodka.'

Mel poured him one. Matt held the glass, looked at it, shook his head. Drinking away his problems. Could he be a bigger cliché? He threw back the vodka and let the warmth coast through him. He nodded for another, but Mel was already on the case. Matt threw that one back too.

He started to feel better. Or to say the same thing in another way: He started to feel less. His eyes slowly swerved from side to side. He felt, as he did in most places, slightly out of place – a spy in enemy territory. He was not really comfortable anywhere anymore – his old softer world or his new hardened one. So he straddled both. Truth was, he was only comfortable – pitiful as it sounded – when he was with Olivia.

Damn her.

Third shot down the hatch. The buzzing started in the base of his skull.

Yo, check out the big man throwing back the booze.

He already felt a bit wobbly. He wanted that. Just make it go away, he thought. Not forever. He wasn't drinking away the blues. He was postponing them, for just one more night, just until Olivia came home and explained to him why she was in a motel room with another man, why she lied about it, why the guy knew that he had told her about the pictures.

Like that. The little things.

He pointed for another. Mel, rarely one to converse or hand out advice, poured.

'You're a beautiful man, Mel.'

'Hey, thanks, Matt. I get that a lot, but it still means something, you know?'

Matt smiled and looked at the glass. Just for a night. Just let it go.

A big moose came back from the can, accidentally bumping into Matt as he walked past. Matt startled to, gave the moose the eye. 'Watch it,' Matt said.

The moose grunted an apology, diffusing the moment. Matt was almost disappointed. One would think he'd be smarter – that Matt, better than anyone, knew the danger in fisticuffs of any sort – but not tonight. Nope, tonight fisticuffs would be most welcome, yes indeed.

Screw the consequences, right?

He looked for Stephen McGrath's ghost. He often sat on the next bar stool. But Stephen was nowhere to be found tonight. Good.

Matt was not a good drinker. He knew that. He could not hold his liquor. He was already past buzzed and nearing inebriation. The key, of course, was knowing when to stop – maintaining the high without the aftermath. It was a line many people tried to find. It was a line most tripped over.

Tonight he really didn't care about the line.

'Another.'

The word came out slurred. He could hear it. It was hostile too. The vodka was making him angry or, more likely, letting him be. He was actually hoping for trouble now, even while he feared it. The anger was making him focus. Or at least that was what he wanted to believe. His thinking was no longer muddled. He knew what he wanted. He wanted to hit someone. He wanted a physical confrontation. It didn't matter if he crushed someone or someone crushed him.

He didn't care.

Matt wondered about this – this taste for violence. About its origins. Maybe his old chum Detective Lance Banner was right. Prison changes you. You go in one guy, even if you're innocent, but you come out . . .

Detective Lance Banner.

The keeper of the Livingston gate, the dumb hick bastard.

Time passed. It was impossible to say how much. He eventually signaled for Mel to come over and total him up. When he hopped off the stool, the inside of Matt's skull screamed in protest. He grabbed the bar, got his bearings. 'Later, Mel.'

'Good seeing you, Matt.'

He weaved his way out, one name ringing repeatedly in his head.

Detective Lance Banner.

Matt remembered an incident in second grade when he and Lance had both been seven. During a recess game of Four Squares – the dumbest game since Tetherball – Lance's pants had split. What made it worse, what made it one of those wholly horrifying childhood incidents, was that Lance had not worn underwear that day. A nickname had been born, one that Lance hadn't been able to shake until middle school: 'Keep It in Your Pants, Lance.'

Matt laughed out loud.

Then Lance's voice came back to him: *'We have a nice neighborhood here.'*

'That so?' Matt said out loud. 'Do all the kids wear underwear now, Lance?'

Matt laughed again at his own joke. The noise echoed in the tavern, but nobody looked up.

He pushed the door open. It was night now. He stumbled down the street, still cracking up at his own joke. His car was parked near his house. A couple of his quasi-neighbors stood near it, both drinking out of brown paper bags.

One of the two . . . *homeless* was the politically correct term they used nowadays, but these guys preferred the old standby *winos,* called out to him. 'Yo, Matt.'

'How are you, Lawrence?'

'Good, man.' He held out the bag. 'Need a swig?'

'Nah.'

'Yo.' Lawrence made a waving motion with his hand. 'Looks like you been having your fill anyway, huh?'

Matt smiled. He reached into his pocket and peeled off a twenty. 'You two get some of the good stuff. On me.'

A broad smile broke out on Lawrence's face. 'Matt, you's all right.'

'Yeah. Yeah, I'm very special.'

Lawrence laughed at that one like it was a Richard Pryor special. Matt waved and walked away. He dug into his pocket and pulled out his car keys. He looked at the keys in his hand, at the car, and then he stopped.

He was plastered.

Matt was irrational right now. He was stupid. He'd love to beat the hell out of someone – Lance Banner being number two on his list (Charles Talley was number one, but Matt didn't know how to find him) – but he was not *that* stupid. He wouldn't drive in this condition.

Lawrence said, 'Yo, Matt, you wanna hang with us?'

'Maybe later, guys.'

Matt spun around and headed back toward Grove Street. The number 70 bus hit Livingston. He waited at the stop, swaying with the wind. He was the only one there. Most of the people were traveling from the other direction – exhausted domestics trudging back from the wealthier environs to their far more humble abodes.

Welcome to the flip side of the burbs.

When bus 70 pulled up, Matt watched the tired women descend, zombielike. Nobody spoke. Nobody smiled. Nobody was there to greet them.

The bus ride was maybe ten miles, but what a ten miles. You went from the decay of Newark and Irvington and suddenly it was like you hit another universe. The change happened in a snap. There was Maplewood and Milburn and Short Hills and finally Livingston. Matt thought again about distance, about geography, about the truly thinnest of lines.

Matt rested his head against the bus window, the vibration working like a strange massage. He thought about Stephen McGrath and that terrible night in Amherst, Massachusetts. He thought about his hands around Stephen's neck. He wondered how hard he squeezed. He wondered if he could have let go as they fell, if that would have made a difference. He wondered if maybe, just maybe, he gripped the neck even tighter.

He wondered about that a lot.

Matt got off at the circle on Route 10 and walked toward Livingston's favorite watering hole, the Landmark. The lot on Northfield Avenue was chock full of minivans. Matt sneered. No thin line here. This was not Mel's. This was a goddamn wussy bar, if ever he saw one. He pushed open the door.

Lance Banner would be here.

The Landmark was, of course, nothing like Mel's. It was brightly lit. It was loud. Outkast sang about roses smelling like boo-boo – safe ghetto music. There was no cracked vinyl, no peeling paint, no sawdust on the floor. The Heineken signs worked. So did the Budweiser clock, complete with moving Clydesdales. Very little hard liquor was being served. Pitchers of beer lined the tables. At least half the men were dressed in softball uniforms with various sponsors – Friendly's Ice Cream, Best Buy, Burrelle's Press Clipping – and enjoying a post-rec-league-game celebration with teammates and opponents alike. There was a smattering of college kids home on break from Princeton or Rutgers or – gasp – maybe Matt's almost alma mater, Bowdoin.

Matt stepped inside and when he did, nobody turned around. Not at first. Everyone was laughing. Everyone was boisterous and red-faced and healthy. Everyone talked at the same time. Everyone smiled and swore too casually and looked soft.

And then he saw his brother, Bernie.

Except, of course, it wasn't Bernie. Bernie was dead. But man, it looked like him. At least from the back. Matt and Bernie used to come here with fake IDs. They'd laugh and be boisterous and talk at the same time and swear too casually. They'd watch those other guys, the rec-league softball players, and listen to them talk about their kitchen additions, their careers, their kids, their boxes at Yankee Stadium, their experiences coaching Little League, the lamentations over their declining sex lives.

As Matt stood there, thinking about his brother, the energy of the place shifted. Someone recognized him. A ripple began. Murmurs followed and heads turned. Matt looked around for Lance Banner. He didn't see him. He spotted the table with the cops – you could just tell that was what they were – and recognized one of them as the cop-kid Lance had braced him with yesterday.

Still heavily under the influence, Matt tried to keep his walk steady. The cops gave their best laser glares as he approached. The glares didn't faze him. Matt had seen much worse. The table grew silent as he approached the cop-kid.

Matt stopped in front of him. The kid did not step back. Matt tried not to sway.

'Where's Lance?' Matt asked.

'Who wants to know?'

'Good one.' Matt nodded. 'Say, who writes your lines?'

'What?'

'"Who wants to know?" That's funny stuff, really. I mean, I'm standing in front of you, I'm asking you directly, and you come up, bang, on the spot, no time to think, with, "Who wants to know?"' Matt moved in closer. 'I'm standing right here – so who the hell do you think wants to know?'

Matt heard the sound of chair legs scraping the floor,

but he didn't look away. The cop-kid glanced toward his buddies, then back at Matt. 'You're drunk.'

'So?'

He got into Matt's face now. 'So you want me to haul your ass downtown and give you a Breathalyzer?'

'One' – Matt raised his index finger – 'Livingston's police station is not downtown. It's more midtown. You've been watching too many repeats of *NYPD Blue*. Two, I'm not driving, numbnuts, so I'm not sure what a Breathalyzer is supposed to do for you. Three, while we're on the subject of breath and you standing in my face and all, I have mints in my pocket. I'm going to slowly reach for them so you can have one. Or even the whole pack.'

Another cop stood. 'Get out of here, Hunter.'

Matt turned toward him and squinted. It took him a second to recognize the ferret-faced man. 'My God, it's Fleisher, right? You're Dougie's little brother.'

'Nobody wants you here.'

'Nobody . . . ?' Matt turned from one man to the other. 'Are you guys for real? You going to run me out of town now? You' – Matt snapped, pointed – 'Fleisher's little brother, what's your first name?'

He didn't answer.

'Never mind. Your brother Dougie was the biggest pothead in my class. He dealt to the whole school. We called him Weed, for crying out loud.'

'You talking trash about my brother?'

'I'm not talking trash. I'm talking truth.'

'You want to spend the night in jail?'

'For what, asswipe? You going to arrest me on some trumped-up charge? Go ahead. I work for a law firm. I'll sue your ass back to the high school equivalency exam you probably never passed.'

More chair scrapes. Another cop stood. Then another. Matt's heart started doing a quick two-step. Someone reached and grabbed his wrist. Matt pulled away. His right hand formed a fist.

'Matt?'

This voice was gentle and struck a distant chord deep inside of him. Matt glanced behind the bar. Pete Appel. His old friend from high school. They'd played together at the Riker Hill Park. The park was a converted Cold War missile base. He and Pete used to play rocket ships on the cracked concrete launch pads. Only in New Jersey.

Pete smiled at him. Matt relaxed the fist. The cops all stayed in place.

'Hey, Pete.'

'Hey, Matt.'

'Good to see you, man.'

'You too,' Pete said. 'Look, I'm getting off now. Why don't I give you a lift home, okay?'

Matt looked at the cops. Several were red-faced, ready to go. He turned back to his old friend. 'That's okay, Pete. I'll find my way.'

'You sure?'

'Yeah. Look, man, sorry if I caused you any trouble.'

Pete nodded. 'Good to see you.'

'You too.'

Matt waited. Two of the cops made a space. He did not look back as he walked out into the lot. He sucked in the night air and started down the street. Soon he broke into a run.

He had a specific destination in mind.

17

Lance Banner was still smiling at Loren. 'Come on, get in,' he said. 'We'll talk.'

She took one more look at Marsha Hunter's house and then slid into the passenger seat. Lance started driving around the old neighborhood.

'So,' he said, 'what did you want with Matt's sister-in-law?'

She swore Lance to secrecy but still tossed him only the bare bones – that she was investigating the suspicious death of Sister Mary Rose, that they weren't sure that there was even a murder yet, that Sister Mary Rose had possibly placed a phone call to Marsha Hunter's residence. She did not tell him about the implants or the fact that they didn't know the nun's real identity.

For his part, Lance informed her that Matt Hunter was married now, that he currently worked as a 'low-level, shat-upon' paralegal in his brother's old law firm. Matt Hunter's wife, Lance said, was from Virginia or Maryland, he couldn't remember which. Lance also added, with a little too much enthusiasm, that he would be happy to help Loren look into this case.

Loren told him not to bother, that this was her investigation, that if he thought of something he should let her know. Lance nodded and drove her back to her own car.

Before Loren stepped out, she said, 'Do you remember him? I mean, as a kid?'

'Hunter?' Lance frowned. 'Yeah, sure, I remember him.'

'He seemed like a pretty straight shooter.'

'So do a lot of killers.'

Loren reached for the door handle, shaking her head. 'You really believe that?'

Lance said nothing.

'I read something the other day,' Loren said. 'I don't remember the details, but the basic premise was that by the age of five, much of our future self is determined: how well we'll do in schools, if we'll grow up to be a criminal, our capacity to love. You buy that, Lance?'

'Don't know,' he said. 'Don't much care.'

'You've caught a lot of bad guys, right?'

'Yeah.'

'You ever look into their past?'

'Sometimes.'

'Seems to me,' Loren said, 'that I always find something. There's usually a pretty obvious case of past psychosis or trauma. On the news, the neighbors are always like, 'Gee, I didn't know that nice man was chopping up little kids – he always seemed so polite.' But you go back, you ask their schoolteachers, you ask their childhood friends, they almost always tell a different story. They're never surprised.'

Lance nodded.

'So what about it?' she asked. 'You see anything in his past that makes Matt Hunter a killer?'

Lance thought about it. 'If it was all determined by the age of five, we wouldn't have jobs.'

'That's not an answer.'

'Best I can do. You try to profile based on how a third-grader played on the monkey bars, we're all screwed.'

He had a point. Either way Loren needed to keep her eye on the ball – right now that meant tracking down Matt Hunter. She got back into her car and started south.

There was still time to get to Lockwood Corp. in Wilmington, Delaware, before it was too dark.

She tried to reach Matt Hunter at the law firm, but he was gone for the day. She called his house and left a message on the machine: 'Matt, this is Loren Muse. I'm an investigator with the Essex County prosecutor's office. We knew each other a lifetime ago, at Burnet Hill. Could you give me a call as soon as possible?'

She left both her mobile and office numbers before hanging up.

The usually two-hour ride to Delaware took her an hour and twenty minutes. Loren didn't use the siren, but she did keep the small detachable flashing blue light on for the entire journey. She liked speeding – what's the point in being in law enforcement if you can't drive fast and carry a gun?

Randal Horne's office was a cookie-cut attorney spread. His firm took up three floors in a warehouse of office buildings, one next to the other, an unending drone of boxed sameness.

The receptionist at Horne, Buckman and Pierce, a classic battle-ax who was comfortably past her prime, eyed Loren as if she'd recognized her from a sex offender poster. Full frown in place, the battle-ax told her to sit.

Randal Horne kept her waiting for a full twenty minutes – a classic, if not transparent, lawyer mind game. She passed the time reading the thrilling magazine selection, which consisted of various issues of *The Third Branch*, the newsletter of federal courts, and the *American Bar Association Journal*. Loren sighed. What she wouldn't give for something with Lindsay, or Colin, on the cover.

Horne finally came out to the reception area and moved so that he stood directly over her. He was younger than she'd imagined, though he had that kind of shiny face Loren usually associated with Botox or Jermaine Jackson. His hair was a little too long, slicked back and curling around the neck. His suit was impeccable, though the lapels looked a little wide. Maybe that was back in.

He skipped the introductions: 'I don't really see that we have anything to discuss, Ms. Muse.'

Randal Horne stood close to her so that she couldn't really stand. That was okay. He was trying to do the height thing with her. Loren was all of five-one as it was, so she was used to it. Part of her was tempted to smash her palm into his groin, just to get him to back up, but no, let him have his play.

The battle-ax receptionist – she looked about fifteen years too old to play the prison matron in B-movies – watched the scene play out, the hint of a smile on her dry, lipstick-caked lips.

Loren said, 'I'd like the identity of the woman who purchased the breast implants with the serial number 89783348.'

'In the first place,' Horne said, 'these are very old records. SurgiCo didn't keep the woman's name on record, only the doctor who performed the procedure.'

'Fine, that'll be enough.'

Horne crossed his arms. 'Do you have a subpoena, Detective?'

'It's on its way.'

He gave her his smuggest expression, which was saying something. 'Well then,' he said, 'I'll return to my office. Please inform Tiffany here when you have it, will you?'

The battle-ax preened, smiled widely. Loren pointed at her and said, 'You have lipstick on your teeth.' Then she turned her attention back to Randal Horne. 'Do you mind telling me why you require a subpoena?'

'There are all sorts of new patient privacy laws. We at the Lockwood Corporation believe in following them.'

'But this woman is dead.'

'Still.'

'There are no medical secrets here. We know that she had implants. We're just trying to identify the body.'

'There must be other ways, Detective.'

'We're trying, believe me. But so far . . .' Loren shrugged.

'Unfortunately that does not change our position.'

'But your position, with all due respect, seems a tad fluid, Mr. Horne.'

'I'm not sure I understand your point.'

'Hold on a sec.' Loren started pulling folded papers out of her back pockets. 'I had time on the ride down here to check the New Jersey cases. It seems that your company has always cooperated with law enforcement in the past. You released records on a cadaver found last July in Somerset County. A Mr. Hampton Wheeler, age sixty-six, had his head and fingers cut off in order to avoid identification, but the killer forgot he had a pacemaker. Your company helped the authorities ID him. There was another case –'

'Detective . . . Muse, is it?'

'Inspector.'

'Inspector Muse. I'm very busy. Please make yourself comfortable. When your subpoena arrives, please feel free to tell Tiffany.'

'Wait.' Loren glanced at the battle-ax. 'Tiffany – I mean, that can't be her real name, right?'

'If you'll excuse me . . .'

'Mr. Horne, you already know I have no subpoena coming – that I was bluffing.'

Randal Horne said nothing.

Loren looked down and spotted the issue of *The Third Branch*. She frowned and turned toward Horne. This time she did stand. 'You didn't think I was bluffing,' she said, her words coming slowly. 'You knew it.'

Horne took a step back.

'But in reality,' Loren went on, more to herself than to him, 'it could have been true. It would have been tough timing, sure, but I could have called a federal judge on my way down here. The subpoena would be a no-brainer. Any member of the bench would have rubber-stamped it in five minutes. No judge in their right mind would refuse unless . . .'

Randal Horne waited. It was almost as if he hoped she'd put it together.

'Unless someone on the federal level – the FBI or U.S. attorney's office – shut you down.'

Horne cleared his throat and checked his watch. 'I really have to go now,' he said.

'Your company was cooperating with us at first. That's what Eldon said. Suddenly you stopped. Why? Why would you suddenly change your mind unless the feds told you to?' She looked up. 'Why would the feds care about this case?'

'That isn't our concern,' he said. Horne then put his hand to his mouth as if he'd been aghast at his own indiscretion. Their eyes met and she knew that he'd done her a favor. Horne wouldn't say any more. But he had said enough.

The FBI. They were the ones who had shut her down.

And maybe Loren understood why.

Back at her car Loren ran it through her head.

Who did she know at the FBI?

She had some acquaintances there, but nobody who could help on this level. The found-a-lead tingle rushed through her. This was big, no question about it. The FBI had been looking into this case. For some reason they wanted to find whoever was pretending to be Sister Mary Rose, leaving trip wires and calling cards everywhere, even with the company who supplied her breast implants.

She nodded to herself. Sure, this was mere speculation, but it made sense. Start with the victim: Sister Mary Rose had to be some sort of fugitive or witness. Someone valuable to the FBI.

Okay, good. Go on.

A long time ago Sister Mary Rose (or whatever her real name was) ran off – hard to say how long ago, but she'd been teaching at St. Margaret's, according to Mother Katherine, for seven years. So it had to be at least that long.

Loren stopped, considered the implications. Sister Mary Rose had been a fugitive for at least seven years. Had the feds been looking for her all that time?

It added up.

Sister Mary Rose had gone into deep, deep hiding. She'd changed her identity, for certain. Probably started off in Oregon, at that conservative convent Mother Katherine had mentioned. Who knows how long she was there?

Doesn't matter. What does matter is that seven years ago, for whatever reason, she chose to come east.

Loren rubbed her hands together. Oh, this is good.

So Sister Mary Rose moves to New Jersey and starts teaching at St. Margaret's. By all accounts she's a good teacher and nun, caring and devoted, living a quiet life. Seven years pass. Maybe she thinks she's safe now.

Maybe she gets careless and reaches out to someone from her old life. Whatever.

Somehow, some way, her past catches up with her. Someone learns who she is. And then someone breaks into her small convent room, tortures her, and then suffocates her with a pillow.

Loren paused, almost as if she were offering up a respectful moment of silence.

Okay, she thought, so now what?

She needed to get the identity from the feds.

How?

Only thing she could think of was classic quid pro quo: Give them something in return. But what did she have?

Matt Hunter, for one.

The feds were probably at least a day or two behind her. Would they have the phone logs yet? Doubtful. And if they did, if they knew about the call to Marsha Hunter, would they have already figured in a Matt Hunter connection?

Very doubtful.

Loren hit the highway and picked up her cell phone. It was dead. She cursed the damn thing. The greatest lie – right up there with 'the check is in the mail' and 'your call is very important to us' – is the stated battery life of a cell phone. Hers was supposed to last a week on standby. She was lucky if the cursed thing gave her thirty-six hours.

She flipped open the glove compartment and pulled out the charger. One end she jammed into the cigarette lighter, the other into her phone. The phone's LCD jumped to life and informed her that there were three messages waiting.

The first was from her mother. 'Hi, sweetheart,' Mom said in a voice strangely tender. It was her public voice, the one she usually saved for when she thought someone might overhear and thus judge her maternal skills. 'I thought I'd order us a pizza from Renato's and pick up a movie at Blockbuster – the new Russell Crowe is out on DVD – and, I don't know, maybe we could have a girls' night, just the two of us. Would you like that?'

Loren shook her head, tried not to be moved, but the tears were there, right below the surface. Her mom. Every time she wanted to write her off, to dismiss her from her life, to hold a grudge, to blame her once and for all for Dad's death, she came along and said something surprising and pulled herself back from the brink.

'Yeah,' Loren said softly in the car. 'I'd like that a lot.'

The second and third messages blew that idea out of the water. They were both from her boss, County Prosecutor Ed Steinberg, and were short and to the point. The first one said: 'Call me. Now.' The second one said: 'Where the hell are you? Call me. Doesn't matter what the hour. Disaster on the way.'

Ed Steinberg was not one for overstatement or for having people call at all hours. He was old-fashioned in that approach. Loren had his home number somewhere – not on her, unfortunately – but she had never used it. Steinberg didn't like to be bothered during off hours. His motto was: Get a life, it can wait. He was usually out of the office by five o'clock and she couldn't recall a time when she'd seen him in his office after six.

It was six thirty now. She decided to try his office line first. Thelma, his secretary, might still be there. She'd know how to reach him. After one ring, the phone was picked up by Ed Steinberg himself.

This was not a good sign.

'Where are you?' Steinberg asked.

'On the way back from Delaware.'

'Come straight back here. We got a problem.'

18

Las Vegas, Nevada
FBI Field Office
John Lawrence Bailey Building
Office of the Special Agent in Charge

For Adam Yates it started out as another day.

At least, that was what he wanted to believe. In a larger sense, no day was ever just another for Yates – at least, not for the past ten years. Each day felt like borrowed time, waiting eternally for the proverbial ax to fall. Even now, when most rational people would conclude that he'd successfully put his past mistakes behind him, the fear still gnawed in the back of his brain, tormenting him.

Yates had been a young agent then, working undercover. Now here he was, ten years later, the SAC – Special Agent in Charge – for all of Nevada, one of the FBI's most plum positions. He had risen up the ranks. In all that time, there had not been the smallest inkling of trouble.

So heading into work that morning, it seemed to be another day.

But when his chief advisor, Cal Dollinger, walked into his office, even though neither had spoken about the incident in nearly a decade, something in his old friend's face told him that this was indeed *the* day, that all others had merely been leading up to this.

Yates glanced quickly at the photograph on his desk.

It was a family shot – he, Bess, the three kids. The girls were in their teens now, and no amount of training adequately prepares a father for that. Yates stayed seated. He wore his casual uniform – khakis, no socks, brightly hued polo shirt.

Cal Dollinger stood over his desk and waited. Cal was huge – six-seven and nearly three hundred pounds. Adam and Cal went way back, having first met as eight-year-olds in Mrs. Colbert's third-grade class at Collingwood Elementary School. Some men called them Lenny and George, referring to the Steinbeck characters in *Of Mice and Men*. There might be some truth to it – Cal was big and impossibly strong – but where Lenny had a gentleness, Cal had none. He was a rock, both physically and emotionally. He could indeed kill a rabbit by petting it, but he wouldn't care much.

But their bond was even stronger than that. You go back enough years, you pull each other out of enough fires, you become like one. Cal could be cruel, no question about it. But like most violent men, it was just a question of black and white. Those in his very small white zone – his wife, his kids, Adam, Adam's family – he'd protect with his dying breath. The rest of the world was black and inanimate, a distant backdrop.

Adam Yates waited, but Cal could wait longer.

'What is it?' Adam finally asked.

Cal's eyes swept the room. He feared listening devices. He said, 'She's dead.'

'Which one?'

'The older.'

'Are you sure?'

'Her body was found in New Jersey. We ID'd her by the serial numbers on the surgical implants. She was living as a nun.'

'You're kidding.'

Cal did not smile. Cal did not kid.

'What about' – Yates didn't even want to say Clyde's name – 'him?'

Cal shrugged. 'No idea.'

'And the tape?'

Cal shook his head. It was as Adam Yates had expected. It wouldn't end easily. It would never end at all. He cast one more glance at his wife and children. He looked about his spacious office, the commendations on the wall, his nameplate on the desk. All of it – his family, his career, his entire life – seemed wispy now, like holding smoke in a hand.

'We should go to New Jersey,' he said.

19

Sonya McGrath was surprised to hear the key in the lock.

Today, more than a decade after her son's death, the photographs of Stephen were still in the same frames on the same side tables. Other photographs had been added, of course. When Michelle, Sonya's oldest daughter, got married last year, they naturally took photographs. Several were framed over the fireplace. But no pictures of Stephen had ever been taken down. They could pack away his things, repaint his room, give his clothes to charity, sell his old car, but Sonya and Clark could never touch those photographs.

Her daughter Michelle, like many brides, had chosen to do the standard group photographs before the marriage ceremony. The groom, a nice guy named Jonathan, had a large extended family. They took all the usual shots. Sonya and Clark had gamely posed – with their daughter, with their daughter and soon-to-be son-in-law, with Jonathan's parents and the new bride and groom, whatever, but they balked when the photographer called for the 'McGrath family photograph,' the one that would have consisted of Sonya and Clark and Michelle and Cora, Michelle's younger sister, because all any of them would ever see, even after this joy-filled day, was the giant hole in the 'McGrath family photograph' where Stephen still belonged.

The big house was silent tonight. It had been that way since Cora started college. Clark was 'working late again' – a euphemism for 'sleeping with the bimbette' – but Sonya didn't care. She didn't question his hours because their home was even lonelier, even more silent, when Clark was here.

Sonya swirled the brandy in the snifter. She sat alone in the new theater room, in the dark, cuing up a movie on DVD. She'd rented something with Tom Hanks – his presence, even in crummy movies, oddly comforted her – but she hadn't hit the play button yet.

God, she thought, am I really this pitiful?

Sonya had always been a popular woman. She had many true and wonderful friends. It would be easy to blame them, to say that they slowly disengaged themselves from her after Stephen's death, that they had tried to be dutiful but after a while, you can only take so much, and so they made one excuse, and then another, gradually drifting away, cutting ties.

But that would not be fair to them.

It might be true in some small part – there had certainly been a detachment of sorts – but Sonya had been far more responsible for that than any of her friends. She pushed them away. She did not want comfort. She did not want company or camaraderie or commiseration. She didn't want to be miserable either, but perhaps that was the easiest and ergo best alternative.

The front door opened.

Sonya turned on the small lamp next to her movie-theater recliner. It was dark outside, but in this airless room that didn't matter. The shades blocked out all light. She heard the footsteps in the marble foyer and then on the polished hardwood floors. They were coming toward her.

She waited.

A moment later, Clark stepped into the room. He said

nothing, just stood there. She studied him for a moment. Her husband looked somehow older, or maybe it had been a long time since she had really studied the man she'd married. He'd chosen not to go distinguished gray and took to coloring his hair. The coloring was done, as with all things Clark, meticulously, but it still didn't look right. His skin had an ashen tone. He looked thinner.

'I was just going to put on a movie,' she said.

He stared at her.

'Clark?'

'I know,' he said.

He did not mean that he knew that she was putting on a movie. He meant something else entirely. Sonya did not ask for clarification. There was no need. She sat very still.

'I know about your visits to the museum,' he went on. 'I've known for a long time.'

Sonya debated how to reply. Countering with an 'I know about you too' was the obvious move, but it would be both too defensive and entirely irrelevant. This was not about an affair.

Clark stood, his hands at his sides, his fingers itching but not clenching.

'How long have you known?' she asked.

'A few months.'

'So how come you didn't say anything before now?'

He shrugged.

'How did you find out?'

'I had you followed,' he said.

'Followed? You mean like you hired a private investigator?'

'Yes.'

She crossed her legs. 'Why?' Her voice raised a notch, stung by this strange betrayal. 'Did you think I was sleeping around?'

'He killed Stephen.'

'It was an accident.'

'Really? Is that what he tells you when you have your little lunches? Do you discuss how he accidentally murdered my son?'

'Our son,' she corrected him.

He looked at her then, a look she had seen before but never directed at her. 'How could you?'

'How could I what, Clark?'

'Meet with him. Offer him forgiveness –'

'I've never offered him anything of the sort.'

'Comfort then.'

'It's not about that.'

'Then what is it about?'

'I don't know.' Sonya rose to her feet. 'Clark, listen to me: What happened to Stephen was an accident.'

He made a noise of derision. 'Is that how you comfort yourself, Sonya? By telling yourself it was an accident?'

'Comfort myself?' A dark chill ripped through her. 'There is no comfort, Clark. Not for a second. Accident, murder – Stephen is dead either way.'

He said nothing.

'It was an accident, Clark.'

'He's convinced you of that, eh?'

'Actually, just the opposite.'

'What's that supposed to mean?'

'He's no longer sure himself. He feels tremendous guilt.'

'Poor baby.' Clark made a face. 'How can you be so naïve?'

'Let me ask you something,' Sonya said, moving closer to him. 'If they fell another way, if the angle had been different or if Stephen had twisted his body and Matt Hunter had hit his head on that curb –'

'Don't even start with that.'

'No, Clark, listen to me.' She took another step. 'If it had gone another way, if Matt Hunter ended up dead and Stephen had been found on top of him –'

'I'm not in the mood to play hypotheticals with you, Sonya. None of that matters.'

'Maybe it does to me.'

'Why?' Clark countered. 'Weren't you the one who said that either way Stephen is dead?'

She said nothing.

Clark crossed the room, moving past her, keeping enough distance so that he did not so much as brush up against her. He collapsed into a chair and lowered his head into his hands. She waited.

'Do you remember the case of that mother drowning her kids in Texas?' he asked.

'What does that have to do with anything?'

'Just' – he closed his eyes for a moment – 'just bear with me, okay? Do you remember that case? This over-worked mother drowned her kids in the tub. I think there were four or five of them. Awful story. The defense made an insanity plea. Her husband supported her. Do you remember, on the news?'

'Yes.'

'What did you think?'

She said nothing.

'I'll tell you what I thought,' he continued. 'I thought, who cares? I don't mean that to sound cold. I mean, what's the difference? If this mother was found insane and spent the next fifty years in a loony bin or if she was found guilty and spent the rest of her life in jail or on death row – what does it matter? Either way you killed your own children. Your life is over, isn't it?'

Sonya closed her eyes.

'That's how it is with Matt Hunter to me. He killed our son. If it was an accident or intentional, I only know that our boy is dead. The rest doesn't matter. Do you understand that?'

More than he could ever know.

Sonya felt the tears escape from her eyes. She looked at her husband. Clark was in so much pain. Just go, she wanted to say. Bury yourself in your work, in your mistress, in whatever. Just go.

'I'm not trying to hurt you,' she said.

He nodded.

'Do you want me to stop seeing him?' she asked.

'Would it matter if I did?'

She did not reply.

Clark rose and left the room. A few seconds later, Sonya heard the front door close, leaving her yet again all alone.

20

Loren Muse made even better time on the way back from Wilmington, Delaware, to Newark. Ed Steinberg was alone in his office on the third floor of the new county courthouse.

'Shut the door,' her boss said.

Steinberg looked disheveled – loose tie, collar button undone, one sleeve rolled up higher than the other – but that was pretty much his normal look. Loren liked Steinberg. He was smart and played fair. He hated the politics of the job but understood the necessity of the game. He played it well.

Loren found her boss sexy in that cuddly-bear, hairy-Vietnam-vet-on-his-Harley vein. Steinberg was married, of course, with two kids in college. Cliché but true: The good ones were always taken.

When Loren was young, her mother would warn her to wait: 'Don't get married young,' Carmen would slur through the daytime wine. Loren never consciously followed that advice, but she realized somewhere along the way that it was idiotic. The good men, the ones who wanted to commit and raise children, were scooped up early. The field became thinner and thinner as the years went by. Now Loren had to settle for what one of her friends called 'retreads' – overweight divorcées who were making up for the years of high school rejection or those still cowering from the anguish of their first marriage or those semi-decent guys who were interested – and why not? – in some young waif who'd worship them.

'What were you doing in Delaware?' Steinberg asked.

'Following a lead on our nun's identity.'

'You think she's from Delaware?'

'No.' Loren quickly explained about the implants' identification code, the initial cooperation, the stonewalling, the connection to the feds. Steinberg stroked his mustache as if it were a small pet. When she finished, he said, 'The SAC in the area is a fed named Pistillo. I'll call him in the morning, see what he can tell me.'

'Thank you.'

Steinberg stroked his mustache some more. He looked off.

'Is that what you needed to see me about?' she asked. 'The Sister Mary Rose case?'

'Yes.'

'And?'

'The lab guys dusted the nun's room.'

'Right.'

'They found eight sets of prints,' he said. 'One set matched Sister Mary Rose. Six others matched various nuns and employees of St. Margaret's. We're running those through the system, just in case, see if anybody had a record we don't know about.'

He stopped.

Loren came over to the desk and sat down. 'I assume,' she said, 'you got a hit on the eighth set?'

'We did.' His eyes met hers. 'That's why I called you back here.'

She spread her hands. 'I'm all ears.'

'The prints belong to a Max Darrow.'

She waited for him to say more. When he stayed quiet, she said, 'I assume this Darrow has a record?'

Ed Steinberg shook his head slowly. 'Nope.'

'Then how did you get a match?'

'He served in the armed forces.'

In the distance, Loren could hear a phone ring. Nobody answered it. Steinberg leaned back in his big leather chair. He tilted his chin to look up. 'Max Darrow isn't from around here,' he said.

'Oh?'

'He lived in Raleigh Heights, Nevada. It's near Reno.'

Loren considered that. 'Reno's a pretty long way from a Catholic school in East Orange, New Jersey.'

'Indeed.' Steinberg was still looking up. 'He used to be on the job.'

'Darrow was a cop?'

He nodded. 'Retired. Detective Max Darrow. Worked homicide in Vegas for twenty-five years.'

Loren tried to fit that into her earlier theory about Sister Mary Rose being a fugitive. Maybe she was from the Vegas or Reno area. Maybe she'd stumbled across this Max Darrow sometime in the past.

The next step seemed pretty obvious: 'We need to locate Max Darrow.'

Ed Steinberg's voice was soft. 'We already have.'

'How's that?'

'Darrow is dead.'

Their eyes met and something else clicked into place. She could almost see Trevor Wine pulling up his belt. How had her patronizing colleague described his murder victim?

'A retired white guy . . . a tourist.'

Steinberg nodded. 'We found Darrow's body in Newark, near that cemetery off Fourteenth Avenue. He was shot twice in the head.'

21

It finally started to rain.

Matt Hunter had stumbled from the Landmark Bar and Grill and headed back up Northfield Avenue. Nobody followed him. It was late and dark and he was drunk, but that didn't matter. You always know the streets near where you grew up.

He made the right on Hillside Avenue. Ten minutes later he arrived. The Realtor's sign was still out front, reading UNDER CONTRACT. In a few days this house would be his. He sat on the curb and stared at it. Slow raindrops the size of cherries pounded down on him.

Rain reminded him of prison. It turned the world gray, drab, shapeless. Rain was the color of jail asphalt. Since the age of sixteen Matt wore contact lenses – was wearing them now – but in prison he'd stayed with glasses and kept them off a lot. It seemed to help, making his prison surroundings a blur, more unformed gray.

He kept his eyes on the house he'd planned to buy – this 'saltbox charmer' as the ad had called it. Soon he'd move in with Olivia, his beautiful, pregnant wife, and they'd have a baby. There'd probably be more kids after that. Olivia wanted three.

There was no picket fence in the front, but there might as well have been. The basement was unfinished, but Matt was pretty good with his hands. He'd do it himself. The swing set in the back was old and rusty and would need to be thrown out. While they were two years away from purchasing a replacement, Olivia had already located the exact brand she wanted – something with cedar wood – because they guaranteed no splinters.

Matt tried to see all that – that future. He tried to imagine living inside this three-bedroom abode with the kitchen that needed updating, a roaring fire, laughter at the dinner table, the kid coming to their bed because a nightmare had scared her, Olivia's face in the morning. He could almost see it, like one of Scrooge's ghosts was showing him the way, and for a second he almost smiled.

But the image wouldn't hold. Matt shook his head in the rain.

Who had he been kidding?

He didn't know what was going on with Olivia, but one thing he knew for certain: It marked the end. The fairy tale was over. As Sonya McGrath had said, the images on the camera phone had been his wake-up call, the reality check, the 'It's all a joke on you!' moment, when deep down inside, he'd always known that.

You don't come back.

Stephen McGrath was not about to leave his side. Every time Matt started to pull away, Dead Stephen was there, catching up from behind, tapping him on the shoulder.

'I'm right here, Matt. Still with you . . .'

He sat in the rain. He idly wondered what time it was. Didn't much matter. He thought about that damned picture of Charles Talley, the mysterious man with the blue-black hair, his mocking whispers on the phone. To what end? That was what Matt could not get around or figure out. Drunk or sober, in the comfort of his home or heck, outside in the pouring rain, the drought finally over. . . .

And that was when it struck him.

Rain.

Matt turned and looked up, encouraging the drops now. Rain. Finally. There was rain. The drought had ended with a massive fury.

Could the answer be that simple?

Matt thought about it. First thing: He needed to get home. He needed to call Cingle. Didn't matter what the time. She'd understand.

'Matt?'

He hadn't heard the car pull up, but the voice, even now, even under these conditions, well, Matt couldn't help but smile. He stayed on the curb. 'Hey, Lance.'

Matt looked up as Lance Banner stepped out of a minivan.

Lance said, 'I heard you were looking for me.'

'I was.'

'Why?'

'I wanted to fight you.'

Now it was Lance's turn to smile. 'You wouldn't want to do that.'

'Think I'm afraid?'

'I didn't say that.'

'I'd kick your ass.'

'Which would only prove me right.'

'About?'

'About how prison changes a man,' Lance said. 'Because before you went in, I'd have beaten you with two broken arms.'

He had a point. Matt stayed seated. He still felt pretty wasted and didn't fight the feeling. 'You always seem to be around, Lance.'

'That I am.'

'You're just so damn helpful.' Matt snapped his fingers. 'Hey, Lance, you know who you're like now? You're like that Block Mom.'

Lance said nothing.

'Remember that Block Mom on Hobart Gap Road?' Matt asked.

'Mrs. Sweeney.'

'Right. Mrs. S. Always peering out the window, no matter what time it was. Big sourpuss on her face, complaining about the kids cutting through her yard.' Matt pointed at him. 'You're like that, Lance. You're like a great big Block Mom.'

'You been drinking, Matt?'

'Yup. That a problem?'

'Not in and of itself, no.'

'So why are you always out and about, Lance?'

He shrugged. 'I'm just trying to keep the bad out.'

'You think you can?'

Lance didn't reply to that.

'You really think that your minivans and good schools are, what, some kind of force field, warding off evil?' Matt laughed too hard at that one. 'Hell, Lance, look at me, for chrissake. I'm the poster boy proving that's a load of crap. I should be on your warn-the-teens tour, you know, like when we were in high school and the cops would make us look at some car smashed up by a drunk driver. That's what I should be. One of those warnings to the youngsters. Except I'm not sure what my lesson would be.'

'Not to get into fights, for one.'

'I didn't get in a fight. I tried to break one up.'

Lance fought back a sigh. 'You want to retry the case out here in the rain, Matt?'

'No.'

'Good. Then how about I give you a lift home?'

'Not going to arrest me?'

'Maybe another time.'

Matt took one last look at the house. 'You may be right.'

'What about?'

'About my belonging.'

'Come on, Matt, it's wet out. I'll drive you home.'

Lance came up behind him. He put his hands under Matt's armpits and lifted. The man was powerful. Matt stumbled to a wobbly stand. His head spun. His stomach gurgled. Lance helped him to the car and into the front passenger seat.

'You get sick in my car,' Lance said, 'you'll wish I arrested you.'

'Ooo, tough guy.' Matt cracked the window, enough for a breeze but not enough to let in the rain. He kept his nose near the opening like a dog. The air helped. He closed his eyes and leaned his head against the window. The glass was cool against his cheek.

'So why the drinking binge, Matt?'

'Felt like it.'

'You do that a lot? Drink yourself stupid?'

'You an AA counselor too, Lance? You know, along with your gig as the Block Mom?'

Lance nodded. 'You're right. Change of subject.'

The rain let up a little. The wipers slowed down a notch. Lance kept both hands on the wheel.

'My oldest daughter is thirteen. You believe that?'

'How many kids you got, Lance?'

'Three. Two girls and a boy.' He took one hand off the wheel and fumbled for his wallet. He extracted three photographs and handed them to Matt. Matt studied them, searching as he always did, for echoes of the parent. 'The boy. How old is he?'

'Six.'

'Looks just like you did at that age.'

Lance smiled. 'Devin. We call him Devil. He's wild.'

'Like his old man.'

'Guess, yeah.'

They fell into silence. Lance reached for the radio then decided against it. 'My daughter. The oldest. I'm thinking of putting her in Catholic school.'

'She at Heritage now?' Heritage had been the middle school they'd attended.

'Yeah, but, I don't know, she's a little wild. I heard St. Margaret's in East Orange is supposed to be good.'

Matt looked out the window.

'You know anything about it?'

'About Catholic school?'

'Yeah. Or St. Margaret's.'

'No.'

Lance had both hands on the wheel again. 'Say, do you know who went there?'

'Went where?'

'St. Margaret's.'

'No.'

'Remember Loren Muse?'

Matt did. It was that way with people you went to elementary school with, even if you never saw them after graduation. You recall the name and face instantly. 'Sure. Tomboy, hung out with us for a while. Then she kinda faded away. Her father died when we were kids, right?'

'You don't know?'

'Know what?'

'Her old man committed suicide. Blew his brains out in their garage when she was in like eighth grade. They kept it a secret.'

'God, that's awful.'

'Yeah, but she's doing okay. She works in the prosecutor's office in Newark now.'

'She's a lawyer?'

Lance shook his head. 'An investigator. But after what

happened with her father, well, Loren hit a rough patch too. St. Margaret's helped, I think.'

Matt said nothing.

'But you don't know anybody who went to St. Margaret's?'

'Lance?'

'Yeah.'

'This subtlety act. It's not really playing. What are you trying to ask me here?'

'I'm asking if you know anything about St. Margaret's.'

'You want me to write your daughter a letter of recommendation?'

'No.'

'Then why are you asking me these questions?'

'How about a Sister Mary Rose? Taught social studies there. Do you know her?'

Matt shifted so that he faced Lance full on. 'Am I a suspect in some kind of crime?'

'What? We're just having a friendly conversation here.'

'I don't hear a no, Lance.'

'You have a very guilty conscience.'

'And you're still evading my question.'

'You don't want to tell how you knew Sister Mary Rose?'

Matt closed his eyes. They weren't far from Irvington now. He leaned his head back against the headrest. 'Tell me more about your kids, Lance.'

Lance did not reply. Matt closed his eyes and listened to the rain. It brought him back to what he'd been thinking before Lance Banner showed up. He needed to call Cingle as soon as he could.

Because, strangely enough, the rain could hold the key to what Olivia was doing in that hotel room.

22

Matt thanked Lance for the ride and watched him pull away.

As soon as the minivan was out of sight, he headed inside, grabbed his phone, and started dialing Cingle's cell. He checked the time. It was nearly eleven o'clock. He hoped that she was awake, but even if she wasn't, well, once he explained, she'd understand.

The phone rang four times and then went into Cingle's simple voice mail message:

'Me. You. Tone.'

Damn.

He left Cingle a message: 'Call me back, it's urgent.' He hit the button for 'other options' and plugged in his home number. Maybe she'd get the page.

He wanted to download the images from his camera phone onto his hard drive, but like a dummy he'd left the USB cord at work. He searched the computer room for the cord that came with Olivia's phone, but he couldn't find it.

It was then that he noticed the phone's message light was blinking. He picked it up and hit play. There was only one message and after the day he'd had, it hardly surprised him.

'Matt, this is Loren Muse. I'm an investigator with the Essex County prosecutor's office. We knew each other a lifetime ago, at Burnet Hill. Could you give me a call as soon as possible?'

She left two numbers – office and cell.

Matt put the phone back in its cradle. So Lance was trying to get a jump on his county counterpart. Or they were working together. Whatever. He wondered what it could be about. Lance had said something about St. Margaret's in East Orange. Something about a nun there.

What could it possibly have to do with him?

Whatever, it couldn't be good.

He didn't want to speculate. He also didn't want to get caught unawares. So he headed into the computer room and ran a classic Google search. He searched for St. Margaret's in East Orange and got too many hits. He tried to remember the nun's name. Sister Mary Something. He added that into the mix. 'Sister Mary' 'St. Margaret's' 'East Orange.'

No relevant hits.

He sat back and thought it through. Nothing came to him. He wouldn't call Loren back. Not yet. It could wait until morning. He could say that he was out drinking – Lance would back that up – and forgot to check his messages.

His head started clearing. He thought about his next move. Even though he was alone in the house, Matt checked the corridor and closed the door. Then he opened the closet door, reached toward the back, and pulled out the lockbox. The combination was 878 because those numbers had absolutely no link to his life. He'd just made them up on the spot.

Inside the lockbox was a gun.

He stared at it. The semiautomatic was a Mauser M2. Matt had bought it off the streets – it's not hard to do – when he got out of jail. He'd told no one – not Bernie, not Olivia, not Sonya McGrath. He was not sure how to explain why he owned it. One would again think that his past would have taught him the danger of such actions. It had, he supposed, but with a twist. Now that Olivia was having a baby, yes, he'd have to get rid of the gun. But he wasn't sure that he'd be able to go through with it.

The prison system has its share of critics. Most problems are obvious and, to some extent, organic, what with the fact that you are, for the most part, caging bad people with other bad people. But the one thing that was definitely true was that prison taught you all the wrong skills. You survive by being aloof, by isolating yourself, by fearing any alliance. You are not shown how to assimilate or become productive – just the opposite. You learn that no one can be trusted, that the only person you can truly count on is yourself, that you must be ready to protect yourself at all times.

Having the gun gave Matt a strange feeling of comfort.

He knew it was wrong. He knew the odds were much greater that the gun would lead to disaster rather than salvation. But there it was. And now, with the world caving in on him, he was eyeing it for the first time since he'd bought it.

The phone startled him. He quickly closed the lockbox, as if someone had suddenly entered the room, and picked up the receiver.

'Hello?'

'Guess what I was doing when you called.'

It was Cingle.

'I'm sorry,' Matt said. 'I know it was late.'

'No, no. Guess. C'mon. Okay, forget it, I'll tell you. I was putting out for Hank. He takes forever. I was getting so bored I almost picked up mid, er, thrust. But men, well, they're so sensitive, you know?'

'Cingle?'

'What's up?'

'The pictures you downloaded from my phone.'

'What about them?'

'Do you have them?'

'You mean the files? They're at the office.'

'Did you blow them up?'

'My tech guy did, but I haven't had a chance to study them.'

'I need to see them,' Matt said. 'Blown up, that is.'

'Why?'

'I have a thought.'

'Uh oh.'

'Yes, uh oh. Look, I know it's late, really late, but if you could meet me down at your office –'

'Now?'

'Yes.'

'I'm on my way.'

'I owe you.'

'Time and a half,' Cingle said. 'See you in forty-five minutes.'

He grabbed his keys – he was sober enough now to drive – jammed his cell phone and wallet into his pocket, started for the door. Then he remembered the Mauser semiautomatic. It was still on the desktop. He considered his next move.

He picked up the gun.

Here was something that they never tell you: Holding a gun feels great. On television, the average person always acts all repulsed when the gun is first handed to them. They make a face and say, 'I don't want that thing!' But the truth is, having a gun in your hand – the cold steel against your skin, the weight in your palm, the very shape, the way your hand naturally coils around the grip, the way your index finger slides into the trigger loop –

it feels not only good, but right and even natural.

But no, he shouldn't.

If he somehow got caught carrying a piece, with his record, there would be huge problems. He knew that.

But he still jammed the gun into the waist of his pants.

When Matt opened his front door, she was walking up the stoop. Their eyes met.

Matt wondered if he would have recognized her had he not just heard her name from Lance and listened to the message on the machine. Hard to say. The hair was still short. That tomboyish quality remained. She looked very much the same to him. Again there was something to that – to running into adults you only knew as kids in elementary school, how you can still recognize them by seeing the small child there.

Loren Muse said, 'Hey, Matt.'

'Hey, Loren.'

'Long time.'

'Yeah.'

She managed a smile. 'Do you have a second? I need to ask you a few questions.'

23

Standing on his front stoop, Matt Hunter asked, 'Is this about that nun at St. Margaret's?'

Loren was startled by that one, but Hunter held up his hand.

'Don't get excited,' he said. 'I know about the nun because Lance already questioned me.'

She should have known. 'So you want to fill me in?'

Matt shrugged, didn't say anything. She pushed past him, stepped into his foyer, and took a look around. Books were piled everywhere. Some had fallen, looking like crumbling towers. There were framed photographs on the table. Loren studied them. She picked one up.

'This your wife?'

'Yes.'

'Pretty.'

'Yes.'

She put the picture down and turned to him. It would be corny to say that his past was written on his face, that prison had somehow not only changed the inside, but the outside as well. Loren wasn't a fan of that stuff. She didn't believe the eyes were the windows to the soul. She had seen killers with beautiful, kind eyes. She had met brilliant people who had that open-eyed vacancy thing going on. She had heard jurors say, 'I knew he was innocent the minute he walked in the court – you can just tell' and knew that it was total, awful nonsense.

But that said, there was something in Matt Hunter's

stance, in the tilt of the chin maybe, in the line of the mouth. The damage, the defensiveness, emanated from him. She couldn't put her finger on why, but it was there. Even if she hadn't known that he'd served hard time after a fairly comfortable childhood, would she still feel this unmistakable vibe?

She thought the answer was yes.

Loren couldn't help but think back to Matt as a kid, a good, goofy, sweet-natured kid, and a pang of sorrow skipped through her.

'What did you tell Lance?' she asked.

'I asked him if I was a suspect.'

'A suspect in what?'

'In anything.'

'And what did he say?'

'He was evasive.'

'You're not a suspect,' she said. 'Not yet anyway.'

'Whew.'

'Was that sarcasm?'

Matt Hunter shrugged. 'Could you ask your questions quickly? I have to be someplace.'

'Have to be someplace' – she repeated, making a production of checking her watch – 'at this hour?'

'I'm something of a party animal,' he said, stepping back onto the stoop.

'I somehow doubt that.'

Loren followed. She glanced about the neighborhood. There were two men drinking out of brown paper bags and singing an old Motown classic.

'That the Temptations?' she asked.

'Four Tops,' he said.

'I always mix those two up.'

She turned back to him. He spread his hands.

'Not exactly Livingston, is it?' Matt said.

'I heard you're moving back.'

'It's a nice town to raise a family.'

'You think?'

'You don't?'

She shook her head. 'I wouldn't go back.'

'That a threat?'

'No, that's meant to be literal. I, me, Loren Muse, would never want to live there again.'

'To each his own then.' He sighed. 'We done with the small talk now?'

'Guess so.'

'Fine. So what happened to this nun, Loren?'

'We don't know yet.'

'Come again?'

'Did you know her?'

'I don't even remember what Lance told me her name was. Sister Mary Something.'

'Sister Mary Rose.'

'What happened to her?'

'She died.'

'I see. So how do I fit in?'

Loren debated how to play this. 'How do you think?'

He sighed and started to walk past her. 'Good night, Loren.'

'Wait, okay, that was dumb. Sorry.'

Matt turned back to her.

'Her phone logs.'

'What about them?'

'Sister Mary Rose made one call we can't figure out.'

Matt's face showed nothing.

'Did you know her or not?'

Matt shook his head. 'No.'

'Because the log shows that she placed a call to your sister-in-law's residence in Livingston.'

He frowned. 'She called Marsha?'

'Your sister-in-law denied receiving any calls from anyone at St. Margaret's. I also talked to that Kylie girl who rents from her.'

'Kyra.'

'What?'

'Her name is Kyra, not Kylie.'

'Right, whatever. Anyway, I know you stay there a lot. I know, in fact, that you stayed there last night.'

Matt nodded. 'So you figured – drumroll, please – that I must be the one this nun called,' he finished for her.

She shrugged. 'Makes sense.'

Matt took a deep breath.

'What?'

'Isn't this the part where I get all angry and say it only makes sense because you have a bias against an ex-con, even though he's served his time and paid his debt to society?'

That made her smile. 'What, you just want to skip the indignation? Move right to your denial?'

'It would speed things up,' he said.

'So you don't know Sister Mary Rose?'

'No. For the record, I don't know any Sister Mary Rose. I don't even think I know any nuns. I don't know anybody connected with St. Margaret's, except, well, according to Lance, you went there, so I guess the answer would be: only you. I have no idea why Sister Mary Rose would call Marsha's house or even if indeed she called Marsha's house.'

Loren decided to shift tracks. 'Do you know a man named Max Darrow?'

'Did he call Marsha too?'

'How about a straight answer, Matt? Do you know a Max Darrow from Raleigh Heights, Nevada, yes or no?'

Jolt. Loren saw it. A small one – the smallest of tells on Matt's face. But it was there – a slight widening in the eyes. He recovered in less than a second.

'No,' he said.

'Never heard of him?'

'Never. Who is he?'

'You'll read about him in the paper tomorrow. You mind telling where you were yesterday? I mean, before you got to Marsha's house.'

'Yes, I do mind.'

'How about telling me anyway?'

He looked off, closed his eyes, opened them again. 'This is beginning to sound more like a full-fledged, suspectlike interrogation, Detective Muse.'

'Inspector Muse,' she said.

'Either way, I think I've answered enough questions for tonight.'

'So you're refusing?'

'No, I'm leaving.' Now it was Matt's turn to check his watch. 'I really have to go.'

'And I assume you're not going to tell me what you're up to?'

'You assume correctly.'

Loren shrugged. 'I could always follow you.'

'I'll save you the time. I'm heading to the MVD offices in Newark. What I do once I'm inside remains my own business. Have a pleasant night.'

He started down the stairs.

'Matt?'

'What?'

'This might sound weird,' Loren said, 'but it was good seeing you. I mean, I wish it were under different circumstances.'

He almost smiled. 'Same here.'

24

Nevada, Matt thought. Loren Muse had asked him about a man from Nevada.

Twenty minutes after leaving Loren on his stoop, Matt was in Cingle's office. He'd spent the drive running the interrogation through his head. One word kept coming back to him:

Nevada.

Max Darrow, whoever the hell he was, was from Nevada.

And Olivia had been checking a Web site for a newspaper called the *Nevada Sun News*.

Coincidence?

Yeah, right.

The offices at MVD were silent. Cingle sat at her desk, wearing a black Nike sweat suit. Her hair was swept back in a long ponytail. She hit the power button to boot up the computer.

'Have you heard anything about the death of a nun at St. Margaret's?' he asked.

Cingle frowned. 'That the church in East Orange?'

'Yes. It's also a school.'

'Nope.'

'How about anything involving a man named Max Darrow?'

'Like what?'

Matt quickly explained the questions from his old classmates Lance Banner and Loren Muse. Cingle sighed and took notes. She said nothing, only raising an eyebrow when he mentioned finding a computer cookie leading to a stripper Web site. 'I'll look into it.'

'Thanks.'

She swiveled the computer monitor so they could both view it. 'Okay, so what do you want to see?'

'Can you blow up the still shot of Charles Talley that came in on my cell phone?'

She started moving the mouse and clicking. 'Let me explain something quickly.'

'I'm listening.'

'This enhancement program. Sometimes it's a miracle worker, sometimes a total piece of crap. When you take a digital picture, the quality is dependent on the pixels. That's why you get a camera with as many pixels as possible. Pixels are dots. The more dots, the clearer the picture.'

'I know all this.'

'Your camera phone has a pretty crappy pixel reading.'

'I know that too.'

'So you know that the more you blow up the image, the less clear it becomes. This software program uses some kind of algorithm – yeah, I know, big word. Put simply, it guesses what should be there based on whatever clues it comes up with. Coloring, shading, ridges, lines, whatever. It's far from exact. There's a lot of trial and error. But that said . . .'

She pulled up the picture of Charles Talley. This time Matt skipped the blue-black hair, the smirk, the entire face. He ignored the red shirt and white walls. He only had eyes for one thing.

He pointed at it. 'See this?'

Cingle put on a pair of reading glasses, squinted, looked at him. 'Yes, Matt,' she said deadpan. 'We call it a window.'

'Can you blow it up or enhance it any more?'

'I can try. Why, you think there's something out that window?'

'Not exactly. Just do it, please.'

She shrugged, placed the cursor over it, blew it up. The window now took up half the screen.

'Can you make it any clearer?'

Cingle hit something called fine tune. Then she looked at Matt. He smiled at her.

'Don't you see?'

'See what?'

'It's gray. That much I could tell on the camera phone. But now look. There are raindrops on the window.'

'So?'

'So this picture was sent to me yesterday. You see any rain yesterday? Or the day before?'

'But wait, isn't Olivia supposed to be in Boston?'

'Maybe she was, maybe she wasn't. But there hasn't been rain in Boston either. There hasn't been rain anywhere in the Northeast.'

Cingle sat back. 'So what does it mean?'

'Hold up, check something else first,' Matt said. 'Bring up the camera phone video and play it slowly.'

Cingle minimized the photograph of Charles Talley. She started clicking icons again. Matt felt the rush. His leg started shaking. His head began to clear.

The video started playing. Matt tried to watch the woman with the platinum-blonde wig. Later, maybe he'd go through it step-by-step, confirm that it was indeed Olivia. He remained fairly certain that it was. But that wasn't the issue right now.

He waited until the woman started moving, waited for the flash of light.

'Hit pause.'

Cingle was quick. She hit it with the light still there.

'Look,' he said.

Cingle nodded. 'Well, I'll be damned.'

The sun was bursting through the window.

'The photograph and the video weren't taken at the same time,' she said.

'Exactly.'

'So what happened? They downloaded the first picture onto Olivia's phone or maybe took a picture of a picture?'

'Something like that.'

'I still don't get it.'

'I'm not sure I do either. But . . . start the tape rolling again. Slow motion.'

Cingle did as he asked.

'Stop.' He looked at it. 'Blow up the guy's left hand.'

It was a shot from the palm side of the hand. Again it was blurry when she first blew it up. She used the software enhancer. The hand came more into focus.

'Just skin,' Matt said.

'So?'

'No ring or wedding band. Let's switch back to our photograph of Charles Talley.'

This one was easier. The photograph had a better resolution. The figure of Charles Talley was larger. His hand was up, palm wide open, almost as if stopping traffic.

The backside of a ring was clearly visible.

'My God,' Cingle said. 'It's a setup.'

Matt nodded.

'I mean, I don't know what's going on in this video, but they wanted you to think this Charles Talley guy was having an affair with Olivia. Do you have any idea why?'

'None. Did you find anything more on Talley?'

'Let me check my e-mail. Something should be in by now.'

While Cingle started up her online service, Matt took out his cell phone. He once again hit the speed dial for Olivia. The small warmth was back in his chest. He smiled. Yes, there were problems – Olivia was still in a hotel room with a strange man – and, okay, maybe he was still just a touch high from the remnants of vodka, but there was hope now. The curtain of doom seemed to be parting.

This time, Olivia's recorded voice sounded melodic to him. He waited for the beep and said, 'I know you didn't do anything wrong. Please call me.' He looked over at Cingle. She was pretending not to listen. 'I love you,' he finished.

'Aw, how sweet,' Cingle said.

A male voice from her computer shouted: 'You've got mail.'

'Anything?' Matt asked.

'Give me a second.' She started scanning the e-mails. 'Not much yet, but, okay, it's something. Talley has three assault convictions, arrested twice more but the cases were dropped. He was suspected – man, this guy is creepy – of beating his landlord to death. Talley last served time at a state prison called – get this – Lovelock.'

'That name rings a bell. Where is it?'

'Doesn't say. Hold on, let me do a quick search.' Cingle started typing, hit return. 'Jesus.'

'What?'

She looked up at him. 'It's in Lovelock, Nevada.'

Nevada. Matt felt the floor drop away. Cingle's cell phone chirped. She lifted it into view, read the LCD screen.

'Give me a second, okay?'

Matt might have nodded. He felt numb.

Nevada.

And then another stray thought – another wild, possible connection to Nevada – came to him: During his freshman year of college, hadn't he gone with some friends to Nevada?

Las Vegas, to be more specific.

It was there, on that trip so many years ago, that he first met the love of his life. . . .

He shook his head. Uh uh, no way. Nevada is a big state.

Cingle hung up the phone and started typing on her computer.

'What?' he said.

Her eyes were still on the monitor. 'Charles Talley.'

'What about him?'

'We know where he is.'

'Where?'

She hit the return button and squinted. 'According to Mapquest, less than four miles from where you're now standing.' She took off her reading glasses and looked up at him. 'Talley has been staying at the Howard Johnson's by Newark Airport.'

25

'You sure?' Matt asked.

Cingle nodded. 'Talley's been there at least two nights. Room 515.'

Matt tried to put some of the pieces together. Nothing fit. 'Do you have the phone number?'

'The Howard Johnson's? I can look it up online.'

'Do that.'

'You're going to just call him?'

'Yes.'

'And say what?'

'Nothing yet. I just want to see if it's the same voice.'

'The same voice as what?'

'The guy who called me whispering about what he was about to do to Olivia. I just want to know if it was Charles Talley.'

'And if it was?'

'Hey, you think I have a long-term plan here?' Matt said. 'I'm barely winging it.'

'Use my phone. The caller ID is blocked.'

Matt picked up the receiver. Cingle read off the number. The operator answered on the third ring. 'Howard Johnson's, Newark Airport.'

'Room 515, please.'

'One moment.'

With the first ring his heart began to pick up its pace. The third ring was cut off midway. Then he heard a voice say, 'Yeah.'

Matt calmly replaced the receiver.

Cingle looked up at him. 'Well?'

'It's him,' Matt said. 'It's the same guy.'

She frowned, crossed her arms. 'So now what?'

'We could study the video and picture more,' Matt said.

'Right.'

'But I don't know what that would tell us. Suppose I'm wrong. Suppose it was Talley in both the video and the picture. Then we need to talk to him. Suppose it was two different men. . . .'

'We still need to talk to him,' Cingle said.

'Yes. I don't see where we have any choice. I have to go over there.'

'*We* have to go over there.'

'I'd rather go alone.'

'And I'd rather shower with Hugh Jackman,' Cingle said, standing. She took out her hair tie, tightened the ponytail, put the tie back in. 'I'm coming.'

Further argument would just delay the inevitable. 'Okay, but you stay in the car. Man-to-man, alone, maybe I can get something out of him.'

'Fine, whatever.' Cingle was already on her way to the door. 'I'll drive.'

The ride took five minutes.

The Howard Johnson's could have been located near an uglier stretch of freeway, but not without a dumping permit. Or maybe they already had one. On one side of Frontage Road was the New Jersey Turnpike Exit 14 toll plaza. On the other side was the parking lot for Continental Airlines employees. Take Frontage Road a few hundred more feet, and you were at the Northern State Prison, conveniently located – more convenient than the

Howard Johnson's even – to Newark Airport. Perfect for the quick getaway.

Cingle pulled up to the lobby entrance.

'You sure you want to go alone?' she asked.

'Yes.'

'Give me your cell phone first,' she said.

'Why?'

'I have this friend – a financial bigwig on Park Avenue. He taught me this trick. You put on your cell phone. You call mine. You leave it on and connected. I put the mute feature on my phone. Now it's like a one-way intercom. I can hear what you say and do. If there's any trouble, just shout.'

Matt frowned. 'A financial bigwig needs to do this?'

'You don't want to know.'

Cingle took Matt's phone, dialed in her number, answered her phone. She handed his cell phone back to him. 'Attach it to your belt. If you're in trouble, just yell for help.'

'Okay.'

The lobby was empty. Not a surprise considering the hour. He heard a bell ding when the glass door slid open. The night shift receptionist, an unshaven blob who resembled an overstuffed laundry bag, staggered into view. Matt waved to him without slowing, trying to look as if he belonged. The receptionist returned the wave, staggered back.

Matt reached the elevator and pushed the call button. There was only one working elevator car. He heard it start toward him with a grunt, but it took its time coming. Images again started flashing through his head. That video. The platinum-blonde wig. He still had no idea what it all meant, no clue at all.

Yesterday Cingle had compared all this to stepping

into a fight – you couldn't predict the outcome. But here he was, about to open a door literally, and in truth he had no idea what he'd find behind it.

A minute later, Matt stood in front of the door to Room 515.

The gun was still on him. He debated taking it out and hiding it behind his back, but no, if Talley saw it, this would all go wrong. Matt lifted his hand and knocked. He listened. A noise came from down the corridor, a door opening, maybe. He turned.

Nobody.

He knocked again, harder this time.

'Talley?' he shouted. 'You in there? We need to talk.'

He waited. Nothing.

'Please open up, Talley. I just want to talk to you, that's all.'

And then a voice came from behind the door, the same voice he'd heard on the phone: 'One second.'

The door to Room 515 opened.

And suddenly, standing in front of him, with that blue-black hair and knowing scowl, was Charles Talley.

Talley stood in the doorway, talking on his mobile phone. 'Right,' he said to whoever was on the other end. 'Right, okay.'

He gestured with his chin for Matt to step inside.

And that was exactly what Matt did.

26

Loren thought about the jolt.

Matt had tried to cover it, but he'd reacted to the name Max Darrow. The question was, of course, why.

She actually took up Matt's challenge and semi-followed him – that is, she drove ahead and planted herself near the offices of MVD. She knew that the owner of the private investigation firm was an ex-fed. He had a reputation for discretion, but maybe he could be squeezed.

When Matt pulled in – just as he'd said – there were two other cars in the lot. Loren wrote down the license plate numbers. It was late. There was no reason to hang around now.

Twenty minutes later, Loren arrived home. Oscar, her oldest cat, nestled up for an ear scratch. Loren obliged but the cat quickly grew bored, meowed his impatience, and crept into the dark. There was a time when Oscar would dart away, but age and bad hips had ended that. Oscar was getting old. The vet had given Loren that look during the last checkup, the one that said she'd better start preparing. Loren blocked on it. In movies, it was always the kids who were, à la Old Yeller and its subsequent ripoffs, devastated by the loss of a pet. In reality kids get bored with pets. Lonely adults feel the loss most acutely. Like Loren.

It was freezing in the apartment. The air conditioner rattled against the windowsill, dripping water and keeping the room at a good temperature to store meat. Mom was asleep on the couch. The television was still on, playing an infomercial for some contraption guaranteed to give you six-pack abs. She flicked off the air conditioner. Her mother did not budge.

Loren stood in the doorway and listened to her mother's smoke-phlegm snore. The grating sound was something of a comfort – it eased Loren's own desire to light up. Loren didn't wake her mother. She didn't fluff her pillow or pull a blanket over her. She just watched for a few moments and wondered for the umpteenth time what she felt for this woman.

Loren made herself a ham sandwich, wolfed it down over the sink in the kitchen, and poured a glass of Chablis from a jug-shaped bottle. The garbage, she saw, needed to be taken out. The bag was overflowing, not that that ever stopped her mother from trying to stuff more into it.

She ran the dish under the faucet and lifted the garbage can with a sigh. Her mother still did not stir; there was no disturbance or variance in her phlegm-snore cycle. She took the bag to the Dumpster outside. The outside air was sticky. The crickets hummed. She tossed the bag on the heap.

When she got back to her apartment her mother was awake.

'Where were you?' Carmen asked.

'I had to work late.'

'And you couldn't call?'

'Sorry.'

'I was worried sick.'

'Yeah,' Loren said. 'I saw how it affected your sleep.'

'What's that supposed to mean?'

'Nothing. Good night.'

'You're so inconsiderate. How could you not call? I waited and waited –'

Loren shook her head. 'I'm kinda getting tired of it, Mom.'

'Of what?'

'Your constantly berating me.'

'You want to throw me out?'

'I didn't say that.'

'But that's what you want, isn't it? To have me gone?'

'Yes.'

Carmen opened her mouth and put her hand to her chest. There was probably a time when men would react to such theatrics. Loren remembered all those photographs of the young Carmen – so lovely, so unhappy, so sure she deserved more.

'You'd throw out your own mother?'

'No. You asked if I wanted to. I do. But I won't.'

'Am I that horrible?'

'Just . . . just stay off my back, okay?'

'I just want you to be happy.'

'Right.'

'I want you to find someone.'

'You mean a man.'

'Yes, of course.'

Men – that was Carmen's answer to everything. Loren wanted to say, 'Yeah, Mom, look at how ecstatically happy men have made you,' but she bit down.

'I just don't want you to be alone,' her mother said.

'Like you,' Loren said, wishing she hadn't.

She did not wait for the response. She headed into the bathroom and started getting ready for bed. When she came out, her mother was back on the couch. The television was off. The air conditioner was back on.

Loren said, 'I'm sorry.'

Her mother did not reply.

'Were there any messages?' Loren asked.

'Tom Cruise called twice.'

'Fine, good night.'

'What, you think that boyfriend of yours called?'

'Good night, Mother.'

Loren headed into the bedroom and switched on the laptop. While it booted up, she decided to check the caller ID. Nope, Pete, her new boyfriend, hadn't called – hadn't called, for that matter, in three days. In fact, other than those that had emanated from her office, there had been no new calls at all.

Man, that was pitiful.

Pete was a nice enough guy, on the overweight side and sort of sweaty. He worked some district job for Stop & Shop. Loren could never figure out what he did exactly, probably because it really didn't interest her much. They were nothing steady, nothing serious, the kind of relationship that just glides along, that scientific principle about a body in motion will keep moving. Any friction would pretty much stop it in its tracks.

She glanced around the room, at the bad wallpaper, the nondescript bureau, the Kmart snap-together night table.

What kind of life was this?

Loren felt old and without prospects. She considered moving out west – to Arizona or New Mexico, someplace warm and new like that. Start fresh with great weather. But the truth is, she didn't like the outdoors all that much. She liked the rain and cold because they gave her an excuse to stay inside and watch a movie or read a book guilt-free.

The computer sprang to life. She checked her e-mail. There was a message from Ed Steinberg sent within the hour:

Loren,
I don't want to get into Trevor Wine's file on Max
Darrow without involving him. We'll do that in the
morning. Here are the prelims. Get some sleep, I'll
see you at nine a.m.

— Boss

A file was attached. She downloaded the document and decided to print it out. Reading too much on a computer monitor made her eyes ache. She grabbed the pages out of her printer and slipped under the covers. Oscar managed to jump on the bed, but Loren could see him wince from the effort. The old cat cuddled next to her. Loren liked that.

She scanned the documents and was surprised to see that Trevor Wine had already come up with a decent hypothesis for the crime. According to the notes, Max Darrow, a former detective with the Las Vegas Police Department and current resident of Raleigh Heights, Nevada, had been found dead in a rental car near the Hebrew cemetery in Newark. According to the report, Max Darrow had been staying at the Newark Airport Howard Johnson's. He had rented a car from someplace called LuxDrive. The car, a Ford Taurus, had been driven, per the speedometer, eight miles in the two days the car had been in Darrow's possession.

Loren turned to the second page. Here was where things got interesting.

Max Darrow was found shot dead in the driver's seat of the rental car. No one had called it in. A patrol car had spotted the bloodstains on the window. When Darrow was found, his pants and boxers were pulled down around his ankles. His wallet was gone. The report stated that Darrow was wearing no jewelry when found, implying that he'd probably been robbed of those items too.

According to the preliminary report – everything was still preliminary – the blood found in the car, especially the trajectory on the windshield and driver-side window, showed that Darrow had been shot while sitting in the driver's seat of the car. Splatters were also found on the inside of his pants and boxers, which would be consistent with the man having his pants pulled down before the gun fired, not after.

The working theory was obvious: Max Darrow had decided to get lucky – or more likely, to buy some 'get lucky.' He had picked up the wrong prostitute who waited for the right moment – pants down – and then rolled him. Something had gone wrong then, though it was hard to say what. Maybe Darrow, being an ex-cop, had tried to make a hero play. Maybe the prostitute was simply too strung out. Whatever, she ends up shooting and killing Darrow. She takes what she can find – wallet, jewelry – and runs.

The investigative team, in cooperation with the Newark Police Department, would squeeze the prostitution trade. Someone would know what happened. They'd talk.

Case solved.

Loren put down the report. Wine's theory made sense if you didn't know about Darrow's fingerprints being found in Sister Mary Rose's room. Still, now that Loren knew that the lead theory was crap – what did she have left? Well, for one thing, this was probably a pretty clever setup.

Play it out for a second.

You want to kill Darrow. You get in a car with him. You put a gun to his head. You tell him to drive to a sleazy part of town. You make him pull down his pants

– anyone who'd ever watched any forensic TV show would know that if you pulled the pants down after the shooting, the blood splatters would show that. Then you shoot him in the head, take his money and jewelry, make it look like a robbery.

Trevor Wine had bought it.

In a vacuum Loren probably would have come to the same conclusion.

So what would be the next logical step?

She sat up in bed.

Wine's theory had been that Max Darrow had done some cruisin' and picked up the wrong girl. But if that wasn't the case – Loren was sure of that much – how did the killer get in the car with Darrow in the first place? Wouldn't it be most logical to assume that Darrow was with his killer from the beginning of his car trip?

That meant Darrow probably knew his killer. Or at least did not view him as a threat.

She checked the mileage again. Only eight miles. Assuming he used it the day before, well, that meant that he hadn't driven very far.

There was something else to consider: Another set of fingerprints had been found in Sister Mary Rose's room – more specifically, on her body.

Okay, Loren thought, suppose Darrow was working with someone else – a partner maybe. They'd stay together, right? Or near each other, at the very least.

Darrow had been staying at the Howard Johnson's.

She checked the file. The rental car company LuxDrive – they had a counter at the same hotel.

So that was where it all started. At the Howard Johnson's.

Most hotels have security cameras. Had Trevor Wine checked out the ones at the Howard Johnson's yet?

Hard to say, but it would definitely be worth it for her to check it out.

Either way, it could wait until morning, right?

She tried to sleep. She sat in bed and closed her eyes. She did this for well over an hour. From the other room, she heard her mother's snores. The case was heating up. Loren felt the buzz in her blood. She pushed back the covers and got out of bed. There was no way she could sleep. Not now. Not when there was something of a clue in the air. And tomorrow she'd have a whole new set of problems, what with Ed Steinberg calling the feds and Trevor Wine getting involved.

She might be taken off the case.

Loren threw on her sweats, grabbed her wallet and ID. She tiptoed outside, started up her car, and headed for the Howard Johnson's.

27

Nothing worse than crappy porn.

Lying in the motel room bed, that was what Charles Talley had been thinking before the phone rang. He'd been watching some weirdly edited porno on the Spectravision Pay-Per-View channel. It had cost him $12.95, but the damn movie cut out all the good stuff, all the close-ups and, well, genitalia both male and female.

What the hell is this crap?

Worse yet, the movie, in order to make up for the lost time, kept replaying over and over the same parts. So the girl would be like sliding down to her knees and then they'd show this guy's face tilting back and then they'd go back to the girl sliding down, the guy's face, the girl sliding down . . .

It was maddening.

Talley was about to call down to the front desk, give them a piece of his mind. This was the friggin' United States of America. A man has a right to watch porn in the privacy of his own hotel room. Not this chicken-ass soft stuff. Real porn. Hardcore action. This stuff, this soft porn – might as well be put on the Disney Channel.

That was when the phone rang. Talley checked his watch.

About time. He'd been waiting for this callback for hours now.

Talley reached for the phone, put it to his ear. On the screen the girl was panting the exact same way for, what, ten minutes now. This crap was beyond boring.

'Yeah.'

Click. Dial tone.

A hang-up. Talley looked at the receiver as if it might give him a second response. It didn't. He put the receiver down and sat up. He waited for the phone to ring again. After five minutes passed, he started to worry.

What was going on here?

Nothing had turned out as planned. He'd flown in from Reno, what, three days ago now? Hard to remember exactly. His assignment yesterday had been clear and easy: Follow this guy named Matt Hunter. Keep a tail on him.

Why?

He had no idea. Talley had been told where to start off – parked outside some big law office in Newark – and to follow Hunter wherever he went.

But the guy, this Matt Hunter, had spotted the tail almost immediately.

How?

Hunter was strictly an amateur. But something had gone very wrong. Hunter had made him right away. And then, worse – much worse – when Talley called him a few hours ago, Matt Hunter knew who he was.

He had used Talley's full name, for chrissake.

This confused Talley.

He didn't handle confusion well. He placed some calls, tried to find out what was going on, but nobody had picked up.

That confused him even more.

Talley had few talents. He knew strippers and how to handle them. He knew how to hurt people. That was pretty much it. And really, when you thought about it, those two things went together. You want to keep a strip joint running and happy, you need to know how to put on the hurt.

So when things got muddled – as they were now – that was always his fallback position. Violence. Hurting someone and hurting them bad. He had spent time in prison for only three assault beefs, but in his life Talley guessed that he'd probably beaten or maimed fifty plus. Two had died.

His preferred method of putting on the hurt involved stun guns and brass knuckles. Talley reached into his bag. First he pulled out his brand-new stun gun. It was called the Cell Phone Stun Gun. The thing looked, as the name suggested, exactly like a cell phone. Cost him sixty-nine bucks off the Web. You could take it anywhere. You could have it out and put it to your ear like you were talking and bam, you press a button and the 'antenna' on the top wallops your enemy with 180,000 volts.

Then he pulled out his brass knuckles. Talley preferred the newer designs with the wider impact area. They not only spread out your area of collision, they put less pressure on your hand when you laid into someone good.

Talley put both the stun gun and brass knuckles on the night table. He went back to his movie, still holding out hope that the porno flick would improve. Every once in a while he would glance at his weapons. There was arousal there too, no doubt about it.

He tried to think about what to do next.

Twenty minutes later, there was a knock on his hotel room door. He checked the bedside clock. It was nearly one in the morning. He quietly slid off the bed.

There was another knock now, more urgent.

He tiptoed to the door.

'Talley? You in there? We need to talk.'

He peeked through the peephole. *What the . . . ?*

It was Matt Hunter!

Panic flooded in. How the hell had Hunter tracked him down?

'Please open up, Talley. I just want to talk to you, that's all.'

Talley did not think. He reacted. He said, 'One second.'

Then he crept back toward the bed and slipped the brass knuckles on his left hand. In the right, he held the cell phone to his ear, as if he were in the middle of the conversation. He reached for the knob. Before he turned, he looked into the peephole.

Matt Hunter was still there.

Talley planned his next three moves. That was what the greats did. They planned ahead.

He would open the door, pretending he was on the phone. He would signal for Hunter to come forward. As soon as he was in range, Talley would hit him with the stun gun. He'd aim for the chest – a big target with the most surface area. At the same time he'd have the left hand prepared. With the brass knuckles, he'd use an uppercut to the ribs.

Charles Talley opened the door.

He started talking on the phone, pretending someone was on the other line. 'Right,' Talley said into the stun gun. 'Right, okay.'

He gestured with his chin for Matt Hunter to step inside.

And that was exactly what Matt Hunter did.

28

Matt hesitated in the doorway to Room 515 but not for very long.

He had no choice here. He couldn't stay in the corridor and try to talk to him. So he started to move inside. He still was not sure how to present this, what role Talley was playing. Matt had decided to play it fairly straight and see where it led. Did Talley know he was part of a setup? Was he the guy in the video – and if so, why had the other picture been taken at an earlier time?

Matt entered.

Charles Talley was still talking on his mobile phone. As the door started to close, Matt said, 'I think we can help each other out.'

And that was when Charles Talley touched his chest with the cell phone.

It felt like Matt's entire body had suddenly short-circuited. His spine jolted upright. His fingers splayed. His toes went rigid. His eyes widened.

He wanted the cell phone away. Off him. But he couldn't move. His brain shouted. His body would not listen.

The gun, Matt thought. *Get your gun.*

Charles Talley reeled back a fist. Matt could see it. Again he tried to move, tried to at least turn away, but the electrical voltage must have stopped certain brain synapses from firing. His body simply wouldn't obey.

Talley punched him in the bottom point of the rib cage.

The blow landed against the bone like a sledgehammer. The pain burst through him. Matt, already falling, dropped onto his back.

He blinked, his eyes watering, and looked up into the smiling face of Charles Talley.

The gun . . . get the damn gun. . . .

But his muscles were in spasm.

Calm yourself. Just relax. . . .

Standing over him, Talley had the cell phone in one hand. He wore brass knuckles on the other.

Matt idly wondered about his own cell phone. The one on his belt. Cingle was on the other end, listening. He opened his mouth to call out to her.

Talley hit him again with what must have been a stun gun.

The volts raced through his nervous system. His muscles, including those in his jaws, contracted and quaked uncontrollably.

His words, his cry for help, never made it out.

Charles Talley smiled down at him. He showed him the fist with the brass knuckles. Matt could only look up and stare.

In prison, some of the guards used to carry stun guns. They worked, Matt had learned, by overloading and thus disrupting the internal communication system. The current mimics the body's own natural electrical impulses, confusing them, telling the muscles to do a great deal of work, depleting energy.

The victim is left helpless.

Matt watched Talley pull back his fist. He wanted to grab his Mauser M2 and blow the bastard away. The weapon was just there, in his waistband, but it might as well have been out of state.

The fist headed toward him.

Matt wanted simply to raise an arm, wanted to roll away, wanted to do anything. He couldn't. Talley's punch was aimed straight for Matt's chest. Matt watched as it moved as though it were in slow motion.

The knuckles smashed into his sternum.

It felt as if the bones had caved in on his heart. Like his sternum was made of Styrofoam. Matt opened his mouth in a silent, anguished scream. His air was gone. His eyes rolled back.

When Matt's eyes finally regained focus, the brass knuckles were heading toward his face.

Matt struggled, but he was weak. Too weak. His muscles still wouldn't obey. His internal communication network remained shut down. But something primitive, something base, was still there, still had enough survival instincts to at the very least turn away from the blow.

The brass knuckles scraped off the back of his skull. The skin burst open. Pain exploded in his head. His eyes closed. This time they did not reopen. From somewhere far away he heard a voice, a familiar voice, shout, 'No!' But that was probably not real. Between the electrical currents and the physical punishment, the brain's wiring was probably conjuring up all sorts of strange delusions.

There was another blow. Maybe another. Maybe there were more, but Matt was too far away to notice.

29

'Talley? You in there? We need to talk.'

Cingle Shaker perked up when she heard Matt's voice through the cell phone. The sound wasn't great, but she could make out enough.

'Please open up, Talley. I just want to talk to you, that's all.'

The reply was muffled. Too muffled to make out. Cingle tried to clear her head and concentrate. Her car sat double-parked by the front entrance. It was late. Nobody would bother her.

She debated heading inside now. That would be the smart play. Matt was on the fifth floor. If something went wrong, it would take her a while to get up there. But Matt had been fairly adamant. He felt his best chance was to brace this Talley guy alone. If she was spotted before they talked, that would only complicate matters.

But now that there was a muffled voice, Cingle could be reasonably sure that Talley was not in the lobby. In fact, from her vantage point, nobody was in the lobby.

She decided to head in.

Surveillance was far from Cingle's forte. She was simply too noticeable. She had never been a Rockette or dancer of any sort – yes, she'd heard all the rumors – but she had given up trying to dress herself down years ago. Cingle had started developing at a young age. By twelve, she could pass for eighteen. Boys loved her, girls hated her. With all the years of enlightenment, that was pretty much the norm.

Neither one of those attitudes bothered her much. What did bother her, especially at that young age, were the looks of older men, even relatives, even men she trusted and loved. No, nothing ever happened. But you learn at a young age how longing and lust can twist a mind. It is rarely pretty.

Cingle was just about in the lobby when, through the phone, she heard a strange sound.

What the hell was that?

The lobby's glass doors slid open. A little bell dinged. Cingle kept the phone pressed against her ear. Nothing. There was no sound, no talking at all.

That couldn't be good.

A sudden crashing sound came through the earpiece, startling her. Cingle picked up her pace, ran for the elevator bank.

The guy behind the desk waddled out, saw Cingle, pulled in his gut and smiled. 'May I help you?'

She pushed the call button.

'Miss?'

There was still no talking coming from the phone. She felt a chill on her neck. She had to risk it. Cingle put the phone to her mouth. 'Matt?'

Nothing.

Damn, she'd put on the mute button. She'd forgotten about that.

Yet another strange sound – a grunt maybe. Only more muffled. More choked.

Where the hell was that damn elevator?

And where the hell was that mute button?

Cingle found the mute button first. It was on the bottom right-hand corner. Her thumb fumbled before touching down. The little mute icon disappeared. She put the phone to her mouth.

'Matt?' she shouted. 'Matt, are you okay?'

Another strangled cry. Then a voice – not Matt's – said, 'Who the hell . . . ?'

From behind her, the night man asked, 'Is something wrong, miss?'

Cingle kept pressing the elevator call button. *Come on, come on . . .*

Into the phone: 'Matt, are you there?'

Click. Silence now. Absolute silence. Cingle's heart beat as though trying to break free.

What should she do?

'Miss, I really have to ask you –'

The elevator door opened. She jumped inside. The night man stuck his arm out and stopped the door from closing. Cingle's gun was in her shoulder holster. For the first time ever in the line of duty, she pulled it out.

'Let go of that door,' she said to him.

He obeyed, taking his hand away like it didn't belong to him.

'Call the police,' she said. 'Tell them you have an emergency on the fifth floor.'

The doors slid closed. She pressed the five button. Matt might not be happy about that, about getting the police involved, but it was her call now. The elevator groaned and started ascending. It seemed to move one foot up, two feet down.

Cingle held the gun in her right hand. With her finger off the trigger, she repeatedly pushed the five button on the elevator console. Like that would help. Like the elevator would see that she was in a hurry and pick up speed.

Her cell phone was in her left hand. She quickly re-dialed Matt's cell phone.

No ring, just his recorded voice: 'I'm not available right now –'

Cingle cursed, pressed the end button. She positioned her body directly in front of the crack in the door so as to get out of the elevator in mid-opening and as soon as humanly possible. The elevator buzzed with each floor, a signal for the blind, and finally came to a halt with a ding.

She hunched over like a sprinter starting in the standing position. When the doors started sliding open, Cingle pried them apart with both hands and pulled herself through.

She was in the corridor now.

Cingle could only hear the footsteps, not see anyone. It sounded like someone running the other way.

'Halt!'

Whoever it was did not let up. Neither did she. Cingle ran down the hall.

How long? How long since she'd lost contact with Matt?

From down the corridor Cingle heard a heavy door bang open. Emergency door, she bet. To the stairwell.

Cingle was counting off the room numbers as she ran. When she reached Room 511, she could see far enough up ahead to see that the door to Room 515 – two doors ahead of her – was wide open.

She debated what to do – follow whoever was running down the stairs or check in Room 515 – but only briefly.

Cingle hurried, turned the corner, gun drawn.

Matt was flat on his back, his eyes closed. He was not moving. But that wasn't the really shocking thing.

The really shocking thing was who was with him.

Cingle almost dropped her gun.

For a moment she just stood there and stared in disbelief. Then she stepped fully into the room. Matt had still not moved. Blood was pooling behind his head.

Cingle's gaze stayed locked on the other person in the room.

The person kneeling next to Matt.

The face was tearstained. The eyes were red.

Cingle recognized the woman right away.

'Olivia.'

30

Loren Muse took the Frontage Road exit off Route 78 and pulled into the Howard Johnson's lot. A car was double-parked by the front entrance.

She hit the brake.

That car, a Lexus, had been in the MVD lot less than an hour ago.

This could not be a coincidence.

She maneuvered her vehicle by the front door and snapped her gun onto her belt. The shield was already there. The handcuffs dangled off her back. She hurried toward the car. No one inside. The keys were still in the ignition. The door was unlocked.

Loren opened the Lexus's door.

Was this a legal search? She thought it might be. The keys were in plain view in the ignition. The car was unlocked. She was helping out here. That had to make it legit somehow, right?

She pulled her sleeves up over her hands, forming makeshift mittens so she wouldn't leave fingerprints. She dropped open the glove compartment and tried to paw through the paperwork. It didn't take long. It was a company car, belonging to MVD. But the paperwork from the Midas Muffler dealer showed that it had been brought in by someone named Cingle Shaker.

Loren knew the name. The guys in the county office discussed her with a tad too much zeal. Said she had a body that could knock a movie rating from PG to R.

So what was her connection to Hunter?

Loren took the car keys with her – no sense in giving Ms. Shaker a chance to run off without them having a little chat. She headed inside and approached the desk. The man behind it was breathing in uneven gulps.

'You guys are back?' he asked.

'Back?'

Not her best line of interrogation, but it was a start.

'The other cops left, what, an hour ago maybe. With the ambulance.'

'What other cops?'

'You're not with them?'

She approached him. 'What's your name?'

'Ernie.'

'Ernie, why don't you tell me what happened here?'

'It's like I told the other guys.'

'Now tell me.'

Ernie sighed dramatically. 'Okay, fine, it's like this. First this guy comes dashing into the hotel.'

'When?' Loren interrupted.

'What?'

'What time was this?'

'I don't know. Two hours ago maybe. Don't you know all this?'

'Go on.'

'So this guy, he goes into the elevator. He goes up. Couple minutes later, this big chick comes flying in and runs over to the elevator.' He coughed into his fist. 'So, you know, I call out to her. Ask her if everything is okay. You know, doing my job and all.'

'Did you ask the guy if everything was okay?'

'What? No.'

'But you asked the' – Loren made quote marks with her fingers – 'big chick?'

'Hold up a sec. She wasn't big really. She was tall. I don't want you to think she was fat or anything. Give you the wrong idea. She wasn't. Not fat at all. Just the opposite. Like a chick in one of those Amazon movies, you know?'

'Yeah, Ernie, I think I got the picture.' Sounded like Cingle Shaker. 'So you asked Miss Amazon if everything was okay?'

'Right, yeah, like that. And this girl, this *tall* girl, she pulls a gun on me – a gun! – and tells me to call the cops.'

He paused now, waiting for Loren's jaw to drop in shock.

'And that's what you did?'

'Hell, yeah. I mean, she pulled a gun on me. You believe that?'

'I'll try to, Ernie. So then what happened?'

'She's in the elevator, right? She holds the gun on me until the doors close. So then I called the cops. Like she said to do. Two Newark guys were eating next door. They were here in no time. I told them she'd gone up to the fifth floor. So they went up.'

'You said something about an ambulance?'

'They must have called for one.'

'They? You mean, the cops?'

'Nah. Well, I mean, maybe. But I think it was the women in the room who made the call.'

'What room?'

'Look, I didn't go up there. I didn't see it or anything.' Ernie's eyes narrowed into thin slits. 'This is secondhand knowledge you're asking about now. Aren't you only supposed to ask me what I actually saw or have direct knowledge of?'

'This isn't a courtroom,' she snapped. 'What was going on upstairs?'

'I don't know. Someone got beaten up.'

'Who?'

'I just said. I don't know.'

'Man, woman, black, white?'

'Oh, I see what you mean. But I don't get it. Why are you asking me? Why can't you –?'

'Just tell me, Ernie. I don't have time to make a bunch of calls.'

'Not a bunch of calls, but you could just radio the cops who were here before, the Newark guys –'

Her voice was steel. 'Ernie.'

'Okay, okay, relax. It was a man, all right? White. I'd say mid-thirties. They wheeled him out on a stretcher.'

'What happened to him?'

'Someone beat him up, I guess.'

'And this all happened on the fifth floor?'

'I guess so, yeah.'

'And you said something about women in the room. That they might have called the ambulance.'

'Yeah. Yeah, I did say that.' He smiled like he was proud of himself. Loren wanted to draw her gun too.

'How many women, Ernie?'

'What? Oh, two.'

'Was one of them the tall girl who pulled the gun on you?'

'Yeah.'

'And the other?'

Ernie looked left. He looked right. Then he leaned closer and whispered, 'I think it might have been the guy's wife.'

'The guy who got beaten up?'

'Uh huh.'

'Why do you say that?'

His voice stayed soft. 'Because she went with him. In the ambulance.'

'So why are we whispering?'

'Well, I'm trying to be whatchya call discreet.'

Loren matched the whisper. 'Why, Ernie? Why are we being whatchya call discreet?'

'Because that other woman – the wife, I mean – she's been staying here for the past two nights. He, the husband, hasn't been.' He leaned over the desk. Loren got a whiff of whatchya call chronic halitosis. 'All of a sudden the husband rushes in, there's a fight of some kind . . .' He stopped, raised both eyebrows as though the implications were obvious.

'So what happened to the Amazon girl?'

'The one who pulled the gun on me?'

'Yes, Ernie,' Loren said, fighting off her growing impatience. 'The one who pulled the gun on you.'

'The cops arrested her. Cuffed her and everything.'

'The woman you think might be the wife, the one who stayed here the past two days. You have a name?'

He shook his head. 'No, sorry, I never heard it.'

'Didn't she register?'

Ernie's eyes lit up. 'Sure. Sure, she did. And we take an imprint of a credit card and everything.'

'Great.' Loren rubbed the bridge of her nose with her index finger and thumb. 'So – shot in the dark here, Ernie – why don't you look up the name for me?'

'Yeah, sure, I can do that. Let me see.' He turned to the computer and started typing. 'I think she was in Room 522. . . . Wait, here it is.'

He turned the monitor so Loren could see.

The occupant of Room 522 was named Olivia Hunter. Loren just stared at the screen for a moment.

Ernie pointed to the letters. 'It says Olivia Hunter.'

'I can see that. What hospital did they go to?'

'Beth Israel, I think they said.'

Loren handed Ernie her card with her cell phone number on it. 'Call me if you think of anything else.'

'Oh, I will.'

Loren rushed out for the hospital.

31

Matt Hunter woke up.

Olivia's face was there.

There was no question that this was real. Matt didn't have one of those moments where you wonder if it's a dream or not. The color was drained from Olivia's face. Her eyes were red. He could see the fear and the only thing Matt could think – not about answers, not about explanations – the only thing he could think clearly is, 'How do I make it better?'

The lights were bright. Olivia's face, still beautiful, was framed by what looked like a white shower curtain. He tried to smile at her. His skull throbbed like a thumb hit with a hammer.

She was watching him. He saw her eyes well up with tears. 'I'm sorry,' she whispered.

'I'm fine,' he said.

He felt a little la-dee-dah. Painkillers, he thought. Morphine or something similar. His ribs ached but it was a dull ache. He remembered the man in the hotel room, Talley, he of the blue-black hair. He remembered the paralyzing feeling, the dropping to the floor, the brass knuckles.

'Where are we?' he asked.

'Emergency room, Beth Israel.'

He actually smiled. 'I was born here, you know.' Yep, he was definitely on something – a muscle relaxant, painkiller, something. 'What happened to Talley?' he asked.

'He ran away.'

'You were in his room?'

'No. I was down the hall.'

He closed his eyes for just a moment. That last part did not compute – she was down the hall? – so he tried to clear his mind.

'Matt?'

He blinked a few times and tried to refocus. 'You were down the hall?'

'Yes. I saw you go into his room, so I followed you.'

'You were staying at that hotel?'

Before she could reply, the curtain was pulled open. 'Ah,' the doctor said. He had an accent – Pakistani or Indian, maybe. 'How are we feeling?'

'Like a million bucks,' Matt said.

The doctor smiled at them. His name tag read PATEL. 'Your wife told me that you were assaulted – that she thought the perpetrator might have used a stun gun.'

'I guess.'

'That's good, in a way. Stun guns don't leave permanent damage. They only temporarily incapacitate.'

'Yeah,' Matt said. 'I live under a lucky star.'

Patel chuckled, checked something on the chart. 'You suffered a concussion. The rib is probably cracked, but I won't know that until we do an X-ray. It doesn't matter much – bad bruise or break, you can only treat it with rest. I already gave you something for the pain. You may need more.'

'Okay.'

'I'm going to keep you overnight.'

'No,' he said.

Patel looked up. 'No?'

'I want to go home. My wife can look after me.'

Patel looked at Olivia. She nodded. He said, 'You

understand I don't recommend this?'

Olivia said, 'We do.'

On TV, the doctor always fights the 'wanna-go-home' patient. Patel didn't. He simply shrugged. 'Okay, you sign the release forms, you're out of here.'

'Thanks, Doc,' Matt said.

Patel shrugged again. 'Have a nice life then.'

'You too.'

He left.

'Are the police here?' Matt asked.

'They just left, but they'll be back.'

'What did you tell them?'

'Not much,' she said. 'They assumed it was some kind of marital spat. You caught me with another man, something like that.'

'What happened to Cingle?'

'They arrested her.'

'What?'

'She drew her gun to get past the clerk at the front desk.'

Matt shook his aching head. 'We have to bail her out.'

'She said not to, that she'd take care of it.'

He started to sit up. Pain tore down the back of his skull like a hot knife.

'Matt?'

'I'm okay.'

And he was. He'd been beaten worse. Much worse. This was nothing. He could play through it. He sat all the way up and met her eyes. She looked as if she were steeling herself for a blow.

Matt said, 'This is something bad, isn't it?'

Olivia's chest hitched. The tears welling began to escape. 'I don't know yet,' she said. 'But yeah. Yeah, it's pretty bad.'

'Do we want the police involved?'

'No.' The tears had started running down her cheeks. 'Not until I tell you everything.'

He swung his feet off the bed. 'Then let's hurry the hell out of here.'

Loren counted six people on line at the ER reception desk. When she cut to the front, all six grunted their disapproval. Loren ignored them. She slammed her badge down on the desk.

'You had a patient brought in here a little while ago.'

'You're kidding.' The woman behind the desk looked up over the half-moon reading glasses and let her eyes travel over the packed waiting room. 'A patient, you say?' She chewed gum. 'Gee, I guess you caught us. We did have a patient brought in here a little while ago.'

The line snickered. Loren's face reddened.

'He was an assault victim. From Howard Johnson's.'

'Oh, him. I think he's gone.'

'Gone?'

'Checked himself out a few minutes ago.'

'Where did he go?'

The woman gave her flat eyes.

'Right,' Loren said. 'Never mind.'

Her cell phone rang. She picked it up and barked, 'Muse.'

'Uh, hi, are you the policewoman who was here before?'

Loren recognized the voice. 'Yes, Ernie. What's up?'

There was a low moan. 'You have to come back here.'

'What is it? Ernie?'

'Something happened,' he said. 'I think . . . I think he's dead.'

32

Matt and Olivia had filled out the necessary paperwork, but neither of them had a car. Matt's was still parked at the MVD lot. Olivia's was at the Howard Johnson's. They called a taxi and waited outside by the entrance.

Matt sat in a wheelchair. Olivia stood next to him. She looked straight forward, not at him. It was hot and sticky, but Olivia still stood with her arms wrapped around herself. She wore a sleeveless blouse and khaki pants. Her arms were toned and tan.

The taxi pulled up. Matt struggled to his feet. Olivia tried to help, but he waved her off. They both got into the backseat. Their bodies did not touch. They did not hold hands.

'Good evening,' the driver said, eyes in the rearview. 'Where to?'

The driver was dark-skinned and spoke with some sort of African accent. Matt gave him their address in Irvington. The driver was chatty. He was from Ghana, he told them. He had six children. Two of them lived here with him, the rest were back in Ghana with his wife.

Matt tried to be responsive. Olivia stared out her window and said nothing. At one point Matt reached for her hand. She let him take it, but it felt lifeless.

'Did you visit Dr. Haddon?' Matt asked her.

'Yes.'

'And?'

'Everything is fine. It should be a normal pregnancy.'

From the front seat, the driver said, 'Pregnancy? You're having a baby?'

'Yes, we are,' Matt said.

'Is this your first?'

'Yes.'

'Such a blessing, my friend.'

'Thank you.'

They were in Irvington now, on Clinton Avenue. Up ahead the light turned red. The driver cruised to a stop.

'We make a right here, yes?'

Matt had been glancing out the window, preparing to say yes, when something snared his gaze. Their house was indeed down the street on the right. But that wasn't what had captured his attention.

There was a police car parked on the street.

'Hold up a second,' Matt said.

'Pardon me?'

Matt cranked open the window. The police car's engine was running. He wondered about that. He looked to the corner. Lawrence the Wino was staggering with his customary brown bag, singing the old Four Tops classic 'Bernadette.'

Matt leaned out the window. 'Hey, Lawrence.'

'. . . And never find the love I've found in y –' Lawrence stopped mid-lyric. He cupped his hand over his eyes and squinted. A smile broke out on his face. He stumbled toward them. 'Matt, mah man! Look at you, all fine and fancy in a taxi.'

'Yep.'

'You been out drinking, right? I remember from before. Didn't want to drink and drive, am I right?'

'Something like that, Lawrence.'

'Whoa.' Lawrence pointed to the bandage on Matt's head. 'What happened to you? You know who you look like, with your head wrapped like that?'

'Lawrence –'

'That dude marching in that old picture, the one playing the flute. Or is it the one on the snare? I can never remember. Had his head wrapped, just like you. What was that picture called again?'

Matt tried to get him on track. 'Lawrence, do you see that cop car over there?'

'What' – he leaned closer – 'he did that to you?'

'No, nothing like that. I'm fine, really.'

Lawrence was perfectly positioned to block the car's view of Matt's face. If the cop happened to look this way, he'd probably figure Lawrence was panhandling.

'How long has he been parked there?' Matt asked.

'I don't know. Fifteen, twenty minutes maybe. Time flies by now, Matt. Older you get, the faster it goes by. You listen to Lawrence.'

'Has he gotten out of the car?'

'Who?'

'The cop.'

'Oh, sure. Knocked on your door too.' Lawrence smiled. 'Oh, I see. You in trouble, ain't you, Matt?'

'Me? I'm one of the good guys.'

Lawrence loved that one. 'Oh, I know that. You have a good night now, Matt.' He leaned into the window a little. 'You too, Liv.'

Olivia said, 'Thank you, Lawrence.'

Lawrence saw her face and paused. He looked at Matt and straightened up. His voice grew softer. 'You take care now.'

'Thanks, Lawrence.' Matt sat forward and tapped the driver. 'Change of destination.'

The driver said, 'Will I get in trouble for this?'

'Not at all. I was in an accident. They want to talk to me

about how I got hurt. We'd rather wait until morning.'

The driver wasn't buying it, but he didn't seem ready to argue either. The light turned green. The taxi started up, heading straight instead of right.

'So where to?'

Matt gave him the address of MVD in Newark. He figured that they could pick up his car and find a place to go and talk. The question was, where? He checked his watch. It was three in the morning.

The driver pulled into MVD's lot. 'This is good, yes?'

'Fine, thanks.'

They got out of the car. Matt paid the man. Olivia said, 'I'll drive.'

'I'm fine.'

'Right, fine. You just got beaten up and you're high on meds.' Olivia put out her palm. 'Give me the keys.'

He did. They got into the car and started out.

'Where are we going?' Olivia asked.

'I'm going to call Marsha, see if we can crash there.'

'You're going to wake up the kids.'

He managed a small smile. 'Grenades in their pillows wouldn't wake up those two.'

'And what about Marsha?'

'She won't mind.'

But Matt suddenly hesitated. He really didn't worry about waking Marsha – there had been plenty of late-night calls over the years – but now he wondered if she would be alone tonight, if maybe he wouldn't be inter-rupting something. He also – and this was really weird – started worrying about something else right now.

Suppose Marsha got remarried.

Paul and Ethan were still young. Would they call the guy Daddy? Matt wasn't sure if he could handle that. More to the point, what role would Uncle Matt have in this new life, this new family? All of this was silly, of course. He was getting way ahead of himself. It was hardly the time either, what with his other problems right now. But the thoughts were there, in his head, knocking to come out of some back closet.

He pulled out his cell phone and pushed the second number on his speed dial. As they hit Washington Avenue, Matt noticed two cars going past them in the opposite direction. He turned and watched them pull into the MVD lot. The cars were from the Essex County prosecutor's office. They were the same make and model Loren had been using earlier in the evening.

This couldn't be good.

The phone was picked up on the second ring.

Marsha said, 'I'm glad you called.' If she'd been sleeping, she hid it pretty well.

'Are you alone?'

'What?'

'I mean . . . I know the kids are there –'

'I'm alone, Matt.'

'I don't mean to pry. I just want to make sure I'm not interrupting anything.'

'You're not. You never will be.'

That should have set his mind at ease, he guessed. 'Do you mind if Olivia and I crash at your place tonight?'

'Of course not.'

'It's a long story, but basically I was assaulted tonight –'

'Are you okay?'

The pain was starting to ebb back into his head and ribs. 'I got a few bumps and bruises, but I'll be fine. Thing is, the police want to ask some questions and we're just not ready for that yet.'

'Does this have anything to do with that nun?' Marsha asked.

'What nun?'

Olivia's head snapped toward him.

'There was a county investigator here today,' Marsha said. 'I should have called you, but I guess I was hoping it was no big deal. Hold on, I have her card here someplace . . .'

Matt's mind, both exhausted and scrambled, remembered now. 'Loren Muse.'

'Right, that's the name. She said a nun made a phone call to the house.'

'I know,' he said.

'Muse reached you?'

'Yes.'

'I figured she would. We were just talking and then, I don't know, she spotted your picture on the refrigerator and suddenly she starts asking Kyra and me all these questions about how often you visit.'

'Don't worry, I straightened it out. Look, we'll be there in twenty minutes.'

'I'll get the guest room ready.'

'Don't go to any trouble.'

'No trouble. I'll see you in twenty minutes.'

She hung up.

Olivia said, 'What's this about a nun?'

Matt told her about Loren's visit. Olivia's face lost even more color. By the time he finished, they were in Livingston. The roads were completely empty of both cars and pedestrians. There was no one about. The only lights coming from the homes were those downstairs lamps set on timers to fool burglars.

Olivia remained silent as she pulled into Marsha's driveway. Matt could see Marsha's silhouette through the curtain in the downstairs foyer. The light above the garage was on. Kyra was awake. He saw her look out.

Matt slid down the car window and waved up to her. She waved back.

Olivia turned off the ignition. Matt checked his face in the visor mirror. He looked like hell. Lawrence was right. What with the bandage wrapped around his head, he did resemble the soldier playing the flute in Willard's *Spirit of '76*.

'Olivia?'

She said nothing.

'Do you know this Sister Mary Rose?'

'Maybe.'

She stepped out of the car. Matt did the same. The outside lights – Matt had helped Bernie install the motion detectors – snapped on. Olivia came around to him. She took his hand and held it firmly.

'Before I say anything else,' she began, 'I need you to know something.'

Matt waited.

'I love you. You are the only man I've ever loved. Whatever happens now, you have brought me a happiness and joy I once thought was impossible.'

'Olivia –'

She put her finger to his lips. 'I just want one thing. I want you to hold me. Hold me right now. Just for a minute or two. Because after I tell you the truth, I'm not sure you will ever want to hold me again.'

33

When Cingle got to the police station she used her phone call to reach her boss, Malcolm Seward, the president of Most Valuable Detection. Seward was retired FBI. He opened MVD ten years ago and was making a small fortune.

Seward was not thrilled about the late-night call. 'You pulled a gun on the guy?'

'It's not like I would have shot him.'

'How reassuring.' Seward sighed. 'I'll make some calls. You'll be out in an hour.'

'You're the best, Boss.'

He hung up.

She went back to her holding cell and waited. A tall officer unlocked the holding cell door. 'Cingle Shaker.'

'Right here.'

'Please follow me.'

'Anywhere, handsome.'

He led her down the hallway. She expected this to be it – the bail hearing, the quick release, whatever – but that wasn't the case.

'Please turn around,' he said.

Cingle cocked an eyebrow. 'Shouldn't you buy me dinner first?'

'Please turn around.'

She did. He cuffed her hands.

'What are you doing?'

He didn't speak. He escorted her outside, opened the

back door of his squad car, and pushed her in.

'Where are we going?'

'The new court building.'

'The one on West Market?'

'Yes, ma'am.'

The ride was short, less than a mile. They took the elevator to the third floor. The words OFFICE OF THE ESSEX COUNTY PROSECUTOR were stenciled on the glass. There was a big trophy case by the door, the kind you see in a high school. Cingle wondered about that, about what a trophy case was doing in a prosecutor's office. You prosecute killers and rapists and drug dealers and the first thing you see when you enter is a bunch of trophies celebrating softball wins. Weird.

'This way.'

He led her through the waiting area, past the double doors. When they stopped, she peeked inside a small, windowless space. 'An interrogation room?'

He said nothing, just held the door. She shrugged and entered.

Time passed. A lot of time, actually. They had confiscated her possessions, including her watch, so she didn't really know how much. There was no one-way mirror either, like you usually see on TV. They used a camera here. There was one mounted in the corner of the wall. From the monitoring room, you could zoom the camera in or change the angle, whatever. There was one sheet of paper taped down at a funny angle. That was the guide spot, she knew, where you put the release statement so that the camera could tape you signing it.

When the door finally opened, a woman – Cingle assumed that it was a plainclothes investigator – stepped into the room. She was a tiny thing, maybe five-one, 110 pounds tops. Sweat drenched her body. It looked like she'd just stepped out of a steam room. Her blouse stuck to her chest. There was dampness under her pits. A thin coat of perspiration made her face glisten. She wore a gun on her belt and had a manila folder in her hand.

'I'm Investigator Loren Muse,' the woman said.

Wow, that was fast. Cingle remembered the name — Muse was the one who'd questioned Matt earlier this evening.

'Cingle Shaker,' she said.

'Yes, I know. I have a few questions.'

'And I'm going to choose not to answer them right now.'

Loren was still catching her breath. 'Why's that?'

'I'm a working private investigator.'

'And who would your client be?'

'I don't have to tell you.'

'There is no such thing as PI-client privilege.'

'I'm aware of the law.'

'So?'

'So I choose not to answer any questions at this time.'

Loren dropped the manila folder on the table. It stayed closed. 'Are you refusing to cooperate with the county prosecutor's office?'

'Not at all.'

'Then please answer my question. Who is your client?'

Cingle leaned back. She stretched out her legs and crossed her ankles. 'You fall in a pool or something?'

'Oh, wait, I get it. Because I'm wet? Good one, really. Should I get a pen, you know, in case you come up with more gems?'

'No need.' Cingle pointed to the camera. 'You can just watch the tape.'

'It's not on.'

'No?'

'If I wanted to tape this, I'd have you sign the release.'

'Is anybody in the monitoring room?'

Loren shrugged, ignored the question. 'Aren't you curious about how Mr. Hunter's doing?'

Cingle didn't bite. 'Tell you what. I won't ask any questions if you don't.'

'I don't think so.'

'Look, Inspector . . . Muse, is it?'

'Yes.'

'What's the big deal here? It was a simple assault. That hotel probably has three a week.'

'Yet,' Loren said, 'it was serious enough for you to pull a gun on a man?'

'I was just trying to get upstairs before it got any more dangerous.'

'How did you know?'

'Pardon me?'

'The fight was on the fifth floor. You were outside in your car. How did you know that someone was in trouble?'

'I think we're done.'

'No, Cingle, I don't think we are.'

Their eyes met. Cingle did not like what she saw. Loren pulled out the chair and sat down. 'I've just spent the last half an hour in the stairwell of the Howard Johnson's. It's not air-conditioned. In fact, it's hot as hell. That's why I look like this.'

'Am I supposed to know what you're talking about?'

'It's not a simple assault, Cingle.'

Cingle eyed the manila folder. 'What's that?'

Loren dumped out the folder's contents. They were photographs. Cingle sighed, picked one up, froze.

'I assume you recognize him?'

Cingle stared at the two pictures. The first was a head-shot. No question about it – the dead man was Charles

Talley. His face looked like raw meat. The other was a full body shot. Talley was sprawled on what looked like metal steps. 'What happened to him?'

'Two shots to the face.'

'Jesus.'

'Feel like talking now, Cingle?'

'I don't know anything about this.'

'His name is Charles Talley. But you knew that, right?'

'Jesus,' Cingle said again, trying to put it together. Talley was dead. How? Hadn't he just assaulted Matt?

Loren put the pictures back in the manila folder. She folded her hands and leaned closer. 'I know you're working for Matt Hunter. I also know that right before you headed for that hotel you two met in your office for a very late-night chat. Would you care to tell me what you discussed?'

Cingle shook her head.

'Did you kill this man, Ms. Shaker?'

'What? Of course not.'

'How about Mr. Hunter? Did he kill him?'

'No.'

'How do you know?'

'Excuse me?'

'I didn't even tell you when he was killed.' Loren tilted her head. 'How could you possibly know that he wasn't involved in the man's death?'

'That's not what I meant.'

'What did you mean?'

Cingle took a breath. Loren did not.

'How about retired detective Max Darrow?'

'Who?' But Cingle remembered that name from Matt. He had asked her to check him out.

'Another dead man. Did you kill him? Or did Hunter do it?'

'I don't know what . . .' Cingle stopped, crossed her arms. 'I have to get out of here.'

'That's not going to happen, Cingle.'

'Are you charging me with something?'

'As a matter of fact, we are. You threatened a man with a loaded handgun.'

Cingle crossed her arms and tried to regain her composure. 'Old news.'

'Ah, but see, you're no longer getting sped through the system. You'll be kept overnight and arraigned in the morning. We're going to prosecute this to the full extent of the law. You'll only lose your license if it all breaks your way, but my bet is, you'll serve jail time.'

Cingle said nothing.

'Who assaulted Mr. Hunter tonight?'

'Why don't you ask him?'

'Oh, I will. Because – and this is interesting – when we found Mr. Talley's corpse he had a stun gun and a pair of brass knuckles. There was fresh blood on the brass knuckles.' Loren did that head tilt again, moving in a little closer. 'When we run a DNA test, whose blood do you think will match?'

There was a knock on the door. Loren Muse held the gaze a moment longer before she opened it. The man who escorted Cingle from the station was there. He was holding a cell phone.

'For her,' the man said, gesturing toward Cingle. Cingle looked at Loren. Loren's face gave away nothing. Cingle took the phone and put it to her ear. 'Hello?'

'Start talking.'

It was her boss, Malcolm Seward.

'It's a sensitive case.'

'I'm on the computer network now,' Seward said. 'Which case number?'

'There isn't a case number yet.'

'What?'

'With all due respect, sir, I don't feel comfortable talking with the authorities here.'

She heard Seward sigh. 'Guess who just called me, Cingle. Guess who called me at home at three in the morning.'

'Mr. Seward –'

'Actually, no, don't guess. I'll tell you because, hey, it's three in the morning and I'm too tired for games. Ed Steinberg. Ed Steinberg himself called me. Do you know who that is?'

'Yes.'

'Ed Steinberg is the Essex County prosecutor.'

'I know.'

'He's also been my friend for twenty-eight years.'

'I know that too.'

'Good, Cingle, then we're on the same wavelength here. MVD is a business. A very successful business, or so I like to think. And a big part of our effectiveness – yours and mine – depends on working with these people. So when Ed Steinberg calls me at home at three in the morning and tells me he's working on a triple homicide –'

'Hold up,' Cingle said. 'Did you say triple?'

'You see? You don't even know how deep this doo-doo goes. Ed Steinberg, my old pal, very much wants your cooperation. That means I, your boss, very much want your cooperation. Do I make myself clear?'

'I guess so.'

'Guess? What, am I being too subtle here, Cingle?'

'There are mitigating factors.'

'Not according to Steinberg. Steinberg tells me this all involves some ex-con. That true?'

'He works at Carter Sturgis.'

'Is he a lawyer?'

'No, he's a paralegal.'

'And he served time for manslaughter?'

'Yes, but –'

'Then there's nothing to discuss. There's no privilege here. Tell them what they want to know.'

'I can't.'

'Can't?' There was an edge in Seward's tone now. 'I don't like to hear that.'

'It's not that simple, Mr. Seward.'

'Well, then let me simplify it for you, Cingle. You have two choices: Talk or clean out your desk. Bye now.'

He hung up the phone. Cingle eyed Loren. Loren smiled at her.

'Everything all right, Ms. Shaker?'

'Peachy.'

'Good. Because as we speak, our techno people are on their way to MVD's office. They'll comb through your hard drive. They'll scrutinize every document you've got in there. Prosecutor Steinberg is right now calling back your boss. He'll find out what files you accessed recently, who you talked to, where you've been, what you've been working on.'

Cingle stood slowly, towering over Loren. Loren did not back up a step. 'I have nothing more to say.'

'Cingle?'

'What?'

'Sit your ass down.'

'I prefer to stand.'

'Fine. Then listen up because we're coming to the end of our conversation. Did you know I went to school with Matt Hunter? Elementary school, actually. I liked him. He was a good kid. And if he's innocent, nobody will be more anxious to clear his name than yours truly. But your keeping mum like this, well, Cingle, it suggests you might be hiding something. We have Talley's brass knuckles. We know Matt Hunter was at the murder scene tonight. We know he got into some kind of fight in Room 515 – that was Mr. Talley's room. We also know that Mr. Hunter was out drinking at two bars this evening. We know that the DNA test on the brass knuckles will show that the blood is Hunter's. And, of course, we know that Mr. Hunter, a convicted felon, has something of a history of getting into fights where someone ends up dead.'

Cingle sighed. 'Is there a point to this?'

'Sure is, Cingle, and here it comes: Do you really think I need your help to nail him?'

Cingle started tapping her foot, looking for a way out. 'Then what do you want from me?'

'Help.'

'Help with what?'

'Tell me the truth,' Loren said. 'That's all I ask. Hunter is already as good as indicted. Once he's in the system – him being an ex-con and all – well, you know how that'll go.'

She did. Matt would freak. He'd go nuts if they lock him up – his greatest fear come to fruition.

Loren moved a little closer. 'If you know something that might help him,' she said, 'now is the time to say it.'

Cingle tried to think it through. She almost trusted this little cop, but she knew better. That was what Muse wanted – playing good cop and bad cop in one package. Christ, an amateur could see through this charade and yet Cingle was almost ready to bite.

Key word: almost.

But Cingle also knew that once they got into her office computer, there would be huge problems. The last files she accessed were the photographs from Matt's cell phone. Pictures of the murder victim. A video of the murder victim and Matt Hunter's wife.

Those would be the final nails in any ex-con's coffin.

As Investigator Muse had pointed out, they already had enough with the physical evidence. The photographs would add one thing more: motive.

Cingle had her own career to worry about too. This had started out as a favor to a friend, just another case. But how far was she willing to go? What should she be willing to sacrifice? And if Matt had nothing to do with the murder of Charles Talley, wouldn't cooperating right from the get-go help bring the truth to light?

Cingle sat back down.

'You have something to say?'

'I want to call my lawyer,' Cingle said. 'Then I'll tell you everything I know.'

34

'I haven't charged you with anything,' Loren said.

Cingle crossed her arms. 'Let's not play semantics games, okay? I asked for my lawyer. The interview is over. The end. *El fin*.'

'If you say so.'

'I say so. Get me a phone, please.'

'You're entitled to call an attorney.'

'That's who I plan on calling.'

Loren thought about this. She didn't want Cingle warning Hunter. 'You mind if I dial the number for you?'

'Suit yourself,' Cingle said. 'I'll need a phone book though.'

'You don't know your attorney's home number by heart?'

'No, sorry.'

It took another five minutes. Loren dialed and handed her the phone. She could always check the call log later, make sure she didn't sneak another call in. She turned off the microphone and moved into the monitoring room. Cingle, wise in the ways of the camera, turned her back to the lens, just in case someone could read lips.

Loren started working the phones. First she tried the cop sitting in front of Hunter's residence in Irvington. He informed her that Matt and Olivia Hunter still weren't home. Loren knew that this was not good news. She started a quiet search because she didn't want to sound off too many alarm bells yet.

She'd need to get a subpoena for both Matt and Olivia Hunter's recent credit card transactions – run it through TRW. If they were on the run, they'd probably need to access money at an ATM or check into a motel – something.

From the monitoring screen, Loren could see that Cingle had finished her phone call. Cingle held the phone up to the camera and signaled for someone to hit the audio switch. Loren complied.

'Yes?'

Cingle said, 'My attorney is on his way.'

'Sit tight then.'

Loren switched off the intercom. She leaned back. Exhaustion was starting to set in. She was nearing the wall. She needed a little shut-eye or her brain would start going hazy. Cingle's attorney wouldn't be here for at least half an hour. She crossed her arms, threw her feet on the desk, and closed her eyes, hoping to doze for just a few minutes, just until the attorney showed.

Her cell phone rang. She startled up and put it to her ear.

It was Ed Steinberg. 'Hey.'

'Hey,' she managed.

'The private eye talking?'

'Not yet. She's waiting for her lawyer.'

'Let her wait then. Let them both wait.'

'Why, what's up?'

'The feds, Loren.'

'What about them?'

'We're meeting them in an hour.'

'Who?'

'Joan Thurston.'

That made her drop her feet to the floor. 'The U.S. attorney herself?'

'In the flesh. And some hotshot SAC from Nevada. We're meeting them at Thurston's office to discuss your phony nun.'

Loren checked the clock. 'It's four in the morning.'

'Thank you, Mistress of the Obvious.'

'No, I mean, I'm surprised you'd call the U.S. attorney that early.'

'Didn't have to,' Steinberg said. 'She called me.'

When Ed Steinberg arrived, he looked at Loren and shook his head. Her hair was frizzed out from the humidity. The sweat had dried, but she was still a mess.

'You look,' Steinberg said, 'like something I once left in the bottom of my gym locker.'

'Flattering, thank you.'

He motioned at her with both his hands. 'Can't you – I don't know – do something about your hair?'

'What, this a singles' club now?'

'Evidently not.'

The ride from the county prosecutor's office to the U.S. attorney's was three blocks. They entered via the well-guarded private underground garage. There were very few cars at this hour. The elevator dropped them on the seventh floor. The stencil on the glass read:

UNITED STATES ATTORNEY
DISTRICT OF NEW JERSEY
JOAN THURSTON
UNITED STATES ATTORNEY

Steinberg pointed at the top line and then the bottom line. 'Kinda redundant, no?'

Despite the power of the office, the waiting room was done up in Early American Dentist. The carpet was threadbare. The furniture managed to be neither fashionable nor functional. There were a dozen different issues of *Sports Illustrated* on the table and nothing else. The walls seemed to plead for a paint job. They were stained and barren, except for the photographs of past U.S. attorneys, a remarkable lesson in what not to wear and how not to pose when taking a picture for posterity.

No receptionist was sitting guard at this hour. They knocked and were buzzed into the inner sanctum. It was much nicer in here, a totally different feel and look, like they'd stepped through a wall into Diagon Alley.

They turned right and headed toward the corner office. A man – an enormous man – stood in the corridor. He had a buzz cut and a frown. He stood perfectly still and looked as if he could double as a squash court. Steinberg stuck out his hand. 'Hi, I'm Ed Steinberg, county prosecutor.'

Squash Court took the hand but he did not look happy about it. 'Cal Dollinger, FBI. They're waiting.'

That was the end of that conversation. Cal Dollinger stayed where he was. They turned the corner. Joan Thurston greeted them at the door.

Despite the early hour U.S. Attorney Joan Thurston looked resplendent in a charcoal gray business suit that seemed to have been tailored by the gods. Thurston was mid-forties and, in Loren's view, excessively attractive. She had auburn hair, broad shoulders, tapered waist. She had two sons in their early teens. Her husband worked at Morgan Stanley in Manhattan. They lived in ritzy Short Hills with a vacation home on Long Beach Island.

In short: Joan Thurston was what Loren wanted to be when she grew up.

'Good morning,' Thurston said, which felt weird because outside her windows, the skies were still night black.

She shook Loren's hand firmly, meeting her eye and softening it with a smile. She gave Steinberg a hug and buss on the cheek. 'I'd like you to meet Adam Yates. He's the FBI Special Agent in Charge of the Las Vegas office.'

Adam Yates wore freshly ironed khakis and a bright pink shirt that might be the norm on Worth Avenue in Palm Beach but not Broad Street in Newark. He wore loafers without socks, his legs too casually crossed. He had that whole Old World, came-over-on-the-Mayflower thing going on, what with the receding ash-blond hair, the high cheekbones, the eyes so ice blue she wondered if he was wearing contacts. His cologne smelled like freshly cut grass. Loren liked it.

'Please sit,' Thurston said.

Thurston had a spacious corner office. On one wall – the least noticeable wall – was a smattering of diplomas and awards. They were put out of the way, almost as if to say, 'Hey, I need to put them up but I don't like to put on airs.' The rest of the office was personal. She had photographs of her children and her husband, all of whom – big surprise – were gorgeous. Even the dog. There was a white guitar autographed by Bruce Springsteen hanging behind her head. On the bookshelf were the usual assortment of law books, along with autographed baseballs and footballs. All the local teams, of course. Joan Thurston had no photographs of herself, no news clippings, no Lucite-block awards in view.

Loren sat down carefully. She used to tuck her heels underneath her to gain a few inches, but she'd read a business self-help book about how women sabotage their own careers, and one of the rules said that a woman must never sit on her heels. It looked unprofessional. Usually Loren forgot that rule. Something about seeing Joan Thurston brought it all back.

Thurston came around and half-sat/half-leaned against the front lip of her desk. She folded her arms and focused her attention on Loren.

'Tell me what you have so far.'

Loren glanced at Ed Steinberg. He nodded.

'We have three dead people. The first, well, we don't know her real name. That's why we're here.'

'This would be Sister Mary Rose?' Thurston asked.

'Yes.'

'How did you stumble across her case?'

'Pardon?'

'I understand that the death was originally ruled of natural causes,' Thurston said. 'What made you look into it deeper?'

Steinberg took that one. 'The Mother Superior personally asked Investigator Muse to look into it.'

'Why?'

'Loren is an alum of St. Margaret's.'

'I understand that, but what made this Mother Superior . . . what's her name?'

'Mother Katherine,' Loren said.

'Mother Katherine, right. What made her suspect foul play in the first place?'

'I'm not sure she suspected anything,' Loren said. 'When Mother Katherine found Sister Mary Rose's body, she tried to resuscitate her with chest compressions and discovered that she had breast implants. That didn't mesh with Sister Mary Rose's history.'

'So she came to you to find out what was up?'

'Something like that, yes.'

Thurston nodded. 'And the second body?'

'Max Darrow. He was a retired Vegas police officer now residing in the Reno area.'

They all looked at Adam Yates. He stayed still. So,

Loren thought, this would be the game. They'd roll over and maybe, just maybe, the feds would award them with a tiny doggie treat.

Thurston asked, 'How did you connect Max Darrow to Sister Mary Rose?'

'Fingerprints,' Loren said. 'Darrow's fingerprints were found in the nun's private quarters.'

'Anything else?'

'Darrow was found dead in his car. Shot twice at point-blank range. His pants were down around his ankles. We think the killer tried to make it look like a prostitute rolled him.'

'Fine, we can go into the details later,' Thurston said. 'Tell us how Max Darrow connects to the third victim.'

'The third victim is Charles Talley. For one thing, both Talley and Darrow lived in the Reno area. For another, they were both staying at the Howard Johnson's near Newark Airport. Their rooms were next door to one another's.'

'And that's where you found Talley's body? At the hotel?'

'Not me. A night custodian found him in the stairwell. He'd been shot twice.'

'Same as Darrow?'

'Similar, yes.'

'Time of death?'

'It's still being worked on, but sometime tonight between eleven p.m. and two a.m. The stairwell had no air-conditioning, no windows, no ventilation – it had to be over a hundred degrees in there.'

'That's why Investigator Muse here looks like that,' Steinberg said, gesturing with both hands as if he were presenting a soiled prize. 'From being in that sauna.'

Loren shot him a look and tried to hold back from

smoothing her hair. 'The heat makes it more difficult for our ME to pinpoint a better time frame.'

'What else?' Thurston asked.

Loren hesitated. Her guess was that Thurston and Yates probably knew – or at least, could readily learn – most of what she'd already told them. So far, this had all been about getting up to speed. All that she really had left – all that she'd have that they probably wouldn't – was Matt Hunter.

Steinberg held up a hand. 'May I make a suggestion?'

Thurston turned toward him. 'Of course, Ed.'

'I don't want to have any jurisdictional hassles here.'

'Neither do we.'

'So why don't we just pool our resources on this one? Totally open communication both ways. We tell you what we know, you tell us what you know. No holding back.'

Thurston glanced at Yates. Adam Yates cleared his throat and said, 'We have no problem with that.'

'Do you know the real identity of Sister Mary Rose?' Steinberg asked.

Yates nodded. 'We do, yes.'

Loren waited. Yates took his time. He uncrossed his legs, tugged at the front of his shirt as if trying to get some air.

'Your nun – well, she's not even close to being a nun, believe me – was one Emma Lemay,' Yates said.

The name meant nothing to Loren. She looked at Steinberg. He, too, had no reaction to the name.

Yates continued: 'Emma Lemay and her partner, a cretin named Clyde Rangor, disappeared from Vegas ten years ago. We did a fairly massive search for both of them but turned up nothing. One day they were there, the next – poof – they were both gone.'

Steinberg asked, 'How did you know we found Lemay's body?'

'The Lockwood Corporation had her silicone implants marked. The NCIC now puts everything they can into the national database. Fingerprints, you know about. DNA and descriptions, those have been in there for a while. But now we're working on a national database for medical devices – any kind of joint replacements, surgical implants, colostomy bags, pacemakers – mostly to help identify Jane and John Does. You get the model number, you put it in the system. It's new, pretty experimental. We're trying it out on a select few that we're very anxious to locate.'

'And this Emma Lemay,' Loren said. 'You were anxious to locate her?'

Yates had a good smile. 'Oh, yes.'

'Why?' Loren asked.

'Ten years ago Lemay and Rangor agreed to turn on a nasty perennial RICO top-ten asswipe, guy named Tom "Comb-Over" Busher.'

'Comb-Over?'

'That's what they call him, though not to his face. Been his nickname for years, actually. Used to be, he had this comb-over going. You know, when he started going bald. But it just kept growing. So now he kinda twirls it around and around, looks like he stuck a cinnamon swirl on top of his head.'

Yates chuckled. Nobody else did.

Thurston said, 'You were talking about Lemay and Rangor?'

'Right. So anyway, we nailed Lemay and Rangor on pretty serious drug charges, pressed them like hell, and for the first time, we got someone on the inside to flip. Clyde Rangor and Comb-Over are cousins. They started working with us, taping conversations, gathering evidence. And then. . . .' Yates shrugged.

'So what do you think happened?'

'The most likely scenario was that Comb-Over got wind of what was up and killed them. But we never really bought that.'

'Why not?'

'Because there was evidence – lots of it, actually – that Comb-Over was searching for Lemay and Rangor too. Even harder than we were. For a while it was like the race was on, you know, who'd find them first. When they never turned up, well, we figured we lost the race.'

'This Comb-Over. He still on the streets?'

'Yes.'

'And what about Clyde Rangor?'

'We have no idea where he is.' Yates shifted in his chair. 'Clyde Rangor was a major whack-job. He managed a couple of strip clubs for Comb-Over and had a rep for enjoying the occasional, uh, rough session.'

'How rough?'

Yates folded his hands and placed them in his lap. 'We suspect that some of the girls didn't recover.'

'When you say didn't recover –'

'One ended up in a catatonic state. One – the last one, we think – ended up dead.'

Loren made a face. 'And you were cutting a deal with this guy?'

'What, you want us to find someone nicer?' Yates snapped.

'I –'

'Do I really need to explain to you how trading up works, Investigator Muse?'

Steinberg stepped in. 'Not at all.'

'I didn't mean to imply. . . .' Loren bit back, her face

reddening, upset with herself for sounding so amateurish. 'Go on.'

'What else is there? We don't know where Clyde Rangor is, but we believe that he can still provide valuable information, maybe help us take Comb-Over down.'

'How about Charles Talley and Detective Max Darrow? Any idea how they fit in?'

'Charles Talley is a thug with a record for brutality. He handled some of the girls in the clubs, made sure they kept in line, didn't steal much, shared their, uh, tips with the house. Last we heard he was working for a dump in Reno called the Eager Beaver. Our best guess is, Talley was hired to kill Emma Lemay.'

'By this Comb-Over guy?'

'Yes. Our theory is that somehow Comb-Over found out that Emma Lemay was pretending to be this Sister Mary Rose. He sent Talley here to kill her.'

'And what about Max Darrow?' Loren asked. 'We know he was in Lemay's quarters. What was his role?'

Yates uncrossed his legs and sat up. 'For one thing, we think Darrow, though a fairly solid cop, might have been crooked.'

His voice drifted off. He cleared his throat.

'And for another,' Loren prompted.

Yates took a deep breath. 'Well, Max Darrow . . .' He looked at Thurston. She didn't nod, didn't move, but Loren got the impression that, as she had done with Steinberg, Yates was looking for an okay. 'Let's just say that Max Darrow is connected into this case in another way.'

They waited. Several seconds passed. Loren finally said, 'How?'

Yates rubbed his face with both hands, suddenly looking exhausted. 'I mentioned before that Clyde Rangor was into rough trade.'

Loren nodded.

'And that we think he killed his last victim.'

'Yes.'

'The victim was a small-time stripper and probable hooker, named . . . hold on, I have it here . . .' – Yates pulled a small leather notepad from his back pocket, licked his finger, flipped through the pages – 'named Candace Potter, aka Candi Cane.' He snapped the notebook shut. 'Emma Lemay and Clyde Rangor disappeared soon after her body was found.'

'And how does that fit in with Darrow?'

'Max Darrow was the homicide investigator in charge of the case.'

Everyone stopped.

'Wait a second,' Ed Steinberg began. 'So this Clyde Rangor murders a stripper. Darrow catches the case. A few days later, Rangor and his girlfriend Lemay vanish. And now, what, ten years later, we get Darrow's fingerprints at Emma Lemay's murder scene?'

'That pretty much sums it up, yes.'

There was more silence. Loren tried to digest this.

'Here's the important thing,' Yates continued, leaning forward. 'If Emma Lemay still had materials pertinent to this case – or if she left information on the whereabouts of Clyde Rangor – we believe that Investigator Muse is in the best position to find it.'

'Me?'

Yates turned toward her. 'You have a relationship with her colleagues. Lemay lived with the same group of nuns for seven years now. The Mother Superior clearly trusts you. What we need you to concentrate on is that angle – in finding out what Lemay knew or what she had.'

Steinberg looked at Loren and shrugged. Joan Thurston

moved around her desk. She opened a mini-fridge. 'Anybody want a drink?' she asked.

They didn't reply. Thurston shrugged, grabbed a bottle, began to shake it. 'How about you, Adam? You want something?'

'Just a water.'

She tossed him a bottle.

'Ed? Loren?'

They both shook their heads. Joan Thurston twisted off the cap and took a deep sip. She moved back in front of her desk.

'Okay, time to stop the dance,' Thurston said. 'What else have you learned, Loren?'

Loren. Already calling her Loren. Again she checked with Steinberg. Again he nodded.

'We found several connections between all of this and an ex-con named Matt Hunter,' Loren said.

Thurston's eyes narrowed. 'Why does that name ring a bell?'

'He's local, from Livingston. His case made the papers years back. He got into a fight at a college party –'

'Oh, right, I remember,' Thurston interrupted. 'I knew his brother Bernie. Good lawyer, died much too young. I think Bernie got him a job at Carter Sturgis when he got out.'

'Matt Hunter still works there.'

'And he's involved in this?'

'There are connections.'

'Such as?'

She told them about the phone call from St. Margaret's to Marsha Hunter's residence. They did not seem all that impressed. When Loren started filling them in on what she'd learned this very night – that Matt Hunter had, in all likelihood, gotten into a fight with Charles

Talley at the Howard Johnson's – they sat up. For the first time Yates started jotting notes in the leather pad.

When she finished, Thurston asked, 'So what do you make of it, Loren?'

'Truth? I don't have a clue yet.'

'We should look at this guy Hunter's time in prison,' Yates said. 'We know Talley was in the system too. Maybe they met along the way. Or maybe Hunter somehow got involved with Comb-Over's people.'

'Right,' Thurston said. 'Could be that Hunter is the one cleaning up the loose ends for Comb-Over.'

Loren kept quiet.

'You don't agree, Loren?'

'I don't know.'

'What's the problem?'

'This may sound hopelessly naïve, but I don't think Matt Hunter is working as some kind of hit man. He has a record, yes, but that's from a fight at a frat party fifteen years ago. He had no priors and has been clean ever since.'

She did not tell him that they'd gone to school together or that her 'gut' didn't like it. When other investigators used that rationale, Loren wanted to gag.

'So how do you explain Hunter's involvement?' Thurston asked.

'I don't know. It might be a more personal thing. According to the front-desk guy, his wife was staying at the hotel without him.'

'You think it's a lovers' quarrel?'

'It could be.'

Thurston looked doubtful. 'Either way, we all agree that Matt Hunter is involved?'

Steinberg said, 'Definitely.' Yates nodded hard. Loren stayed still.

'And right now,' Thurston continued, 'we have more than enough to arrest and indict. We have the fight, the call, all that. We'll get DNA soon linking him to the dead man.'

Loren hesitated. Ed Steinberg did not. 'We got enough to arrest.'

'And with Hunter's record, we can probably get a no-bail situation. We can put him in the system and keep him there for a little while, right, Ed?'

'I'd bet on it, yeah,' Steinberg said.

'Pick him up then,' Joan Thurston said. 'Let's get Hunter's ass back behind bars pronto.'

35

Matt and Olivia were alone in Marsha's guest room.

Nine years ago Matt had spent his first night as a free man in this room. Bernie had brought him home. Marsha had been outwardly polite, but looking back on it, there must have been some serious reservations. You move into a house like this to escape people like Matt. Even if you know he's innocent, even if you think he's a good guy and got a bad break, you don't want your life enmeshed with his. He is a virus, a carrier of something malevolent. You have children. You want to protect them. You want to believe, as Lance Banner did, that the manicured lawns can keep this element out.

He thought about his old college buddy Duff. At one time Matt had believed that Duff was tough. Now he knew better. Now he could kick Duff's ass around the corner without breaking a sweat. He wasn't being boastful. He didn't think that with any pride. It was just a fact of life. His buddies who thought they were tough – the Duffs of the world – man, they had no idea.

But tough as Matt had become, he'd spent his first night of freedom in this room crying. He couldn't exactly say why. He had never cried in prison. Some would say that he simply feared showing weakness in such a horrible place. That was part of it, maybe. Maybe it was just a 'saving up' outlet, that now he was crying for four years of anguish.

But Matt didn't think so.

The real reason, he suspected, had more to do with fear and disbelief. He could not accept that he was really free, that prison was really behind him. It felt like a cruel hoax, that this warm bed was an illusion, that soon they'd drag him back and lock him away forever.

He'd read how interrogators and hostage-takers try to break spirits by holding mock executions. That would work, Matt thought, but what would undoubtedly be more effective, what would unquestionably make a man crack, would be the opposite – pretending you were going to set him free. You get the guy dressed, you tell him that his release has been all arranged, you say good-bye and blindfold him and drive him around and then, when they stop and take him inside and pull off his blind-fold, he finds that he is back where he started, that it was all a sick joke.

That was how it felt.

Matt sat now on the same queen-size mattress. Olivia stood with her back to him. Her head was lowered. Her shoulders were still high, still proud. He loved her shoulders, the sinew of her back, the knot of gentle muscles and supple skin.

Part of him, maybe most of him, wanted to say, 'Let's just forget it. I don't need to know. You just said that you love me. You just told me that I am the only man you ever loved. That's enough.'

When they arrived Kyra had come out and met them in the front yard. She had been concerned. Matt remembered when she first moved in over the garage. He'd noted that she was 'just like the Fonz.' Kyra had no idea what he'd been talking about. Funny what you think about when you're terrified. Marsha looked concerned too, especially when she saw Matt's bandages and noticed his tentative step. But Marsha knew him well enough to know that now was not the time for questions.

Olivia broke the silence. 'Can I ask you something?'

'Sure.'

'You said something on the phone about receiving pictures.'

'Yes.'

'May I see them, please?'

He took out his cell phone and held it up. Olivia turned and took it from him without touching his skin. He watched her face now. She concentrated in that way he knew so well. Her head tilted a little to the side, the same as it always did when something confused her.

'I don't understand this,' she said.

'Is that you?' he asked. 'With the wig?'

'Yes. But it wasn't like that.'

'Like what?'

Her eyes stayed on the camera. She hit the replay button, watched the scene again, shook her head. 'Whatever you want to think of me, I never cheated on you. And the man I met with. He was wearing a wig too. So he could look like the guy in the first picture, I guess.'

'I figured that.'

'How?'

Matt showed her the window, the gray skies, the ring on the finger. He explained about the drought and about blowing up the pictures in Cingle's office.

Olivia sat next to him on the bed. She looked so damn beautiful. 'So you knew.'

'Knew what?'

'Deep in your heart, despite what you saw here, you knew that I'd never cheat on you.'

He wanted to reach out and take her in his arms. He could see her chest hitching a little, trying to hold it together.

Matt said, 'I just need to ask you two questions before you begin, okay?'

She nodded.

'Are you pregnant?' he asked.

'Yes,' she said. 'And before you ask the second question – yes, it's yours.'

'Then I don't care about the rest. If you don't want to tell me, you don't have to. It doesn't matter. We can just run off, I don't care.'

She shook her head. 'I don't think I can run again, Matt.' She sounded so worn. 'And you can't just do that either. What about Paul and Ethan? What about Marsha?'

She was right, of course. He didn't know how to put it. He shrugged and said, 'I just don't want things to change.'

'Neither do I. And if I could come up with a way around this, I would. I'm scared, Matt. I've never been so scared in my life.'

She turned to him. She reached out and cupped the back of his head. She leaned forward and kissed him. She kissed him hard. He knew that kiss. It was the prelude. Despite what was happening, his body reacted, began to sing. The kiss grew hungrier. She moved closer, pressed against him. His eyes rolled back.

They turned a little, and Matt's ribs suddenly screamed. Pain shot down his side. He stiffened. His low cry chased the moment away. Olivia released him, pulled away. She lowered her eyes.

'Everything I've ever told you about me,' she said, 'was a lie.'

He did not react. He was not sure what he had expected her to say – not this – but he just sat and waited.

'I didn't grow up in Northways, Virginia. I didn't go

to UVA – I didn't even go to high school. My father wasn't the town doctor – I don't know who my father was. I never had a nanny named Cassie or any of that. I made it all up.'

Outside the window a car turned onto the street, the headlights dancing against the wall as it passed. Matt just sat there, still as a stone.

'My real mother was a strung-out junkie who gave me to Child Services when I was three. She died from an OD two years later. I bounced around from foster home to foster home. You don't want to know what they were like. I did that until I ran away when I was sixteen. I ended up near Las Vegas.'

'When you were sixteen?'

'Yes.'

Olivia's voice had taken on a strange monotone now. Her eyes were clear, but she stared straight ahead, two yards past him. She seemed to be waiting for a reaction. Matt was still fumbling, trying to take this all in.

'So those stories about Dr. Joshua Murray . . . ?'

'You mean the young girl with the dead mother and the kindly father and the horses?' She almost smiled. 'Come on, Matt. I got that from a book I read when I was eight.'

He opened his mouth but nothing came out. He tried again. 'Why?'

'Why did I lie?'

'Yes.'

'I didn't really lie so much as . . .' She stopped, looked up . . . 'so much as died. I know that sounds melodramatic. But becoming Olivia Murray was more than just a fresh start. It was like I was never that other person. The foster child was dead. Olivia Murray of Northways, Virginia, took her place.'

'So everything . . .' He put his hands up. 'It was all a lie?'

'Not us,' she said. 'Not how I feel about you. Not how I act around you. Nothing about us was ever a lie. Not one kiss. Not one embrace. Not one emotion. You didn't love a lie. You loved me.'

Loved, she had said. You loved me. The past tense.

'So when we met in Las Vegas, you weren't in college?'

'No,' she said.

'And that night? At the club?'

Her eyes met his. 'I was supposed to be working.'

'I don't understand.'

'Yeah, Matt. Yeah, you do.'

He remembered the Web site. The stripper site.

'You danced?'

'Danced? Well, yes, the politically correct term is exotic dancer. All the girls use that term. But I was a stripper. And sometimes, when they made me. . . .' Olivia shook her head. Her eyes started to water. 'We'll never get past this.'

'And that night,' Matt said, a surge of anger coursing through him, 'what, I looked like I had money?'

'That's not funny.'

'I'm not trying to be funny.'

Her voice had steel in it now. 'You have no idea what that night meant to me. It changed my life. You never got it, Matt.'

'Never got what?'

'Your world,' she said. 'It's worth fighting for.'

He wasn't sure what she meant – or if he wanted to know what she meant. 'You said you were in foster homes.'

'Yes.'

'And that you ran away?'

'My last foster home encouraged this line of work. You can't imagine how badly you want to get out. So they told us where to go. My last foster mother's sister – she ran the club. She got us fake IDs.'

He shook his head. 'I still don't see why you didn't tell me the truth.'

'When, Matt?'

'When what?'

'When should I have told you? That first night in Las Vegas? How about when I came to your office? Second date? Engagement? When should I have told you?'

'I don't know.'

'It wasn't that easy.'

'It wasn't easy for me to tell you about my time in prison either.'

'My situation involves more than me,' she said. 'I made a pact.'

'What kind of pact?'

'You have to understand. I might have been able to risk it, if it was just me. But I couldn't risk it for her.'

'Who?'

Olivia looked away and didn't say anything for a long time. She took a piece of paper out of her back pocket, unfolded it slowly, and handed it to him. Then she turned her face away from him again.

Matt took the piece of paper and turned it over. It was an article printed out from the *Nevada Sun News* Web site. He read it. It didn't take long.

WOMAN SLAIN

Las Vegas, NV – Candace Potter, age 21, was found slain in a trailer park off Route 15. The cause of death was strangulation. Police would not comment about the possibility of sexual assault. Ms. Potter worked as a dancer

*at the Young Thangs, a nightclub on the outskirts of
the city, using the stage name Candi Cane. Authorities
said the investigation was ongoing and that they were
following up some promising leads.*

Matt looked up. 'I still don't get it.' Her face was still
turned away from him. 'You promised this Candace
person?'

She chuckled without humor. 'No.'

'Then who?'

'What I said before. About not really lying to you.
About it being more like I died.'

Olivia turned toward him.

'That's me,' she said. 'I used to be Candace Potter.'

36

When Loren got back to the county prosecutor's office, Roger Cudahy, one of the techno guys who'd gone to Cingle's office, was sitting with his feet up on her desk, his hands folded behind his head.

'Comfy?' Loren said.

His smile was wide. 'Oh yeah.'

'Don't we look like the proverbial cat who ate the proverbial canary.'

The smile stayed. 'Not sure that proverbial applies, but again: Oh yeah.'

'What is it?'

With his hands still behind his head, Cudahy motioned toward the laptop. 'Take a look.'

'On the laptop?'

'Oh yeah.'

She moved the mouse. The darkened screen came to life. And there, filling up the entire screen, was a snapshot of Charles Talley. He was holding his hand up. His hair was blue-black. He had a cocky grin on his face.

'You got this off Cingle Shaker's computer?'

'Oh yeah. It came from a camera phone.'

'Nice work.'

'Hold up.'

'What?'

Cudahy continued to grin. 'As Bachman Turner Overdrive used to sing, you ain't seen nothing yet.'

'What?' Loren said.

'Hit the arrow key. The right one.'

Loren did it. The shaky video started up. A woman in a platinum-blonde wig came out of the bathroom. She moved toward the bed. When the video was finished, Cudahy said, 'Comments?'

'Just one.'

Cudahy put out his palm. 'Lay it on me.'

Loren slapped him five. 'Oh yeah.'

37

'It was about a year after I met you,' Olivia said.

She stood across the room. The color was back in her face. Her spine was straighter. It was as though she was gaining strength, telling him all this. For his part, Matt tried not to process yet. He just wanted to absorb.

'I was eighteen years old, but I'd already been in Vegas for two years. A lot of us girls lived in old trailers. The manager of the club, an evil man named Clyde Rangor, had a couple of acres a mile down the road. It was just desert. He put up a chain-link fence, dragged in three or four of the most beaten-down trailers you'd ever seen. And that's where we lived. The girls, they came and went, but at this time I was sharing the trailer with two people. One was new, a girl named Cassandra Meadows. She was maybe sixteen, seventeen years old. The other was named Kimmy Dale. Kimmy was away that day. See, Clyde used to send us out on road trips. We'd strip in some small town, do three shows a day. Easy money for him. Good tips for us, though Clyde kept most of that too.'

Matt needed to get his bearings, but there was just no way. 'When you started there, you were how old?' he asked.

'Sixteen.'

He tried not to close his eyes. 'I don't understand how that worked.'

'Clyde was connected. I don't really know how, but they'd find hard-up girls from foster homes in Idaho.'

'That's where you're from?'

She nodded. 'They had contacts in other states too. Oklahoma. Cassandra was from Kansas, I think. The girls would basically be funneled to Clyde's place. He'd give them fake IDs and put them to work. It wasn't difficult. We both know that nobody really cares about the poor, but little children are, at least, sympathetic. We were just sullen teenagers. We had nobody.'

Matt said, 'Okay, go on.'

'Clyde had this girlfriend named Emma Lemay. Emma was sort of a mother figure to all the girls. I know how that sounds, but when you consider what we'd had in the past, she almost made you believe it. Clyde used to beat the hell out of her. He'd just walk by, you'd see Emma flinch. I didn't realize it then, but that victimization . . . it made us relate, I guess. Kimmy and I liked her. We all talked about one day getting out – that's all we ever talked about. I told her and Kimmy about meeting you. About what that night meant to me. They listened. We all knew it would never happen, but they listened anyway.'

There was a sound from outside of the room. A tiny cry. Olivia turned toward it.

'That's just Ethan,' Matt said.

'Does he do that a lot?'

'Yes.'

They waited. The house fell silent again.

'One day I was feeling sick,' Olivia said. Her voice had again moved into a distant monotone. 'It's not like they give you nights off, but I was so nauseous I could barely stand, and, well, girls throwing up on stage didn't do much for business. Since Clyde and Emma weren't around, I checked with the guy at the door. He said I could leave. So I walked back to the Pen – that's what we called the trailer area. It was around three in the afternoon. The sun was still strong. I could almost feel my skin being baked.'

Olivia smiled wistfully then. 'You know what's odd? Well, I mean, the whole thing is odd, but you know what just struck me?'

'What?'

'The degrees. Not the temperature degrees. But the degrees that change everything. The little ifs that become the big ones. You know about those better than anyone. If you had just driven straight back to Bowdoin. If Duff hadn't spilled the beer. You know.'

'I do.'

'It's the same thing here. If I hadn't been sick. If I had just danced like I did every night. Except in my case, well, I guess different people would say different things. But I'd say my ifs saved my life.'

She was standing by the door. She eyed the knob as if she wanted to flee.

Matt said, 'What happened when you got back to the Pen?'

'The place was empty,' Olivia said. 'Most of the girls were already at the club or in town. We usually finished around three in the morning and slept to noon. The Pen was so depressing, we got the hell out of there as soon as we could. So when I came back, it was silent. I opened the door to my trailer and the first thing I saw was blood on the floor.'

He watched closely now. Olivia's breathing had deepened, but her face was smooth, untroubled.

'I called out. That was stupid, I guess. I probably should have just started screaming and ran, I don't know. Another if, right? Then I looked around. The trailers had two rooms, but they're set up backwards, so you first walk into the bedroom where the three of us slept. I had the lower bunk. Kimmy's was on the top. Cassandra, the new girl, her bed was against the far wall. Kimmy was neat as a pin. She was always getting on us about not cleaning up. Our lives were dumps, she'd say, but that didn't mean we had to live in one.

'Anyway, the place was totally trashed. The drawers had all been dumped out, clothes everywhere. And there, near Cassandra's bed, where the blood trailed off, I could see two legs on the floor. I ran over and I just pulled up short.'

Olivia looked him straight in the eye. 'Cassandra was dead. I didn't need to feel for a pulse. Her body was on its side, almost in a fetal position. Both eyes were open, staring at that wall. Her face was purple and swollen. There were cigarette burns on her arms. Her hands were still hog-tied with duct tape behind her back. You have to remember, Matt. I was eighteen years old. I may have felt older or looked older. I may have had too much life experience. But think about that. I'm standing there looking at a dead body. I was frozen. I couldn't move. Even when I heard the sounds coming from the other room, even when I heard Emma scream out, "Clyde, don't!".'

She stopped, closed her eyes, let loose a deep breath.

'I turned just in time to see a fist flying at my face. There was no time to react. Clyde didn't pull the punch at all. His knuckles landed flush on my nose. I actually heard the crack more than I felt it. My head snapped back. I fell back and landed on top of Cassandra – that was probably the worst part of all. Landing on her dead body. Her skin was all clammy. I tried to crawl off her. Blood was flowing down into my mouth.'

Olivia paused, swallowing air, trying to catch her breath. Matt had never felt more incompetent in his life.

He did not move, did not say anything. He just let her gather herself.

'Clyde rushed over and looked down on me. His face . . . I mean, he usually had this smirk. I'd seen him give Emma Lemay the backside of his hand lots of times. I know this sounds foreign to you. Why didn't we act? Why didn't we do something? But his beatings weren't unusual to us. They were normal. You have to understand that. This was all any of us knew.'

Matt nodded, which felt totally inadequate, but he understood this thinking. Prisons were filled with this sort of rationale – it wasn't so much that you did something awful as that the awful was simply the norm.

'Anyway,' Olivia went on, 'the smirk was gone. If you think rattlesnakes are mean, you never met Clyde Rangor. But now, standing over me, he looked terrified. He was breathing hard. There was blood on his shirt. Behind him – and this is a sight I'll never forget – Emma just stood with her head down. Here I was, bleeding and hurt, and I was looking past the psycho with the clenched fists at his other victim. His real victim, I guess.

'"Where's the tape?" Clyde asked me. I had no idea what he meant. He stomped down hard on my foot. I howled in pain. Then Clyde shouted, 'You playing games with me, bitch? Where is it?'

'I tried to scramble back, but I bumped up into the corner. Clyde kicked Cassandra's body out of the way and followed. I was trapped. I could hear Emma's voice in the distance, meek as a lamb, 'Don't, Clyde. Please.' With his eyes still on me, Clyde reeled on her. He had the full weight of his body in the blow. The back of his hand split Emma's cheek wide open. She tumbled back and out of sight. But it was enough for me. The distraction gave me the chance to act. I lashed out with my foot and managed to kick the spot right below his knee. Clyde's leg buckled. I got to my feet and rolled over the bed. See, I had a destination in mind. Kimmy kept a gun in the room. I didn't like it, but if you think I had it tough, Kimmy had it worse. So she was always armed. She had two guns. She kept this mini-revolver, a twenty-two in her boot. Even onstage. And Kimmy had another gun under her mattress.'

Olivia stopped and smiled at him.

'What?' Matt said.

'Like you.'

'What do you mean?'

'You don't think I know about your gun?'

He had forgotten all about it. He checked his pants. They'd taken them off him in the hospital. Olivia calmly opened her purse. 'Here,' she said.

She handed him the gun.

'I didn't want the police to find it and trace it back to you.'

'Thanks,' he said stupidly. He looked at the gun, tucked it away.

'Why do you keep it?' she asked.

'I don't know.'

'I don't think Kimmy did either. But it was there. And when Clyde went down, I dove for it. I didn't have much time. My kick hadn't incapacitated Clyde – it'd just bought me a few seconds. I dug my hand under the top bunk's mattress. I heard him shout, 'Crazy whore, I'm gonna kill you.' I had no doubt he would. I'd seen Cassandra. I'd seen his face. If he caught me, if I didn't get the gun, I was dead.'

Olivia was looking off now, her hand raised as though she were back in that trailer, digging for that gun. 'My hand was under the mattress. I could almost feel his breath on my neck. But I still couldn't find the gun. Clyde grabbed my hair. He was just starting to pull when my fingers felt the metal. I gripped for all I was worth as he tugged me back. The gun came with me. Clyde saw it. I didn't have a real grip on it. My thumb and forefinger were wrapped around the butt of the gun. I tried to snake my finger around the trigger. But Clyde was on me. He grabbed my wrist. I tried to fight him off. He was too strong. But I didn't let go. I held on. And then he dug his thumbnail into my skin. Clyde had these really long, sharp fingernails. See this?'

Olivia made a fist, tilted it back so that he could see the crescent-white scar on the underside of her wrist. Matt had noticed it before. A lifetime ago, she'd told him it was from a fall off a horse.

'Clyde Rangor did that. He dug his fingernail in so deep that he drew blood. I dropped the gun. He still had me by the hair. He flung me onto the bed and jumped on top of me. He grabbed me by the neck and began to squeeze. He was crying now. That's what I remember. Clyde was squeezing the life out of me and he was crying. Not because he cared or anything like that. He was scared. He was choking me and I could hear him pleading, "Just tell me where it is. Just tell me . . ."'

Olivia gently put her own hand up to her throat now. 'I struggled. I kicked, I flailed, but I could feel the power draining out of me. There was nothing behind my blows anymore. I could feel his thumb pushing down on my throat. I was dying. And then I heard the gun go off.'

Her hand dropped to the side. The antique clock in the dining room, a wedding gift to Bernie and Marsha, started to chime. Olivia waited, let it finish playing.

'The gun wasn't loud. It was more like the crack of a bat. I guess that's because it was a twenty-two, I don't know. For a second, Clyde's grip somehow tightened. His face looked more surprised than pained. He let go of me. I started gagging, choking. I rolled to the side, gasping for air. Emma Lemay was standing behind him. She pointed the gun at him and it was like all those years of abuse, all those beatings, they just boiled over. She didn't cower. She didn't look down. Clyde spun toward her, enraged, and she fired again, right in his face.

'Then Emma pulled the trigger one more time and Clyde Rangor was dead.'

38

Motive.

Loren now had motive. If the video was any indication, Charles Talley, a scumbag by anyone's calculations, had not only slept with Matt Hunter's wife – Loren was betting that it was Olivia Hunter in that video with the blonde wig – but he'd gone through the trouble of sending the pictures to Matt.

Mocking him.

Pissing him off.

Calling him out, if you will.

It added up. It made perfect sense.

Except too many things in this case made perfect sense at first. And then, after a few minutes, they didn't anymore. Like Max Darrow being rolled by a prostitute. Like the murder of Charles Talley looking like a common jealous-husband scenario when, if that indeed was the case, how do you explain the connection to Emma Lemay and the Nevada FBI and all the rest of the stuff she'd learned at Joan Thurston's office?

Her cell phone trilled. The number was blocked.

'Hello?'

'So what's up with this APB on Hunter?'

It was Lance Banner.

'Do you ever sleep?' she asked.

'Not in the summer. I prefer winter hibernation. Like a bear. So what's up?'

'We're looking for him.'

'Stop with all specifics, Loren. I mean, no, really, I can't handle all that detail.'

'It's a long story, Lance, and I've had a long night.'

'The APB was mainly on the Newark wire.'

'So?'

'So has anyone checked out Hunter's sister-in-law's?'

'I don't think so.'

'I live right down the block,' Lance Banner said. 'Consider me on the way.'

39

Neither Matt nor Olivia moved. The story had drained her. He could see that. He almost made a move to come closer, but she put up her hand.

'I saw an old picture of Emma Lemay once,' Olivia began. 'She was so beautiful. She was smart too. If anyone had the wiles to get out of this life, it was Emma. But you see, no one does. I was eighteen, Matt. And I already felt like my life was over. So there we were, me retching, Emma still holding the gun. She stared down at Clyde for a long time and simply waited for me to catch my breath. It took a few minutes. Then she turns to me, all clear-eyed, and says, 'We need to hide his body.'

'I remember shaking my head. I told her I didn't want any part of that. She didn't get upset or raise her voice. It was so strange. She looked so . . . serene.'

Matt said, 'She'd just slain her abuser.'

'That was part of it, sure.'

'But?'

'It was almost as if she'd been waiting for this moment. Like she knew it would one day happen. I said we should call the police. Emma shook her head, calm, in control. The gun was still in her hand. She didn't point it at me. 'We could tell them the truth,' I said. 'That it was self-defense. We'll show them the bruises on my neck. Hell, we'll show them Cassandra.''

Matt shifted in his seat. Olivia saw it and smiled.

'I know,' she said. 'The irony isn't lost on me. Self-defense. Like you claimed. We were both, I guess, at that same fork in the road. Maybe you didn't have a choice, what with all those people around. But even if you did, you came from a different world. You trusted the police. You thought that truth would win out. But we knew better. Emma had shot Clyde three times, once in the back, twice in the face. No one would buy self-defense. And even if they did, Clyde made big money for his mobbed-up cousin. He'd never let us live.'

'So what did you do?' he asked.

'I was confused, I guess. But Emma kept explaining the predicament. We had no choice. Not really. And that was when she hit me with her best argument.'

'What?'

'Emma said, "What if it all goes well?"'

'What if what all goes well?' Matt asked.

'What if the police believe us and Clyde's cousin leaves us alone?'

She stopped, smiled.

'I don't get it,' Matt said.

'Where would we be? Emma and me. Where would we be if it all worked out?'

Matt saw it now. 'You'd be where you were.'

'Right. This was our chance, Matt. Clyde had a hundred thousand dollars hidden at the house. Emma said we'd take it. We'd split up and run. We'd start anew. Emma already had a destination in mind. She'd been planning on leaving for years, but she never had the courage. Neither did I. Neither did any of us.'

'But now you had to.'

Olivia nodded. 'She said that if we hid Clyde, they'd figure the two of them ran off together. They'd be looking for a couple. Or they'd think they were both killed and buried together. But she needed my help. I said,

'What about me? Clyde's friends know what I look like. They'll hunt me down. And how do we explain Cassandra being dead?'

'But Emma already had that covered. She said, "Give me your wallet." I dug into my pocket and pulled it out. She took out my ID – back in those days, Nevada didn't require you to have pictures on the ID – and she jammed it into Cassandra's pocket. "When is Kimmy coming back?" she asked me. In three days, I told her. Plenty of time, she said. Then she said, "Listen to me. Neither you nor Cassandra has any real family. Cassandra's mother threw her out years ago. They don't talk."

'I said, "I don't understand."

'"I've been thinking about this for years," Emma said. "Whenever he beat me. Whenever he choked me until I passed out. Whenever he said he was sorry and promised that it would never happen again and that he loved me. Whenever he told me he'd hunt me down and kill me if I ever left. What . . . what if I killed Clyde and buried him and just took the money and ran someplace I knew was safe? What if I made amends, you know, for what I'd done to you girls? You have those fantasies, don't you, Candi? About running away?"'

Matt said, 'And you did.'

Olivia held up her index finger. 'With one difference. I said before that my life already felt over. I disappeared in my books. I tried to keep upbeat. I imagined something different. Because I had something to hold on to. Look, I don't want to make too much of that night in Vegas. But I thought about it, Matt. I thought about the way you made me feel. I thought about the world you lived in. I remember everything you said – about your family, about where you grew up, about your friends and your school. And what you didn't know, what you still don't understand, is that you were describing a place I couldn't let myself imagine.'

Matt said nothing.

'After you left that night, I can't tell you how many times I thought of trying to find you.'

'Why didn't you?'

She shook her head. 'You of all people should understand shackles.'

He nodded, afraid to answer.

'Didn't matter anymore,' Olivia said. 'It was too late for any of that now. Even with shackles, like you said, we had to act. So we came up with a plan. It was simple, really. First, we rolled Clyde's body up in a blanket and dumped it in the back of the car. We padlocked the Pen. Emma knew a place. Clyde had dumped at least two bodies there she said. Out in the desert. We buried him in a shallow grave, way out in this no-man's-land. Then Emma called the club. She made sure all the girls were made to work overtime, so that none of them would be able to go back to the Pen.

'We stopped at her place to shower. I stepped under the warm water and thought, I don't know, I thought it would be weird, showering off the blood, like something out of *Macbeth*.'

A wan smile crossed her face.

'But it wasn't like that?' Matt asked.

Olivia shook her head slowly. 'I had just buried a man in the desert. At night the jackals would dig him up and feast. Carry his bones away. That's what Emma told me. And I didn't care.'

She looked at him as if daring him to challenge her.

'So what did you do next?'

'Can't you guess?'

'Tell me.'

'I . . . I mean, Candace Potter was nothing. There was

no one to even notify in the event of her untimely death. Emma as her employer and almost guardian called the police. She said that one of her girls had been murdered. The police arrived. Emma showed them Cassandra's body. The ID was already in her pocket. Emma identified the body and confirmed that it belonged to one of her girls, Candace 'Candi Cane' Potter. There was no next of kin. No one questioned it. Why should they? Why would anyone make something like this up? Emma and I split the money. I got over fifty grand. Can you imagine? All the girls at the club had fake IDs anyway, so getting a new one was no problem for me.'

'And you just ran off?'

'Yes.'

'What about Cassandra?' Matt asked.

'What about her?'

'Didn't anyone wonder what happened to her?'

'We had a million girls come and go. Emma told everyone she'd quit — been spooked off by the murder. Two other girls got scared and ran off too.'

Matt shook his head, trying to wrap his brain around all this. 'When I met you the first time, you used the name Olivia Murray.'

'Yes.'

'You went back to that name?'

'That was the only time I used it. With you that night. Did you ever read *A Wrinkle in Time*?'

'Sure. In fifth grade, I think.'

'When I was a kid, it was my favorite book. The protagonist was named Meg Murray. That's how I came up with the last name.'

'And Olivia?'

She shrugged. 'It sounded like the direct opposite of Candi.'

'So then what happened?'

'Emma and I made a pact. We would never tell any one the truth – no matter what – because if one of us talked, it could lead to the death of the other. So we swore. I need you to understand how solemnly I made that promise.'

Matt was not sure what to say to that. 'Then you went to Virginia?'

'Yes.'

'Why?'

'Because it was where Olivia Murray lived. It was far away from Vegas or Idaho. I made up a background story. I took courses at the University of Virginia. I didn't officially attend, of course, but this was in the days before strict security. I just sat in on classes. I hung out in the library and cafeteria. I met people. They just figured I was a student. A few years later, I pretended to graduate. I got a job. I never looked back or thought about Candi. Candace Potter was dead.'

'And then, what, I came along?'

'Something like that, yeah. Look, I was a scared kid. I ran away and tried to make a life for myself. A real one. And the truth is, I had no interest in meeting a man. You hired DataBetter, remember?'

Matt nodded. 'I do.'

'I'd had enough of that in my life. But then I saw you and . . . I don't know. Maybe I wanted to go back to the night we met. To some silly dream. You scoff at the idea of living out here, Matt. You don't see that this place, this town, this is the best possible world.'

'And that's why you want to move out here?'

'With you,' she said, her eyes imploring. 'Don't you see? I never bought that soul-mate stuff. You see what I've seen and . . . but maybe, I don't know, maybe our

286

wounds work for us. Maybe the suffering gives us a better appreciation. You learn to fight for what others just take for granted. You love me, Matt. You never really believed I was having an affair. It's why you kept digging for that proof – because despite what I'm telling you here, you and you alone really know me. You're the only one. And yes, I want to move out here and raise a family with you. That's all I want.'

Matt opened his mouth, but no words came out.

'It's okay,' she said with a small smile. 'It's a lot to take in.'

'It's not that. It's just . . .' He couldn't express it. The emotions were still swirling. He needed to let them settle. 'So what went wrong?' he asked. 'After all these years, how did they find you?'

'They didn't find me,' she said. 'I found them.'

Matt was about to ask a follow-up question when another set of car headlights began to skitter across the wall. They slowed a beat too long. Matt raised his hand to quiet her for a moment. They both listened. The sound of an idling engine was faint, but it was there. No mistake.

Their eyes met. Matt moved toward the window and peeked out.

The car was parked across the street. The headlights went off. A few seconds later, so did the car engine. Matt recognized the car right away. He had, in fact, been in that car just a few hours earlier.

It belonged to Lance Banner.

40

Loren burst back into the interrogation room.

Cingle was checking out her own nails. 'Lawyer's not here yet.'

Loren just stared at her for a moment. She wondered what it must be like to look like Cingle Shaker, to have men fawn over you, to know you can pretty much do what you want with them. Loren's mother had a bit of that, but when a woman looked like Cingle Shaker, what must that be like? Would it be a good thing or bad? Would you start to rely on those assets to the detriment of your others? Loren didn't think that was the case with Cingle, but that just made her more of a threat.

'Guess what we found on your office computer?' Loren asked.

Cingle blinked. But it was enough. She knew. Loren took out the photograph of Charles Talley. She also took out a few choice stills from the video. She put them on the table in front of Cingle. Cingle barely glanced at them.

'I'm not talking,' Cingle said.

'Would you nod?'

'What?'

'I'll start talking. You can nod along if you like. Because I think it's all pretty obvious now.' Loren sat down, folded her hands, and put them on the table. 'Our lab guys said these photographs came from a camera phone. So here is how we figured it played out. Charles Talley was a bit of a sicko. We know that. He has a criminal history rather rich in violence and perversion. Anyway, he meets up with Olivia Hunter. I don't know how yet. Maybe you'll tell us when your lawyer arrives. Doesn't matter. Either way, for whatever sick reasons, he gets off on sending a photograph and video to our mutual bud Matt Hunter. Matt brings the pictures to you. You, because you're good at what you do, find out that the guy in the pictures is Charles Talley and that he is currently staying at the Howard Johnson's by Newark Airport. Or maybe you figure out that Olivia Hunter is staying there. I don't know which.'

Cingle said, 'That's not right.'

'But it's close. I don't know the details, and I don't really care why or how Hunter came to you. What is clear is that he did. That he gave you the picture and the video. That you found Charles Talley. That you both drove to confront him at the hotel. That Talley and Hunter got into a fight. That Hunter ended up injured and that Talley ended up dead.'

Cingle looked away.

'You have something to add?' Loren asked.

Loren's cell phone rang again. She pulled it out, flipped it open, and said, 'Hello.'

'It's your friendly neighborhood Lance.'

'What's up?'

'Guess where I am.'

'In front of Marsha Hunter's house?'

'Bingo. Now guess whose car is parked in her driveway.'

Loren straightened up. 'You call for backup?'

'They're on their way.'

She snapped the phone closed. Cingle's eyes were on her.

'That about Matt?'

Loren nodded. 'We're about to arrest him.'

'He's going to freak.'

Loren shrugged, waited.

Cingle bit down on a fingernail. 'You got it wrong.'

'How's that?'

'You think Charles Talley sent those pictures to Matt.'

'He didn't?'

Cingle shook her head very slowly.

'Then who did?'

'Good question.'

Loren sat back. She thought about the photograph, the one of Charles Talley. He had his hand up, almost as if he were embarrassed to have the picture taken. He hadn't shot that picture of himself.

'Doesn't matter. We'll have Matt in custody in a few minutes.'

Cingle stood. She began to pace. She folded her arms. 'Maybe,' she started again, 'the pictures are a big setup.'

'What?'

'Come on, Loren. Use your head here. Don't you think this is all a little too neat?'

'Most murder cases are.'

'Bull.'

'You find a dead man, you check his love life. You find a dead woman, you check her boyfriend or husband. It's usually just that simple.'

'Except Charles Talley wasn't Olivia Hunter's boyfriend.'

'And you figured that out how?'

'I didn't figure it out. Matt did.'

'I'm still waiting for the how.'

'Because the pictures are fakes.'

Loren opened her mouth, closed it, decided to wait her out.

'That's why Matt came to my office tonight. He wanted to blow up the pictures. He realized that they weren't what they appeared to be. He figured it out when it started to rain.'

Loren leaned back and spread her hands. 'You better explain from the beginning.'

Cingle grabbed the photograph of Charles Talley. 'Okay, see the window here, the way the sun shines through it . . . ?'

41

Lance Banner's car stayed parked across the street from Marsha's house.

'You know him?' Olivia asked Matt.

'Yes. We went to school together. He's a cop here in town.'

'He's here to ask about the assault?'

Matt did not reply. That made sense, he guessed. What with Cingle's arrest, the police probably wanted to file a full report. Or maybe Matt's name, as a victim or a witness, had gone out over a police radio and Lance had seen it. Maybe this was simply more harassment.

Either way, it really wasn't a big deal. If Lance came to the door, Matt would send him away. That was his right. They couldn't arrest a victim for not filing a timely report.

'Matt?'

He turned toward Olivia. 'You were saying that they didn't find you. That you found them.'

'Yes.'

'I'm not sure I follow.'

'That's because this is the most difficult part,' Olivia said.

He thought – no, hoped – that she was joking. He was trying to hold on, trying to compartmentalize, rationalize, or just plain block.

'I told a lot of lies,' she said. 'But this last one is the worst.'

Matt stayed by the window.

'I became Olivia Hunter. I told you that already. Candace Potter was dead to me. Except . . . except there was one part of her I could never quite give up.'

She stopped.

'What is it?' Matt asked in a soft voice.

'When I was fifteen I got pregnant.'

He closed his eyes.

'I was so scared, I hid it until it was too late. When my water broke, my foster mother brought me to a doctor's office. They had me sign a bunch of papers. There was a payment made, I don't know how much. I never saw the money. The doctor put me under. I had the baby. When I woke up . . .'

Her voice tailed off. She sort of shrugged it away and said: 'I never even knew if it was a boy or a girl.'

Matt kept his eyes on Lance's car. He felt something at his core rip away. 'What about the father?'

'He ran off when he heard I was pregnant. Broke my heart. He got killed in a car crash a couple of years later.'

'And you never knew what happened to the baby?'

'Never. Not a word. And in many ways I was okay with that. Even if I wanted to interfere in her life, I couldn't – not with my predicament. But that doesn't mean I didn't care. Or wonder what happened to her.'

There was a moment of silence. Matt turned and faced his wife.

'You said "her."'

'What?'

'Just now. First you said you didn't know if it was a boy or girl. Then you said you didn't want to interfere in *her* life and that you wondered what happened to *her*.'

Olivia said nothing.

'How long have you known you had a girl?'

'Just a few days.'

'How did you find out?'

Olivia took out another sheet of paper. 'Do you know anything about online adoption support groups?'

'No, not really.'

'There are these boards where adoptive kids can post looking for their biological parents and vice versa. I always checked. Just out of curiosity. I never thought I'd find anything. Candace Potter was long dead. Even if her child searched for her biological mother, she'd learn that and give up. Besides, I couldn't say anything anyway. I had my pact. Finding me could only bring my child harm.'

'But you checked the boards anyway?'

'Yes.'

'How often?'

'Does that matter, Matt?'

'I guess not.'

'You don't understand why I did it?'

'No, I do,' he said, though he was not sure if that was the truth. 'So what happened?'

Olivia handed him the sheet of paper. 'I found this post.'

The paper was wrinkled and had clearly been opened and closed many times. The date on the top was from four weeks ago. It read:

This is an urgent message and must be kept in strict confidence. Our daughter was adopted eighteen years ago at the office of Dr. Eric Tequesta in Meridian, Idaho, on February 12th. The birth mother's name is Candace Potter, who is deceased. We have no information on the father.

Our daughter is very sick. She desperately needs

a kidney donation from a blood relative. We are
searching for any blood relatives who might be a
match. Please, if you are a blood relative of the late
Candace Potter, please contact us at . . .

Matt kept reading and rereading the post.

'I had to do something,' Olivia said.

He nodded numbly.

'I e-mailed the parents. At first I just pretended to be
an old friend of Candace Potter's, but they wouldn't release any information to me. I didn't know what to do.
So I wrote again and said I was indeed a blood relative.
And then it all took a weird turn.'

'How?'

'I think . . . I don't know . . . suddenly the parents got
cagey. So we agreed to meet in person. We set up a time
and place.'

'In Newark?'

'Yes. They even booked the room for me. I had to
check in and wait for them to contact me. I did. Some
man finally called and told me to go to Room 508. When
I got there, the man said he needed to search my bag.
That's when he took the phone out, I guess. Then he told
me to change in the bathroom and put on a wig and a
dress. I didn't get why, but he said we were going someplace and he didn't want anyone recognizing either one
of us. I was too afraid not to listen. He put on a wig too,
a black one. When I came out he told me to sit on the
bed. He walked toward me, just like you saw. When he
got to the bed, he stopped and said he knew who I was.
If I wanted to save my daughter's life, I'd have to trans-
fer money to his account. I should get it ready.'

'Did you?'

'Yes.'

'How much?'

'Fifty thousand dollars.'

He nodded, feigning calm. All the money they had. 'So then what?'

'He told me he'd need more. Another fifty thousand. I told him I didn't have that kind of money. We argued. I finally said he'd get more money when I saw my daughter.'

Matt looked off.

'What?' she asked.

'Weren't you starting to wonder?'

'About?'

'If this was all a con of some sort.'

'Of course,' Olivia said. 'I read about these con men who'd pretend to find information on MIAs in Vietnam. They'd get the family to give them money to continue the search. The families wanted it to be true so badly that they couldn't see it was all a ruse.'

'So?'

'Candace Potter was dead,' she said. 'Why would someone try to con money from a dead woman?'

'Maybe someone figured out you were alive.'

'How?'

'I don't know. Emma Lemay might have said something.'

'Suppose she did. Then what? Nobody knew, Matt. The only person in Vegas I told was my friend Kimmy, but even she didn't know all that information – the date of birth, the town in Idaho, the name of the doctor. I didn't even remember the doctor's name until I saw it in that post. The only people who would know all that were my daughter or her adoptive parents. And even if it was some sort of scam, what with the wig and all, I had to follow it up. I mean, somehow my daughter had to be involved. Don't you see that?'

'I do,' he said. He also saw that her logic was somewhat flawed, but now was not the time to point that out. 'So now what?'

'I insisted on seeing my daughter. So he set up a meet. That's when I'm supposed to bring the rest of the money.'

'When?'

'Tomorrow at midnight.'

'Where?'

'In Reno.'

'Nevada?'

'Yes.'

Again Nevada. 'Do you know a man named Max Darrow?'

She said nothing.

'Olivia?'

'He was the man in the black wig. The one I met with. I knew him back in Vegas too. He used to hang at the club.'

Matt was not sure what to make of that. 'Where in Reno?'

'The address is 488 Center Lane Drive. I have a plane ticket. Darrow said I shouldn't tell anyone. If I'm not there . . . I don't know, Matt. They said they would hurt her.'

'Hurt your daughter?'

Olivia nodded. The tears were back in her eyes. 'I don't know what's going on. I don't know if she's sick or if they kidnapped her or hell, if she's somehow in on it. But she's real and she's alive and I have to go to her.'

Matt tried to take it in, but it wasn't happening. His cell phone rang. Matt automatically reached to snap it off, but then he thought better of it. At this hour it was probably Cingle. She could be in trouble, need his help. He checked the caller ID. Private number. Could be the police station.

'Hello?'

'Matt?'

He frowned. It sounded like Midlife. 'Ike, is that you?'

'Matt, I just got off the phone with Cingle.'

'What?'

'I'm on the way to the county prosecutor's office now,' Midlife said. 'They want to interrogate her.'

'She called you?'

'Yeah, I guess, but I think that had more to do with you.'

'What are you talking about?'

'She wanted to warn you.'

'About what?'

'I wrote it down, hold on. Okay, first off, you asked her about a man named Max Darrow? He's been murdered. They found him shot dead in Newark.'

Matt looked at Olivia. She said, 'What is it?'

Midlife was still talking. 'But worse, Charles Talley is dead. They found his body at the Howard Johnson's. They also found a set of bloody brass knuckles. They're running DNA tests on them now. And within the hour, they'll have the photographs off your cell phone.'

Matt said nothing.

'Do you understand what I'm telling you, Matt?'

He did. It didn't take long. They'd put it together like this: Matt, an ex-con who'd already served time for killing a man in a fight, gets these mocking photographs on his cell phone. His wife was clearly shacking up with Charles Talley. Matt used a private eye to find out where they were. He charged into the hotel late at night. There was a fight. There'd be at least one witness – the guy at the front desk. Probably a security video. They'd have physical evidence too. His DNA is probably all over the dead man.

There would be holes in their case. Matt could show them the gray window and explain about the drought. He also didn't know what time Talley had been killed, but if Matt was lucky, the murder took place when he was in the ambulance or at the hospital. Or maybe he'd have an alibi in the taxi driver. Or his wife.

Like that would hold up.

'Matt?'

'What is it?'

'The police are probably searching for you now.'

He glanced out the window. A police car pulled up next to Lance's. 'I think they already found me.'

'You want me to arrange a peaceful surrender?'

A peaceful surrender. Trust the authorities to straighten it out. Do the law-abiding thing.

That worked so well before, didn't it?

Fool me once, shame on me. Fool me twice . . .

And suppose he did come clean. Then what? They'd have to tell everything, including Olivia's past. Forget about the fact that Matt swore, *swore,* he'd never let himself go back to prison. Olivia had indeed committed a crime. She'd, at best, helped dispose of a dead body. Not to mention the fact that Max Darrow, who had also been murdered, had been blackmailing her. How would that look?

'Ike?'

'Yes.'

'If they know we communicated, you could get nailed for aiding and abetting.'

'Nah, Matt, I really can't. I'm your attorney. I'm giving you the facts and encouraging you to surrender. But what you do . . . well, I can't control that. I can only be shocked and outraged. You see?'

He did. He looked out the window again. Another

squad car pulled up. He thought about being back in prison. In the window reflection, he saw Stephen Mc-Grath's ghost. Stephen winked at him. Matt felt the tightness in his chest.

'Thanks, Ike.'

'Good luck, pal.'

Midlife hung up the phone. Matt turned to Olivia. 'What is it?' she asked.

'We have to get out of here.'

42

Lance Banner approached Marsha Hunter's front door.

Two tired uniforms were with him now. Both men had facial stubble nestled in that cusp between needing a shave and trendy, the end of an uneventful Livingston night shift. They were young guys, fairly new on the force. They walked in silence. He could hear them breathing hard. Both men had put on weight recently. Lance was not sure why that happened, why the new recruits always gained weight during their first year with the force, but he'd be hard-pressed to find examples where that didn't happen.

Lance was conflicted here. He was having second thoughts about his run-in with Matt yesterday. Whatever his past crime, whatever he may have become, Hunter had not deserved being subject to Banner's clumsy and stupid harassment. And it had been stupid, no question about it, intimidating a purported interloper like some redneck sheriff in a bad movie.

Last night Matt Hunter had scoffed at Lance's seemingly Pollyanna-ish attempt to keep evil out of his fair town. But Matt got it wrong. Lance wasn't naïve. He understood that there was no protective force field around the fertile suburban sprawl. That was the point. You work hard to make a life for yourself. You meet up with like-minded people and build a great community. Then you fight to keep it. You see a potential problem, you don't let it fester. You remove it. You're proactive.

That was what he'd been doing with Matt Hunter. That was what men like Lance Banner did for their hometowns. They were the soldiers, the front line, the few who took night duty so that the others, including Lance's own family, could sleep soundly.

So when his fellow cops started talking about doing something, when Lance's own wife, Wendy, who had gone to school with Matt Hunter's younger sister and thought she was a 'Queen Bitch,' started getting on his case about a convicted killer moving into their neighborhood, when one of the town councilmen had offered up the sternest of suburban worries – 'Lance, do you realize what it'll do to property values?' – he had acted.

And now he wasn't sure if he regretted it or not.

He thought about his conversation with Loren Muse yesterday. She'd asked him about young Matt Hunter. Had Lance seen any early signs of psychosis there? The answer was a pretty firm no. Hunter had been soft. Lance remembered him crying at a Little League game when he dropped a fly ball. His father had comforted him while Lance marveled at what a big baby the kid was. But – and this might seem the opposite of Loren's study on early signs of trouble – men can indeed change. It was not all decided by age five or whatever Loren had told him.

The catch was, the change was always, *always,* for the worse.

If you discover a young psychotic, he will never turn himself around and become productive. Never. But you can find plenty of guys, nice guys who grew up with the right values, quality guys who respected the law and loved thy neighbor, gentle guys who found violence abhorrent and wanted to stay on the straight and narrow – you find lots of guys like this who end up doing terrible things.

Who knew why? Sometimes it was, as in Hunter's case, just a question of bad luck, but then again it's all about luck, isn't it? Your upbringing, your genes, your life experience, conditions, whatever – they're all a crapshoot. Matt Hunter had been in the wrong place at the wrong time. That didn't matter anymore. You could see it in his eyes. You could see it in the way Hunter walked, the early gray in his hair, the way he blinked, the tightness in his smile.

Bad follows some people. It hooks into them and never lets them go.

And simple as it sounded, you don't want those people around you.

Lance knocked on Marsha Hunter's door. The two uniforms stood behind him in vee formation. The sun had begun its ascent. They listened for a sound.

Nothing.

He saw the doorbell. Marsha Hunter, he knew, had two young children. If Matt wasn't here, he'd feel bad about waking them, but that couldn't be helped. He pressed the bell and heard the chime.

Still nothing.

Just for the heck of it, Lance tried the door, hoping it might be unlocked. It wasn't.

The officer on Lance's right started shifting his feet. 'Kick it in?'

'Not yet. We don't even know if he's here.'

He rang the bell again, keeping his finger pressed against it until it rang a third time too.

The other cop said, 'Detective?'

'Give it a few more seconds,' he said.

As if on cue, the foyer light snapped on. Lance tried to look through the pebble glass, but the view was too distorted. He kept his face pressed against it searching for movement.

'Who is it?'

The female voice was tentative – understandable under the circumstances.

'It's Detective Lance Banner, Livingston Police. Could you open the door, please?'

'Who?'

'Detective Lance Banner, Livingston Police. Please open the door.'

'Just a minute.'

They waited. Lance kept peering through the pebble glass. He could make out a hazy figure coming down the stairs now. Marsha Hunter, he assumed. Her steps were as tentative as her voice. He heard a bolt slide and a chain rattle and then the door was opened.

Marsha Hunter had a bathrobe tied tightly around her waist. The robe was old and terrycloth. It looked like it belonged to a man. Lance wondered for a brief second if it had been her late husband's. Her hair was mussed. She wore no makeup, of course, and while Lance had always considered her an attractive woman, she could have used the touches.

She looked at Lance, then at the two officers at his wing, then back to Lance. 'What do you want at this hour?'

'We're looking for Matt Hunter.'

Her eyes narrowed. 'I know you.'

Lance said nothing.

'You coached my son last year in rec soccer. You have a boy Paul's age.'

'Yes, ma'am.'

'Not ma'am,' she said, her voice sharp. 'My name is Marsha Hunter.'

'Yes, I know.'

'We're your neighbors, for crying out loud.' Marsha

again took in the uniformed men before returning her gaze to Lance. 'You know I live alone with two young boys,' she said, 'yet you wake us up like storm troopers?'

'We really need to talk to Matt Hunter.'

'Mommy?'

Lance recognized the boy coming down the stairs. Marsha gave Lance a baleful eye before turning to her son. 'Go to bed, Ethan.'

'But, Mom . . .'

'I'll be up in a moment. Go back to bed.' She turned back to Lance. 'I'm surprised you don't know.'

'Don't know what?'

'Matt doesn't live here,' she said. 'He lives in Irvington.'

'His car is in your driveway.'

'So?'

'So is he here?'

'What's going on?'

Another woman was at the top of the stairs.

'Who are you?' Lance asked.

'My name is Olivia Hunter.'

'Olivia Hunter as in Mrs. Matt Hunter?'

'Excuse me?'

Marsha looked back at her sister-in-law. 'He was just asking why your car is in the driveway.'

'At this hour?' Olivia Hunter said. 'Why would you want to know that?'

'They're looking for Matt.'

Lance Banner said, 'Do you know where your husband is, Mrs. Hunter?'

Olivia Hunter started to move down the stairs. Her steps, too, were deliberate. Maybe that was the tip-off. Or maybe it was her clothes. She was, after all, wearing clothes. Regular clothes. Jeans and a sweatshirt. Not nightclothes. No robe, no pajamas. At this hour.

That didn't make sense.

When Lance glanced back at Marsha Hunter, he saw it. A small tell on her face. Damn, how could he have been so stupid? The turning on the light, the walking down the stairs, the slow walk right now . . . it had all taken too long.

He spun to the uniformed cops. 'Check around back. Hurry.'

'Wait,' Olivia shouted too loudly. 'Why are your men going to the backyard?'

The cops started running – one toward the right, one to the left. Lance looked at Marsha. She stared back at him defiantly.

That was when they heard a woman's scream.

'What's going on?' Olivia asked.

'That was Midlife,' Matt said. 'Charles Talley and Max Darrow are both dead.'

'Oh, my God.'

'And unless I'm mistaken,' he continued, gesturing toward the window, 'these guys are here to arrest me for their murders.'

Olivia closed her eyes, tried to ride it out. 'What do you want to do?'

'I have to get out of here.'

'You mean, *we* have to get out of here.'

'No.'

'I'm going with you, Matt.'

'You're not the one they want. They have nothing on you. At worst they think you cheated on your husband. You just refuse to answer any questions. They can't hold you.'

'So you're just going to run?'

'I have no choice.'

'Where will you go?'

'I'll figure that out. But we can't communicate. They'll be watching the house, tapping the phone.'

'We need a plan here, Matt.'

'How about this,' he said. 'We meet up in Reno.'

'What?'

'Tomorrow at midnight. The address you said – 488 Center Lane Drive.'

'You still think there's still a chance that my daughter . . . .'

'I doubt it,' Matt said. 'But I also doubt Darrow and Talley were doing this on their own.'

Olivia hesitated.

'What?'

'How are you going to get across the country that fast?'

'I don't know. If I can't make it, we'll figure out something later. Look, it's not a great plan, but we don't have time for anything better.'

Olivia took a step forward. He felt it again in his chest, the gentle thrum. She had never looked so beautiful or vulnerable. 'Do we have time for you to say you still love me?'

'I do love you. More than ever.'

'Just like that?'

'Just like that,' he said.

'Even after . . . ?'

'Even after.'

She shook her head. 'You're too good for me.'

'Yeah, I'm a prince.'

Olivia laughed through the sob. He put his arms around her.

'We'll get into this later, but right now we need to find your daughter.'

Something she had said – about this life being worth fighting over. It resonated in him, even more than the revelations. He would fight. He would fight for both of them.

Olivia nodded, wiped her tears. 'Here. I only have twenty dollars.'

He took it. They risked a glance out the window. Lance Banner was approaching the front door, flanked by two cops. Olivia moved in front of him as if readying to take a bullet.

'You sneak out back,' Olivia said. 'I'll wake up Marsha, tell her what's going on. We'll try to stall them.'

'I love you,' he said.

She gave him the crooked smile. 'Good to hear.' They kissed hard and quick. 'Don't let anything happen to you,' she said.

'I won't.'

He headed downstairs and started toward the back door. Olivia was already in Marsha's room. It wasn't right to drag Marsha into this, but what choice did they have? From the kitchen he could see another police car pull up to the front.

There was a knock on the door.

No time. Matt had something of a plan. They were not far from the East Orange Water Reservation, which was basically a forest. Matt had gone through it count-less times as a child. Once inside he'd be difficult to find. He'd be able to work his way toward Short Hills Road and from there, well, suffice to say that he needed out-side help.

He knew where to go.

His hand was on the back-door knob. Matt heard Lance Banner ring the bell. He turned the knob and pushed open the door.

Someone was standing right there, already in the doorway. He nearly jumped out of his skin.

'Matt?'

It was Kyra.

'Matt, what are –?'

He signaled her to stay quiet and beckoned her inside.

'What's going on?' Kyra whispered.

'What are you doing awake?'

'I – ' She shrugged. 'I saw police cars. What's going on?'

'It's a long story.'

'That investigator who came by today. She asked me about you.'

'I know.'

They both heard Marsha shout: 'Just a minute.'

Kyra's eyes widened. 'You're trying to run away?'

'It's a long story.'

Her eyes met his. He wondered what Kyra was going to do here. He didn't want to involve her. If she screamed, he would understand. She was just a kid. She had no role in any of this, no real reason to trust him.

'Go,' Kyra whispered.

He didn't wait or say thank you. He started outside. Kyra followed, veering the other way back toward her room above the garage. Matt saw the swing set he'd put up with Bernie a lifetime ago. It'd been ridiculously hot the day they assembled it. They'd both had their shirts off. Marsha had waited on the porch with beers. Bernie had wanted to put in one of those ziplines, but Marsha had nixed that, claiming, correctly in Matt's view, that they were dangerous.

What you remember.

The yard was too open – there were no trees, no bushes, no rocks. Bernie had cleared out a lot of the brush with the anticipation of putting in a swimming pool – another dream, albeit a small one, that died with him. There were white bases laid out in the shape of a baseball diamond and two small soccer goals. He started to cross the yard. Kyra had gone back inside the garage.

Matt heard a commotion.

'Wait!' The voice belonged to Olivia. She was intentionally shouting so that he would hear. 'Why are your men going to the backyard?'

There was no time to hesitate. He was out in the open. Make a mad run for it? There was little choice. He sprinted into the neighbor's yard. Matt avoided the flower beds, which were a strange thing to worry about at a time like this, but he did it anyway. He risked a glance behind him.

A policeman had made the turn into the backyard.

Damn.

He hadn't been spotted. Not yet. He searched for a place to hide. The neighbors had a toolshed. Matt leaped behind it. He pressed his back against it, like he'd seen done in the movies. A pointless move. He checked his waistband.

The gun was there.

Matt risked a peek.

The cop was staring directly at him.

Or at least he appeared to be. Matt quickly pulled back. Had the cop seen him? Hard to say. He waited for someone to yell, 'Hey, he's right there, right in the next yard behind that toolshed!'

Nothing happened.

He wanted to take another look.

He couldn't risk it.

He stayed and waited.

Then he heard a voice – another cop, he guessed: 'Sam, you see some –?'

The voice cut out like a radio turned off.

Matt held his breath. He strained his ears. Footsteps? Was he hearing footsteps? He couldn't say for sure. He debated sneaking another glance. If they were on their way toward him, what harm would it do? Either way he'd be nailed.

It was too quiet back here.

If the cops were actively searching for him, they'd be calling out to one another. If they were being quiet, quiet like this, there was only one explanation.

He'd been spotted. They were sneaking up on him.

Matt listened again.

Something jangled. Like something on a policeman's belt.

No question now – they were coming for him. His heart picked up pace. He could feel it hammering in his chest. Caught. Again. He pictured what would happen: the rough handling, the handcuffs, the back of the cruiser . . .

Jail.

Fear gripped him. They were coming. They'd take him away and throw him back into that pit. They'd never listen. They'd lock him up. He was an ex-con. Another man was dead after a fight with Matt Hunter. Forget everything else. This one would be a slam dunk.

And what would happen to Olivia if he was caught?

He couldn't even explain the truth, even if he wanted to, because then she would end up in jail. And if there was one thing that terrified him more than his own incarceration . . .

Matt wasn't sure how it happened, but suddenly the Mauser M2 was in his hand.

Calm down, he told himself. We're not shooting anybody here.

But he could still use the threat, couldn't he? Except that there were several cops here, four or five at a minimum, more probably on the way. They'd draw their weapons too. Then what? Were Paul and Ethan awake?

He slid to the back part of the toolshed. He risked a peek out from the back.

Two cops were no more than six feet away from him.

He had been spotted. No way around that. They were headed right toward him.

There was no escape.

Matt gripped the gun and got ready to sprint when his gaze was snagged by something in Marsha's backyard.

It was Kyra.

She must have been watching the whole time. She was standing near her door at the garage. Their eyes met. Matt saw something that looked like a small smile on her face. He almost shook his head no, but he didn't.

Kyra screamed.

The scream shattered the air and rang in the ears. The two cops turned toward her – and away from him. She screamed again. The cops sprinted toward her.

'What's wrong?' one of the cops yelled.

Matt did not hesitate now. He used Kyra's diversion and sprinted in the opposite direction, toward the woods. She screamed again. Matt never looked back, not until he was deep in the trees.

43

Sitting with her feet on her desk, Loren Muse decided to call Max Darrow's widow.

It was three or four in the morning in Nevada – Loren could never remember if Nevada was two hours or three behind – but she suspected that a woman whose husband gets murdered probably sleeps uneasily.

She dialed the number. It went into voice mail. A man's voice said, 'Max and Gertie can't answer your call right now. We're probably out fishing. Leave a message, okay?'

The voice from the grave made her pause. Max Darrow, retired cop, was a human being. Simple, but you forget that sometimes. You get caught up in the details, in the puzzle pieces. A life has been lost here. Gertie will have to change that message. She and Max won't be going fishing anymore. Sounded like a small thing but it was a life, a struggle, a world now shattered.

Loren left a message with her phone number and hung up.

'Hey, what are you working on?'

It was Adam Yates, the FBI chief from Vegas. He'd driven to the county prosecutor's office with her after their meeting with Joan Thurston. Loren looked up at him. 'Just a few strange developments.'

'Such as?'

She told him about her conversation with Cingle Shaker. Yates grabbed a chair from a nearby desk. He sat, never taking his eyes off hers. He was one of those guys. Big on eye contact.

When she finished, Yates frowned. 'I just can't see how this Hunter guy fits in.'

'He should be in custody soon. Maybe we'll learn something then.'

Yates nodded, kept up with the eye contact.

Loren said, 'What?'

'This case,' Yates said. His voice was soft now. 'It means a great deal to me.'

'Any reason in particular?'

'Do you have children?' he asked.

'No.'

'Married?'

'No.'

'You gay?'

'Jesus, Yates.'

He held up his hand. 'That was stupid, sorry.'

'Why all the questions?'

'You don't have kids. I don't think you'll understand.'

'Are you for real?'

Yates held up the hand again. 'I don't mean that the way it sounded. I'm sure you're a good person and all.'

'Gee, thanks.'

'It's just that . . . when you have kids, it just changes things.'

'Do me a favor, Yates. Please don't give me that having-children-alters-you spiel. I listen to that crap enough from my painfully few friends.'

'It's not that.' He paused. 'Actually I think single people make better cops. You can focus.'

'Speaking of which . . .' She picked up some papers and pretended to be busy.

'Let me ask you something, Muse.'

She waited.

'When you wake up,' Yates went on, 'who's the first person you think about?'

'Excuse me?'

'Okay, it's morning. You open your eyes. You start getting out of bed. Who is the first person you think about?'

'Why don't you tell me?'

'Well, not to be insulting, but the answer is you, right? There's nothing wrong with that. You think about you. That's normal. All single people do that. You wake up and wonder what you're going to do that day. Oh, sure, you might take care of an elderly parent or something. But here's the thing. When you have a child, you are never number one again. Someone is more important than you. It changes your worldview. It has to. You think you know about protect and serve. But when you have a family . . .'

'Is there a point to this?'

Adam Yates finally stopped with the eye contact. 'I have a son. His name is Sam. He's fourteen now. When he was three years old, he got meningitis. We thought he might die. He was in the hospital in this great big bed. It was too big for him, you know? It looked like it would swallow him up. And me, I just sat next to him and watched him get worse.'

He gulped a breath and swallowed hard. Loren let him take his time.

'After a couple of hours, I picked Sam up and held him in my arms. I didn't sleep. I didn't put him down. I just kept holding him. My wife says it was three full days. I don't know. I just knew that if I kept Sam in my arms, if I kept watching him, then death couldn't take him away from me.'

Yates seemed to drift off.

315

Loren spoke softly. 'I still don't see the point.'

'Well, here it is,' he said, his voice back to normal. He locked eyes again. His pupils were pinpricks. 'They threatened my family.'

Yates put his hand to his face, then back down as if he wasn't sure where he wanted to put it. 'When I first started this case,' he went on, 'they set their sights on my wife and kids. So you understand.'

She opened her mouth, said nothing.

The phone on the desk rang. Loren picked it up.

Lance Banner said, 'We lost Matt.'

'What?'

'That kid who lives with them. Kyra, whatever. She started screaming and. . . . Anyway, his wife is here. She says that she was driving the car, not him, and that she doesn't know where he is.'

'That's crap.'

'I know it.'

'Bring her in.'

'She refuses to come.'

'Excuse me?'

'We have nothing on her.'

'She's a material witness in a murder investigation.'

'She's lawyering up. She says we either have to arrest her or let her go.'

Her cell phone chirped. Loren checked the caller ID. The call was originating from Max Darrow's house.

'I'll get back to you.' She hung up the office phone and clicked on the mobile. 'Investigator Muse.'

'This is Gertie Darrow. You left me a message?'

Loren could hear the tears in her voice. 'I'm sorry about your loss.'

'Thank you.'

'I don't mean to disturb you at such a terrible time, but

I really need to ask you a few questions.'

'I understand.'

'Thank you,' Loren said. She grabbed a pen. 'Do you know why your husband was in Newark, Mrs. Darrow?'

'No.' She said it as though it was the most painful word she ever uttered. 'He told me he was visiting a friend in Florida. A fishing trip, he said.'

'I see. He was retired, yes?'

'That's right.'

'Could you tell me if he was working on anything?'

'I don't understand. What does this have to do with his murder?'

'This is just routine –'

'Please, Investigator Muse,' she interrupted, her voice up a notch. 'My husband was a police officer, remember? You're not calling me at this hour for routine questions.'

Loren said, 'I'm trying to find a motive.'

'A motive?'

'Yes.'

'But . . .' And then she quieted down. 'The other officer. The one who called before. Investigator Wine.'

'Yes. He works in my office.'

'He told me that Max was in a car, that' – there was a choke in the voice but she kept it together – 'that he had his pants down.'

Loren closed her eyes. So Wine had already told her. She understood, she guessed. In today's society of openness, you couldn't even spare a widow anymore. 'Mrs. Darrow?'

'What?'

'I think that was a setup. I don't think there was any prostitute. I think your husband was murdered for some other reason. And I think it might involve an old case of his. So I'm asking you: Was he working on anything?'

There was a brief silence. Then: 'That girl.'

'What?'

'I knew it. I just knew it.'

'I'm sorry, Mrs. Darrow. I'm not sure what you mean.'

'Max never talked about business. He never brought it home. And he was retired. She had no reason to come around.'

'Who?'

'I don't know her name. She was a young thing. Maybe twenty.'

'What did she want?'

'I told you. I don't know. But Max . . . after she left, he was like a madman. He started going through old files.'

'Do you know what the files referred to?'

'No.' Then: 'Do you really think this could have something to do with Max's murder?'

'Yes, ma'am. I think it might have everything to do with it. Does the name Clyde Rangor mean anything to you?'

'No, I'm sorry.'

'How about Emma Lemay or Charles Talley?'

'No.'

'Candace Potter?'

Silence.

'Mrs. Darrow?'

'I saw that name.'

'Where?'

'On his desk. There was a file. Must have been a month ago. I just saw the word 'Potter.' I remember because that was the name of the bad guy in *It's a Wonderful Life*. Remember? Mr. Potter?'

'Do you know where the file is now?'

'I'll go through the cabinets, Investigator Muse. If it's still here, I'll find it for you and call back.'

44

Matt learned how to steal cars in prison. Or at least, that was what he thought.

There was a guy named Saul two cells over who had a fetish for joyriding with stolen cars. He was about as decent a guy as you'd meet in prison. He had his demons – his seemingly more innocuous than most – but the demons did him in. He got arrested for stealing a car when he was seventeen, then again when he was nineteen. On his third go-round, Saul lost control of the vehicle and killed someone. He'd already had two priors so he got a life sentence.

'All that stuff you see on TV?' Saul had told him. 'That's all crap, unless you want a specific make. Otherwise, you don't jam the lock. You don't use tools. And you don't hot-wire. That only works on old cars anyway. And with all the alarms, you try most of that stuff, the car will lock down on you.'

'So what do you do?' Matt asked.

'You use a person's car keys. You open the door like a human being. You drive away.'

Matt made a face. 'Just like that?'

'No, not just like that. What you do is, you go to a crowded parking lot. Malls work great, though you gotta look out for the rent-a-cops circling around. Those big superstores are even better. You find an area where people won't be watching you much. You just keep walking and running your hand over a front tire or under the bumper. People leave their keys there. They also keep them in those cute magnets under the driver's-side fender. Not everyone. But hey, at least one in fifty. You do that enough, you'll find a key. *Voilà*.'

Matt wondered. His prison info was at least nine years old and perhaps obsolete. He had been on foot for more than an hour – first making his way through the woods and now keeping off main roads. When he reached the corner of Livingston Avenue, he grabbed a bus to the campus of Bergen Community College in Paramus. The ride took about an hour. Matt slept for all of it.

Bergen Community was a commuter school. There were tons of cars driven by carefree coeds. Security was almost nonexistent. Matt began his search. It took almost an hour, but as Saul promised, Matt eventually hit pay dirt in the form of a white Isuzu with a quarter tank of gas. Not bad. The keys had been hidden in one of those magnets above the front tire. Matt got into the car and drove toward Route 17. He didn't know Bergen County all that well. It might be smarter to go north over the Tappan Zee but he chose the route he knew over the George Washington Bridge.

He was on his way to Westport, Connecticut.

When he reached the GWB, he worried that the toll booth operator would recognize him – he even went so far as to rip the bandage off his head and replace it with a New York Rangers cap he found in the backseat – but that didn't happen. He switched on the radio and listened to the news – first, 1010 WINS for twenty-two minutes, then CBS 880. In the movies they always interrupt for a special bulletin when a man is at large. But neither station said anything about him. In fact, there was nothing on any of it – nothing about Max Darrow or Charles Talley or a fleeing suspect.

He needed money. He needed a place to sleep. He needed some meds. The pain had been held in check by the flow of adrenaline. That was ebbing now. He'd only slept about an hour in the past twenty-four, and the preceding night, what with the pictures on his camera phone, hadn't brought him much slumber either.

Matt checked the money. He had thirty-eight bucks. Hardly enough. He couldn't use his ATM or credit cards. The police would be able to track those down. Ditto with getting help from close friends or relatives, not that he had many he could really depend on.

There was, however, one person Matt could go to whom the police would never suspect.

When he got off at the Westport exit, he slowed down. He had never been invited here, but he knew the address. When he first got out of prison, he actually drove past this particular road several times, but he never had the courage to turn onto the block.

Now he took a right and then another and pulled slowly down the quiet, tree-lined street. His pulse started kicking up again. He checked the driveway. Her car was the only one there. He considered using his cell phone, but no, the police would be able to access that too. Maybe he should just knock. He thought about it, but in the end he decided to play it safe. He drove back toward town and spotted a pay phone. He dialed the number.

Sonya McGrath answered on the first ring. 'Hello?'

'It's me,' he said. 'Are you alone?'

'Yes.'

'I need your help.'

'Where are you?'

'I'm about five minutes from your house.'

*

Matt pulled into the McGraths' driveway.

There was a rusted basketball hoop near the garage. The shredded netting had not been replaced in a very long time. The hoop didn't fit in with the surroundings. It was old and unkempt where the rest of the house was so posh, so updated. For a moment Matt stopped and stared at the basketball hoop. Stephen McGrath was there. He was shooting with nice form, his eyes locked on the front rim. Matt could see the backspin on the ball. Stephen was smiling.

'Matt?'

He turned around. Sonya McGrath stood on the front step. She looked over to see where he'd been staring and her face fell.

'Tell me,' Sonya said.

He did – but as he did, he noticed the devastation in her face did not fade. He had seen her take blows like this before. She always came back, if not all the way, then enough. That wasn't happening now. Her face maintained that horrid pallor. It wouldn't change. Matt saw it, but he couldn't stop himself. He kept talking and explaining what he was doing here and somewhere along the line Matt had an almost out-of-body experience where he rose above them and actually heard what he was saying and how it must sound to her. But he still did not stop. He just kept talking while a small voice inside his brain urged him to shut the hell up. But he didn't listen. He'd trudged on, figuring that he'd somehow make it through.

But in the end, when you cut through it all, his words sounded like this: Another fight, another death.

When he finally wound down, Sonya McGrath just watched him for several seconds. Matt could feel himself wither and die under the glare.

'You want me to help you?' she said.

And there it was. So simply stated. He could hear it now, how not only ridiculous it sounded, but how outrageous. How obscene.

He didn't know what to do.

'Clark found out about our meetings,' she said.

He was going to say I'm sorry or something similar, but it didn't feel appropriate. He kept quiet now and waited.

'Clark thinks I'm after comfort. He has a point, I guess, but I don't think that's it. I think I needed closure. I think I needed to forgive you. And I can't.'

'I should go,' he said.

'You should turn yourself in, Matt. If you're innocent, they'll –'

'They'll what?' he said, his tone edgier than he'd wanted. 'I've tried that route already, remember?'

'I do.' Sonya McGrath tilted her head to the side. 'But were you innocent then, Matt?'

He looked back at the basketball hoop. Stephen had the ball in his hand. He stopped mid-shot, turned, and waited for Matt's answer.

'I'm sorry,' Matt said, turning away from them both. 'I have to go.'

45

Loren Muse's cell phone rang. It was Max Darrow's widow calling back.

'I found something,' she said.

'What?'

'It looks like an autopsy file on Candace Potter,' Gertie Darrow said. 'I mean, it is an autopsy. It's signed by the old medical examiner. I remember him. He was a very nice man.'

'What does it say?'

'It says a lot of things. Height, weight. You want me to read it all to you?'

'How about a cause of death?'

'It says something here about strangulation. It also says something about a severe beating and trauma to the head.'

That fit in with what they already had. So what had Max Darrow noticed after all these years? What had sent him to Newark, to Emma Lemay as Sister Mary Rose? 'Mrs. Darrow, do you have a fax machine?'

'There's one in Max's office.'

'Could you fax me the file?'

'Of course.'

Loren gave her the fax number.

'Investigator Muse?'

'Yes.'

'Are you married?'

Loren held back a sigh. First Yates, now Mrs. Darrow. 'No, I'm not.'

'Ever been?'

'No. Why do you ask?'

'I believed the other investigator. Mr. Wine, is it?'

'That's right.'

'What he said about Max being in the car with, well, a woman of questionable morals, as we used to say.'

'Right.'

'I just wanted to let you know.'

'Know what, Mrs. Darrow?'

'See, Max, well, he wasn't always a good husband, you know what I mean?'

'I think so,' Loren said.

'What I'm trying to say is Max had done that in the past. In a car like that. More than once. That's why I was so quick to believe. I thought you should know. Just in case this doesn't pan out.'

'Thank you, Mrs. Darrow.'

'I'll fax it over now.'

She hung up without saying anything more. Loren stood and waited by the fax machine.

Adam Yates came back with two Cokes. He offered her one, but she shook him off. 'Uh, what I said before, about not having kids –'

'Forget it,' Loren said. 'I know what you were trying to get at.'

'Still stupid of me to put it that way.'

'Yeah. Yeah, it was.'

'What's going on here?'

'Max Darrow was looking into Candace Potter's autopsy.'

Yates frowned. 'What does that have to do with this?'

'Not a clue, but I doubt it's a coincidence.'

The phone rang and the fax machines began their mating screech. The first sheet churned out slowly. There was no cover letter. That was good. Loren hated the waste of paper. She grabbed the sheet and started searching for the conclusion. In truth she read very little else in autopsy reports. Weights of livers and hearts might interest some people, but she was only interested in what they meant to her case.

Adam Yates read over her shoulder. It all seemed pretty normal.

'You see anything?' she asked.

'No.'

'Me neither.'

'This could be a dead end.'

'Probably is.'

Another sheet came in. They both started reading it.

Yates pointed midway down the right-hand column. 'What's this over here?'

There was check mark in the middle of the body description.

Loren read it out loud: 'No ovaries, testes hidden, probable AIS.'

'AIS?'

'It stands for Androgen Insensitivity Syndrome,' Loren said. 'I had a friend in college who had it.'

'What's the relevance of that?' Yates asked.

'I'm not sure. AIS women look and feel like typical females and for all practical purposes, they're considered female. They can legally marry and adopt.' She stopped, tried to think it through.

'But?'

'But in short it means that Candace Potter was genetically male. She had testes and XY chromosomes.'

He made a face. 'You mean she was, what, a transsexual?'

'No.'

'Then, what, she was a guy?'

'Genetically, yes. But probably not in any other way. Oftentimes an AIS woman doesn't know she's any different until she reaches puberty and doesn't menstruate. It's not that uncommon. There was a Miss Teen USA a few years back who was AIS. Many believe Queen Elizabeth I and Joan of Arc and a slew of supermodels and actresses have it, but that's really nothing more than speculation. Either way you can lead a perfectly normal life. In fact, if Candace Potter was a prostitute, perverse as this sounds, it may even have benefited her.'

'Benefited her how?'

Loren looked up at him. 'Women with AIS can't get pregnant.'

46

Matt drove away. Sonya McGrath headed back inside. Their relationship, if there had ever been one, was over. It felt odd and yet, despite the honesty and raw emotion, anything built on such misery was bound to cave. It was all too fragile. They were simply two people needing something that neither could ever get.

He wondered if Sonya would call the police. He wondered if it mattered.

God, he'd been stupid to come here.

He was hurting badly. He needed to rest. But there was no time. He'd have to push through. He checked the gas gauge. It was near empty. He stopped at a nearby Shell station and used the rest of his money to fill the tank.

During his ride, he thought about the bombshell Olivia had just dropped on him. At the end of the day, as weird or naïve as this might sound, he wondered what it really changed. He still loved Olivia. He loved the way she frowned when she checked herself in the mirror, that little smile she made when she was thinking of something funny, the way she rolled her eyes when he made a clumsy double entendre, the way she tucked her feet under when she read, the way she took deep, almost cartoon breaths when she was irritated, the way her eyes welled up with tears when they made love, the way his heart pumped a little faster when she laughed, the way he'd catch her studying him when she thought he wouldn't notice, the soft way her eyes closed when she listened to a favorite song on the radio, the way her hand would just take his at any time without hesitation or embarrassment, the way her skin felt, the charge at her touch, the way she'd drape a leg over him on the lazy mornings, the way her chest felt pressed against his back when they slept, the way when she slipped out of bed in the early morning she'd kiss his cheek and make sure the blankets still covered him.

What about any of that was different now?

The truth was not always freeing. Your past was your past. He had not, for example, told her about his stint in prison to illuminate the 'real Matt' or 'take their relationship to the next level' – he told her because she would undoubtedly find out anyway. It didn't mean a thing. If he hadn't told her, wouldn't their relationship be equally strong?

Or was this all a giant rationalization?

He stopped at an ATM near Sonya's house. He had no choice now. He needed money. If she called the police, well, they'd know he'd been in this area anyway. If they traced it down, he'd be long gone by the time they arrived. He didn't want to use the credit card at a gas station. They might get his license plate number that way. As it was, if he could get the money and put distance between himself and this ATM, he figured that he'd be all right.

The ATM had a max of a thousand dollars. He took it.

Then he started thinking of a way to get to Reno.

Loren drove. Adam Yates sat in the passenger seat.

'Explain this to me again,' he said.

'I have a source. A man named Len Friedman. A year ago we found two dead women in a hooker alley, both young, both black, both had their hands cut off so that we couldn't get an ID off fingerprints. But one of the girls had a strange tattoo, a logo from Princeton University, on her inner thigh.'

'Princeton?'

'Yes.'

He shook his head.

'Anyway, we put that in the papers. The only person who came forward was this Len Friedman. He asked if she also had a rose petal tattoo on her right foot. That hadn't been released. So our interest, to put it mildly, was piqued.'

'You figured he was the perp.'

'Sure, why not? But it turns out that both women were strippers – or as Friedman calls them, erotic dancers – at a dump called the Honey Bunny in Newark. Friedman is an expert on all things stripper. It's his hobby. He collects posters, bios, personal information, real names, tattoos, birthmarks, scars, I mean everything. A full database. And not just on the local trade. I assume you've walked the Vegas Strip?'

'Sure.'

'You know how they pass out cards advertising strippers and prostitutes and whatever.'

'Hey, I live there, remember?'

She nodded. 'Well, Len Friedman collects them. Like baseball cards. He gathers information on them. He travels for weeks at a time visiting these places. He writes what some consider academic essays on the subject. He also collects historical material. He has a brassiere belonging to Gypsy Rose Lee. He has stuff that dates back more than a century.'

Yates made a face. 'He must be a lot of fun at parties.'

Loren smiled. 'You have no idea.'

'What's that supposed to mean?'

'You'll see.'

They fell into silence.

Yates said, 'I'm really sorry again. About what I said before.'

She waved him off. 'How many kids do you have anyway?'

'Three.'

'Boys, girls?'

'Two girls, one boy.'

'Ages?'

'My daughters are seventeen and sixteen. Sam is fourteen.'

'Seventeen- and sixteen-year-old girls,' Loren said. 'Yikes.'

Yates smiled. 'You have no idea.'

'You have pictures?'

'I never carry pictures.'

'Oh?'

Yates shifted in his seat. Loren glanced at him out of the corner of her eye. His posture was suddenly rigid. 'About six years ago,' he began, 'I had my wallet stolen. I know, I'm head of an FBI field office and I'm dumb enough to get pickpocketed. Sue me. Anyway, I went nuts. Not because of the money or the credit cards. But all I kept thinking about was, some slimeball has pictures of my kids. My kids. He probably just took the cash and dumped the wallet in the garbage. But suppose he didn't. Suppose he kept the pictures. You know, for his own amusement. Maybe he, I don't know, stared at the pictures longingly. Maybe he even put his fingers on their faces, caressed them.'

Loren frowned. 'Talk about being a lot of fun at parties.'

Yates chuckled without humor. 'Anyway, that's why I never carry pictures.'

They turned off of Northfield Avenue in West Orange. It was a nicely aging town. Most of the newer burbs had landscapes that looked somehow phony, like a recent hair transplant. West Orange had lush lawns and ivy on the walls. The trees were tall and thick. The houses were not cookie-cutter – there were Tudors, next to capes, next to Mediterranean style. They were all a little past due, not in prime condition, but it all seemed to work.

There was a tricycle in the driveway. Loren pulled up behind it. They both got out. Someone had set up one of those baseball net – retrievers in the front yard. Two mitts sat in the fetal position on the grass.

Yates said, 'Your source lives here?'

'Like I said, you have no idea.'

Yates shrugged.

A woman straight out of the Suzy Homemaker hand-book answered the door. She wore a checkered apron and a smile Loren usually associated with religious fervor. 'Len's in the workroom downstairs,' she said.

'Thank you.'

'Would you like some coffee?'

'No, that's okay.'

'Mom!'

A boy of maybe ten ran into the room. 'Kevin, we have guests.'

Kevin smiled like his mother. 'I'm Kevin Friedman.' He stuck out his hand and met Loren's eye. The shake was firm. He turned to Yates, who seemed startled. He shook too and introduced himself.

'Very nice to meet you,' Kevin said. 'Mom and I are making some banana bread. Would you care for a slice?'

'Maybe later,' Loren said. 'We, uh . . .'

'He's down that way,' Suzy Homemaker said.

'Right, thanks.'

They opened the basement door. Yates muttered, 'What did they do to that boy? I can't even get my kids to say hello to me, forget strangers.'

Loren muffled a laugh. 'Mr. Friedman?' she called out.

He stepped into view. Friedman's hair had gone a shade grayer since the last time she'd seen him. He wore a light blue button-down sweater and khakis. 'Nice to see you again, Investigator Muse.'

'Same here.'

'And your friend?'

'This is Special Agent in Charge Adam Yates from Las Vegas.'

Friedman's eyes lit up when he heard the location. 'Vegas! Welcome then. Come, let's sit and see if I can help you out.'

He opened a door with a key. Inside was everything stripper. There were photographs on the wall. Documents of one kind or another. Framed panties and bras. Feathered boas and fans. There were old posters, one advertising Lili St. Cyr, and her 'Bubble Bath Dance,' another for Dixie Evans, 'The Marilyn Monroe of Burlesque,' who was appearing at the Minsky-Adams Theater in Newark. For a moment Loren and Yates just looked around and gaped.

'Do you know what that is?' Friedman gestured toward a big feathered fan he kept in a museum-style glass cube.

'A fan?' Loren said.

He laughed. 'Not just a fan. Calling this a fan would be like' – Friedman thought about it – 'like calling the Declaration of Independence a piece of parchment. No, this very fan was used by the great Sally Rand at the Paramount Club in 1932.'

Friedman waited for a reaction, didn't get one.

'Sally Rand invented the fan dance. She actually performed it in the 1934 movie *Bolero*. The fan is made from real ostrich feathers. Can you believe that? And that whip over there? It was used by Bettie Page. She was called the Queen of Bondage.'

'By her mother?' Loren couldn't resist.

Friedman frowned, clearly disappointed. Loren held up an apologetic hand. Friedman sighed and moved toward his computer.

'So I assume this involves an erotic dancer from the Vegas area?'

'It might,' Loren said.

He sat at his computer and typed something in. 'Do you have a name?'

'Candace Potter.'

He stopped. 'The murder victim?'

'Yes.'

'But she's been dead for ten years.'

'Yes, we know.'

'Most people believe she was killed by a man named Clyde Rangor,' Friedman began. 'He and his girlfriend Emma Lemay had a wonderful eye for talent. They co-managed some of the best low-rent but talent-loaded gentlemen's clubs anywhere.'

Loren sneaked a glance at Yates. Yates was shaking his head in either amazement or repulsion. It was hard to tell which. Friedman saw it too.

'Hey, some guys get into NASCAR,' Friedman said with a shrug.

'Yeah, what a waste,' Loren said. 'What else?'

'There were bad rumors about Clyde Rangor and Emma Lemay.'

'They abused the girls?'

'Sure, I mean, they were mob connected. This isn't unusual in the business, unfortunately. It really taints the overall aesthetic, you know what I mean?'

Loren said, 'Uh huh.'

'But even among thieves there is a certain code. They purportedly broke it.'

'In what way?'

'Have you seen the new commercials for Las Vegas?' Friedman asked.

'I don't think so.'

'The ones that say, 'What goes on in Vegas stays in Vegas'?'

'Oh wait,' Loren said. 'I've seen them.'

'Well, gentlemen's clubs take that motto to a fanatical extreme. You never, ever tell.'

'And Rangor and Lemay told?'

Friedman's face went dark. 'Worse. I –'

'Enough,' Yates said, cutting him off.

Loren turned toward Yates. She gave him a what-gives shrug.

'Look,' Yates continued, checking his watch, 'this is all interesting, but we're a little pressed for time here. What can you tell us about Candace Potter specifically?'

'May I ask a question?' Friedman said.

'Shoot.'

'She's been dead a long time. Has there been a new development in the case?'

'There might have been,' Loren said.

Friedman folded his hands and waited. Loren took the chance.

'Did you know that Candace Potter may have been' – she decided to go with a more popular though inaccurate term – 'a hermaphrodite?'

That got him. 'Wow.'

'Yes.'

'You're sure?'

'I've seen the autopsy.'

'Wait!' Friedman shouted it in the same way an editor in an old movie would shout, 'Hold the presses!' 'You have the actual autopsy?'

'Yes.'

He licked his lips, tried not to look too anxious. 'Is there any way I can get a copy?'

'It can probably be arranged,' Loren said. 'What else can you tell us about her?'

Friedman started typing on the computer. 'The information on Candace Potter is sketchy. For the most part she went by the stage name Candi Cane, which, let's face it, is a horrible name for an exotic dancer. It's too much, you know? Too cute. You know what a good name is? Jenna Jameson, for example. You've probably heard of her. Well, Jenna started as a dancer, you know, before she got into porn. She got the name Jameson from a bottle of Irish whiskey. See? It's classier. It has more oomph, you know what I mean.'

'Right,' Loren said, just to say something.

'And Candi's solo act was not the most original either. She dressed like a hospital candy striper and carried a big lollipop. Get it? Candi Cane? I mean, talk about clichéd.' He shook his head in the manner of a teacher let down by a prized pupil. 'Professionally she'll be better remembered for a dual act where she was known as Brianna Piccolo.'

'Brianna Piccolo?'

'Yes. She worked with another dancer, a statuesque African American named Kimmy Dale. Kimmy, in the act, went by the name Gayle Sayers.'

Loren saw it. So did Yates.

'Piccolo and Sayers? Please tell me you're kidding.'

'Nope. Brianna and Gayle did a sort of exotic dance rendition of the movie *Brian's Song*. Gayle would tearfully say, 'I love Brianna Piccolo,' you know, like Billy Dee did on the dais in the movie. Then Brianna would be lying sick in a bed. They'd help each other undress. No sex. Nothing like that. Just an exotic artistic experience. It had great appeal to those with an interracial fetish, which, frankly, is nearly everyone. I think it was one of the finest political statements made in exotic dance, an early display of racial sensitivity. I never saw the act in person, but my understanding was that it was a moving portrayal of socioeconomic –'

'Yeah, moving, I get it,' Loren interrupted. 'Anything else?'

'Sure, of course, what do you want to know? The Sayers-Piccolo number was usually the opening act for Countess Allison Beth Weiss IV, better known as Jewish Royalty. Her act – get this – was called 'Tell Mom It's Kosher.' You've probably heard of it.'

A waft of banana bread was reaching them down here. The smell was wonderful, even in this appetite-reducing atmosphere. Loren tried to get Friedman back on track. 'I mean anything else about Candace Potter. Anything that can illuminate what happened to her.'

Friedman shrugged. 'She and Kimmy Dale were not only dance partners but also real-life roommates. In fact, Kimmy Dale paid for the funeral to save Candi from – pardon the unintentional pun here – a potter's grave. Candi is buried at Holy Mother in Coaldale, I think. I've visited the tombstone to pay my respects. It's quite a moving experience.'

'I bet. Do you keep track of what happens to exotic dancers after they leave the business?'

'Of course,' he said, as if she'd asked a priest if he ever went to Mass. 'That's often the most interesting part. You wouldn't believe the variety of life roads they take.'

'Right, so what happened to this Kimmy Dale?'

'She's still in the business. A true warhorse. She no longer has the looks. She's – again pardon the unintentional pun – slid down the pole, if you will. The headline days are over. But Kimmy still has a small following. What she loses in not being, say, toned or hard-bodied she makes up for in experience. She's out of Vegas though.'

'Where is she?'

'Reno, last I heard.'

'Anything else?'

'Not really,' Friedman said. Then he snapped his fingers. 'Hold on, I have something to show you. I'm quite proud of this.'

They waited. Len Friedman had three tall file cabinets in the corner. He opened the second drawer of the middle one and began to finger through it. 'The Piccolo and Sayers act. This is a rare piece and it's only a color reproduction off a Polaroid. I'd really like to find more.' He cleared his throat as he continued his search. 'Do you think, Investigator Muse, that I could get a copy of that autopsy?'

'I'll see what I can do.'

'It would really add to my studies.'

'Studies. Right.'

'Here it is.' He took out a photograph and placed it on the table in front of them. Yates looked at it and nodded. He turned to Loren and saw the expression on her face.

'What?' Yates said.

Friedman added, 'Investigator Muse?'

Not in here, Loren thought. Not a word. She stared at the late Candace Potter aka Candi Cane aka Brianna Piccolo aka the Murder Victim.

'This is definitely Candace Potter?' she managed.

'Yes.'

'You're sure?'

'Of course.'

Yates looked a question at her. Loren tried to blink it away.

Candace Potter. If this really was Candace Potter, then she wasn't a murder victim. She wasn't dead at all. She was alive and well and living in Irvington, New Jersey, with her ex-con husband Matt.

They'd had it all wrong. Matt Hunter wasn't the connection here. Things were finally starting to make some sense.

Because Candace Potter had a new alias now.

She was Olivia Hunter.

47

Adam Yates tried to maintain his cool.

They were back outside now, on the Friedmans' front lawn. That had been much too close a call. When that Friedman cuckoo had started yammering about never ever telling, well, it could have ended right there – Yates's career, his marriage, even his freedom. Everything.

Yates needed to take control.

He waited until he and Loren Muse were back in the car. Then, calmly as he could, Yates asked, 'So what was that all about?'

'Candace Potter is still alive,' Muse said.

'Pardon me?'

'She's alive and well and married to Matt Hunter.'

Yates listened to Loren's explanation. He felt his insides tremor. When she finished he asked to see the autopsy. She handed it to him.

'No photos of the victim?'

'It's not the whole file,' Loren said. 'It's just the pages that concerned Max Darrow. My guess is he somehow learned the truth – that Candace Potter hadn't been killed all these years ago. Maybe it had something to do with the fact that the real victim was an AIS female.'

'Why would Darrow have checked that now? I mean, after ten years?'

'I don't know. But we need to talk to Olivia Hunter.'

Adam Yates nodded, trying to take this in. It was impossible for him to fathom. Olivia Hunter was the dead stripper named Candace Potter. Candi Cane. She had been there that night, he was sure of it.

It was likely now, very likely, that Olivia Hunter had the videotape.

That meant he had to take Loren Muse out of the equation. Right now.

Yates glanced at the autopsy report again. Muse drove. The height, weight, and hair color matched, but the truth seemed obvious now. The real victim had been Cassandra Meadows. She'd been dead all along. He should have figured that. She wouldn't have been smart enough to vanish.

Len Friedman had been right when he talked about the honor of thieves. Yates had counted on that, he guessed, which in hindsight was beyond stupid. People in that business respect confidentiality not out of any sense of honor but because of profit. If you get a reputation for talking, you lose your clientele. Simple as that. The only thing was, Clyde Rangor and Emma Lemay had found a way to make even more money. Ergo the 'honor of thieves' nonsense went right out the window.

Yates didn't do it a lot, but over the years, he'd cheated on Bess. Yates never really considered it a big deal. It was beyond compartmentalizing – beyond the usual 'sex was one thing, making love another.' Sex with Bess was fine. Even after all these years. But a man needs more. Check all the history books – that one is a given. No great men were sexually monogamous. It was as simple and as complicated as that.

And in truth there was nothing wrong with it. Do wives really get upset if their husband occasionally watches, for example, an X-rated film? Was that a crime? An act worthy of divorce? A betrayal?

Of course not.

Hiring a prostitute was really no different. A man might use pictures or 900-lines or whatever as outside stimuli. That was all this was. Many wives understood this. Yates might even be able to explain it to Bess.

If that was all it had been.

Rangor and Lemay – they should rot in hell.

Yates had been looking for Rangor, Lemay, Cassandra, and that damn tape for ten years. Now there was a twist. At least two of them were dead. And Candace Potter was suddenly in the mix.

What did she know?

He cleared his throat and looked at Loren Muse. First step: Remove her from the case. So how to handle this . . . ? 'You said you knew Matt Hunter?'

'Yes.'

'You shouldn't do the interview with his wife then.'

Loren frowned. 'Because I used to know him?'

'Yes.'

'That was in elementary school, Adam. I don't think I've spoken to him since we were ten.'

'Still. There's a connection.'

'So?'

'So the defense can use it.'

'How?'

Yates shook his head.

'What?'

'You seem like a decent investigator, Muse. But every once in a while, your naïveté is absolutely startling.'

Her grip on the wheel tightened. He knew that his words had stung.

'Go back to the office,' he said. 'Cal and I will take over this part of the investigation.'

'Cal? Was he that lug in Joan Thurston's office this morning?'

'He's a damn good agent.'

'I'm sure.'

They fell into silence. Loren was trying to think of a way out of this. Yates waited, knowing how to work this now.

'Look, I know the way,' Loren said. 'I'll drive you to Hunter's house and stay outside in case –'

'No.'

'But I want –'

'Want?' Yates cut her off. 'Who do you think you're talking to, Investigator Muse?'

She fumed in silence.

'This is now a federal investigation. Most of this case, in fact, seems to lead back to Nevada. Either way it clearly crosses state lines and certainly pissant county lines. You're a county investigator. You get that? There's county, then state, then federal. I'll demonstrate this with a bar graph, if you'd like. But you don't give the orders here. I do. You'll go back to your office and if I deem it appropriate, I'll keep you informed of what is occurring in my investigation. Do I make myself clear?'

Loren fought to keep her voice steady. 'You wouldn't even know about Olivia Hunter being Candace Potter if it wasn't for me.'

'Oh, I see. Is that what this is about, Muse? Your ego? You want the credit? Fine, it's yours. I'll put a gold star next to your name on the board, if you like.'

'That's not what I meant.'

'That's sure as hell how it sounded to me. Naïve and a glory hound. Quite a winning combination.'

'That's not fair.'

'That's not . . .' Yates laughed. 'Are you kidding me? Fair? How old are you, Muse, twelve? This is a federal investigation into murder and racketeering and you're worried about my playing fair with a lowly county investigator? You'll drive me back to your office immediately and' – enough stick, a little carrot – 'if you want to participate in this investigation, your current assignment will be to find out anything you can on that other whore, the black one she roomed with.'

'Kimmy Dale.'

'Yes. Find out exactly where she is, what her story is, everything you can. You will not talk to her, however, without talking to me first. If you don't like it, I'll have you removed from the case. Understood?'

She responded as if there were nails in her mouth: 'Understood.'

He knew that she would take it. Loren wanted to remain in the loop. She'd settle for marginalized, hoping she'd make it back onto the center stage. Truth was, she was a damn fine investigator. Yates would try to steal her away when this was all over. He'd flatter her and let her have all the credit and then, good as she was, she probably wouldn't look too closely at the details.

At least that was what he hoped.

Because so far, those who had died had not been innocent – they'd been trying to hurt him. Loren Muse was different. He really didn't want her harmed. But as old a philosophy as it was, in the end, if it comes down to us or them, it is always us.

Loren Muse pulled the car into the lot and got out without a word. Yates let her huff off. He called Cal Dollinger, the only man he trusted with this sort of information. He quickly explained what he needed to. Cal did not need much detail.

Adam flashed on a painful memory – the hospital when Sam had meningitis. What he left out of the story he'd told Loren was Cal's part in the nightmare. Cal, too, had refused to leave the hospital. Adam's oldest friend had pulled up a stiff metal chair and stayed outside Sam's door for three straight days, not saying a word, just sitting there on guard, making certain that if Adam needed anything, he'd be ready.

'You want me to go alone?' Cal asked.

'No, I'll meet you at the Hunters' house,' Yates said, his voice soft. 'We'll get the tape. Then we end this.'

48

Olivia Hunter held it together until Midlife had been able to extricate her from Detective Lance Banner. Now that she was back in her own home she let her defenses down. She cried silently. Tears ran down her cheeks. Olivia could not stop them. She did not know if they came from joy, relief, fear, what. She only knew that sitting down and trying to stop them would be a waste of time.

She had to move.

Her suitcase was still at the Howard Johnson's. She simply packed another. She knew better than to wait. The police would be back. They would want answers.

She had to get to Reno right now.

She couldn't stop crying, which was unlike her yet understandable, she guessed, under the circumstances. Olivia was physically and emotionally spent. She was pregnant, for one thing. For another, she was worried about her adopted daughter. And finally, after all this time, she had told Matt the truth about her past.

The pact was over. Olivia had broken it when she responded to that online post – more than that, she had been directly responsible for the death of Emma Lemay. It was Olivia's fault. Emma had done a lot wrong in her life. She had hurt many people. Olivia knew that she'd tried to make up for it, that she'd truly spent her last years making amends. She didn't know where that put Emma on the Great Ledger in the Sky, but if anyone earned redemption, she assumed that Emma Lemay had.

But the thing Olivia could not get over, the thing that was really making the tears waterfall down her cheeks, was the look on Matt's face when she told him the truth.

It had not been what she'd imagined at all.

He should have been upset. He probably was. How could he not be? From the first time they met in Vegas, Olivia had always loved the way he looked at her – as if God had never created anything more spectacular, more – for lack of a better word – pure. Olivia naturally expected that look to vanish or at least dim once he learned the truth. She figured that his faded-blue eyes would harden, grow cold.

But that hadn't happened.

Nothing had changed. Matt had learned that his wife was a lie, that she had done things that would make most men turn away forever in disgust. And he had reacted with unconditional love.

Over the years Olivia had gained enough distance to see that her awful upbringing made her, like so many of the girls she worked with, lean toward self-destruction. Men who grew up like that, in different foster homes and under what could best be described as poor situations, usually reacted with violence. That was how abused men showed rage – by striking out, with physical brutality.

Women were different. They used more subtle forms of cruelty or, as in most cases, directed the rage inward – they cannot hurt someone else so they hurt themselves. Kimmy had been like that. Olivia – no, Candi – had been like that too.

Until Matt.

Maybe it was because of the years he spent in jail. Maybe, like she said before, it had to do with their mutual wounds. But Matt was the finest man she had ever known. He truly didn't sweat the small stuff. He lived in the moment. He paid attention to what mattered. He didn't let the trappings get in the way. He ignored the superfluous and saw what was really there. It made her see past it too – at least, in herself.

Matt didn't see the ugly in her – still didn't see it! – ergo, it was not there.

But as Olivia packed, the cold hard truth was obvious. After all the years and all the pretending, she had not rid herself of that self-destructive bent. How else to explain her actions? How stupid had she been – searching online for Candace Potter like that?

Look at the damage she'd wrought. To Emma, of course. To herself, yes, but more to the point, to the only man she'd ever loved.

Why had she insisted on poking at the past?

Because, in truth, she couldn't help herself. You can read all the pro-choice, pro-adoption, pro-life arguments – over the years, Olivia had ad nauseum – but there was one basic truth: Getting pregnant is the ultimate fork in the road. Whatever you choose, you will always wonder about the path not taken. Even though she was very young, even though keeping the child would have been impossible, even though the decision was ultimately made by others, no day passed without Olivia wondering about that gigantic what-if.

No woman simply skates by that one.

There was a knock on the door.

Olivia waited. A second knock. There was no peephole, so she went to a nearby window, pushed the lace curtain to the side, and peered out.

There were two men at her door. One looked like he'd just walked out of an L.L. Bean catalogue. The second man was enormous. He wore a suit that didn't seem to fit him quite right, but then again, judging by his looks, no suit would. He had a military buzz cut and no neck.

The enormous man turned to the window and caught her eye. He nudged the smaller man. The smaller man turned too.

'FBI,' the normal-size one said. 'We'd like to speak to you for a moment.'

'I have nothing to say.'

The L.L. Bean man stepped toward her. 'I don't think that's a wise position to take, Mrs. Hunter.'

'Please refer all questions to my attorney, Ike Kier.'

The man smiled. 'Maybe we should try again.'

Olivia did not like the way he said that.

'My name is Special Agent in Charge Adam Yates from the Las Vegas office of the Federal Bureau of Investigation. This' – he gestured to the big man – 'is Special Agent Cal Dollinger. We would very much like to speak with Olivia Hunter or, if she prefers, we can arrest one Candace Potter.'

Olivia's knees buckled at the sound of her old name. A smile cracked the big man's rock face. He was enjoying the moment.

'Up to you, Mrs. Hunter.'

There was no choice now. She was trapped. She'd have to let them in, would have to talk.

'Let me see your identification please.'

The big man walked over toward the window. Olivia had to fight off the desire to step back. He reached into his pocket, took out his ID, slammed it hard enough against the glass to make her jump. The other man, the one named Yates, did likewise. The IDs looked legitimate, though she knew how easy it was to buy fakes.

'Slide your business card under the door. I'd like to call your office and verify who you are.'

The big man, Dollinger, shrugged, the stilted smile still

locked in place. He spoke for the first time: 'Sure thing, Candi.'

She swallowed. The big man reached into his wallet, plucked out a card, slid it under the door. There was no reason to go ahead and call the number. The card had a raised seal and looked too legitimate – plus there had been no hesitation on the part of Cal Dollinger, who, according to the card, was indeed a special agent out of the Las Vegas office.

She opened the door. Adam Yates entered first. Cal Dollinger ducked in as if he were entering a teepee. He stayed by the door, hands folded in front of him.

'Nice weather we're having,' Yates said.

And then Dollinger closed the door.

49

Loren Muse fumed.

She'd been about to call Ed Steinberg and complain about Yates's treatment of her, but in the end she decided against it. Little lady can't take care of herself. Needs to call her boss for help. No, she wouldn't play into that.

She was still part of the investigation. Fine, that was all she wanted. A foot in the door. She started digging up all she could on the roommate, Kimmy Dale. It wasn't too difficult. Kimmy had a record for prostitution. Despite what people thought, prostitution was not legal in Clark County, where Las Vegas is.

One of Dale's old probation officers, an old-timer named Taylor, was in early. He remembered her.

'What can I tell you?' Taylor began. 'Kimmy Dale had a bad family history, but what girl out here doesn't? You ever listen to Howard Stern on the radio?'

'Sure.'

'Ever listen when he has strippers on? He always kinda jokingly asks, 'And you were first abused at what age?' and the thing is, they always have an answer. They always were. They sit there and say it's great getting naked and they made their own choice, blah blah, but there's always something in the background. You know what I mean?'

'I do.'

'So Kimmy Dale was another classic case. She ran away from home and started stripping when she was probably fourteen, fifteen tops.'

'Do you know where she is now?'

'She moved out to Reno. I got a home address if you want.'

'I do.'

He gave her Kimmy Dale's home address. 'Last I heard she works out of a place called the Eager Beaver, which, believe it or not, is not as classy as the name would lead you to believe.'

Eager Beaver, she thought. Wasn't that where Yates said Charles Talley worked?

Taylor said, 'Nice town, Reno. Not like Vegas. Don't get me wrong. I love Vegas. We all do. It's awful and horrible and mobbed up, but we don't leave. You know what I'm saying?'

'I'm calling you from Newark, New Jersey,' she said. 'So yeah, I know what you mean.'

Taylor laughed. 'Anyway, Reno is actually a pretty nice place to raise a family nowadays. Good weather because it's below the Sierra Nevada mountains. Used to be divorce capital of the USA and have more millionaires per capita than anywhere in the country. You ever been?'

'Nope.'

'Are you cute?'

'Adorable.'

'So come out to Vegas. I'll show you around.'

'Next plane, I'm there.'

'Wait, you're not one of those 'I-hate-men' feminazis, are you?'

'Only when I don't get enough sleep.'

'So what's this about?'

Her cell phone began to ring. 'I'll fill you in later, okay? Thanks, Taylor.'

'We'll stay at the Mandalay Bay. I know a guy. You'll love it.'

'Right, soon, bye.'

She hung up and hit the answer button.

'Hello?'

Without preamble, Mother Katherine said, 'She was murdered, wasn't she?'

Loren was about to hem and haw again, but something in Mother Katherine's tone told her it would be a waste of time. 'Yes.'

'Then I need to see you.'

'Why's that?'

'I wasn't allowed to say anything before. Sister Mary Rose was very specific.'

'Specific about what?'

'Please come by my office as soon as you can, Loren. I need to show you something.'

'What can I do for you, Agent Yates?' Olivia asked.

By the door, Cal Dollinger's eyes swept the room. Adam Yates sat and rested his elbows on his thighs. 'You own a lot of books,' Yates said.

'Very observant.'

'Are they yours or your husband's?'

Olivia put her hands on her hips. 'Yes, I can see how that would be relevant, so let me clear your mind. Most of the books belong to me. Are we done?'

Yates smiled. 'You're very amusing,' he said. 'Isn't she amusing, Cal?'

Cal nodded. 'Most strippers and whores, they're bitter. But not her. She's a slice of sunshine.'

'Sunshine indeed,' Yates added.

Olivia did not like the way this was going. 'What do you want?'

'You faked your own death,' Yates said. 'That's a crime.'

She said nothing.

'That girl who really died,' he went on. 'What was her name?'

'I don't know what you're talking about.'

'Her name was Cassandra, wasn't it?' Yates leaned in a little. 'Were you the one who murdered her?'

Olivia held her ground. 'What do you want?'

'You know.'

Yates's hands tightened into fists, then relaxed. She glanced at the door. Cal remained calm, a statue.

'I'm sorry,' she said. 'I don't.'

Yates tried a smile. 'Where's the tape?'

Olivia stiffened. She flashed back to that trailer. There had been a horrible smell when she and Kimmy first moved into it, as if small animals had died in the walls. Kimmy had bought some heavy potpourri – much too perfumed. It tried to mask something that could never really be hidden. The smell came back to her now. She saw Cassandra's crumpled body. She remembered the fear on Clyde Rangor's face as he asked:

'Where's the tape?'

She tried to keep her voice from cracking. 'I don't know what you're talking about.'

'Why did you run away and change your name?'

'I needed a fresh start.'

'Just like that?'

'No,' Olivia said. 'Nothing about it was "just like that."' She stood. 'And I don't want to answer any more questions until my attorney is present.'

Yates looked up at her. 'Sit down.'

'I want you both out of here.'

'I said sit down.'

She looked over at Cal Dollinger again. Still playing statue. He had eyes with nothing behind them. Olivia did as Yates said. She sat.

'I was going to say something like, "You got a nice life here, you wouldn't want me to spoil it all for you," ' Yates began. 'But I'm not sure that will work. Your neighborhood is a cesspool. Your house is a dump. Your husband is an ex-con wanted in a triple murder.' He gave her the smile. 'One would have thought you'd have made the most of your new start, Candi. But amazingly you did just the opposite.'

He was intentionally trying to antagonize her. Olivia wouldn't let that happen. 'I'd like you both to leave now.'

'You don't care who learns your secret?'

'Please leave.'

'I could arrest you.'

That was when she decided to take the chance. Olivia put out her hands, as if ready to be cuffed. Yates did not move. He could arrest her, of course. She wasn't sure of the exact law or the statute of limitations, but she had clearly interfered with a murder investigation – she had, in fact, pretended to be the victim. It would be more than enough to hold her.

But that wasn't what Yates wanted.

Clyde's pleading voice: *'Where's the tape?'*

Yates wanted something else. Something Cassandra had died for. Something Clyde Rangor had killed for. She looked into his face. The eyes were steady. His hands kept clenching and unclenching.

Her wrists were still together in front of her. She waited another second, then dropped them back to her sides. 'I don't know anything about any tapes,' she said.

Now it was Yates's turn to study her. He took his time. 'I believe you,' he said.

And for some reason the way he said it scared her more than anything else.

'Please come with us,' Yates said.

'Where?'

'I'm taking you in.'

'On what charge?'

'You want the list alphabetically?'

'I'll need to call my attorney.'

'You can call him from the precinct.'

She was not sure how to play this. Cal Dollinger took a step toward her. When she took a step back, the big man said, 'You want me to drag you out of here in cuffs?'

Olivia stopped. 'That won't be necessary.'

They headed outside. Yates took the lead. Dollinger stayed next to her. Olivia checked the streets. The giant brown beer bottle was in the sky. For some reason it gave her comfort. Yates walked ahead. He unlocked the car door, slid in, started it up. He turned back and looked at Olivia and suddenly it hit her.

She recognized him.

Names fled easily, but faces were her prisoners for life. When she'd danced it became a way of numbing herself. She'd studied the faces. She'd memorize them, classify them by their level of boredom and enjoyment, try to remember how many times they'd been there. It had been a mental exercise, a way to distract herself.

Adam Yates had been to Clyde's club.

She may have hesitated or maybe Cal Dollinger was just attuned to what was going on around him. She was about to flee, just start running until her legs gave out, but Dollinger put a firm hand on her arm. He squeezed the spot above her elbow just hard enough to get her attention. She tried to pull away, but it was like pulling your arm out of a concrete block.

She couldn't move.

They were almost at the car now. Cal picked up speed. Olivia's eyes skimmed the street, pausing on Lawrence.

He was standing on the corner, swaying with another man she didn't know. Both of them had brown paper bags in their hand. Lawrence looked at her and started to raise his hand to wave.

Olivia mouthed the words: Help me.

Lawrence's face didn't change. There was no reaction at all. The other man made a joke. Lawrence laughed long and hard and slapped his thigh.

He hadn't seen her.

They approached the car. Olivia's mind raced. She did not want to get in with them. She tried to slow her walk. Dollinger gave her arm a quick, painful pinch.

'Keep moving,' the big man told her.

They reached the back door. Dollinger opened it. She tried to hold her ground, but his grip was simply too strong. He pushed her into the backseat.

'Yo, got a dollar?'

The big man took a quick glance. It was Lawrence. Dollinger started turning away, dismissing the panhandler, but Lawrence grabbed his shoulder.

'Yo, man, I'm hungry. Got a dollar?'

'Buzz off.'

Lawrence put his hands on the big man's chest. 'I'm just asking for a dollar, man.'

'Let go of me.'

'A dollar. Is that too much to –'

And that was when Dollinger let go of her arm.

Olivia hesitated but not for long. When both of Dollinger's hands gripped Lawrence by the front of his shirt, she was ready. She jumped up and started to run.

'Run, Liv!'

Lawrence didn't have to tell her twice.

Dollinger dropped Lawrence and spun around. Lawrence jumped on the big man's back. Dollinger shrugged him off like dandruff. Then Lawrence did something truly foolish. He hit Dollinger with the brown bag. Olivia could hear the clunk from the beer bottle inside. Dollinger turned around and punched Lawrence in the sternum. Lawrence went down hard.

Dollinger shouted, 'Stop! FBI!'

I don't think so, big man.

Olivia heard the car take off. The tires squealed as Yates peeled out. She glanced behind her.

Dollinger was catching up to her. And he had a gun in his hand.

Her lead was maybe fifty feet. She ran as hard as she could. This was her neighborhood. She'd have the advantage, right? She cut down a back alley. It was empty – nobody else in sight. Dollinger followed. She risked a look back. He was gaining on her and didn't look the least bit put out.

She spun forward and ran harder, pumping her arms.

A bullet whizzed by her. Then another.

Oh, God. He's shooting!

She had to get out of the alley. Had to find people. He wouldn't just shoot her in front of a lot of people.

Would he?

She veered right back onto the street. The car was there. Yates sped toward her. She rolled over a parked car and onto the sidewalk. They were at the old Pabst Blue Ribbon factory. Soon it would be gone, replaced with yet another no-personality shopping center. But right now the broken-down ruins could be a haven.

Wait, where was that old tavern?

She swerved to the left. It was down the second alley. She remembered that. Olivia did not dare look behind her, but she could hear his footsteps now. He was gaining.

'Stop!'

Like hell, she thought. The tavern. Where the hell was that tavern?

She turned right.

Bingo, there it was!

The door was on the right. She wasn't far from it. She ran hard. She grabbed the handle as Dollinger made the turn. She pulled the door open and fell inside.

'Help!'

There was one person inside. He was cleaning glasses behind the bar. He looked up in surprise. Olivia stood and quickly threw the bolt.

'Hey,' the bartender shouted, 'what's going on here?'

'Someone is trying to kill me.'

The door shook. 'FBI. Open up!'

Olivia shook her head. The bartender hesitated, then gestured toward the back room with his head. She ran for it. The bartender picked up a shotgun as Dollinger kicked the door open.

The bartender was startled by the size of the man. 'Jesus H. Christ!'

'FBI! Drop it.'

'Let's just slow down, buddy . . .'

Dollinger pointed his gun at the bartender and fired twice.

The bartender went down, leaving only a splash of blood on the wall behind him.

Oh my God oh my God oh my God!

Olivia wanted to scream.

No. Go. Hurry.

She thought about the baby inside her. It gave her the extra spurt. She dove into the back room where the bartender had gestured.

Gunfire raked the wall behind her. Olivia dropped to the floor.

She crawled toward the back door. It was made of heavy metal. There was a key in the lock. In one move she pulled the door open and twisted the key so hard that it broke in the knob. She rolled back into the sunlight. The door closed and locked automatically behind her.

She heard him twisting the knob. When that didn't work, he began to pound on the door. This time the door would not give way easily. Olivia ran, keeping off the main streets, looking out for both Yates's car and Dollinger on foot.

She saw neither. Time to get the hell out of here.

Olivia walk-jogged for another two miles. When a bus drove by, she hopped on, not much caring where it took her. She got off in the center of Elizabeth. Taxis were lined up by the depot.

'Where to?' the driver asked her.

She tried to catch her breath. 'Newark Airport, please.'

50

As Matt crossed into Pennsylvania in the white Isuzu, he was amazed at how much of what he'd thought of as useless information he'd retained from prison. Of course, prison is not the great education in all things crime many thought it was. You have to keep in mind that the inhabitants had all been, well, caught, and thus any claimed expertise had something of a shadow cast over it.

He had also never listened too closely. Criminal activities did not interest him. His plan, which he'd maintained for nine years, was to stay away from anything even remotely unlawful.

That had changed.

Saul's stolen car method had borne fruit. And now Matt remembered other law-evading lessons from his time behind bars. He stopped in the parking lot of a Great Western off Route 80. No security, no surprise. He did not want to steal another car, just a license plate. He wanted a license plate with the letter P in it. He got lucky. There was a car in the employee lot with a plate that began with the letter P. The employee car would work well, he thought. It was eleven a.m. Most places would be in early- to mid-shift by then. The employee owner would probably be inside for several more hours at a minimum.

He stopped in a Home Depot and bought thin black electric tape, the kind you use to repair phone cords.

Making sure no one was watching, he ripped a strip and put it on the letter P, turning it into the letter B. It wouldn't hold up under close scrutiny, but it should be good enough to get him where he was going.

Harrisburg, Pennsylvania.

There was no choice. Matt had to get to Reno. That meant flying on an airplane. He knew that would be risky. The prison tips for evading detection, even if good in their heyday, were all pre-9/11. Security had changed a lot since then, but there were still methods. He just had to think it through, move fast, and be more than a little lucky.

First, he tried a little old-fashioned confusion and mayhem. He used a pay phone back on the New Jersey border to make flight reservations from Newark Airport to Toronto. Maybe they'd track that down and figure he was an amateur. Maybe not. He hung up, moved to another pay phone, and made his other reservation. He wrote down his booking number, hung up, and shook his head.

This was not going to be easy.

Matt pulled into the Harrisburg airport parking lot. The Mauser M2 was still in his pocket. No way he could take it with him. Matt jammed the weapon under the front passenger seat because, if things did not go as planned, he might be back. The Isuzu had served him well. He wanted to write a note to its owner, explaining what he had done and why. With luck there'd be a chance to explain in the future.

Now to see if his plan worked. . . .

But first, he needed sleep. He bought a baseball cap in the souvenir store. Then he found a free chair in the arrivals area, folded his arms across his chest, closed his eyes, pulled the brim low across his face. People slept in airports all the time, he figured. Why would anyone bother him?

He woke up an hour later, feeling like absolute hell. He headed upstairs to the departure level. He bought some extra-strength Tylenol and Motrin, took three of each. He cleaned up in the bathroom.

The line at the ticket sales counter was long. That was good, if the timing worked. He wanted the staff to be busy. When it was his turn, the woman behind the desk gave him that distracted smile.

'To Chicago, Flight 188,' he said.

'That flight leaves in twenty minutes,' she said.

'I know. There was traffic and –'

'May I see your picture ID, please?'

He gave her his driver's license. She typed in 'Hunter, M.' This was the moment of truth. He stood perfectly still. She frowned and typed some more. Nothing happened. 'I don't see you in here, Mr. Hunter.'

'That's odd.'

'Do you have your booking number?'

'I sure do.'

He handed the one he'd gotten when he made the reservation on the phone. She typed in the letters: YTIQZ2. Matt held his breath.

The woman sighed. 'I see the problem.'

'Oh?'

She shook her head. 'Your name is misspelled on the reservation. You're listed here as Mike, not Matt. And the last name is Huntman, not Hunter.'

'Honest mistake,' Matt said.

'You'd be surprised how often it happens.'

'Nothing would surprise me,' he said.

They shared a world-is-full-of-dopes laugh. She printed out his ticket and collected the money. Matt smiled, thanked her, and headed to the plane.

There was no nonstop from Harrisburg to Reno, but that might work in his favor. He didn't know how the airline computer system meshed with the federal government's, but two short flights would probably work better than one long one. Would the computer system pick up his name right away? Matt doubted it – or maybe hope sprang eternal. Thinking logically, the whole thing would have to take some time – gathering the information, sorting it, getting it to the right person. A few hours at a minimum.

He'd be in Chicago in one.

It sounded good in theory.

When he landed safely at O'Hare in Chicago, he felt his heart start up again. He disembarked, trying not to look conspicuous, planning an escape route in case he saw a row of police officers at the gate. But no one grabbed him when he came off the plane. He let out a long breath. So they hadn't located him – yet. But now came the tricky part. The flight to Reno was longer. If they put together what he'd done the first time, they'd have plenty of time to nail him.

So he tried something slightly different.

Another long line at the airline purchasing desk. Matt might need that. He waited, snaking through the velvet ropes. He watched, seeing which employee looked most tired or complacent. He found her, on the far right. She looked bored past the point of tears. She examined IDs, but there was little spark in her eyes. She kept sighing. She kept glancing around, clearly distracted. Probably had a personal life, Matt thought. Maybe a fight with the husband or her teenage daughter or who knew what?

Or maybe, Matt, she's very astute and just has a tired-looking face.

Still, what other options were there? When Matt got to the front of the line and his agent wasn't free, he faked looking for something and told the family behind him to go ahead. He did that one more time and then it was his agent's turn to say, 'Next.'

He approached as inconspicuously as possible. 'My name is Matthew Huntler.' He handed her a piece of paper with the booking number on it. She took it and started typing.

'Chicago to Reno/Tahoe, Mr. Huntler.'

'Yes.'

'ID, please.'

This was the hardest part. He had tried to set it up as smoothly as possible. M. Huntler was a member of their frequent-flier club – Matt had signed him up a few hours ago. Computers don't know from subtlety. Humans sometimes do.

He gave her his wallet. She did not look at it at first. She was still typing into the computer. Maybe he'd get lucky here. Maybe she wouldn't even check his ID.

'Any luggage to check?'

'Not today, no.'

She nodded, still typing. Then she turned toward his ID. Matt felt his stomach tumble. He remembered something Bernie had sent him by e-mail several years ago. It said:

Here's a fun test. Read this sentence:

FINISHED FILES ARE THE RESULT OF YEARS OF SCIENTIFIC STUDY COMBINED WITH THE EXPERIENCE OF YEARS.

Now count the F's in that sentence.
He had done it and ended up with four. The real answer

was six. You don't see every letter. That's not how we're built. He was counting on something like that here. Hunter, Huntler. Would someone really catch the difference?

The woman said to him. 'Aisle or window.'

'Aisle.'

He'd made it. The security check went even easier – after all, Matt had already been ID'd at the counter, right? The security guard looked at his picture, at his face, but he didn't come up with the fact that the ID said Hunter while the boarding pass read Huntler. Typos are made all the time anyway. You see hundreds or thousands of boarding passes each day. You really wouldn't notice such a small thing.

Once again Matt got to his plane right as the gate was about to close. He settled into his aisle seat, closed his eyes, and didn't wake up until the pilot announced their descent into Reno.

The door to Mother Katherine's office was closed.

This time there was no flashback for Loren. She pounded hard on the door and put her hand on the knob. When she heard Mother Katherine say, 'Come in,' she was ready.

The Mother Superior had her back to the door. She did not turn around when Loren entered. She merely asked, 'Are you sure Sister Mary Rose was murdered?'

'Yes.'

'Do you know who did it?'

'Not yet.'

Mother Katherine nodded slowly. 'Have you learned her real identity?'

'Yes,' Loren said. 'But it would have been easier if you'd just told me.'

She expected Mother Katherine to argue, but she didn't. 'I couldn't.'

'Why not?'

'Unfortunately it was not my place.'

'She told you?'

'Not exactly, no. But I knew enough.'

'How did you figure it out?'

The old nun shrugged. 'Some of her statements about her past,' she said. 'They didn't add up.'

'You confronted her?'

'No, never. And she never told me her true identity. She said it would endanger others. But I know that it was sordid. Sister Mary Rose wanted to move past it. She wanted to make amends. And she did. She contributed much to this school, to these children.'

'With her work or with finances?'

'Both.'

'She gave you money?'

'The parish,' Mother Katherine corrected. 'Yes, she gave quite a bit.'

'Sounds like guilt money.'

Mother Katherine smiled. 'Is there any other kind?'

'So that story about chest compressions . . . ?'

'I already knew about the implants. She told me. She also told me that if someone learned who she really was, they'd kill her.'

'But you didn't think that happened.'

'It appeared to be death by natural causes. I thought it best to leave it alone.'

'What changed your mind?'

'Gossip,' she said.

'What do you mean?'

'One of our sisters confided to me that she had seen a man in Sister Mary Rose's room. I was suspicious, of course, but I couldn't prove anything. I also needed to protect the school's reputation. So I needed this investigated quietly and without my betraying Sister Mary Rose's trust.'

'Enter me.'

'Yes.'

'And now that you know she was murdered?'

'She left a letter.'

'For whom?'

Mother Katherine showed her the envelope. 'A woman named Olivia Hunter.'

Adam Yates was closing in on panic.

He parked a good distance from the old brewery and waited while Cal quickly cleaned up. The clues would be gone. Cal's weapon could not be traced. The license plates they were using would lead to nowhere. Some crazy person might identify a huge man chasing a woman but there would be no practical way of linking them with the dead bartender.

Perhaps.

No, no perhaps about it. He had been in worse scrapes. The bartender had pulled a rifle on Cal. It would have his fingerprints on it. The untraceable gun would be left behind. They would both be out of state in a matter of hours.

They would get through it.

When Cal sat in the passenger seat, Adam said, 'You messed up.'

Cal nodded. 'I did at that.'

'You shouldn't have tried to shoot her.'

He nodded again. 'A mistake,' he agreed. 'But we can't let her go. If her background comes out –'

'It's going to come out anyway. Loren Muse knows about it.'

'True, but without Olivia Hunter, it doesn't lead any-place. If she's caught, she will try to save herself. That may mean looking into what happened all those years ago.'

Yates felt something inside him start to tear. 'I don't want to hurt anyone.'

'Adam?'

He looked at the big man.

'It's too late for that,' Dollinger said. 'Us or them, re-member?'

He nodded slowly.

'We need to find Olivia,' Dollinger said. 'And I do mean we. If other agents arrest her . . .'

Yates finished it for him. 'She may talk.'

'Precisely.'

'So we call her in as a material witness,' Yates said. 'Tell them to keep an eye on the nearby airports and train stations but not to do anything until they notify us.'

Cal nodded. 'Already done.'

Adam Yates considered his options. 'Let's head back to the county office. Maybe Loren found something use-ful on that Kimmy Dale.'

They had driven about five minutes when the phone rang. Cal picked it up and barked, 'Agent Dollinger.'

Cal listened closely.

'Let her land. Have Ted follow her. Do not, repeat, do not, approach. I'll be on the next plane out.'

He hung up.

'What?'

'Olivia Hunter,' he said. 'She's already on a plane to Reno.'

'Reno again,' Yates said.

'Home of the deceased Charles Talley and Max Darrow.'

369

'And maybe the tape.' Yates made a right up ahead. 'All the signs are pointing west, Cal. I think we better get to Reno too.'

51

The taxi driver worked for a company called Reno
Rides. He pulled to a full stop, shifted in park, turned
around, and looked Olivia up and down. 'You sure this
is the place, ma'am?'

Olivia could only stare.

'Ma'am?'

An ornate cross dangled from the taxi's rearview mirror. Prayer cards wallpapered the glove compartment.

'Is this 488 Center Lane Drive?' she asked.

'It is.'

'Then this is the place.' Olivia reached into her purse.
She handed him the money. He handed her a pamphlet.

'You don't have to do this,' he said.

The pamphlet was church-affiliated. John 3:16 was
on the cover. She managed to smile.

'Jesus loves you,' the driver said.

'Thank you.'

'I'll take you anywhere else you want to go. No
charge.'

'It's okay,' Olivia said.

She stepped out of the taxi. The driver gave her a for-
lorn look. She waved as he departed. Olivia cupped a
hand over her eyes. The sign of tired neon read:

EAGER BEAVER – NUDE DANCING.

Her body began to quake. Old reaction, she guessed.
She had never been in this place, but she knew it. She

knew the dirty pickups that littered the lot. She knew the men trudging in mindlessly, the low lights, the sticky feel of the dance pole. She headed toward the door, knowing what she'd find inside.

Matt feared prison – going back. This, right in front of her, was her prison.

Candi Cane lives another day.

Olivia Hunter had tried to exorcise Candace 'Candi Cane' Potter years ago. Now the girl was back in a big bad way. Forget what experts tell you: You can indeed wipe away the past. Olivia knew that. She could jam Candi in some back room, lock the door, destroy the key. She had almost done it – would have done – but there'd been one thing that always kept that door, no matter how hard she pushed, from closing all the way.

Her child.

A chill scrambled down her back. Oh, God, she thought. Was her daughter working here?

Please no.

It was four p.m. Still plenty of time before the midnight meeting. She could go somewhere else, find a Starbucks maybe or get a motel room, grab some sleep. She had caught a little shut-eye on the plane out here, but she could definitely use more.

When she first landed, Olivia called FBI headquarters and asked to speak to Adam Yates. When she was connected to the office of the Special Agent in Charge, she hung up.

So Yates was legit. Dollinger too, she supposed.

That meant that two FBI agents had tried to kill her.

There would be no arrest or capture. She knew too much.

The last words Clyde had said to her came back: *'Just tell me where it is. . . .'*

It was starting to make some sense. There were rumors about Clyde making tapes for blackmail. He'd probably blackmailed the wrong guy – either Yates or somebody close to them. Somehow that led him to poor Cassandra. Did she have the tapes? Was she in them?

Standing there, reading the sign about the $4.99 EAGER BEAVER BUFFET! Olivia nodded to herself.

That was it. It had to be. She started walking toward the front door.

She should wait, come back.

No.

She got a curious look at the door. Women do not come to these places alone. Every once in a while a man might bring a girlfriend. The girlfriend would be trying to show she was hip. Or maybe she had lesbian tendencies. Whatever. But women never came in alone.

Heads turned when she entered, but not as many as you'd think. People reacted slowly at places like this. The air was syrupy, languid. The lights were down. Jaws remained slack. Most patrons probably assumed that she was either a working girl on her downtime or a lesbian waiting for her lover's shift to end.

The Human League's 'Don't You Want Me' played over the sound system, a song that had been an already aged classic when Olivia had danced. Retro, she guessed, but she had always liked the track. In this place, the lyrics were supposed to be a sexy come-on, but if you listened closely, Phil Oakey, the lead singer, made you feel the pain and shock of having your heart broken. The title wasn't repeated with lust. It was repeated with shattering disbelief.

Olivia took a seat in a back booth. There were three dancers onstage right now. Two looked off at nothing. One worked a customer, feigning passion, inviting him to jam dollar bills into her G-string. The man complied. She took in the audience and realized that nothing had changed in the decade since she'd worked rooms like these. The men were of the same variety. Some had the blank faces. Some had the glazed smile. Some tried a cocky look, a swagger in their expression, as if they were somehow above it all. Others aggressively downed their beers, staring at the girls with naked hostility, as if demanding an answer to the eternal question, 'Is that all there is?'

The girls onstage were young and on drugs. You could tell. Her old roommate Kimmy had two brothers who OD'd. Kimmy wouldn't tolerate drug use. So Olivia – no, Candi – took to drinking, but Clyde Rangor had made her stop when she started stumbling onstage. Clyde as a rehab counselor. Weird, but there you have it.

The grease from the awful lunch buffet took to the air, becoming more a skin coating than a smell. Who ate that stuff? she wondered. Buffalo wings dating back to the Carter administration. Hot dogs that sit in water until, well, until they were gone. French fries so oily it makes picking them up a near impossibility. Fat men circled the dishes and piled their Styrofoam plates to dizzying heights. Olivia could almost see their arteries hardening in the dim light.

Some strip joints called themselves 'gentlemen's clubs,' and businessmen wore suits and acted above the riffraff. There was no such pretense at the Eager Beaver. This was a place where tattoos outnumbered teeth. People fought. The bouncers had bigger guts than muscle because muscle was show and these guys would seriously kick your ass.

Olivia was not scared or intimidated, but she wasn't sure what she was doing here. The girls onstage began their rotation. The dancer at the one spot went offstage.

A bubbly young girl came on in the three spot. No way was she legal age. She was all legs, moving on the high heels like a colt. Her smile looked almost genuine, so Olivia figured that the life had not yet been ripped out of her.

'Get you something?'

The waitress looked at the oddity that was Olivia with a wary eye.

'Coca-Cola please.'

She left. Olivia kept her eye on the bubbly young girl. Something about her brought back memories of poor Cassandra. Just the age, she guessed. Cassandra had been far prettier. And then, as she looked at the three girls still onstage, the obvious question hit her:

Was one of these girls her daughter?

She looked at their faces for any sort of resemblance and saw none. That meant nothing, of course. She knew that. The waitress delivered the Coke. Olivia just let it sit there. There was no way she'd drink from any of these glasses.

Ten minutes later the girls rotated again. Another new girl. Probably running a five shift – three girls on, two girls off, fairly steady rotation. Could be a six shift. She wondered about Matt, about how he'd find his way out here. He had seemed so confident that he'd be able to make it, or had that been false bravado for her sake?

The dancer in the two spot worked some guy with a toupee so bad it looked like it had a zipper. Probably handing him that old favorite about working her way through school, Olivia thought. Why guys got off on the idea that a girl was a student always amazed her. Did they need a spot of purity to offset their filth?

The girl who'd been in the one spot when Olivia entered came out from the back. She approached a man who had a chicken wing sticking out of his mouth. The man dropped the chicken wing, wiped his hands on his jeans. The girl took the man by the hand and disappeared into a corner. Olivia wanted to follow her. She wanted to grab all of these girls and drag them out into the sunshine.

Enough.

She signaled to the waitress to bring over a check. The waitress broke away from a bunch of laughing locals. 'Three-fifty,' she said.

Olivia stood, reached into her purse, and took out a five. She was just about to hand it to the waitress, just about ready to leave this dark, awful place, when the dancers shifted again. A new girl came out from the back.

Olivia froze. Then a small groan, a groan of quiet, strong anguish, escaped from her lips.

The waitress said, 'Miss, you okay?'

Walking on the stage, taking the number three position.

It was Kimmy.

'Miss?'

Olivia's legs almost gave way. She sat back down. 'Get me another Coke.'

She had not touched her last one but if that bothered the waitress, she hid it pretty well. Olivia simply stared. For several seconds, she let the swirl of emotions twist through her. Regret, of course. Deep sadness to see Kimmy still up on that stage after all this time. Guilt for what Olivia had been forced to leave behind. But there was joy too at seeing her old friend. Olivia had visited a couple of Web sites in recent weeks, trying to see if Kimmy was dancing. She'd found nothing, which, Olivia had hoped, meant that Kimmy was no longer in the business. Now she could see the truth: Kimmy had just been too low-level to earn even a mention.

Olivia could not move.

Despite what one might think, it was not hard to forge friendships in that life. Most of the girls genuinely liked one another. They were like army buddies, bonding while trying to stay alive. But no one had been like Kimmy Dale. Kimmy had been her closest friend, the only one she still missed, still thought about, still wished that she could talk to. Kimmy had made her laugh. Kimmy had kept her off cocaine. Kimmy had even kept the gun in their trailer that ended up saving Olivia's life.

Olivia smiled in the dark. Kimmy Dale, the clean freak, her sometimes dance partner, her confidante.

And then the guilt and sadness roared back.

The years hadn't been kind, but then again no years ever had been to Kimmy Dale. Her skin sagged. There were lines around her mouth and eyes. A pattern of small bruises dotted her thighs. She wore too much makeup now, like the old 'hangers-on' they used to dread becoming. That had been their greatest fear: being one of the old hangers-on who couldn't see it was time to get out of the business.

Kimmy's stage dance hadn't changed – the same few steps, the moves a little slower now, more lethargic. The same high black boots she had always favored. There was a time when Kimmy would work the crowd better than anyone – she had a terrific smile – but there was no posturing anymore. Olivia kept back.

Kimmy thinks I'm dead.

How, she wondered, would Kimmy react to seeing this . . . this ghost? Olivia wondered what to do. Should she reveal herself – or just stay here in the shadows, wait another thirty minutes, slip out when she was sure Kimmy couldn't see her?

She sat there and watched her friend and considered

her next step. It was obvious. Everything was coming out now. The pact with Emma was over. Yates and Dollinger knew who she was. There was no reason to hide anymore. There was no one left to protect and maybe, just maybe, there was still someone she could save.

When Kimmy was on the final leg of her rotation, Olivia waved over the waitress.

'The dancer on the right,' Olivia said.

'The black one?'

'Yeah.'

'We call her Magic.'

'Okay, good. I want a private session with her.'

The waitress cocked an eyebrow. 'You mean in the back?'

'Right. A private room.'

'Fifty bucks extra.'

'No problem,' Olivia said. She had picked up cash at the ATM in Elizabeth. She handed the girl an extra ten for her own troubles.

The waitress stuffed the bill in her cleavage and shrugged. 'Go back and to the right. Second door. It's got a B on it. I'll send Magic over in five minutes.'

It took longer. There was a couch and a bed in the room. Olivia did not sit. She stood there and waited. She was shaking. She heard people walking past her door. On the sound system, Tears for Fears noted that everybody wants to rule the world. No kidding.

There was a knock on the door.

'You in there?'

The voice. No question who it was. Olivia wiped her eyes.

'Come in.'

The door opened. Kimmy stepped inside. 'Okay, let me tell you the price –'

She stopped.

For several seconds, they both just stood there and let the tears roll down their cheeks. Kimmy shook her head in disbelief.

'It can't be . . .'

Candi – not Olivia now – finally nodded. 'It's me.'

'But . . .'

Kimmy put a hand to her mouth and began to sob. Candi spread her arms. Kimmy nearly collapsed. Candi grabbed her and held on.

'It's okay,' she said softly.

'It can't be . . .'

'It's okay,' Olivia said again, stroking her friend's hair. 'I'm here. I'm back.'

52

Loren's flight went to Reno via Houston.

She had bought the ticket with her own money. She was taking a huge chance – the kind of chance that might indeed force her to leave her job and move out to someplace like New Mexico or Arizona – but the facts were there. Steinberg needed to play it more by the book. She understood that, agreed with it on some level.

But in the end she knew that this was the only way to go.

Yates, a powerful fed, was up to something.

Her suspicions first took flight when Yates abruptly turned nasty after leaving Len Friedman's house. He had suddenly pretended to be an irrational ass – not an unusual thing for a big-time federal agent, she knew – but it just didn't ring true. It seemed forced to her. Yates feigned control, but she sensed a panic there. You could almost smell it on him.

Yates clearly did not want her to see or talk to Olivia Hunter.

Why?

And when she thought about it, what had brought on that hissy fit in the first place? She remembered something that had happened in Friedman's basement – something that had seemed small and unimportant at the time. Yates had gone out of his way to steer the conversation away from what Rangor and Lemay used to do that Friedman had referred to as 'worse' than telling on their clientele. At the time she'd just been annoyed by Yates's interruption. But then you add in the way he threw her off the case and you had . . .

Well, okay, you still had nothing.

After visiting Mother Katherine, Loren had called Yates's cell phone. She had not gotten an answer. She had tried Olivia Hunter's residence. No answer there either. And then a report came over the radio, about a murder in Irvington, in a tavern not far from where the Hunters lived. There was not much yet, but there was some talk about a huge man running down the street chasing a woman.

A huge man. Cal Dollinger, whom Yates said he was bringing with him to question Olivia Hunter, was a huge man.

Again, on its own it meant very little.

But add it to what she knew.

She'd called Steinberg then and asked, 'Do you know where Yates is?'

'No.'

'I do,' she said. 'I checked with my airport source.' Newark Airport was, after all, in Essex County. The office had several contacts there. 'He and that Goliath are on a plane heading to the Reno-Tahoe airport.'

'And I care because?'

'I'd like to follow them,' she said.

'Come again?'

'Yates is up to something.'

She told Steinberg what she knew. She could almost see him frowning.

'So let me get this straight,' her boss said. 'You think that Yates is somehow involved in all this? Adam Yates, a decorated FBI agent. Wait, no, scratch that: a dedicated Special Agent in Charge, the top fed in Nevada. You base this on – A – his mood. B, that a big person might have been seen somewhere near but not even at a murder scene in Irvington. And C, that he's flying back to his home state. That about cover it?'

'You should have heard him playing good cop-bad cop, boss.'

'Uh huh.'

'He wanted me off the case and away from Olivia Hunter. I'm telling you: Yates is bad, boss. I know it.'

'And you know what I'm going to say, right?'

Loren did. 'Gather evidence.'

'You got it.'

'Do me one favor, boss.'

'What?'

'Check on Yates's story about Rangor and Lemay turning state's witness.'

'What about it?'

'See if it's true.'

'What, you think he made that up?'

'Just check it.'

He hesitated. 'I doubt it'll do any good. I'm a county guy. That's RICO. They don't like to talk.'

'Ask Joan Thurston then.'

'She'll think I'm nuts.'

'Doesn't she already?'

'Yeah, well, that's a point,' he said. He cleared his throat. 'One more thing.'

'Yes, boss.'

'You thinking of doing something stupid?'

'Who, me?'

'As your boss, you know I won't authorize anything. But if you're off the clock and I'm none the wiser . . .'

'Say no more.'

She hung up. Loren knew that the answers were in Reno. Charles Talley worked at the Eager Beaver in Reno.

Kimmy Dale did too. Now Yates and Dollinger were on their way there. So Loren made sure that she was off the clock. Then she booked a flight and rushed to the airport. Before she boarded, she made one more phone call. Len Friedman was still in his basement office.

'Hey,' Friedman said. 'Is this about getting me Candi Cane's autopsy?'

'It's yours, if you answer a few more questions. You said something about "what goes on in Vegas stays in Vegas."'

'Yes.'

'When I asked if you meant that Clyde Rangor and Emma Lemay were telling on patrons, you said, "Worse."'

There was silence.

'What did you mean, Mr. Friedman?'

'It's just something I heard,' he said.

'What?'

'That Rangor had a scheme going.'

'You mean like a blackmail scheme?'

'Yeah, something like that.'

He went quiet.

'How like that?' she asked.

'He made tapes.'

'Of?'

'Of what you think.'

'His clients having sex with women?'

Again there was a brief silence.

'Mr. Friedman?'

'Yes,' he said. 'But . . .'

'But what?'

'But' – his voice grew soft – 'I'm not sure you'd call them women.'

She frowned. 'They were men?'

'No, not like that,' Friedman said. 'Look, I don't even know if it's true. People make stuff up all the time.'

'And you think that's the case here?'

'I don't know, that's all I'm saying.'

'But you heard rumors?'

'Yes.'

'So what are these rumors?' Loren asked. 'What did Rangor have on those tapes?'

53

Matt got off the plane and hurried out of the airport. Nobody stopped him. He felt a rush. He'd done it. He'd made it to Reno with hours to spare.

He grabbed a taxi. '488 Center Lane Drive.'

They drove in silence. When they pulled up to the address, Matt stared out the window at the Eager Beaver. He paid the driver, got out, and headed inside.

Fitting, he thought to himself.

While he had not expected 488 Center Lane Drive to be a strip joint, he was not all that surprised either. Olivia was missing something in all of this. He understood that. He even understood why. She wanted to find her child. It had blinded her a bit. She couldn't see what was so obvious to him: This was about more than an adoption or even a scam to extort money.

It all came back to the pictures on his camera phone.

If you're the family with a sick daughter, you are not interested in making a husband jealous. If you're a lowlife crook after a big payday, you don't care about breaking up a marriage.

But this had to be about more than that. Matt wasn't sure what exactly, but he knew that it was something bad – something that made whoever was behind this want to drag them back to a place like this.

He headed inside and found a table in the corner. He looked around, hoping to see Olivia. He didn't. Three girls slowly undulated onstage. He tried to imagine his beautiful wife, the one who made everyone lucky enough to encounter her feel somehow blessed, up there like that. Oddly enough it wasn't that hard to picture. Rather than confusing him, something about Olivia's shocking confessions made it all click. It was why she had such a zest for things most found too ordinary, why she so badly wanted a family, a home, the life in the suburbs. She yearned for what we consider both our normalcy and our dream. He understood that better now. It made more sense to him.

That life. The life they were trying to make together. She was right: It was worth fighting for.

A waitress came by and Matt asked for coffee. He needed the caffeine fix. She brought it over. It was surprisingly good. He sipped it and watched the girls and tried to put some of the facts together. Nothing was really coming to him.

He stood and asked if there was a pay phone. The bouncer, a fat man with a pockmarked face, pointed with his thumb. Matt had a prepaid phone card. He always carried it – another holdover from what he'd learned in the pen, he guessed. The truth was, you could trace a phone card. You could find out where it came from and even who bought it. Eventually. Best example was when prosecutors traced a call made with a phone card in the Oklahoma bombing case. But it took time. It could be used to prosecute, but Matt wasn't worried about that anymore.

His cell phone was off. If you keep it on, there are ways to figure out where you are. Cell-phone tracking, even without making a call, is a reality. He pressed in the digits for the 800 number, then his code, then Midlife's private line at the office.

'Ike Kier.'

'It's me.'

'Don't say anything you don't want someone else to hear.'

'Then you do the talking, Ike.'

'Olivia is okay.'

'Did they hold her?'

'No. She's, uh, gone.'

That was good to hear. 'And?'

'Hold on.' He passed the phone.

'Hey, Matt.'

It was Cingle.

'I talked to that investigator friend of yours. I hope you don't mind, but they had my ass over a barrel.'

'That's okay.'

'Nothing I said will hurt you anyway.'

'Don't worry about it,' he said.

Matt was looking off in the direction of the club's entrance. Cingle was telling him something else, something about Darrow and Talley, but there was a sudden rush in his ears.

Matt almost dropped the phone when he saw who'd just walked into the Eager Beaver.

It was Loren Muse.

Loren Muse flashed her badge at the fat guy at the door.

'I'm looking for one of your dancers. Her name is Kimmy Dale.'

The fat man just stared at her.

'Did you hear me?'

'Yeah.'

'So?'

'So your ID says New Jersey.'

'I'm still a law enforcement officer.'

The fat man shook his head. 'You're out of your jurisdiction.'

'What are you, a lawyer?'

The fat man pointed at her. 'Good one. Bye, bye now.'

'I said I'm looking for Kimmy Dale.'

'And I said you have no jurisdiction here.'

'You want me to bring someone more local?'

He shrugged. 'If that gets you off, honey, do whatever.'

'I can make trouble.'

'This.' The fat man smiled and pointed at his own face. 'This is me scared.'

Loren's cell phone rang. She took a step to the right. The music blared. She put the phone to her right ear and stuck a finger in her left. Her eyes squinted, as if that'd make the connection better.

'Hello?'

'I want to make a deal with you.'

It was Matt Hunter.

'I'm listening.'

'I surrender to you and only you. We go somewhere and wait until at least one in the morning.'

'Why one in the morning?'

'Do you think I killed Darrow or Talley?'

'You're certainly wanted for questioning.'

'I didn't ask you that. I asked you if you think I killed them.'

She frowned. 'No, Matt. I don't think you have anything to do with it. But I think your wife does. I know her real name. I know she's been hiding and running for a long time. I think that Max Darrow somehow figured out that she was still alive. I think they went after her and that somehow you got caught in the middle.'

'Olivia is innocent.'

'That,' Loren said, 'I'm not sure about.'

'My deal still stands. I surrender to you. We go somewhere else and talk this out until one in the morning.'

'Somewhere else? You don't even know where I am.'

'Yeah,' Matt said. 'I know exactly where you are.'

'How?'

She heard a click. Damn, he hung up. She was about to dial in for an immediate trace when she felt a tap on her shoulder. She turned and he was standing right there, as if he'd just materialized out of thin air.

'So,' Matt said. 'Was I smart to trust you?'

54

When the plane landed, Cal Dollinger took over. Yates was used to that. Most mistook Dollinger as the muscle and Yates as the brains. In truth theirs had always been closer to a more political partnership. Adam Yates was the candidate who stayed clean. Cal Dollinger was behind-the-scenes and willing to get nasty.

'Go ahead,' Dollinger said. 'Make the call.'

Yates called Ted Stevens, the agent they had assigned to follow Olivia Hunter.

'Hey, Ted, you still on her?' Yates asked.

'I am at that.'

'Where is she?'

'You're not going to believe this. Ms. Hunter got off the plane and headed straight to a strip joint called the Eager Beaver.'

'She still there?'

'No, she left with a black stripper. I followed them back to some dump on the west side of town.' Stevens gave him the address. Yates repeated it for Dollinger.

'So Olivia Hunter is still at the stripper's trailer,' Yates asked.

'Yes.'

'Anyone else with them?'

'Nope, just the two of them alone.'

Yates looked at Dollinger. They had discussed how to handle this, how to get Stevens off the case and set it up for what was about to occur. 'Okay, thanks, Ted, you can leave them now. Meet me at the Reno office in ten minutes.'

'Someone else picking them up?' Stevens asked.

'Not necessary,' Yates said.

'What's going on?'

'Olivia Hunter used to work the clubs for Comb-Over. We flipped her yesterday.'

'She knows a lot?'

'She knows enough,' Yates said.

'So what's she doing with the black chick?'

'Well, she promised us that she would try to convince a woman named Kimmy Dale, a black dancer who works at the Eager Beaver, to flip too. Hunter told us that Dale knows a ton. So we gave her rope, see if she was keeping her word.'

'Which it looks like she is.'

'Yeah.'

'So we're in good shape.'

Yates looked over at Dollinger. 'As long as Comb-Over doesn't find out, yeah, I think we're in real good shape. I'll meet you at the office in ten minutes, Ted. We'll talk more.'

Yates pressed the end button. They were in the concourse now, heading for the exit. He and Dollinger walked shoulder to shoulder, as they'd done since elementary school. They lived on the same block in Henderson, outside of Las Vegas. Their wives had been college roommates and were still inseparable. Dollinger's oldest son was best friends with Yates's daughter Anne. He drove her to school every morning.

'There has to be another way,' Yates said.

'There isn't.'

'We're crossing a line here, Cal.'

'We've crossed lines before.'

'Not like this.'

'No, not like this,' Cal agreed. 'We have families.'

'I know.'

'You have to do the math. On one side, you have one person. Candace Potter, an ex-stripper, probably an old coked-out whore, who was involved with lowlifes like Clyde Rangor and Emma Lemay. That's on one side of the equation, right?'

Yates nodded, knowing how this would go.

'On the other side are two families. Two husbands, two wives, three kids of yours, two of mine. You and me, we may not be that innocent. But the rest of them are. So we end one ex-hooker's life, maybe two if I can't get her away from this Kimmy Dale – or we let seven other lives, worthy lives, get destroyed.'

Yates kept his head down.

'Us or them,' Dollinger said. 'In this case, it's not even a close call.'

'I should go with you.'

'No. We need you to be at the office with Ted. You're creating our murder scenario. When Hunter's body is found, it will naturally look like a mob hit to keep an informant quiet.'

They headed outside. Night had begun to settle in now.

'I'm sorry,' Yates said.

'You've pulled my butt out of plenty of fires, Adam.'

'There has to be another way,' Yates said again. 'Tell me there's another way.'

'Go to the office,' Dollinger said. 'I'll call you when it's done.'

55

The smell of potpourri filled Kimmy's trailer.

Whenever Olivia had smelled potpourri over the past decade it brought her back to that trailer outside Vegas. Kimmy's new place still had that same smell. Olivia could feel herself start slipping back in time.

If there were train tracks nearby, this neighborhood was on the wrong side of them. The trailer had siding that seemed to be in mid-shed. Missing windows were covered with plywood. Her rusted car cowered like an abandoned dog. The driveway was oil-stained sand. But the interior, besides the aforementioned odor, was clean and what magazines would dub tastefully furnished. Nothing expensive, of course. But there were little touches. Nice throw pillows. Small figurines.

It was, in short, a home.

Kimmy grabbed two glasses and a bottle of wine. They sat on a futon couch, and Kimmy poured. The air conditioner whirred. Kimmy put her glass to the side. She reached out with both hands and gently placed them on Olivia's cheeks.

'I can't believe you're here,' Kimmy said softly.

Then Olivia told her the whole story.

It took a while. She started with being sick at the club, going back to the trailer early, Cassandra's dead body, Clyde attacking her. Kimmy listened, totally rapt. She did not say a word. She cried sometimes. She shook. But she did not interrupt.

When Olivia mentioned the online post about her daughter, she saw Kimmy go rigid.

'What?'

'I met her,' Kimmy said.

Olivia felt her stomach drop. 'My daughter?'

'She came here,' Kimmy said. 'To my house.'

'When?'

'Two months ago.'

'I don't understand. She came here? Why?'

'She said she started looking for her birth mother. You know, out of curiosity. The way kids do. I told her as nicely as I could that you were dead, but she already knew that. Said she wanted to find Clyde and avenge you, something like that.'

'How would she have known about Clyde?'

'She said – let me think a second – she said that first she went to the cop who handled your homicide.'

'Max Darrow?'

'Right, I think that's the name. She went to him. He told her that he thought Clyde killed you but that nobody knew where Clyde was.' Kimmy shook her head. 'All these years. That son of a bitch has been dead all these years?'

'Yes,' Olivia said.

'It's like hearing Satan died, you know.'

She did. 'What was my daughter's name?'

'She didn't tell me.'

'Did she look sick?'

'Sick? Oh, wait, I see. Because of that online post. No, she looked pretty healthy.' Kimmy smiled then. 'She was pretty. Not flashy. She had spunk though. Just like you. I gave her that picture. You know, the one of us from the Sayers-Pic routine. You remember that?'

'Yeah. Yeah, I do.'

Kimmy just shook her head. 'I just can't believe you're

here. It's like a dream or something. I'm scared you're going to start to fade away and I'm going to wake up in this cockroach hell without you.'

'I'm here,' Olivia said.

'And you're married. And pregnant.' She shook her head some more and let loose a dazzling smile. 'I just can't believe it.'

'Kimmy, do you know a Charles Talley?'

'You mean Chally? Crazy whack-job. He works at the club now.'

'When did you last see him?'

'Oh, I don't know. Week at least.' She frowned. 'Why? What does that bastard have to do with this?'

Olivia was silent.

'What is it, Candi?'

'They're dead.'

'Who?'

'Charles Talley and Max Darrow. They were in on it somehow. I don't know. Something with my daughter coming back tipped them off. They probably wrote that post to find me.' Olivia frowned. Something felt off about that part, but for now she pushed through. 'Darrow wanted money. I gave him fifty thousand. Charles Talley was involved too.'

'You're not making sense.'

'I was supposed to meet with someone tonight,' Olivia said. 'They were supposed to show me my daughter. Only now Darrow and Chally are both dead. And someone is still looking for some tape.'

Again Kimmy's face fell. 'Tape?'

'When Clyde was beating me up, he kept asking, 'Where's the tape?' And then today –'

'Wait a second.' Kimmy held up a hand. 'Clyde asked you that?'

395

'Yes.'

'And that's why he killed Cassandra? To find a video-tape?'

'I think so, yeah. He was going nuts searching for it.' Kimmy started biting her nails.

'Kimmy?'

But her old friend just stood and walked toward the cabinet in the corner.

'What's going on?' Olivia asked.

'I know why Clyde wanted the tape,' Kimmy said, her voice suddenly calm. She pulled open the cabinet door. 'And I know where it is.'

56

Matt led Loren to the Eager Beaver's darkened back booth. They sat down as ABC began to sing 'The Look of Love.' The room was dark. The strippers felt suddenly far away.

'You're not armed, are you?' Matt said.

'I didn't have time to get a weapon approval.'

'You're also here on your own.'

'So?'

Matt shrugged. 'If I wanted to, I could probably still knock you over and run.'

'I'm tougher than I look.'

'I don't doubt it. You were a tough kid.'

'You weren't.'

He nodded. 'So what do you know about my wife?'

'Why don't you start, Matt?'

'Because I've done all the stuff that shows trust so far,' he replied. 'You haven't.'

'Fair point.'

'So?'

Loren thought about it but not for long. There was no reason not to. She truly believed he was innocent and if she was wrong, the evidence would prove it. He wouldn't be able to talk his way out of it. Ex-cons don't have that luxury.

'I know your wife's real name is Candace Potter.'

She started talking. He did too. He interrupted with questions and follow-ups. When Loren reached the part about the Candace Potter autopsy, about the AIS woman, Matt sat up and his eyes widened.

'Say that again.'

'Max Darrow checked off the part about the victim having AIS.'

'Which you said is like being a hermaphrodite?'

'A little, yeah.'

He nodded. 'So that's how Darrow figured it out.'

'Figured out what?'

'That Candace Potter was alive. Look, my wife had a daughter when she was fifteen. The baby was put up for adoption.'

Loren started nodding. 'So somehow Darrow found that out.'

'Exactly.'

'And then he remembers the AIS from the autopsy. If Candace Potter was at one time pregnant –'

'Then it couldn't have been Candace Potter who was murdered,' Matt finished.

'Your wife is supposed to meet with her daughter here tonight?'

'At midnight, right.'

Loren nodded. 'That's why you made this deal with me. That one a.m. thing. So your wife would be able to keep her rendezvous with her daughter.'

'Right,' Matt said.

'Nice of you. To make that sacrifice.'

'Yeah, I'm a prince except . . .' Matt stopped. 'Oh, Christ, think about what we've been saying. It's all a setup. It has to be.'

'I'm not following.'

'Okay, let's say you're Max Darrow. Let's say you fig-ure out that Candace Potter is still alive, that she ran off. How would you find her after all these years?'

'I don't know.'

'You'd try to draw her out, right?'

'Yeah, I guess.'

'And how? By forcing her to show herself. You might post something about her long-lost daughter being on death's door. You, if you're a cop, might be able to find out some details about the hospital, the town, the doctor. Maybe you even find out from the adopted daughter herself, I don't know.'

'Risky,' Loren said.

'Risky how?'

'What would make him think she'd still be looking up her old name like that?'

He thought about that. 'I'm not sure. But of course that's not all you do. You try to follow up on any old leads. You go back over the case step-by-step. But if she's out there, if she's got a computer like everyone else in the free world, maybe she's going to be curious and Google her old name. It's bound to happen, right?'

Loren frowned. So did Matt. The same thing kept troubling him.

'Those pictures on my camera phone,' he said.

'What about them?'

He was thinking about how to put it when the waitress popped up to their booth. 'Another drink?'

Matt took out his wallet. He plucked out a twenty-dollar bill and showed it to her. 'Do you know Kimmy Dale?'

She hesitated.

'I only want a yes or no,' Matt said. 'Twenty bucks.'

'Yes.'

He handed her the twenty and took out another.

'Is she here?'

'Just yes or no again?'

'Right.'

'No.'

He handed it to her. He took out three more. 'You get these if you tell me where she is.'

The waitress thought about it. Matt kept the money in sight.

'Kimmy might be home. I mean, it was weird. Her shift is supposed to run until eleven, but she just ran out an hour ago with some lady.'

Loren turned to him, but Matt did not blink. His face kept still. He took out another twenty. He also took out a photograph of Olivia. 'Was this the lady Kimmy left with?'

The waitress suddenly looked scared. She didn't answer. She didn't have to. Loren was already up and starting for the door. Matt dropped the dollars and followed her.

'What's up?' Matt said.

'Come on,' Loren called back. 'I already have Kimmy Dale's address.'

Kimmy put the videotape into the player. 'I should have known,' she said.

Olivia sat on the futon and waited.

'You remember that closet in the kitchen?' Kimmy asked.

'Yes.'

'Three, maybe four weeks after your murder, I bought this big vat of vegetable oil. I got on a stepladder to put it on the top shelf and behind the lip on top of the door, I saw this' – she pointed with her chin toward the screen – 'stuck up there with duct tape.'

'Have you watched it?'

'Yeah,' she said softly. 'I should have – I don't know –

gotten rid of it. Given it to the police, something.'

'Why didn't you?'

Kimmy just shrugged.

'What's on it?'

She looked like she was about to explain, but then she gestured toward the screen. 'Watch.'

Olivia sat up. Kimmy paced, wringing her hands, not looking at the screen. For a few seconds there was nothing but static. Then it snapped to an all-too-familiar scene.

A bedroom.

It was filmed in black and white. The date and time were stamped in the corner. A man sat on the edge of a bed. She did not recognize him.

A male voice whispered, 'This is Mr. Alexander.'

Mr. Alexander – if that was his real name – started undressing. From stage right, a woman appeared and started to help him.

'Cassandra,' Olivia said.

Kimmy nodded.

Olivia frowned. 'Clyde was taping customers?'

'Yes,' Kimmy said. 'But with a twist.'

'What sort of twist?'

On the screen, both participants were naked. Cassandra was on top of the man now. Her back was arched. Her mouth was open. They could hear her purported cries of passion – they couldn't have sounded more fake if she'd used a cartoon voice.

'I think I've seen enough,' Olivia said.

'No,' Kimmy said, 'I don't think you have.'

Kimmy hit the fast-forward button. The onscreen activities became more hurried. Changing positions, quick shifts. It didn't take all that long. The man was done and dressed in fast-forward seconds. When he left the room,

Kimmy let go of the button. The tape slowed back down to normal speed.

Cassandra moved closer to the camera. She smiled into the lens. Olivia felt her breath grow deep. 'Look at her, Kimmy. She was so young.'

Kimmy stopped pacing. She put a finger to her lips and then pointed it at the screen.

A man's voice came on. 'This is a souvenir for Mr. Alexander.'

Olivia made a face. Sounded like Clyde Rangor trying to disguise his voice.

'Did you have fun, Cassandra?'

'I had lots of fun,' Cassandra said in the flattest monotone. 'Mr. Alexander was just great.'

There was a brief pause. Cassandra licked her lips and glanced toward someone who was out of the shot, as if waiting for her cue. It came soon enough.

'How old are you, Cassandra?'

'I'm fifteen.'

'Are you sure?'

Cassandra nodded. Someone off camera handed her a sheet of paper. 'I just turned fifteen last week. Here's my birth certificate.' She put the document close to the lens. For a moment the picture was blurry, but then someone worked the focus. Cassandra held it up for nearly thirty seconds. Born at the Mercy Medical Center in Nampa, Idaho. Parents were named Mary and Sylvester. Dates were clearly visible.

'Mr. Alexander said he wanted someone fourteen,' Cassandra said, as if reading her lines for the first time, 'but then he said I'd be okay.'

The camera went back to static.

Olivia sat in silence. So did Kimmy. It took a while for the full weight of what Clyde Rangor had done to hit her.

'My God,' she said.

Kimmy nodded.

'Clyde didn't just blackmail them with prostitutes,' Olivia said. 'He set them up with underage girls. He had their birth certificates for proof. He even pretended that the johns were the ones who requested pubescent girls, but either way, even if you claim that you thought the girl was over eighteen, that's a serious crime. This guy, this Mr. Alexander, he didn't just risk being embarrassed or found out. He could be ruined. He could end up in jail.'

Kimmy nodded.

The static ended and another man appeared on the screen.

'This is Mr. Douglas,' the whispery voice said.

Olivia felt her blood go cold. 'Oh, no.'

'Candi?'

She moved closer to the screen. The man. The man on the bed. No question about it. Mr. Douglas was Adam Yates. Olivia watched transfixed. Cassandra entered the room again. She helped him undress. So that was it. That was why Clyde had gotten so desperate. He had taped an important federal officer. He probably didn't know that – not even Clyde Rangor would be that stupid – and when he tried to blackmail him, it had all gone wrong.

'You know him?' Kimmy said.

'Yeah,' Olivia said. 'We just met.'

The front door burst open. Olivia and Kimmy both spun toward the sound.

Kimmy shouted, 'What the . . . ?'

Cal Dollinger closed the door behind him, pulled out his gun, and took aim.

57

Loren had rented a car.

Matt said, 'So how do you think it worked here? Darrow got the ball rolling?'

'It makes the most sense,' she agreed. 'Darrow somehow finds out about your wife having a daughter. He remembers the autopsy. Then he starts to figure out what really happened back then. He knows there was money involved. He hires some muscle to help out.'

'That would be Charles Talley?'

'Right, Talley.'

'And you think he found Olivia when she answered that post online?'

'Yes, but . . .' Loren stopped.

'What?'

'They found Emma Lemay first.'

'As Sister Mary Rose.'

'Yes.'

'How?'

'I don't know. Maybe she was trying to make amends. I mean, I got the whole story on her from the Mother Superior. Sister Mary Rose has lived a good and pious life since she changed IDs. Maybe, I don't know, maybe she saw the post too.'

'And tried to help?'

'Yes. And that might explain that six-minute phone call from St. Margaret's to your sister-in-law's house.'

'She was warning Olivia?'

'Maybe, I don't know. But they probably found Emma Lemay first. The medical examiner says they tortured her. Maybe they wanted money. Or maybe they wanted your wife's name. Whatever, Emma Lemay ends up dead. And when I try to find out her true identity, it sets off warning bells.'

'And this FBI guy. Yates. He hears them?'

'Yes. Or maybe he already knew about Lemay. Maybe he was using that as a cover to come out and get involved, I'm not sure.'

'And you think Yates is trying to cover something up?'

'I have a source who told me about this blackmail taping involving underage girls. He's not sure if they're real. But if they are, yeah, I think that somehow he's tied into all this. I think he took me off the case because I was getting too close. He's in Reno too right now.'

Matt faced front. 'How much longer?'

'Next block.'

The car had barely made the turn when Loren spotted Cal Dollinger near a trailer. He was hunched down, looking through a window. She slammed on the brake. 'Damn.'

'What?'

'We need a weapon.'

'Why? What's wrong?'

'That's Yates's man. By the window.'

Dollinger stood up. They could see him reach into his jacket and pull out a gun. With a speed that defied his bulk, Dollinger moved to the door, pushed against it, and disappeared inside.

Matt did not hesitate.

'Wait, where are you going?'

He didn't look back, didn't break stride. He sprinted toward the house. He could see through the window into the trailer.

Olivia was there.

She stood up suddenly and put up her hands. Another woman – he assumed it was Kimmy Dale – was there too. She opened her mouth to scream. Dollinger was pointing the gun at them.

He fired.

Oh, no. . . .

Kimmy fell. Olivia dived from view. Matt did not let up. Dollinger stood not far from a window. Using all his momentum, realizing that time was past the point of essence, Matt leaped toward the glass. He tucked his chin and led with his forearms.

The glass shattered with surprising ease.

Matt got his legs under him. He landed and again there was no hesitation. Dollinger still had the gun. His mouth had dropped open in surprise. Matt did not want to lose that. He jumped straight at him.

It was like jumping against a cement block. Dollinger barely gave at all.

'Run!' Matt shouted.

Dollinger reacted now. He aimed his gun at Matt. Matt took hold of Dollinger's wrist with both hands. He pulled. So did Dollinger. Even though Matt was using two hands against Dollinger's one, Matt was losing the battle of strength. With his free hand, Dollinger hit Matt in the ribs with an uppercut. Matt felt his belly collapse, the air go out of him. He wanted to collapse and writhe on the floor.

But he wouldn't.

Olivia was here.

So he held on to the wrist with all he had.

Another fist slammed under his rib cage. Matt's eyes watered. He saw dark spots. He was losing consciousness, losing his grip.

A voice screamed, 'Freeze! Police! Drop your weapon!'
It was Loren Muse.

Dollinger let him go. Matt sank to the floor. But only for a second. He looked up at Dollinger. Dollinger had a funny look on his face. He glanced about the room.

Loren Muse was nowhere in sight.

Matt knew how this would go. Dollinger would wonder why she wasn't showing herself. He would remember that she had just flown over from Newark, that she was a county investigator, that the authorities would not let her travel with a gun.

He would realize that Loren didn't have a weapon. That she was bluffing.

Olivia was crawling toward Kimmy Dale. Matt looked over at her. Their eyes met. 'Go,' he mouthed. He looked back up at Dollinger.

Dollinger had put it together now.

He swung his aim back toward Olivia.

'No!' Matt shouted.

He bent his legs and pushed off as if they were two pistons. He knew something about real-life fights. He knew that the good big man almost always beats the good little man. But he didn't care about winning. He cared about saving his wife. He just needed to do enough so that Olivia could get free.

And Matt knew something else.

Even the biggest, strongest men have the same vulnerable spots as the rest of us.

Matt positioned his hand for a palm strike. He leaped up and smacked Dollinger in the heart of the groin. The big man made an oof noise and bent at the waist. He grabbed Matt on his way down. Matt tried to straighten. Dollinger was too big.

Vulnerable spots, he thought. Hit the vulnerable spots.

Matt reared back with his head. The skull landed on Dollinger's nose. Dollinger howled and stood up. Matt looked over at his wife.

What the . . . ?

Olivia had not run away. He couldn't believe it. She was still by Kimmy's side, working on her friend's leg, feverishly trying, he assumed, to stop the bleeding or something.

'Get out!' he shouted.

Dollinger had recovered. The gun was aimed at Matt now.

From the other end of the trailer Loren Muse let out a cry and pounced on Dollinger's back. She reached around for his face. The big man pulled back, his nose and mouth covered with blood. He threw Loren off like a bucking bronco. She landed hard against the wall. Matt jumped up.

Go for the vulnerable . . .

He tried to get Dollinger's eyes and missed. His hand slipped down. They ended up on the big man's throat.

Just like before.

Just like all those years ago, on a college campus in Massachusetts, with a boy named Stephen McGrath.

Matt didn't care.

He squeezed hard. He put his thumb on the hollow of the throat. And he squeezed some more.

Dollinger's eyes bulged. But his gun hand was free now. He raised his weapon toward Matt's head. Matt let go of the throat with one hand. He tried to deflect Dollinger's aim. The gun fired anyway. Something hot sliced into the flesh above Matt's hip.

His leg went slack. His hand dropped off Dollinger's neck.

Dollinger had the gun ready now. He looked into Matt's eyes and started to squeeze the trigger.

A shot rang out.

Dollinger's eyes bulged a little more. The bullet had hit his temple. The big man folded to the floor. Matt spun and looked at his wife.

In her hand she had a small pistol. Matt crawled over to her. They looked down. Kimmy Dale wasn't bleeding from her leg. She was bleeding from a spot just above the elbow.

'You remembered,' Kimmy said.

Olivia smiled.

Matt said, 'Remembered what?'

'Like I told you,' Olivia said, 'Kimmy always kept a gun in her boot. It just took me a few seconds to dig it out.'

58

Loren Muse sat across from Harris Grimes, the assistant director in charge who ran the FBI's Los Angeles field office. Grimes was one of the most powerful federal officers in the region, and he was not a happy man.

'You realize that Adam Yates is a friend of mine,' Grimes said.

'It's the third time you've told me,' Loren said.

They were using a room on the second floor of the Washoe Medical Center in Reno. Grimes narrowed his eyes and chewed on his lower lip. 'Are you being insubordinate, Muse?'

'I've told you what happened three times.'

'And you'll tell it again. Now.'

She did. There was a lot to cover. It took hours. The case wasn't over. There were still plenty of questions. Yates was missing. No one knew where he was. But Dollinger was dead. Loren was learning that he, too, had been well liked by his fellow agents.

Grimes stood and rubbed his chin. There were three other agents in the room, all with legal pads, all keeping their heads down and jotting away. They knew now. No one wanted to believe it, but the videotape of Yates and Cassandra spoke volumes. Grudgingly they were beginning to accept her theory. They just weren't liking it.

'You have any idea where Yates would have gone?' Grimes asked her.

'No.'

'He was last seen at our Reno office on Kietzke Lane maybe fifteen minutes before the incident at Ms. Dale's residence. He checked in with a special agent named Ted Stevens, who'd been told to trail Olivia Hunter when she arrived at the airport.'

'Right. You told me. Can I go now?'

Grimes turned his back and waved his hand. 'Get the hell out of my sight.'

She stood and walked downstairs to the emergency room on the first floor. Olivia Hunter sat by the ER receptionist.

'Hey,' Loren said.

'Hi.' Olivia managed to smile. 'I just came down to check on Kimmy.'

Olivia had suffered no real injuries. Kimmy Dale was finishing up at the other end of the corridor. Her arm was wrapped in a sling. The bullet had missed bone, but there was serious muscle and tissue damage. It would be painful and need hours of rehabilitation. But, alas, in this era of getting people out of the hospital pronto – six days after having his chest cut open Bill Clinton was reading in his backyard – they finished asking their questions and told Kimmy that she could go home but needed to 'stay in town.'

'Where's Matt?' Loren asked.

'He just came out of surgery,' Olivia said.

'Did it go okay?'

'The doctor said he'll be fine.'

The bullet from Dollinger's gun had grazed the neck of Matt's femur just below the hip joint. The doctors needed to put in a couple of bone screws. Fairly minor surgery, they said. He'd be up and out in two days.

'You should get some rest,' Olivia said.

'Can't,' Loren said. 'I'm too wired.'

'Yeah, me too. Why don't you sit with Matt in case he wakes up? I'm just going to get Kimmy settled and then I'll be right up.'

Loren took the elevator to the third floor. She sat next to Matt's bed. She thought about the case, about Adam Yates, about where he was and what he might do.

A few minutes later Matt's eyes blinked open. He looked up at her.

'Hey, hero,' Loren said.

Matt managed a smile. He turned his head to the right.

'Olivia?'

'She's downstairs with Kimmy.'

'Is Kimmy . . . ?'

'She's fine. Olivia's just helping her get settled.'

He closed his eyes. 'There's something I need you to do.'

'Why don't you rest?'

Matt shook his head. His voice was weak. 'I need you to get some phone records for me.'

'Now?'

'The camera phone,' he said. 'The picture. The video. It still doesn't add up. Why would Yates and Dollinger take those pictures?'

'They didn't. Darrow did.'

'Why . . .' He closed his eyes again. 'Why would he?'

Loren thought about that. Then Matt's eyes suddenly opened. 'What time is it?'

She checked her watch. 'Eleven thirty.'

'At night?'

'Of course at night.'

And then Loren remembered. The meeting at midnight. At the Eager Beaver. She quickly grabbed the phone and called down to the emergency room receptionist.

'This is Investigator Muse. I was down there a few moments ago with a woman named Olivia Hunter. She was waiting for a patient named Kimmy Dale.'

'Right,' the receptionist said, 'I saw you.'

'Are they still there?'

'Who, Miss Dale and Miss Hunter?'

'Yes.'

'No, they hurried out the same time you left.'

'Hurried out?'

'Into a taxi.'

Loren hung up. 'They're gone.'

'Give me the phone,' Matt said, still flat on his back. She nestled the phone next to his ear. Matt gave her Olivia's cell number. The phone rang three times before he heard Olivia's voice.

'It's me,' he said.

'Are you okay?' Olivia asked.

'Where are you?'

'You know where.'

'You still think . . .'

'She called, Matt.'

'What?'

'She called Kimmy's cell. Or someone did. She said the meeting was still on, but no cops, no husbands, nobody. We're on our way over now.'

'Olivia, it has to be a setup. You know that.'

'I'll be fine.'

'Loren is on her way.'

'No. Please, Matt. I know what I'm doing. Please.'

And then Olivia hung up.

59

When Olivia and Kimmy arrived, the fat man at the door pointed to Kimmy and said, 'You left early. You got hours to make up.'

Kimmy showed him her arm in a sling. 'I'm hurt.'

'What, you can't get naked with that?'

'You for real?'

'This.' He pointed to his face. 'This is me being real. Some guys get turned on by that kinda thing.'

'An arm in a cast?'

'Sure. Like the guys who get off on amputees.'

'I'm not an amputee.'

'Hey, guys get turned on by a strong wind, you know what I'm saying?' The fat man rubbed his hands together. 'I used to know a guy who got off on toe jam. Toe jam.'

'Nice.'

'So who's your friend?'

'Nobody.'

He shrugged. 'Some cop from New Jersey was asking about you.'

'I know. It's okay now.'

'I want you to go on. With that sling.'

Kimmy looked at Olivia. 'I might be better able to watch up there, you know. Like I won't be noticed.'

414

Olivia nodded. 'Up to you,' she said.

Kimmy disappeared into the back room. Olivia sat at a table. She did not see or notice the crowd. She did not look in the dancer's face for her daughter. There was a rushing in her head. Sadness, an overwhelming sadness, weighed her down.

Call it off, she thought. Walk away.

She was pregnant. Her husband was in the hospital. That was where her life was now. This was in the past. She should leave it there.

But she didn't do that.

Olivia thought again about how the abused always take the path of self-destruction. They simply could not stop themselves. They take it no matter what the consequences, no matter what the danger. Or maybe, as in her case, they take it for the opposite reason – because no matter how much life has tried to beat them down, they cannot let go of hope.

Wasn't there still a chance that tonight she'd be reunited with the baby she'd put up for adoption all those years ago?

The waitress came over to the table. 'Are you Candace Potter?'

There was no hesitation. 'Yes, I am.'

'I have a message for you.'

She handed Olivia a note and left. The message was short and simple:

Go to backroom B now. Wait ten minutes.

It felt like she was walking on stilts. Her head spun. Her stomach churned. She bumped into a man on the way and said, 'Excuse me,' and he said, 'Hey, baby, my pleasure.' The men with him yukked it up. Olivia kept walking. She found the back area. She found the door with the letter B on it, the same one she'd been in just a few hours ago.

She opened it and went inside. Her cell phone rang. She picked it up and said hello.

'Don't hang up.'

It was Matt.

'Are you at the club?'

'Yes.'

'Get out of there. I think I know what's going on –'

'Shh.'

'What?'

Olivia was crying now. 'I love you, Matt.'

'Olivia, whatever you're thinking, please, just –'

'I love you more than anything in the world.'

'Listen to me. Get out of –'

She closed the phone and turned the power off. She faced the door. Five minutes passed. She stayed standing, not moving, not swaying, not looking around. There was a knock on the door.

'Come in,' she said.

And the door opened.

60

Try as he might, Matt couldn't get out of bed.

'Go!' he told Loren.

She radioed the Reno Police Department and ran to her car. Loren was within two miles of the Eager Beaver when her cell phone sounded.

She picked it up and barked, 'Muse.'

'So are you still in Reno?'

It was Adam Yates. His voice was slurred.

'I am.'

'Are they all applauding your genius?'

'I'd say just the opposite.'

Yates chuckled. 'I was, alas, beloved.'

He had definitely been drinking. 'Tell me where you are, Adam.'

'I meant what I said. You know that, right?'

'Sure, Adam. I know.'

'I mean, about them threatening my family. I never said it was physical. But my wife. My kids. My job. That tape was like a big gun. A big gun they were pointing at us all, you know what I mean?'

'I do,' Loren said.

'I was working undercover, pretending to be a rich real estate dealer. So Clyde Rangor figured I was the perfect mark. I never knew the girl was underage. You need to believe that.'

'Where are you, Adam?'

He ignored her question. 'Someone called. Demanded

a payoff in exchange for the tape. So Cal and me, we went to see Rangor. We leaned on him hard. Ah, who am I kidding? Cal did the leaning. He was a good man but he had a violent streak. He once beat a suspect to death. I saved his ass then. He saved my ass, I saved his. That's what makes a friend. He's dead now, isn't he?'

'Yes.'

'Damn.' He started to cry. 'Cal hurt Emma Lemay. Punched her hard in the kidney. That was his warning. We walk in and I think we're just going to talk and he starts off by spinning Lemay and pounding her back like a heavy bag. Rangor, it doesn't bother him. He beat that woman silly anyway. Better her than him, you know?'

Loren was nearly in the parking lot now.

'So Rangor pisses in his pants. Literally, I mean. He's so scared he runs to his cabinet to get the tape. Only it's gone. The girl, he says, the one in the video. Cassandra, her name is. He says she must have stolen it. He says he'll get it. Cal and me, we figure we got the fear of God in him now. He'll do what we say. Next thing we know, Rangor and Lemay and that Cassandra girl, they all disappear. Years pass. I still think about it. I think about it every day. And then we get that call from the NCIC. Lemay's body's been found. And it all comes back. Like I always knew it would.'

'Adam, it's not too late.'

'Yeah, it is.'

She pulled into the lot. 'You still have friends.'

'I know. I called them. That's why I'm calling you.'

'What?'

'Grimes is going to bury the tape.'

'What are you talking about?'

'If it gets out, it destroys my family. It'll destroy those

other guys on the tape too. They were just being johns, you know.'

'You can't just bury the tape.'

'Nobody needs it anymore. Grimes and his guys will arrange it for me. They just need you to cooperate.'

And then she realized what he was about to do. Panic seized her.

'Wait, Adam, listen to me.'

'Cal and I will die in the line of fire.'

'Adam, don't. You have to listen.'

'Grimes will set it up that way.'

'Think about your kids –'

'I am. Our families will get full benefits.'

'My father, Adam.' Loren had tears on her cheeks now. 'He killed himself. Please, you don't know what this will do –'

But he wasn't listening. 'You just have to keep it to yourself, okay? You're a good investigator. One of the best. Please, for my kids.'

'Dammit, Adam, listen to me!'

'Good-bye, Loren.'

And then he hung up the phone.

Loren Muse put the car in park. She stepped outside, crying, shrieking at the skies, and in the distance, she was sure that she could hear the rumble of a gun blast.

61

The door to Backroom B opened. Olivia waited.

When Kimmy walked into the room, the two women just stared at each other. They both had tears in their eyes. Just like a few hours earlier.

But this was nothing like that.

'You knew,' Kimmy said.

Olivia shook her head. 'I thought.'

'How?'

'You acted like you didn't remember Max Darrow. He was one of your clients in the old days. But the main thing is, everyone figures Darrow put that post online. But he wouldn't have known that it'd draw me out. Only a good friend, my best friend, would know I'd still be checking up on my child.'

Kimmy stepped into the room. 'You just left me, Candi.'

'I know.'

'We were supposed to go together. I told you my dreams. You told me yours. We always helped each other out, remember?'

Olivia nodded.

'You promised me.'

'I know I did.'

Kimmy shook her head. 'All these years, I thought you were dead. I buried you, did you know that? I paid for your funeral. I mourned. I cried for months. I did things to Max for free – anything he wanted – just to make sure he tried to find your killer.'

'You have to understand. I couldn't tell. Emma and I –'

'You what?' Kimmy shouted. The sound echoed in the stillness. 'You made a promise?'

Olivia said nothing.

'I died when you died. Do you know that? The dreams. The hope about getting out of this life. It all died when you did. I lost everything. For all those years.'

'How . . . ?'

'. . . did I find out you were alive?'

Olivia nodded.

'Two days after that girl comes to my door, Max comes over. He said that he sent her – that she wasn't really your daughter. He'd just sent her to test me.'

Olivia tried to make sense of that. 'Test you?'

'Yeah. He knew we were close. He figures I know where you are. So he sets me up. He sends me some girl pretending to be your long-lost daughter. Then he watches me, sees if I'm going to call you or something. But all I do is, I go to your grave site and cry.'

'I'm so sorry, Kimmy.'

'Imagine it, okay? Imagine when Max comes to my house and shows me the autopsy. He tells me the dead girl had some kind of freak condition and couldn't possibly have kids. He tells me you aren't dead and you know what I did? I just shook my head. I didn't believe him. I mean, how could I? Candi would never do that to me, I tell him. She'd never just leave me behind like that. But Max shows me the pictures of the dead girl. It's Cassandra. I start to see the truth now. I start putting it together.'

'And you wanted revenge,' Olivia said.

'Yes. I mean . . . I did.' Kimmy shook her head. 'But it all got so crazy, you know?'

421

'You were the one who helped Darrow find me. You had the idea about posting on the adoption Web site. You knew I'd bite.'

'Yes.'

'So you set up that meet. At the motel.'

'Not just me. If it was just me . . .' Kimmy stopped and just stared. 'I was just so hurt, you know.'

Olivia nodded, said nothing.

'So, yeah, I wanted payback. And I wanted a big payday too. I was the one getting the new life this time. It was finally my turn. But once Max and Chally flew out to Jersey' – Kimmy shut her eyes and shook her head as if she might jar something out – 'it all just spun out of control.'

'You were trying to hurt me,' Olivia said.

Kimmy nodded.

'So first, you went after my marriage with that call to my husband's phone.'

'Max came up with that, actually. He was going to use his own camera phone, but then he realized it'd work even better if he could use yours. See, if something went wrong, Chally would be the guy on the camera phone. He'd be holding the bag. But first he needed Chally's help.'

'With Emma Lemay.'

'Right. Chally was dumb muscle. He and Max flew up to get Emma to talk. But she wouldn't give you up. No matter what they did to her. So they kept pushing. And they just pushed too far.'

Olivia closed her eyes. 'So this' – she gestured around the room – 'us being here tonight, this was to be your grand finale, right, Kimmy? You take my money. You break my heart by showing me that there is no daughter, no child. And then what?'

Kimmy said nothing for several seconds. 'I don't know.'

'Yeah, Kimmy, you do.'

She shook her head, but there was nothing behind it.

'Darrow and Chally wouldn't have let me stay alive,' Olivia said.

'Darrow,' Kimmy said softly, 'had nothing to say about it.'

'Because you killed him?'

'Yes.' She smiled. 'Do you know how many times that son of a bitch had his pants down in a car with me?'

'And that's why you killed him?'

'No.'

'Then why?'

'I needed to stop this,' Kimmy said. 'And I needed to strike first.'

'You thought he'd kill you?'

'For this kind of money, Max Darrow would kill his own mother. Yeah, I was hurt when I found out – no, it was more like . . . it was more like I was in shock. But Max, I thought he was just in this with me. But then he started running his own game too. It had to stop.'

'What do you mean?'

'Just . . .' Her whole persona emanated exhaustion. 'Just forget it,' Kimmy said. 'All that matters is, Max didn't like witnesses. I was an unreliable whore. You think he'd risk that?'

'And Charles Talley?'

'Your husband tracked him down. They got into that fight and then he ran away. Chally called me. See, I was staying on the floor below you. He was in a panic, all worried about the cops coming. He was on parole. One more offense and he was in for life. He'd do anything to avoid that. So I told him to wait in the stairwell.'

'You set it up to look like Matt killed him.'

'That had been what Max wanted all along – to set up both Chally and your husband.' She shrugged. 'I figured, might as well stick with the plan.'

Olivia looked at her old friend. She stepped closer. 'I thought about you,' she said. 'You know that.'

'I know,' Kimmy said. 'But that wasn't enough.'

'I was afraid. Emma said if they found out what we'd done, they'd hurt us all. They'd look for the tape again. We didn't have it. They'd kill us.'

'Look at me,' Kimmy said.

'I am.'

She pulled out a gun. 'Look at what I've become.'

'Kimmy?'

'What?'

'I didn't plan it like this,' Olivia said. 'I thought I would die.'

'I know that now.'

'And I'm pregnant.'

Kimmy nodded. 'I know that too.' The gun in her hand shook.

Olivia took another step closer. 'You won't kill the baby.'

Kimmy's face fell. Her voice was barely audible. 'It was the tape.'

'What was, Kimmy?' And then Olivia saw it. 'Oh. Oh, no . . . .'

'That damn tape,' Kimmy said, tears spilling down her face. 'That's what got Cassandra killed. That's what started it all.'

'Oh, God.' Olivia swallowed. 'Cassandra wasn't the one who stole it from Clyde,' she said. 'You were.'

'For us, Candi. Don't you see?' she pleaded. 'That tape was our ticket out. We were going to get a big stash of cash. We'd run away, you and me – just like we talked about. It'd be our turn, you know? And then I come home and someone's murdered you . . . .'

'All that time, all these years, you . . .' Olivia felt her heart break anew. 'You blamed yourself for my death.'

Kimmy managed a nod.

'I'm so sorry, Kimmy.'

'It hurt so bad when I found out you were alive. You understand? I loved you so much.'

Olivia did understand. You grieve, not just for the dead, but for yourself, for what might have been. You think your best friend, the one person you could dream with . . . you think she died because of you. You live with that guilt for ten years and then one day, you learn it was all a lie. . . .

'We can make it okay,' Olivia said.

Kimmy straightened up. 'Look at me.'

'I want to help.'

There was a hard rap on the door. 'Open up! Police!'

'I killed two men,' Kimmy said to her. Then she smiled – a beatific smile that brought Olivia back. 'Look at my life. It's my turn, remember? My turn to escape.'

'Please, Kimmy . . .'

But Kimmy pointed the gun to the floor and fired. There was a moment of panic and then the door burst open. Kimmy spun toward the door and aimed her gun. Olivia screamed, 'No!'

Gun blasts followed. Kimmy spun one more time, like a marionette, and then she dropped to the floor. Olivia fell to her knees and cupped her friend's head. She lowered her lips to Kimmy's ear.

'Don't . . .' Olivia begged.

But now, at long last, it was Kimmy's turn.

62

Two days later, Loren Muse was home in her garden apartment. She was making a ham and cheese sandwich. She grabbed two slices of bread and put them on her plate. Her mother sat on the couch in the next room, watching *Entertainment Tonight*. Loren heard the familiar theme music. She dug into the mayonnaise and began spreading it on the bread when she started to cry.

Loren's sobs were silent. She waited until they passed, until she could talk again.

'Mom.'

'I'm watching my program.'

Loren moved behind her mother. Carmen was munching down a bag of Fritos. Her swollen feet were propped up with a pillow on the coffee table. Loren smelled the cigarette smoke, listened to her mother's raspy breath.

Adam Yates had killed himself. Grimes would not be able to cover it up. The two girls, Ella and Anne, and the boy, Sam, the one Adam had held in the hospital to ward off death – they would know the truth. Not about the videotape. Despite Adam Yates's fear, those images would not be what haunted his children late at night.

'I always blamed you,' Loren said.

No reply. The only sound came from the television.

'Mom?'

'I heard you.'

'This man I just met. He killed himself. He had three kids.'

Carmen finally turned around.

'See, the reason I blamed you was because otherwise –' She stopped, caught her breath.

'I know,' Carmen said softly.

'How come . . .' Loren said, her voice hitching, the tears flowing freely. Her face began to crumble. 'How come Daddy didn't love me enough to want to live?'

'Oh, honey.'

'You were his wife. He could have left you. But I was his daughter.'

'He loved you so much.'

'But not enough to want to live.'

'It's not like that,' Carmen said. 'He was in so much pain. No one could save him. You were the best thing in his life.'

'You.' Loren wiped her face with her sleeve. 'You let me blame you.'

Carmen said nothing.

'You were trying to protect me.'

'You needed to find blame,' her mother said.

'So all these years . . . you took the hit.'

She thought about Adam Yates, about how much he'd loved his children, about how that hadn't been enough either. She wiped her eyes.

'I should call them,' Loren said.

'Who?'

'His children.'

Carmen nodded and spread out her hands. 'Tomorrow, okay? Right now come here. Come sit with me on the couch here.'

Loren sat on the couch. Her mother scooted over.

'It's okay,' Carmen said.

She threw the afghan over Loren. A commercial came on. Loren leaned on her mother's shoulder. She could smell the stale cigarettes, but that was comforting now. Carmen stroked her daughter's hair. Loren closed her eyes. A few seconds later, her mother began to flick the remote.

'Nothing good on,' Carmen said.

With her eyes still closed, Loren smiled and moved in even closer.

Matt and Olivia flew home that same day. Matt had a cane. He limped, but that wouldn't last much longer. When they stepped off the plane, Matt said, 'I think I should go alone.'

'No,' Olivia said. 'We do this together.'

He did not argue.

They took the same Westport exit, pulled down the same street. There were two cars in the driveway this morning. Matt looked at the basketball hoop. There was no sign of Stephen McGrath. Not today.

They headed to the door together. Olivia held his hand. He rang the bell. A minute passed. Then Clark McGrath opened the door.

'What the hell are you doing here?'

Behind him, Sonya McGrath said, 'Who is it, Clark?'

Sonya pulled up short when she saw who it was. 'Matt?'

'I squeezed too hard,' Matt said.

The grounds were hushed. There was no wind, no cars driving by, no pedestrians. It was just four people and maybe one ghost.

'I could have let go. I was so scared. And I thought Stephen was a part of it. And when we landed, I don't know anymore. I could have done better. I held on too long. I know that now. I can't tell you how sorry I am.'

Clark McGrath bit down, his face reddening. 'You think that makes it all okay?'

'No,' Matt said. 'I know it doesn't. My wife is pregnant now. So I understand better. But it has to end, right here and right now.'

Sonya said, 'What are you talking about, Matt?'

He held up a sheet of paper.

'What is that?' Sonya asked.

'Phone records.'

When Matt first woke up in the hospital, he had asked Loren to get these for him. He had maybe an inkling of a suspicion – no more than that. But something about Kimmy's revenge scheme . . . it seemed like something she could never quite pull off on her own. It seemed too focused, too anxious to destroy not only Olivia . . .

. . . but Matt as well.

'These phone records belong to a man named Max Darrow who lived in Reno, Nevada,' Matt said. 'He called your husband's line eight times in the past week.'

'I don't understand,' Sonya said. She turned to her husband. 'Clark?'

But Clark closed his eyes.

'Max Darrow was a police officer,' Matt said. 'Once he found out who Olivia was, he would have investigated her. He would have learned that her husband was a notorious ex-con. He got in contact with you. I don't know how much you paid him, Mr. McGrath, but it just made so much sense. Kill two birds with one stone. Like Darrow's partner told my wife, he was playing his own game. With you.'

Sonya said, 'Clark?'

'He should be in prison,' Clark spat at her. 'Not having lunch with you.'

'What did you do, Clark?'

Matt stepped closer. 'This is over now, Mr. McGrath. I'm going to apologize one more time for what happened.

I know you won't accept it. I understand that. I'm very sorry about Stephen. But here's something I think you'll understand.'

Matt took one more step. The two men were almost nose to nose.

'If you come near my family again,' Matt said, 'I will kill you.'

Matt walked away. Olivia stayed for another second. She looked first at Clark McGrath and then at Sonya, as if hammering home her husband's words. Then she turned away and took her husband's hand and never looked back.

63

Matt drove away from the McGraths'. For a long time they sat in silence. Damien Rice's 'O' was on the car radio. Olivia leaned forward and flipped it off.

'This feels so weird,' she said.

'I know.'

'We just, what, pick up like nothing happened?'

Matt shook his head. 'I don't think so.'

'We start again?'

Matt shook his head. 'I don't think so.'

'Well, as long as we've got that cleared up.'

He smiled. 'You know something.'

'What?'

'We'll be fine.'

'I won't settle for fine.'

'Neither will I.'

'We will be,' Olivia said, 'spectacular.'

They arrived at Marsha's house. She ran out to greet them, threw her arms around them both. Paul and Ethan followed. Kyra stayed by the door, her arms folded.

'My God,' Marsha said, 'what on earth happened to you two?'

'We have a lot to tell you.'

'Your leg . . .'

Matt waved her off. 'It's fine.'

'The cane is cool, Uncle Matt,' Paul said.

'Yeah, way cool,' chimed in Ethan.

They approached the door where Kyra was standing.

431

Matt remembered how she had helped him escape from the backyard. 'Hey, thanks for that scream.'

She blushed. 'You're welcome.'

Kyra took the boys into the yard. Matt and Olivia began to explain. Marsha listened closely. They told her everything. They did not hold back. She seemed grateful. When they were done, Marsha said, 'Let me make you both lunch.'

'You don't have to –'

'Sit.'

They did. Olivia looked off. Matt could see that there was still a giant hole.

'I already called Cingle,' he said.

'Thank you.'

'We'll find your child.'

Olivia nodded, but she didn't believe it anymore. 'I want to visit Emma's grave. Pay my last respects.'

'I understand.'

'I can't believe she ended up so close to us.'

'What do you mean?'

'That was part of our pact. We knew each other's new identities, of course. But we never communicated. I thought she was still at the parish in Oregon.'

Matt felt the tingle start in his spine. He sat up.

Olivia said, 'What's the matter?'

'You didn't know she was at St. Margaret's?'

'No.'

'But she called you.'

'What?'

'As Sister Mary Rose. There were phone records. She called you.'

Olivia shrugged. 'She could have found out where I was, I guess,' she said. 'She knew my name. Maybe she tried to reach me or warn me.'

Matt shook his head. 'Six minutes.'

'What?'

'The call lasted six minutes. And she didn't call our house. She called here.'

'I don't understand.'

And then another voice said, 'She was calling me.'

They both turned. Kyra stepped into the room. Marsha stood behind her.

Kyra said, 'I've been wondering how to tell you.'

Matt and Olivia stayed still as a stone.

'You didn't break the pact, Olivia,' Kyra said. 'Sister Mary Rose did.'

'I don't understand,' Olivia said.

'See, I always knew I was adopted,' Kyra said.

Olivia put her hand to her mouth. 'Oh, my God . . .'

'And once I started looking into it, I found out pretty fast that my birth mother had been murdered.'

A sound escaped Olivia's mouth. Matt sat stunned. Olivia, he thought. She was from Idaho. And Kyra . . . she lived in one of those Midwestern 'I' states. . . .

'But I wanted to learn more about it. So I tracked down the policeman who investigated the death.'

'Max Darrow,' Matt said.

Kyra nodded. 'I told him who I was. He seemed to genuinely want to help. He took all the information – where I was born, the doctor, all that. He gave me Kimmy Dale's address. I visited her.'

'Wait,' Matt said, 'I thought Kimmy said –'

Kyra looked at him, but Matt stopped himself. The answer was obvious. Darrow had been controlling things again by keeping Kimmy in the dark. Why let her know that there really was a daughter in the picture? Maybe Kimmy, already emotionally unhinged, would swing the other way if she knew that the girl who visited her really was Candi's flesh and blood.

'I'm sorry,' Matt said. 'Go on.'

Kyra slowly turned back to Olivia. 'So I visited Kimmy's trailer. She was so nice. And talking to her just made me want to find out more about you. I wanted to . . . I know how this will sound, but I wanted to find your killer. So I kept digging. I kept asking around. And then I got a call from Sister Mary Rose.'

'How . . . ?'

'She was trying to help some of her old girls, I think. Make amends. She heard what I was up to. So she called me.'

'She told you I was still alive?'

'Yes. I mean, it was a total shock. I thought you'd been murdered. And then Sister Mary Rose tells me if I do what she says, I might be able to find you. But we had to play it safe, she said. I didn't want to put you in danger or anything. I just wanted . . . I just wanted a chance to get to know you.'

Matt looked at Marsha. 'You knew?'

'Not until yesterday. Kyra told me.'

'How did you happen to live here?'

'That was part luck,' Kyra said. 'I wanted to find a way to get close to you. Sister Mary Rose was going to try to get me hired at DataBetter. But then we heard Marsha needed a live-in helper. So Sister Mary Rose called someone at St. Philomena's. She gave them my name.'

Matt remembered now that Marsha had met Kyra through her church. A nun would have that kind of pull – who would question that kind of recommendation?

'I wanted to tell you,' Kyra said, her eyes only on Olivia. 'I was just looking for the right time. But then Sister Mary Rose called. Like you said. Three weeks ago. She said it was still too soon – that I shouldn't say anything until she contacted me again. I was scared, but I trusted her. So I listened. I didn't even know she'd been killed. And then the other night, when you both came here so late – I was going to tell you anyway. That's why I came back in from the garage. But Matt was running out.'

Olivia stood, opened her mouth, closed it, tried again. 'So you . . . you're my . . . ?'

'Daughter. Yes.'

Olivia took a tentative step toward Kyra. She reached out with one hand. Then, thinking better of it, she dropped it back to her side.

'Are you okay, Kyra?' Olivia asked.

Kyra smiled, a smile so heartbreakingly close to her mother's Matt wondered how he'd missed it before. 'I'm fine,' she said.

'Are you happy?'

'I am, yes.'

Olivia said nothing. Kyra took another step.

'I'm fine, really.'

And then Olivia started to cry.

Matt looked away. This wasn't about him. He heard the sobs and the shushing sounds of two people trying to comfort each other. He thought about the miles, the pain, the prison, the abuse, the years, and what Olivia had said about this life, this simple life, being worth fighting for.

Epilogue

Your name is Matt Hunter.

A year has passed.

Lance Banner has apologized to you. For several months Lance remains wary, but then one day, at a neighborhood barbecue, he asks you to be his assistant basketball coach. Your nephew, Paul, Lance reminds you with a slap on the back, is on the team too. So what do you say?

You say yes.

You bought the house in Livingston, after all. You work out of it now, consulting on legal matters for Carter Sturgis. Ike Kier is by far your biggest client. He pays you well.

All charges against Cingle Shaker were dropped. Cingle has opened her own private investigation agency called Cingler Service. Ike Kier and Carter Sturgis throw all the business they can her way. She has three investigators working for her now.

Your sister-in-law, Marsha, is now serious with a man named Ed Essey. Ed works in manufacturing. You really don't understand what he does. They plan on marrying soon. He seems nice, this Ed guy. You try to like him, but you can't. He loves Marsha though. He will take care of her. He will probably be the only father Paul and Ethan will remember. They'll be too young to remember Bernie. Maybe that's how it should be, but it kills you. You will always try to be a presence in their lives, but you will become simply an uncle. Paul and Ethan will run to Ed first.

Last time you were in the house, you looked for the picture of Bernie on the refrigerator. It was still there, but it's buried under more recent photographs and report cards and artwork.

You never hear from Sonya or Clark McGrath again.

Their son, Stephen, still visits you sometimes. Not as much as he used to. And sometimes you're even glad to see him.

After you close on the new house, Loren Muse comes over. The two of you sit in the backyard with Corona beers.

'Back in Livingston,' she says.

'Yep.'

'Happy?'

'Towns don't make you happy, Loren.'

She nods.

There is still something hanging over your head. 'What's going to happen to Olivia?' you ask.

Loren reaches into her pocket and pulls out an envelope. 'Nothing.'

'What's that?'

'A letter from Sister Mary Rose née Emma Lemay. Mother Katherine gave it to me.'

You sit up. She hands it to you. You start to read it.

'Emma Lemay put it all on herself,' Loren tells you. 'She and she alone killed Clyde Rangor. She and she alone hid his body. She and she alone lied to the authorities about the identity of the murder victim. She claimed Candace Potter didn't know anything about it. There's more, but that's the gist.'

'You think that will wash?'

Loren shrugs. 'Who's to say otherwise?'

'Thank you,' you say.

Loren nods. She puts down her beer and sits up. 'Now, you want to tell me about those phone records, Matt?'

'No.'

'You think I don't know who Darrow spoke to in Westport, Connecticut.'

'Doesn't matter. You can't prove anything.'

'You don't know that. McGrath probably sent him money. There could be a trail.'

'Let it go, Loren.'

'Wanting revenge is not a defense.'

'Let it go.'

She picks the beer back up. 'I don't need your approval.'

'True.'

Loren looks off. 'If Kyra had just told Olivia the truth in the beginning –'

'They'd probably all be dead.'

'What makes you say that?'

'Emma Lemay's phone call. She told Kyra to stay silent. And I think she had a good reason.'

'That being?'

'I think Emma – or Sister Mary Rose – knew that they were getting close.'

'You saying Lemay took the hit for all of them?'

You shrug. You wonder how they found Lemay and Lemay alone. You wonder why Lemay, if she suspected something, didn't run. You wonder how she stood up to their torture and never gave Olivia away. Maybe Lemay figured one last sacrifice would end it. She wouldn't have known they'd post something about the adoption. She probably figured that she was the only link. And if that link was permanently broken – especially by force – there'd be no way to find Olivia.

But you'll never know for sure.

Loren looks off again. 'Back in Livingston,' she says. You both shake your head. You both sip your beers.

Over the course of the year Loren visits every once in a while. If the weather is cooperating, you two sit outside.

The sun is high on that day a year later. You and Loren are sprawled out in lawn chairs. You both have Sol beers. Loren tells you that they're better than Coronas.

You take a sip and agree.

As always, Loren looks around and shakes her head and says her usual refrain: 'Back in Livingston.'

You are in your backyard. Your wife Olivia is there, planting a flower bed. Your son Benjamin is on a mat next to her. Ben is three months old. He is making a happy cooing noise. You can hear it all the way across the yard. Kyra is in the garden too, helping her mother. She has been living with you for a year now. She plans on staying until she graduates.

So you, Matt Hunter, look at them. All three of them. Olivia feels your eyes on her. She looks up and smiles. So does Kyra. Your son makes another cooing noise.

You feel the lightness in your chest.

'Yeah,' you say to Loren with a silly grin on your face. 'Back in Livingston.'

Acknowledgments

Once again, a nod of gratitude to Carole Baron, Mitch Hoffman, Lisa Johnson, Kara Welsh, and all at Dutton, NAL, and Penguin Group USA; Jon Wood, Malcolm Edwards, Susan Lamb, Jane Wood, Juliet Ewers, Emma Noble, and the gang at Orion; Aaron Priest and Lisa Erbach Vance for all the usual stuff.

A special thanks to Senator Harry Reid of Nevada. He constantly shows me the beauty of his state and her inhabitants, even if, for the sake of drama, I end up putting my own spin on them.

The author also wishes to thank the following for their technical expertise:

- Christopher J. Christie, United States Attorney for the state of New Jersey;
- Paula T. Dow, Essex County (NJ) Prosecutor;
- Louie F. Allen, Chief of Investigators, Essex County (NJ) Prosecutor's Office;
- Carolyn Murray, First Assistant Essex County (NJ) Prosecutor;
- Elkan Abramowitz, attorney extraordinaire;
- David A. Gold, MD, surgeon extraordinaire;
- Linda Fairstein, lotsa-things extraordinaire;
- Anne Armstrong-Coben, MD, Medical Director of Covenant House Newark and just plain extraordinaire;
- And for the third straight book (and final time), Steven Z. Miller, MD, Director of Pediatric Emergency Medicine, Children's Hospital of New York-Presbyterian. You taught me about much more than medicine, my friend. I will miss you always.

All Orion/Phoenix titles are available at your local bookshop or from the following address:

Mail Order Department
Littlehampton Book Services
FREEPOST BR535
Worthing, West Sussex, BN13 3BR
telephone 01903 828503, *facsimile* 01903 828802
e-mail MailOrders@lbsltd.co.uk
(Please ensure that you include full postal address details)

Payment can be made either by credit/debit card (Visa, Mastercard, Access and Switch accepted) or by sending a £ Sterling cheque or postal order made payable to *Littlehampton Book Services*.
DO NOT SEND CASH OR CURRENCY

Please add the following to cover postage and packing

UK and BFPO:
£1.50 for the first book, and 50p for each additional book to a maximum of £3.50

Overseas and Eire:
£2.50 for the first book plus £1.00 for the second book and 50p for each additional book ordered

---

BLOCK CAPITALS PLEASE

name of cardholder _____   *delivery address*
_____   *(if different from cardholder)*

address of cardholder _____   _____

_____   _____

_____   _____

postcode _____   *postcode* _____

[ ] I enclose my remittance for £_____

[ ] please debit my Mastercard/Visa/Access/Switch (delete as appropriate)

card number [ ][ ][ ][ ][ ][ ][ ][ ][ ][ ][ ][ ][ ][ ][ ][ ]

expiry date [ ][ ][ ][ ]   Switch issue no. [ ][ ]

signature _____

prices and availability are subject to change without notice